T0354797

THE MENDER'S TOMB

THE MENDER'S TOMB

ELFDREAMS OF PARALLAN V

ALBTRÄUME...

BENJAMIN TOWE

authorHOUSE®

AuthorHouse™
1663 Liberty Drive
Bloomington, IN 47403
www.authorhouse.com
Phone: 1 (800) 839-8640

Published by AuthorHouse 08/12/2015

ISBN: 978-1-5049-2951-6 (sc)
ISBN: 978-1-5049-2952-3 (hc)
ISBN: 978-1-5049-2950-9 (e)

Library of Congress Control Number: 2015913136

Print information available on the last page.

CONTENTS

Wisps…
Threads…
Threads of Magick…
Threads of fate…
Threads of time…
Threads connecting worlds …
Dreams connecting worlds …
Dreams of Magick…
The Magick of Dreams…
Magick connecting dreams…
Magick connecting worlds…
Dream raiders…
Elf pressure…
Albtraum…
Albträume, elf dreams, nightmares…

PROLOGUE

Menders came into the world with knowledge of their beginning. A mundane world orbited a distant globular star cluster. Simple folk inhabited the lands and stared up at a fantastic sky filled with thousands of stars. Their naïve eyes saw closely gathered bright dots. In reality great distances separated Nature's *suns*. In a blink of those naïve eyes, the skies above the primeval world changed. A massive star collapsed and doomed innumerable neighbors. The cataclysmic event instantly ruined countless civilizations. Forces of Nature overwhelmed both ordinary worlds and worlds of Magick. Many thousands of suns became the great dark sun one day called Orpheus. Meries, one of the outer suns, survived the cataclysm but fell under the influence of massive Orpheus. As a consequence Meries circled through but never left the skies of the ancient simple world. Meries and Orpheus produced cycles of variable light and left the world without total darkness. The simple world experienced very bright light periods, slightly less brilliant amber periods, and darker periods. Dark periods occurred at Meries' nadirs and allowed twinkling points of light to peek through. Comets, shooting stars, and other visitors infrequently appeared in the amber skies. More rarely meteors fell to the land of hunters and gatherers. A third sun wandered unpredictably into the ancient skies. On the odd occasion the gray giant drew near the world. The strange gray rays of the wandering sun Andreas brought vestiges of Magick. The interval of its Approximations remained variable and unpredictable. Meries gave the world bright amber skies. Massive Orpheus influenced the world through gravity. The Gray Wanderer Andreas was the source of Magick for Parallan, the World of the Three Suns.

During an ancient Approximation, a stalwart chap stared into the skies, wondered at the giant sun's nearness, and basked in the gray light of the wandering sun. The primitive bloke heard the muffled roar of the forbidden falls in the distance. His father had warned him to avoid this area. Legends held powerful malevolent spirits lurked in the vicinity of the waterfall and lured unwary passersby to their dooms.

Still curiosity drew the hunter.

His mother gave him the name Seffa Lexin. In a moment of time, the name forever left his memory. A celestial visitor appeared in the gray skies and moved toward the massive gray sun. This remnant of a dead sun traveled rapidly and slammed into the giant Andreas. The cosmic collision dispersed many fragments of the gray sun. Frozen by fear and wonder, the hunter stared upward. A miniscule piece of the gray sun hurdled toward him. The fragment moved quickly, approached to within a hand's distance, paused, hovered briefly, circled him thrice, and then buried into the bewildered simple bloke's left hand, between his fifth and sixth digit. Excruciating pain stole consciousness from him, and the hunter fell to the ground.

Seffa dreamed.

His mind retraced his simple life, but then redness replaced the visions in his mind's eye.

Wisps…
Threads…
Threads of Magick…
Threads of fate…
Threads of time…
Threads connecting worlds …
Dreams connecting worlds …
Dreams of Magick…
The Magick of Dreams…
Magick connecting dreams…
Magick connecting worlds…
Dream raiders…
Elf pressure…
Albtraum…
Albträume, elf dreams, nightmares…

Out of the redness, the unfamiliar face of a beautiful female appeared. The very tall alluring female had creamy skin, soft blue eyes, and coal black hair that fell gracefully down her back and chest. She wore a blazing red dress. The female walked gracefully back and forth across a field of odd green clover with purple flowers. Only orange, red, and blue clover grew in the forests of the World of the Three Suns. Blue flower petals showered around the beautiful female. Mesmerized and unable to move, the sleeping Seffa pondered. Had he dreamt in color before? Where did the unusual plants grow?

The matron spoke pleasantly to the sleeping huntsman, "Behold this pastoral scene. Relax. Release your pain, fear, and doubt. Do you feel your new strength? You have the power to comfort, heal, and restore. Let your eyes feast on my beauty. Don't resist. When you awaken, your mind will be clear and free of memories. Employ your gift. You will know."

Blueness surrounded her lovely face, and the vision faded. Seffa entered deep sleep.

When the sleeper awakened, the gray sun had retreated from the world and the little yellow sun scampered across the sky. The amber brightness of the light period replaced the gray light. Try as he might, the former hunter could not open his eyes. The bewildered fellow crawled defensively into the nearby bushes, hid from view, and waited. Why were his eyes so sensitive? Hours passed. The amber period arrived. Aided by its dimmer light, Seffa squinted and focused on his surroundings. The everred trees, orange and yellow grasses, and amber skies were unchanged. The gray sun was now only a dark speck in the distant horizon, and the little yellow sun approached its nadir. The prolonged dark period approached. Seffa again painfully opened his eyes and welcomed the relative darkness. Twas then the erstwhile hunter noticed the changes in his body. His integument and hair were as white as the snow that covered the great peaks. The six digits on his hands were longer.

Seffa Lexin was forever changed.

His lack of coloration…
His lost memories…
He only remembered the words of the lovely image in his dream.
Who was *she*?
For that matter, who was *he*?
Where was he?

What was his name?

A crudely made spear, bow, and quiver lay on the ground near him. Though his eyes disdained the light, his hearing and smell were acutely heightened. Seffa Lexin heard the thunderous waterfall, the rhythmic beating of a tiny bird's heart high in the red elm above him, and every step of every skittering insect that crawled on the ground within fifty paces. Seffa smelled every nearby flower distinctly. The amnesiac cowered in the red and orange undergrowth.

Seven foragers named Tycar Sillen, Seth Lothan, Cefana, Triaxin, Vantine, Uroxime, and Spectra found and carried him to their cave dwelling. Hushed discussions followed the party's arrival. The pale stranger found the caverns dark and friendly. Enhanced hearing enabled the transformed captive to hear the cave dwellers' conversations and detect sobbing from within the primitive dwelling. Foreboding sadness preceded and overshadowed his arrival.

Young cave dwellers gathered around and stared at him. Had they not beheld a stranger? The cave people perceived him a threat and restrained him. Burly young Triaxin and Vantine stood nearby and carried rather large spears. Females kept little ones at a distance. Fires flickered around the large cave and provided dim light.

An older fellow approached. His weathered face indicated he had seen many seasons. He carried an ornamental spear and wore a crude crown on his highbrow. The crown looked oddly familiar. Seffa remembered little of anything.

A distraught female named Nova Lynn ran to the apparent leader and sobbed, "He worsens. Epidra asks for you, Chief Seff!"

The Chief groaned, "Will I should lose two sons in half a dark period's time? My clan falls apart. The searchers return with no word of my son Seffa Lexin and instead bring this odd being to our safe haven. Now my youngest son clings to life. Bring the newcomer and watch him. Don't touch him or let him touch you! In my 320 dark periods I've not seen such folk. The world gets stranger by the day!"

The chief followed Nova Lynn. Triaxin grunted and motioned with his spear. The stranger followed. Nova Lynn led them through several passages in the natural cavern to a small grotto. Many hides covered the more lavishly furnished grotto's walls and floor.

Three older females worked over a young male. The tribal leader's child was ill.

A beleaguered female stood and sobbed, "My mate, I have labored long. The matrons and I have tried everything. Our son burns from within. Safiten's illness prevents my grieving the loss of Seffa Lexin."

Flickering flames revealed the child's pale face. Perspiration dripped from his body and the sound of his labored breathing resonated through the awkwardly silent cavern. The massive chief ambled over to his son's prone body. Grief overwhelmed Seff Dyner. The broad-shouldered chief dropped to his knees and sobbed.

Crude pottery vessels filled with herbs and unguents surrounded the thick mooler hide on which the child lay. Great mooler herds roamed the valleys. When something mooed, it was usually a mooler. The purplish bovines provided food for the folk of the World of the Three Suns. Hunting, pursuing, and killing the beasts required teamwork and skill.

The boy's mother glowered in the faint light and uttered, "Why have you brought this person to our vigil? *Who* is he?"

The burly chieftain answered, "Epidra, our parties found no sign of Seffa Lexin, but stumbled upon this lone person. I don't know from whence he came. He speaks our tongue. I had just begun to look into him when you summoned me."

Epidra replied, "Seff, I am bereft of my oldest son and my youngest lingers near death. I want you near me when he leaves us."

Seff Dyner somberly said, "I will stay by your side. Traveler, I can't deal with you now. Triaxin, please give the stranger food and water. He's shown no aggression. I think you understand me, stranger. If you try anything, you'll be killed. Do you have a name?"

The pale stranger shook his head negatively.

"Then, be off with him, Triaxin. I must attend my son and mate," the broad-shouldered leader said.

The pale stranger said in monotonic voice, "No. I'll help you. Bring me the fruits of the tetra berry bush. I'll need unripe and all three ripe types of fruit. That's unripe, yellow, red, and green. Gather the violet sap of the crying willow. Bring them to me quickly."

Seff Dyner looked toward his mate and noted her expression of futility and hopelessness. The Chieftain motioned to Seth Lothan and Cefana, and the two hunters ran from the room. The stranger went to the child's side and touched Safiten's hot skin. The youthful cavern dweller barely reacted to the touch of the pale stranger's twelve fingers.

Epidra, Nova Lynn, and two older women Regula and Lantis dabbed the child with cooling sponge plants.

The pale stranger hurriedly prepared poultices and balms from the materials he found among the cavern's supplies. Cefana and Seth Lothan soon returned with clusters of tetra bush berries. The whitish outsider took a large red gourd from Epidra's wares, placed the unripe berries in the hollowed out plant, and crushed them with his fingers. Grayness briefly filled the chamber. The nimble guest then crushed yellow, red, and finally green berries in the vessel and stirred the fruits rapidly.

"In all the woods, only this plant bears green berries. We've always been taught to avoid them. Are they not poisonous?" young Seth Lothan softly asked Cefana.

"Maybe the stranger poisons the chief's son while the chief stands beside him. Let's remain quiet. We may have to kill the blighter yet," Cefana answered.

The stranger thickened the poultice with the crying willow sap and then slowly rubbed the fragrant poultice over the child with his elongated pale digits. Next he gently opened the boy's parched lips and placed a bit of the unguent on his tongue. The child's breathing dramatically improved and soon his fever dissipated. Within a few hundred heartbeats, the boy sat up. Seff Dyner, Epidra, and the entire clan rejoiced.

The pale visitor never changed his blank expression or tone of his voice.

"You *are* a witch! A healer!" Epidra shouted.

"How did you come to know of the poultice?" Lantis asked.

"You must have come from behind the Great Falls!" old Regula declared.

The stranger stood quietly. *Where was his home?*

"I don't care where you come. You saved my son's life and lessened the tragedy of this day," the tribal leader Seff Dyner declared reverently.

The healer answered, "I just…do what I do…"

"Stranger, you speak more strangely than you look. Please tell us your name," the burly leader asked.

"I…don't have a name," the stranger answered.

"You have restored my son and mended his broken body. I will forever call you *Mender*," Epidra marveled.

"We are in your debt. You've earned your freedom. Seth Lothan and Cefana will take you home," Seff Dyner said.

"I have no home," the Mender answered.

"Then you have a home among my people and the name of my lost son. When we stumbled upon you, we found his spear and quiver nearby. He would have never left them unless...but I still have my younger son. Thanks to you. You are now called Lexin," Seff Dyner stated resolutely.

Lexin the first Mender accepted the gracious chief's offer. Lexin enjoyed unnaturally long life and served many generations of Seff Dyner's people. The nodule at the base of his left fifth and sixth finger throbbed when Approximations occurred. Lexin was alone. Yet Menders multiplied and survived through the ages.

Dreams troubled the first Mender Lexin all his days.

Ø ∞ Ø

Fisher, Yannuvia, and Clouse...

The Mender Fisher differed from others of his ilk in that he was now a bit grayish green. After he received the erstwhile Spellweaver's amber blood, more than Fisher's snow-white skin had changed. Fisher was a wee bit Drelvish and had vestiges of emotion, and the Mender struggled with the brief jiffs of feelings he experienced. Nothing in his years of Mender experience prepared him for feelings! Fortunately for Fisher the episodes occurred infrequently. Clouse, the product of Fisher's confinement, was a green pointed-eared Drelvish Menderish Spellweaverish Yannuvish bloke. Clouse arrived in the world with knowledge of Mender folk, but since his emergence from the chrysalis, Clouse's mind's eye had not shared the visions of other Menders. Thus the green guy's knowledge of Menders was fixed at the time of his arrival. Magick touched Clouse. He also emerged with knowledge of Spellweaver Yannuvia's spells and content of the ancient Drelvish spell book *Gifts of Andreas to the People of the Forest*.

Menders understood mending. Menders *were* Magick.

Fisher addressed leaders of Lost Sons in the common area of the Drelvish splinter community. The Mender had paused for a painfully long time. Lost Sons community elder Dienas cleared his throat. Lost Spellweaver and First Wandmaker Yannuvia gently nudged Fisher.

Fisher resumed his dissertation, "Ultra-rare whitish Menders are among the oldest folk of the World of the Three Suns. Given the opportunity, a Mender will heal both a warrior and the warrior's enemy. Mender's nature precludes haughty eyes, a lying tongue, hands that shed innocent blood, feet swift to run into mischief, deceitful witness that utters lies, and sowing discord among brethren. Menders are neither loyal nor disloyal. Menders do not display lust, gluttony, greed, sloth, wrath, envy, and pride. Likewise Menders do not show signs of chastity, temperance, charity, diligence, patience, kindness, and humility. Menders do not seek adultery, fornication, uncleanness, lasciviousness, idolatry, witchcraft, hatred, variance, emulations, wrath, strife, sedition, heresies, envying, murders, drunkenness, reveling, and such things.

"My kind foregoes courtship and mating. I don't mind. Such endeavors waste lots of energies. The approach of the gray sun heralds the time of Menders' confinement. You might call it procreation. A protuberance develops between the base of the fifth and sixth digits of our right upper extremity and grows with each passing cycle of Meries. Successful confinement requires a dark place and potting soil. All Menders are born with some inherent knowledge of confinement, but every Mender's experience differs. I shared the collective knowledge of my kind, but I knew little of confinement until I endured the experience. But I accomplished the deed."

"Clouse is the product not only of my confinement but also the fusion of the erstwhile Spellweaver and me. I lay dormant within my chrysalis, in what some call a pharate state, for what you'd call three seasons of the harvest. I searched the collective consciousness of my kind. I suppose that's what all Menders do when confined. I've endured confinement once. Some Menders have undergone confinement multiple times. For others, it's been a once in a lifetime occurrence. Whether I ever undergo the ordeal again is a matter of conjecture. Confinement begins and ends with Approximations of the Gray Sun Andreas. There have been times when 144, 233, and 377 seasons of the harvest have separated Approximations of Andreas. Menders undergoing confinement in these times lay dormant for 144, or 233, or 377 years. I suppose I am fortunate. My confinement lasted only three years, 24 dark periods, or three harvests of the enhancing plant. Had I lay dormant for centuries, I'd missed seeing the beauty of your matronly lady friends. I'm rambling. Bottom line… I don't understand why Clouse looks like the Wandmaker Yannuvia and not me. He's green and has pointed ears. I had no idea my confinement would result in green, pointed-eared Drelvish spawn. In the annals of time, rare reports tell of Mender blood accidentally touching others and producing *Menderish* folk. My blood touched the Spellweaver-turned-Wandmaker and changed him for the better, in my opinion."

The changes in Yannuvia included the slight grayish-green tint to his skin, points to his ears, sixth finger on his left hand, and little nodule at the base of the new digit. The Spellweaver had noted the presence of the small nodule on his left hand after the journey with Fisher. Drelve-Vydaelians developed identical odd itchy little lumps at the base of their left fifth finger when the Knock Wand appeared in Yannuvia's right hand during his first Wandmaking ceremony.

The nodule did not form on Clouse and Fisher's hands.

CHAPTER 1

UK

Intense gray light bathed Gray Vale when Alexandrina drew her first breath. Pale Mender's hands helped her sea-elfish mother Victoria to bring Alexandrina into the world. Sea elves Victoria and Edward discovered the badly injured Mender, nursed him back to health, and sheltered him in their abode in the sea elf village Elder Ridge, which was hidden among tall reeds in the shadow of the fortified Carcharian center Doug-less.

The Mender Lou Nester arrived in the underworld realm of the Great Sea with an enlarging nodule on his left hand and driven by primordial urges. Populations of luminescent lichen on the ceiling high above provided light to the massive cavern. The light approximated the Dark Period in the Mender's home, the World of the Three Suns. Ultra-rare whitish Menders were among the oldest folk of the World of the Three Suns. The pale healer walked in the company of a rogue Mountain Giant, who in turn had befriended Carcharians. The Giant discovered a door to the under realm of the great sea and had a means to unlock it. The Mender lived for a time with the shark-men and assisted in their birthing area. The pale healer's efforts gained favor with the Carcharian King and access to upper echelon life in Doug-less, the Amphibimen's conurbation. One great honor he achieved was the opportunity to go "Duoth hunting." The pudgy marshmallow men were the Carcharians' favorite prey and considered animalistic scavengers and foragers. Their consumption was usually reserved for the community's elite. The hunt went awry. A well-thrown Duoth bomb splintered the hunting party and rendered the Mender unconscious. Lou Nester fell into the hands of the Duoths. Unbeknownst to the Carcharians their highly intelligent prey communicated telepathically and had the ability to see into other creatures' minds. Duoths termed all other folk Unduothers.

Duoths tended the Mender's injuries and nursed him back to health with natural remedies and a wonderful concoction called Duoth dropping soup. Lou Nester posed no threat to the Duoths and joined them for a while. Duoths possessed stores of herbs, minerals, and naturopathies. The pale healer created healing potions and unguents. The Duoths' leader *Mose6* was unable to decipher the Mender's complex thoughts. The pale wanderer shared the common experience of Menders, and this created a barrier to his mind. The traveler enjoyed speaking aloud and told many stories. Duoths saw inside Unduothers' minds and seldom used their innate ability to translate and understand spoken word. *Mose6*'s encounter with the pale Lou Nester necessitated using this ability. *Mose6* passed along the visitor's stories. Lou Nester averred he was Mender, professed neutrality, and told of an upper world. The Mender asked many questions the Duoths, but received few answers. *Mose6* tired of the Mender's curiosity. The Mender never learned the secrets of Duoth bombs and Duoth dropping soup.

Ineffective communication with the Duoths frustrated Lou Nester and the pale visitor wandered off to the east. There he encountered a denizen of the deep, the Giant Amebus. The Mender was badly injured in his unfortunate liaison with the Amebus but escaped with his life. A Samaritan carried the unconscious Mender to betrothed sea elves named Edward and Victoria. Victoria was laden with child.

Lou Nester lived with the sea elves for a time in Elder Ridge, but the nodule he bore on his left hand grew larger and drove him to accomplish confinement, something Menders did. Confinement required a dark place, potting soil, seclusion, and time. Edward and Victoria led him to the darkness and nurturing soil of Gray Vale. Sea elves visited the area to ponder the stone circle situated halfway up the hillock in the center of the vale. Five stones sat in a circle and tangentially placed near a larger stone. The mysterious circle predated the lore of Elder Ridge's folk. Gray Vale was ordinarily darker than most of the lichen-illuminated underworld. Its fathomless ceiling faded into deep grayness with little points of light. The trio began discussions of preparing a place for Lou Nester's deed.

Then intense grayness enveloped the valley.

A circle of flattened gray stone appeared among the five similar stones of the stone circle that sat on the hillock. A black rod and chuck of black stone appeared in the center of the thirteen-foot diameter circle. The words Circle of Ooranth, Rod of Ooranth, and Stone of Ooranth, and phrase **"Jams gar field"** appeared in Lou Nester, Edward, and Victoria's minds.

Victoria's time to deliver came. The Mender Lou Nester assisted in the birth of the child. The delivery was complicated and the Mender repaid his debt to the sea elves by saving their child by breathing into her tiny mouth. The child drew her first breath from air exhaled from Mender's lungs in the deep gray light saturating Gray Vale. Her parents gave her the name Alexandrina. She became a sister of grayness. Alexandrina had graying of her skin and a tiny nodule on her little left hand.

Lou Nester grew weaker and directed Edward and Victoria to use the Rod and Stone of Ooranth to create building blocks. Edward and Victoria used the rod and stone to construct a small structure upon the central hillock. Touching the small stone with the cylindrical rod and saying **"Jams Gar Field"** replicated the block. Though growing weaker the Mender attended little Alexandrina while her parents worked. Edward and Victoria finished the structure. Lou Nester crawled inside whilst intense grayness still bathed the Vale. The Mender picked up and tasted a pinch of the gray soil.

"Seven parts composted loam. Loam's porosity allows high moisture retention and air circulation. Three parts decayed compacted sphagnum moss, or peat moss. Two parts perlite. Perlite is sterile light weight white aggregate made from volcanic materials. One and a half parts limestone and 12 parts of a mixture of 5 percent nitrogen, 10 percent phosphorus, and 10 percent potassium. Finally a half part bone meal. The potting soil is perfect. Soft potting soil, a dark place, contact with the gray sun, potting soil with precisely mixed ingredients, privacy, and time. All the requirements needed for confinement," Lou Nester rambled expressionlessly.

The Mender dug a shallow pit in the soft potting soil and inserted the swollen nodule on his left hand. Lou Nester curled into a fetal position, pushed his left forearm deeper into the softened soil, and buried the painful swollen area of his left hand. He closed his eyes. Slowly twig-like structures sprang from the Mender's entire body and grew outward and away from his trunk. The adult sea elves munched on sea biscuits. Over a period of three hours, the twigs grew into a dome. Then thin wafer-like structures extended from each twig and grew together. The sea elves took turns at watch and slept in shifts. Three cycles of Meries passed. By then a dome of pale green tissue covered the Mender's body. The cocoon obscured Lou Nester.

Edward carefully extended his left hand and gently touched the hardened cocoon. Edward closed the chamber at the Mender's behest. Edward, Victoria, and Alexandrina lived in Gray Vale whilst Lou Nester was confined. The area was bountiful, and Carcharians did not know its location. The sea elves had no idea how long the Mender would be confined. In three years, after the equivalent of 24 Dark Periods, intense gray light returned. The structure opened and Lou Nester and a second fully grown Mender emerged.

Whilst the gray light concentrated on Gray Vale, four exceptional stones appeared and rotated around the Menders, Edward, Victoria, and three-year-old Alexandrina. The four stones hovered and then revolved around the quintet at about Victoria's eye level. The stones revolved 13 times and then migrated to the area of the stone circle, where they began to revolve around the five stones. Intense gray light illuminated the area around the five stones. A purple light flowed from the larger stone and concentrated on the area in the midst of the five stones. The Circle of Ooranth reappeared on the soil between the stones. Then a gray sphere appeared and hovered directly over the center of the circle on the ground. The sphere emitted auras and droning sounds. The four stones continued to revolve around the stone circle. The quintet made their way down the hillock to the circle on the ground. One by one they stood on the thirteen foot diameter circle of gray stone. The six-foot diameter sphere hummed more loudly. Purple rays flowed from the sphere onto little Alexandrina and moved back and forth from the child to the center of the circle. Little Alexandrina left her mother's side and walked to the center of the circle and stood beneath the hovering sphere. One of the stones left its orbit and moved to the child's side. Runes appeared on the stone.

Ø ∞ Ø

The surface of the sphere changed. First the sphere reflected Alexandrina's face and then letters appeared on its surface. The Menders saw the letters in Mender language. The sea elves saw them in sea elfish. The first phrase read "Xennic Stones." The next phrase read **"Win Stone Church Chill."**

Alexandrina uttered the phrase. The Black Rod of Ooranth hovered briefly and then slipped into the child's tiny left hand. She reached out and touched the hovering stone. The rock decreased in size and she gripped it and uttered "Curse Stone." The Curse Stone meld to the shape of her little hand. She touched the stone with the black rod. Then the black stone of Ooranth hovered and moved near the child. Alexandrina gripped the curse stone in her right hand, held the rod of Ooranth in her left hand, and touched the hovering black stone and said **"Win Stone Church Chill."** A section of black stone shaped like the Rod of Ooranth hovered in front of her. The Stone of Ooranth dropped to the ground. Alexandria released the Curse Stone from her hand. It resumed its original oblate spheroid shape and returned to its orbit. A second stone left its orbit and drew near her hand. The surface of the sphere again reflected her face and then the phrase **"Wood row will son"** appeared. Runes appeared on the stone.

$$Ø ∞ Ø$$

Alexandrina touched the second stone, which again shrank to fit the size and shape of her tiny hand. She said Stone of Masonry, touched the hovering replicated rock with the rod of Ooranth and said, **"Wood row will son."** The young sea elf released the Stone of Masonry. A third stone drew near her. The sphere reflected her charming face and they displayed the phrase **"Lend dawn john son."** Runes appeared on the stone.

$$Ø ∞ Ø$$

Alexandrina said "Light Stone." She touched the Light Stone with the rod of Ooranth, then touched the hovering length of black stone, and said, **"Lend dawn john son."** She released the Light Stone and the fourth stone drew near her. The sphere showed her face and then the phrase **"Eyes Inn Hour."** Runes appeared on the stone.

$$Ø ∞ Ø$$

She uttered the phrase, touched the fourth stone with the rod of Ooranth, and accepted the new stone in her hand, and declared it the Battle Stone. She touched the hovering length of black stone and said **"Eyes Inn Hour."** The hovering rod transformed to a scepter with an ornate handle and vorpal blade. The child released the Battle Stone and Black Rod of Ooranth. She uttered **"Win Stone Church Chill"** and reached out and grasped the scepter. Her face again appeared on the rotating sphere above her head. Then runes appeared.

UK

Ø ∞ Ǿ

The large rotating sphere disappeared in a mauve flash. The four Xennic Stones then vanished. Intense gray light remained all around the five inhabitants of Gray Vale.

One by one they held the scepter UK.

Uttering **"Win Stone Church Chill"** allowed one to touch the scepter UK without activating its curse. Grasping the scepter and muttering **"Wood row will son"** activated the power of "Rock to Mud." Gripping the scepter and saying **"Lend dawn john son"** produced the effect of "Continual Light." Uttering **"Lend dawn john son"** while holding the scepter and pointing it at an enemy's eyes blinded him long enough to facilitate escape. Grasping the artifact and uttering **"Eyes Inn Hour"** created a formidable vorpal weapon. The heavy scepter served as a blunt weapon in its own right.

Little Alexandrina created the scepter UK with the help of four Xennic Stones, the Curse Stone, Stone of Masonry, Light Stone, and Battle Stone. The child held and managed the device with ease.

The second Mender left after a season.

Lou Nester was weakened by his earlier injury and the ordeal of confinement. Tirelessly Edward and Victoria worked at creating blocks and constructed an octagonal structure on the hillock. When the structure was completed, Lou Nester entered and the others closed the door behind him. Alexandrina returned to Elder Ridge with her parents.

CHAPTER 2

Alms Glen: Coming and Going

Four figures stood in an empty grotto without discernible exit.

The Dreamraider Amica grumpily conceded, "There's little left to do here. Step onto this blue stone and you'll leave the cavern and arrive in the outside World of the Three Suns. I can't tell you where or *when* you'll arrive, so I suggest we hold hands and all step together."

The Dreamraider truthfully had no idea how the blue stone would function for the neophytes.

The púca Cupid said, "There's nothing for it. I don't want to hang around in this sealed cavern."

Leprechaun Oilill quickly said, "Wait!"

The leprechaun sprinkled red sand onto the blue tile. The odd quartet held hands. Then on Amica's command they crowded together and stepped onto the blue tile. Blueness surrounded them. Every inchworm length of their skin tingled.

A flash of redness surrounded Amica, Oilill, Kirrie, and Cupid. A moment later the Dreamraider, Leprechaun, she-Drelve, and púca breathed familiar fragrant air and stood inside the red elm where the Sandman saved the poisoned Good Witch. Kirrie's hair had lengthened and grown browner. Oilill's beard was a bit longer but overall the leprechaun appeared no worse for the wear. The púca Cupid felt stiff and sore and his hair had grown several inches. The large red elm, which served as a guest house in Alms Glen, was otherwise vacant. Kirrie peeked through the bark and listened. Drelves performed day to day tasks in the bustling common area surrounding the big red tree. Two she-Drelves talked near the tree. The mature she-Drelves were Betsy and her sister Emmy. Four-year-old Drelvling Betsy narrowly escaped a

7

meandering Droll only a few cycles of Meries before Kirrie's entourage entered the cavern behind Alluring Falls. In what seemed a few days to Kirrie's group Betsy and her twin sister had matured.

Amica cautioned, "Traveling in the red and blue light has changed you. Eleven changes of seasons have passed since we entered the grotto behind Alluring Falls."

Kirrie muttered, "So Yannuvia and the folk of Lost Sons have been gone thirteen years."

Amica stammered, "Uh, yes…"

Kirrie frowned.

Amica continued, "I must go now. From here, getting these t**ds home is a simple task for me. What are your plans Kirrie?"

The she-Drelve replied, "There's nothing for me in Alms Glen. I may go to Meadowsweet and live amongst the Thirttene Friends at Green Vale. Perhaps I'll encounter Shyrra and search for the four stones that disappeared with the Sandman. It'd at least give me purpose."

Amica replied, "Whatever! We must go!"

The Good Witch grabbed Oilill and Cupid and vanished in an instant. Kirrie remained in the red elm for a while and peered through the thick bark. When opportunity presented, she exited the tree, slipped across the common area, and disappeared into the thick brush.

After Kirrie exited the tree the mysterious traveler known as the Sandman returned unnoticed to the inner red elm. The robed figure rubbed the cherry red birthmark on his chin, then interlocked his fingers, and murmured several lyrical phrases. Three ornate staffs positioned by his side. Runes appeared on the staffs. The four elemental stones appeared on the table in the center of the hollow living tree. The Sandman dutifully touched each stone and said, "I thank the Staves of the Four Winds, the Windward Staves, children of the Bloodstone, the Source of Magick."

Then he and the Summoning Stones of Fire, Air, Water, and Earth vanished only to reappear in the foyer of the Old Orange Spruce, the ancestral home of the Teacher of the Drelves, a position now held for thirteen changes of season by Camille Aires life-mate of bowyer and fletcher BJ Aires. The Sandman positioned the four relics in the corners of the anteroom.

Runes appeared on the Windward Staves and Elemental Stones.

Ǿ ∞ Ǿ

Ǿ ∞ Ǿ

∞ Ǿ ∞

Ǿ ∞ Ǿ

∞ Ǿ ∞

The Elemental Stones
(SSF, SSW, SSE, SSA)

The Sandman smiled and again uttered, "I thank the Staves of the Four Winds, the Windward Staves, children of the Bloodstone, the Source of Magick." The traveler and staves disappeared. Gray auras briefly surrounded the four stones.

CHAPTER 3

Treasures for Drelvedom

Three very different suns gave light to Parallan, the world of the Drelves. Total darkness never covered the land. The little yellow sun Meries traversed the sky in sixteen hours. When Meries drew high in the sky, the little star bathed the World of the Three Suns with amber light, warmed the world, and imparted beautiful yellow and orange hues to the skies of Parallan. Rather than a round bright spot, the dark sun Orpheus was akin to a large black unmoving spiraling defect in the sky. Giant Orpheus gave little light but controlled the movement of Meries. Andreas, the Gray Wanderer, appeared in the sky irregularly. Oft times Andreas came into view as a gray speck on the horizon. From time to time the wanderer left the skies altogether. Every now and then the gray sun wobbled a bit closer to the World of the Three Suns.

Eight-hour periods of waxing and waning amber light made up one cycle of Meries. The little yellow sun never left the horizon, but every sixty cycles Meries slunk down in the amber sky and lingered at its zenith for a time of fifteen cycles, or 240 hours. These nadirs of Meries's light were called dark periods. During the dark period the scant light that reached the World of the Three Suns derived mostly from great Orpheus with variable contribution from the Gray Wanderer. Thus the times of greatest light were called light periods, the lesser light were amber periods, and the cyclic extended periods of least illumination were called dark periods.

Some peoples used the arbitrary term "day" to describe one eight hour cycle of bright light and the term "night" to describe the eight hour amber periods. The terms day and night had little meaning during the 240 hour-long time of decreased illumination of the dark period. Most folk simply used the term dark period. But the time from the beginning of one dark period to the beginning of the next was consistently the equivalent of 75 cycles of Meries, or 1200 hours.

On the odd occasion the Gray Wanderer drew near Parallan. Approximations of Andreas gave wondrous gifts to the fauna, flora, and folk of the World of the Three Suns. During these unpredictable Approximations, the Gray Wanderer filled the sky, bathed the land with its deep gray light, and augmented forces of Magick in the world.

Many peoples of Parallan celebrated the significant rituals of their given ilk during dark periods. For instance the Drelves harvested the tubers of the enhancing plant only during the dark period. Vital to the Drelves, the enhancing plant's tubers matured in eight dark periods. Thus, a season of the harvest encompassed eight dark periods, and equaled the time of 600 cycles of Meries; 480 cycles of light and amber periods and the equivalent of 120 cycles of relative darkness. Drelves called the time between harvests a "season of the harvest," a change of season," or a "year."

Drelves usually matured in fifteen to thirty *years* and chose life-mates when they found love. If blessed by good health and bountiful harvests of the disease fighting enhancing root, the forest folk lived to see hundreds of harvests. Teachers oft lived longer, and the ultra-rare Spellweavers had uncommonly long lives. Camille Aires ascended to Teacher from necessity. The browning of her hair slowed as she labored at assigned tasks in the Old Orange Spruce. Either the tree itself or the artifacts it held gave the Teachers extended life. Camille Aires's chronic pain and limp resulted from a nefarious attack by Drolls transformed by Magick. The attack occurred seasons past at the Drelvish sanctuary Sylvan Lake.

Thirteen years after the disappearance of the Spellweaver Yannuvia and folk of Lost Sons and eleven changes of seasons after the destruction of the Kiennish forts by the Fire Wizard Kirrie and odd cherubic merchant, Teacher Camille Aires discovered the four elemental stones (SSF, SSE, SSA, and SSW) in the foyer of the Old Orange Spruce.

The Summoning Stone of Fire (SSF) bore the image of a proud Fire Horse and looked like a rock. Erstwhile Teacher Kirrie had carried the artifact.

The water stone shared the shape and dimensions of the Summoning Stone of Fire (SSF). The ovoid blue Water Stone (SSW) looked more like a glob of water and felt wet. The precise image of a water horse was faintly visible on the surface of the moist watery material. The image mimicked the Kelpie that had destroyed General Saligia's terror the Xorn eleven seasons past. The artifact was a bit bluer than water.

The Teacher's fingers passed into the deep blue artifact but neither disrupted the integrity of the prolate spheroid nor the image of the kelpie. Ever so faintly three runes appeared on the opposite side of the blue ovoid shape.

∞ **Ó** ∞

Camille Aires touched the Air Stone and wrapped her fingers around the scintillating colors. The object had no appreciable weight. The beautiful prolate spheroid had the appearance of a rainbow bent into fattened cigar shape. Its density was similar to the misty equine that had appeared with Kirrie's odd entourage. Runes appeared on its stunning surface.

∞ **Ó** ∞

The Earth Stone (SSE) shared the oblate spheroid shape of the Fire Stone (SSF), Air Stone (SSA), and Water Stone (SSW), but it looked like a clump of red clay. Three runes glowed brightly on its surface.

Ó ∞ **Ó**

The Earth Stone hummed and emitted faint gray light.

Runes appeared on all four oblate spheroids.

Faint beams of grayness emanated from the four devices and surrounded the fatigued Teacher. Her legs grew heavy. Camille closed her eyes and lay down on the oversized chair in the foyer of the Old Orange Spruce and slept. Shapeless grayness entered her dreams.

Wisps...

Threads...

Threads of Magick...

Threads of fate...

Threads of time…
Threads connecting worlds …
Dreams connecting worlds …
Dreams of Magick…
The Magick of Dreams…
Magick connecting dreams…
Magick connecting worlds…
Grayness…

Words formed in the Teacher's mind. "Accept the gift of these Xennic Stones for your people."

Camille managed, "Am I visited by Dreamraiders? Where is the redness and Good Witch?"

The voice answered, "You are visited by the grayness of Andreas. You may call me Xenn."

Grayness gave way to dreams of her youth, running with her beloved BJ in the Red Meadow and picnicking in the shadow of the Lone Oak. Then Camille Aires awakened. Briefly grayness akin to that seen during the Approximation of the Wandering sun Andreas filled the Old Orange Spruce. She had slept only a moment but the fatigue had left her body and mind.

The Teacher Camille Aires summoned Spellweaver Gaelyss and elders of Alms Glen. Elders Blanchard and Debby brought the group together. The artifacts shared the size and prolate spheroid shape of exceptional stones previously seen in Alms Glen. Morganne, Kirrie, and Edkim had initially possessed those artifacts, which had been tied to the mysterious Good Witch. Some benefit came from the stones, but Teacher Edkim fell heroically as he turned the tide of The Lone Oak Battle with the Cold Stone. Kirrie had followed in the footsteps of Gaelyss's prodigal twin brother Yannuvia and fallen under the influence of Fire Magick.

Kirrie, the missing Fire Wizard and erstwhile teacher and former life-mate of Gaelyss, had carried the Summoning Stone of Fire. The stone had the power to summon and control creatures. Kirrie was thought lost after a battle in the skies with a wyvern rider. She returned changed. Fire Magick corrupted the Lost Spellweaver Yannuvia and Kirrie. Though the actions of Kirrie and the odd cherubic merchant

Cupid had saved Drelvedom from General Saligia of Aulgmoor's last assault 11 changes of season earlier, the leaders of Alms Glen still had dread of the device and Fire Magick. Morganne had deserted the folk of Alms Glen and presumably followed Yannuvia and the folk of Lost Sons to who knows where. The artifacts Camille Aires discovered were bizarre, particularly the odd water stone. Thus, the leaders of Alms Glen were very suspicious of the four artifacts, which Camille deemed Xennic Stones, the name relayed to her in her dream.

Gaelyss cast Detection of Evil, Identify, and Dispel Evil dweomers upon the devices. Each spell produced three runes on the stones and an aura of grayness. On the Summoning Stone of Fire (SSF) and Earth Stone (SSE):

$$Ø \infty Ø$$

On the Water Stone (SSW) and Air Stone (SSA):

$$\infty Ø \infty$$

Gaelyss learned nothing more from the spells.

The veteran field commander Sergeant Major Rumsie and Bowyer and Fletcher BJ Aires urged caution. Rumsie and BJ had seen many battles and preferred stealth and tactics to Magick. Rumsie's Rangers had maintained vigilance since the last devastating defeat of Aulgmoor's forces eleven changes of seasons past. Rumors held General Saligia's influence outside Aulgmoor faded and his erstwhile Drollen allies deserted him. Certainly no major forces had gathered near the River Ornash. Rumors circulated of a dark shadow lurking in the river and misty forms floating in the skies. Rumsie's scouts encountered small parties of Drolls and Kiennites meandering through the woods and rarely approaching the charred ruins of Fort Melphat north of the wide meadow and the second destroyed bastion New Aulgmoor to the south of the meadow. Strange stealthy Droll-sized folk from the south appeared more often. The former Teacher Kirrie first described them after seeing them battling Aulgmoor's forces during the conflict eleven years past. Drelvish Rangers hidden among their friendly allies of the forest observed the newcomers' activities. Gaelyss provided assistance through Comprehend Languages Spells and the Rangers Unstoffe, Glinwood, and Vynda bravely approached a scouting party of the mountain folk and learned the newcomers referred to their ilk as "Draiths." Unstoffe and Vynda adhered to Sergeant Major Rumsie's orders and avoided contact with the Draiths. The newcomers skirted the western perimeter of the wide once red meadow and made forays into the forest leading toward Aulgmoor. As time passed the number of parties from the southern mountains increased. No major incursions from Aulgmoor and the Drollen clans had happened since Saligia's crushing defeat, but small parties of Drolls ventured toward the meadow. On rare occasion Drolls encountered the Draiths. The end result was always the same. The unarmed southerners handily defeated the Drolls and seldom suffered casualties. During the first five years after Saligia's defeat and the destruction of the Kiennish fortresses by the Fire Wizards Rumsie's Rangers only rarely encountered Kiennites.

In the sixth season a legion of Drolls led by a massive Kiennite under the banner of Aulgmoor and accompanied by a company of Kiennish archers trekked down the road from Aulgmoor and approached the meadow. The elaborately dressed Kiennite carried the dragon-scale shield Saligia had carried. Ranger Glinwood bravely hid among the branches of a friendly tangleweed and learned the leader was the High Commander of Aulgmoor Cu Seven. Cu Seven's troupe gingerly approached the meadow and clumsily spread out among the less than willing flora. Glinwood avoided the Drolls and Kiennites and scampered up a red elm. The forces of Aulgmoor kept constant vigil toward the south and never approached the Drelves' positions on the eastern side of the meadow. After watching awhile Cu Seven ordered his forces to proceed in single file along the woods opposite Alms Glen.

Rangers posted high in the trees noted these movements. Rumsie feared the time of peace was ending but such was not the case for the Drelves. However, the Drolls and Kiennites encountered a small party of Draiths near the path leading the destroyed fortress south of the meadow. A fierce battle ensued. Though badly outnumbered, the Draiths made short work of Cu Seven's troops. The banner of Aulgmoor once again fluttered in the breezes as the survivors retreated toward the Doombringers. Since that defeat Drolls and Kiennites had not returned in numbers, but scouting parties from the south increased in number and pushed further north of the meadow. The Draiths went as far as the gap that led to Aulgmoor proper. Unlike Kiennites and Drolls the Draiths did little to disrupt the forest.

The forest slowly recovered from the massive destruction suffered at the hands of General Saligia's forces. Eleven years allowed young trees to approach maturity. Mobile flora returned to the propinquity of Alms Glen. Young Drelves were oft called sprouts! The Drelves' symbiotic relationship with the forest encouraged rambling bramble bushes, triffids of all sorts, shrinking violets, rolling rocks, climbing hydrangeas, cardinal climbers, blooming sooners, walkabout bushes, displacer plants, peashooters, and others to return. What remained absent was the power of the forest's greatest defenders, the Tree Herders. Old Yellow, Big Red, and Orange Julian had fallen in the conflicts. The Tree Shepherd of Green Vale differed from the Tree Herder ilk in many ways other than having green leaves. The Tree Shepherd staunchly guarded Green Vale and never left the circle of Thirttene Friends. The Tree Shepherd communicated telepathically as did tree herders, but the enigmatic icon of Green Vale seldom shared his thoughts even with Spellweavers. He'd berated both Spellweaver Yannuvia and Kirrie and termed them "Fire Wizards."

The Drelves were far from complacent. Eleven years of relative peace had allowed Gaelyss to shore up the natural defenses of Alms Glen with his Magick. The gray sun Andreas had remained away, so no new Spellweavers had been born, but Gaelyss was just maturing. The Dreamraiders, Kirrie, and members of her odd entourage had not returned.

Old fears resurfaced with the appearance of the quartet of stones discovered by Camille Aires. The Spellweaver and Teacher were less fearful of the newfound artifacts. After great debate it was decided that the Teacher should store the artifacts with the Annals of Drelvedom. The Spellweaver Gaelyss, now dubbed the Great Defender, placed illusory and protective spells on the four stones. When the stones came within thirteen paces of the Spellbooks stored within the Old Orange Spruce, telltale runes appeared on the four Xennic Stones.

On the Summoning Stone of Fire (SSF) and Earth Stone (SSE):

$$\text{Ø} \infty \text{Ø}$$

On the Water Stone (SSW) and Air Stone (SSA):

$$\infty \text{Ø} \infty$$

When this happened, Camille and Gaelyss carefully placed the Water Stone (SSW), Air Stone (SSA), and Earth Stone (SSE) fourteen paces away from both the cache of spell books and one another. As a further precaution Gaelyss carried the Summoning Stone of Fire (SSF) to his home in Alms Glen proper.

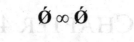

CHAPTER 4

Travels...

The Dreamraider's companions the púca Sean-Cupid and Leprechaun Oilill perceived only the passage of a few heartbeats. Amica Carmisino delivered Oilill and Sean to their homes near Loch Neagh and immediately departed.

Ǿ ∞ Ǿ

Erstwhile Teacher of the Drelves Kirrie arrived in Green Vale. Taller trees and bushes rimmed the roughly circular emerald area. In the entire Drelves' realm only Green Vale nurtured green foliage. A circular valley filled with short shrubby plants dominated the area. A hill occupied the center of the area. Bright green plush grassy moss extended several paces from the tree line and formed a border around the valley. At the edge of the green moss, the terrain followed a gentle fifteen-degree incline for thirty paces to the vale's floor. The gently rolling floor of Green Vale extended several hundred paces and circled the central knoll. A grassy upslope extended fifty paces from the floor to the top of the central hill. Many small rivulets coursed through the landscape. On top of the hillock a geyser erupted from the very center of the hill and bathed the trees with waters of many hues. After the geyser erupted for thirty-nine heartbeats, the thunder ceased and left the area quiet. Shrubby plants filled the hillsides and the floor of the Vale. None grew on the central hill. The plants did not grow in rows. Instead the plants were arbitrarily set in the gently rolling terrain. Very few other plants intermingled with the enhancing plants. Red, yellow, and orange colors typified foliage of the lands of the World of the Three Suns. The only exceptions were

Green Vale and Emerald Island, where deep green plants dominated the flora.

Many peoples of Parallan celebrated the significant rituals of their given ilk during dark periods. Drelves harvested the tubers of the enhancing plant only during the dark period. The enhancing plant's vital tubers matured in eight dark periods. A season of the harvest encompassed eight dark periods and equaled the time of 600 cycles of Meries; 480 cycles of light and amber periods and the equivalent of 120 cycles of relative darkness. Drelves called the time between harvests a "season of the harvest" or a "year."

If blessed by good health and bountiful harvests of the disease fighting enhancing root, the forest folk lived to see hundreds of harvests. Teachers oft lived longer, and ultra-rare Spellweavers had uncommonly long lives. Twin Spellweavers Gaelyss and Yannuvia arrived with an Approximation of Andreas a year before Kirrie's birth.

Tears welled in Kirrie's eyes. She'd encouraged her former life mate Gaelyss and diminished his brother Yannuvia. She'd said,

"Gaelyss, you have done so much for our people. Alms Glen survives. Though we suffered the loss of little Deirdre and noble Balewyn, we have the healthiest and most populous settlement in Drelvedom's history. More healthy people inhabit Alms Glen than any time in old Clarke and Blanchard's memory. Your spells protect and nurture us. Your brother is... was my friend. He angrily addressed the council and challenged you. He has...changed."

Gaelyss and the rest of Drelvedom thought Kirrie dead after her battle with the wyvern rider Encompy Tenet. Kirrie traveled in the red and blue light and returned to Drelvedom on the second anniversary of the Spellweaver Yannuvia and folk of Lost Sons' disappearance. Kirrie's two year absence paralleled the Lost Spellweaver Yannuvia. Gaelyss moved on and took Fadra from Meadowsweet as life mate.

$$Ø \infty Ø$$

Like Yannuvia... Kirrie had returned changed. Grayness touched her. Fire Magick came at a cost. Being at Green Vale and near enhancing plants comforted the former Teacher. The Dark Period began. Soon contingents of Drelves would arrive to harvest mature tubers.

19

Kirrie approached the closest waist high plant and sang in low soothing voice. The plant curled its leaves and retracted barely visible needle-like thorns. Kirrie then tenderly touched the spines of the enhancing plant's upper leaves. The plant pulled its limbs upward and inward, changing from full to thin narrow bush. The ex-Teacher removed a small spade from her pack and knelt at the base of the plant. She delicately inserted the spade into the ground and moved the digging instrument around the base of the plant. The she-Drelve gently pulled the entire plant from the soil, held it aloft, and exposed its roots. The plant emitted gray auras. Kirrie expertly exposed several thumbnail sized tubers dangling from the uncovered roots. She gently pulled tubers from the roots, but very carefully left one tuber undisturbed. The she-Drelve then gently stroked the roots and carefully placed the plant back on the soft dark ground. The enhancing plant's roots plunged back into the soil. Kirrie sang again, and the little bush expanded its branches and reopened its red flowers. Kirrie munched on a purplish tuber and then walked up to the crest of the central hillock.

The ostracized erstwhile Teacher stood before the ancient Tree Shepherd in the circle of Thirttene Friends.

Ø ∞ Ø

I, II, III, IV, V, VI, VII, VIII, IX, X, XI, XII, XIII

∞ Ø ∞

The Thirttene Friends

Ø ∞ Ø

I, II, III, IV, V, VI, VII, VIII, IX, X, XI, XII, XIII

∞ Ø ∞

Ø ∞ Ø I ∞ Ø ∞

The Apple Tree…

Ø ∞ Ø II ∞ Ø ∞

The pear tree…

Ø ∞ Ø **III** ∞ Ø ∞

The snowberry bush…

Ø ∞ Ø **IV** ∞ Ø ∞

The purplanana bush…

Ø ∞ Ø **V** ∞ Ø ∞

The tree Sprite's home, the great green oak…

Ø ∞ Ø **VI** ∞ Ø ∞

The Rainbow luck bush…

Ø ∞ Ø **VII** ∞ Ø ∞

The Tree Shepherd…

Ø ∞ Ø **VIII** ∞ Ø ∞

The Jellybean bush…

Ø ∞ Ø **IX** ∞ Ø ∞

The gem bush…

Ø ∞ Ø **X** ∞ Ø ∞

The silver maple…

Ø ∞ Ø **XI** ∞ Ø ∞

The l'orange tree…

Ø ∞ Ø **XII** ∞ Ø ∞

The Sick Amore…

Ǿ ∞ Ǿ XIII ∞ Ǿ ∞

The toot and see scroll tree…

The Thirttene Friends…
The Tree Shepherd sent an icy telepathic message that chilled Kirrie to the bone, "Fire Wizard!"
Words formed in Kirrie's mind.

"I give you my blood through which you will receive all you seek. You in turn give to me your all."

Ǿ ∞ Ǿ

She thought of the skies over the mutilated Red Meadow whilst aboard the púca Sean in his hippogriff guise…
Sean-hippogriff labored to support her. Kirrie extended her left arm and uttered twenty-one phrases aloud in the dark language of *Grayness*. Gray auras surrounded her. General Saligia and High Commander Cu Seven rode away from the castle at a gallop. Kirrie crushed sulfur and sent a white-hot ball of fire into the structure New Melphat. Tremendous explosions followed. Unsatisfied she smashed another bit of sulfur, uttered the phrases again, and sent an even larger stream of Fire Magick into the structure. Another explosion followed. Anguished screams filled the air. Kirrie attacked a third and then a fourth time. New Melphat lay in molten rubble with no signs of life. Kirrie crushed another piece of sulfur.
The púca pleaded, "Kirrie, no more, please! It's done!"
Kirrie's eyes blazed. She sent a fifth Fire Spell into the rubble.
After each spell words filled her mind.

"I give you my blood through which you will receive all you seek. You in turn give to me your all."

Ǿ ∞ Ǿ

"I give you my blood through which you will receive all you seek. You in turn give to me your all."

Ǿ ∞ Ǿ

"I give you my blood through which you will receive all you seek. You in turn give to me your all."

Ǿ ∞ Ǿ

"I give you my blood through which you will receive all you seek. You in turn give to me your all."

Ǿ ∞ Ǿ

"I give you my blood through which you will receive all you seek. You in turn give to me your all."

Ǿ ∞ Ǿ

Five times the words filled Kirrie's mind.
Then...

"You and I are one."

Ǿ ∞ Ǿ

Kirrie's besieged mind returned to the cavern behind Alluring Walls. The bereft Dream Master had witnessed Kirrie's immolation of his daughter Dee Tenet and then muttered, *"Little Fire Wizard, you'll always bear the contempt of your people, and I suppose that's punishment enough. Fire Magick makes us bedfellows. Your presence may ultimately aid my plans."*

Fire Wizard...
Kirrie exited Green Vale and stood for a moment overlooking the hamlet Meadowsweet. Many memories returned. The Good Witch first visited Kirrie's dreams in Meadowsweet and gave Kirrie the Summoning Stone of Fire (SSF). Kirrie and the Dreamraider shared many experiences, culminating in the fiery destruction of Kiennites'

fortresses with Fire Magick. The Dreamraider chose púca visage during the attack. Thereafter witnesses thought the cherub a powerful sorcerer. Kirrie walked away from Green Vale with no particular plan in mind. The Tree Shepherd had branded her Fire Wizard. So many parallels tied her to Yannuvia. Tiredness took over. A large red oak beckoned.

CHAPTER 5

Kirrie's New Home

Kirrie was very familiar with the route from Alms Glen to Meadowsweet and Green Vale. Drelves had used the red oak tree as a resting point in their travels to Meadowsweet. Kirrie slipped through the bark and curled up on the soft pulpy floor. Sleep came.

Then... redness.
Wisps...
Threads...
Threads of Magick...
Threads of fate...
Threads of time...
Threads connecting worlds ...
Dreams connecting worlds ...
Dreams of Magick...
The Magick of Dreams...
Magick connecting dreams...
Magick connecting worlds...
Dream raiders...
Elf pressure...
Albtraum...
Albträume, elf dreams, nightmares...

The Dreamraider appeared in her Good Witch guise and quipped, "Fire Wizard, indeed! Long time, no see!"

Kirrie said, "You... haven't you invaded my sleep enough? I'm used up. Why appear in my dreams?"

Amica answered, "I enjoy it. I can't penetrate the cloak of Green Vale. Thought you were going to stay there. Maybe shack up with the Dryad."

Kirrie answered, "Things didn't go so well."

Amica asked, "Why are you going to do?"

Kirrie thought back, "No plans. I neither have nor want anything to do."

Amica replied, "Mooler ****! Don't give them the satisfaction. I'd keep going just to spite that ***** Fadra."

Kirrie's eyebrows lifted a bit and she agreed, "Hadn't looked at it that way. But I've nowhere to go. Suppose I could trek to Aulgmoor and roast a few Kiennites. The Fire Spell is festering in my brain. If I'm considered a Fire Wizard, I may as well act the part."

Amica shrugged and said, "I could get into that. Old Saligia cowers behind his walls. Invading his dreams and giving him a nightmare doesn't approach the angst he feels when he is awake. He sees Spellweavers around every corner. Unrest grows among the Drolls and Kiennite warrens. His days are numbered now."

Kirrie couldn't resist saying, "You and your Master used him to your advantage. Didn't you give him the stone he bartered with on the red meadow?"

Amica answered, "Guilty as charged."

Kirrie followed, "You played me against Gaelyss. I mean, you really played me. You played a big role creating in my predicament."

Amica conceded, "Yes, I did. It was all part of the Master's plan."

Kirrie said, "His big plan! That sure fell apart. It would have helped had he told us of his daughter! Killing a child in front of her parent did not make me happy! Though she was a ***** and he is a Fire Demon! No offense intended to parties present!"

Amica returned, "None taken! Couldn't have predicted the arrival of the Sandman! I can't figure him out."

Kirrie said, "I'm enjoyed about as much of this conversation as I can. Why don't you go worry someone else?"

Amica said, "I could just leave. But I can offer you something."

Kirrie asked, "What could you do to help or interest me?"

Amica said, "A home. A chance to malinger and maybe one day get some pay back."

Kirrie ventured, "I've exacted vengeance. I killed thousands of Drolls and Kiennites in a few moments and have no regrets."

Amica smiled wryly and said, "Reminds me of someone. Sleep a bit, my sister of Grayness. We gotta stick together. I'll be here when you wake up. Right outside the tree."

Kirrie said glibly, "Don't go to any trouble."

Amica shrugged. "It's no trouble. I might find a Dryad to pinch."

Blueness surrounded the Good Witch and she left Kirrie's dream. A few hours of restless sleep followed and Kirrie awakened. She threw her orange locks over her shoulder, stretched, and exited the tree. The Good Witch was leaning against the red oak.

Kirrie asked, "Don't you have anything better to do?"

Amica extended her left hand and flipped the ends of Kirrie's long disheveled hair, and said, "No."

Kirrie looked around and said, "I've nothing on my agenda. What's yours?"

Amica answered, "Let's take a little trip. Take my arm."

Kirrie shrugged and grabbed the Good Witch's forearm.

Amica cooed, "Feels nice."

Kirrie impatiently added, "Let's go. Wherever!"

Blueness surrounded Kirrie. In a moment blue gave way to a flash of red. She and her companion arrived at an unassuming cabin tucked into a mountainside. Once inside Kirrie noted odd blue and red inlays in the stone floor. Through a smoky window Kirrie recognized peaks of the Doombringer Mountains and the familiar amber skies of the World of the Three Suns. A large table made of bluewood sat in the center of the room. A thick layer of dust covered the table. Blue and green were unusual colors in the World of the Three Suns. Several blocks of exceptional stone, small capped phials filled with clear, yellow, red, and green liquid, and a container filled with smoky water sat on the table. The blue and red stones were the bluest blues and almost the reddest reds.

Dark gray light filled the room. A large gray sphere about three feet in diameter hovered by the table. The eerie stone slowly rotated and bathed the room with gray and deep mauve auras.

Kirrie watched intently. She slowly walked toward the polished mirror and beheld her reflection. Instead of silver-gray locks, she saw fully brown hair. She looked her mother's age! Drelves began life with silver locks that browned as they grew older. However, she only saw the changes that occurred after her first travel in the blueness and redness. This recent jump with the Dreamraider had only been through space and left time alone.

Amica glanced out the window and spoke, "I'm reprising my Master's role. The dark period commences. Kirrie, you are now kindred of Fire and Grayness. The glorious gift of the Flame Spell requires only your knowledge, a bit of sulfur, and a gesture to direct the dweomer's effects. The Summoning Stone of Fire (SSF) is no longer necessary. It rests now in parts unknown. One does not produce Magick like a crop of Nature. At the beginning of every eighth Dark Period you should revalidate and renew your commitment to Grayness and drink from the Cup of Dark Knowledge. The esyuphee hide sack contains the smoking water of Fire Lake. When the yellow sun Meries reaches its nadir and the dark period begins, the chalice will appear on the table. When the chalice appears on the table, pour some of the water into it."

Kirrie asked, "How much?"

Amica answered, "The cup will let you know when you've added enough. Then you must pour four potions into the chalice and mix them with the water. The order of the potions must be **U**ncolored, **Y**ellow, **R**ed, and **G**reen. The Cup of Dark Knowledge always demands an item of Magick. The waters of Fire Lake will suffice. This will maintain and even enhance your power."

Kirrie replied, "Whoa! What about him? Your Master! He's not going to cotton to my using his chalice. And the little phials and the water will run out!"

Amica answered, "The fluids will replenish. The esyuphee sack is Magick. Though his wrath is unmatched, my Master's eye is blinded to Parallan."

Kirrie countered, "He made his way here before quite handily."

Amica answered, "That happened with the power of the four elemental stones. They are now scattered."

Kirrie said, "With your help he gathered them before."

The Good Witch said, "Doesn't matter if he does. The *Wish* is used. Grayness has touched you. We are sisters of Fire. Your people abandon you. You may as well look after number one. You do have me! I'm in your corner now."

Kirrie scoffed, "What a deal! If I again drink from your Master's cup, I'll be even more beholding to him."

Amica answered, "He cannot reach you in the World of Three Suns. Who knows? You may become more powerful than him."

Kirrie glanced out the window. Meries sat at its nadir and the Dark Period continued. By now Drelves were entering Green Vale to harvest enhancing root tubers. Purple auras filled the cabin. A beautiful gem-laced cup appeared on the table. The ornate twelve inch tall cup's base was six inches in diameter and stem six inches long. Its bowl held little more than half an average tankard of ale. A faint mauve glow surrounded the chalice. A large upward pointing triangle dominated the bowl. Flowing runes covered most of the bowl of the deep red cup. Pristine stones of all colors lined the rim and also adorned the sides of the cup.

Kirrie recognized the goblet, having drunk from the cup in the grotto behind Alluring Falls.

Amica said, "Last time it saved your life. Now, sister, drinking the waters of Fire Lake will strengthen you."

Kirrie stared out the window at the tiny speck that was Meries and felt as insignificant as the little yellow sun. A cursory glance into the mirror noted her brown locks. Gone was the silver of youth. She muttered, "Yes, your Master's cup saved my life, but cut it short at the same time."

Amica stated, "Point taken. Now the chalice offers to maintain your vigor."

Kirrie said, "You imply the cup has free will."

Amica answered, "The Cup of Dark Knowledge is infused with the Master's spirit. It hungers for Magick items and draws power from everything it consumes. It goes wherever and whenever it wants. It'll enjoy coming to you. Every use makes it stronger."

Kirrie returned, "Just like you! The smoking water in the purple sack can't taste worse than the stuff I drank behind Alluring Falls. Though I was barely conscious I still remember quaffing it."

Amica said, "It saved your orange, narrow ***. Look at this place. Great view! Protection and Hallucinatory Terrain dweomers keep trespassers at bay. You will only find fruits of the forest and friendly flora and fauna within 1597 Yardley paces of the cabin. You are a sister of fire. Over time you will become a sister of Grayness. Just perform the task as I've directed when the chalice appears. 832040 minute minuteman heartbeats separate the cup's arrivals. There's no 'beat-to-beat' variability in the little critter's heart rhythm."

Kirrie responded, "I don't give a **** about little timekeepers. Magick pervades the depths of my consciousness. I'd like more knowledge. I'll drink the **** potions."

Kirrie one after the other poured uncolored, yellow, red, and green potions into the chalice and then decanted smoky fluid from the purple esyuphee hide sack into the cup. Auras filled the cavern with each addition. Kirrie eased the ornate vessel to her pale orange lips and gently sipped the smoky warm effervescing liquid. Goose bumps covered her carroty skin and she felt chilled to the bone. She tipped the cup and quaffed the remainder of the liquid.

Amica said, "Done!"

Kirrie shrugged, "Are we just hanging out now? What do I do between the cup's visits?"

Amica answered, "Your specific instructions are to await the cup's return. In between it's your decision. The esyuphee hide is a bottomless cup. It'll refill. You may sip the waters of Fire Lake once a day. It should bring you *closer* to me."

Kirrie said, "I could get accustomed to the smoky taste. Suppose it's a Fire Wizard's drink."

Amica's expression changed. Angst dinged her perfect façade. She quipped, "I must be away!"

Blueness surrounded the Dreamraider and Cup of Dark Knowledge. Both disappeared.

Ǿ ∞ Ǿ

Travels…

Time usually mattered little to the Dreamraider, but the thirteenth anniversary of their departure came to be the arrival of the travelers from Lost Sons. Amica rushed to comply with the Dream Master's instructions and greet the travelers at their destination.

Ǿ ∞ Ǿ

Kirrie stood alone in the cabin and stared impassively at the foreboding Doombringer Peaks. Anger, disappointment, and resentment gave way to boredom. Only the snapping of her fingers broke the silence within the little cabin. Little sparks escaped from her fingertips with each repetition. Rivulets of blue smoke circled about the room. Faint odors of sulfur and mint permeated the cabin. Kirrie soon coordinated her finger snapping to the timing of a minute minuteman's heartbeat. It was the first step to mastering time. Light periods gave way to dark periods and Kirrie ventured outside the cottage after three of Parallan's days. Kirrie did not seek respite. She wandered to the tree line and found some of the Dream Master's markings on the trees. The sojourner had vainly attempted to wall off his progeny from the dangers of the world, but his uncooperative spouse Turrina had led her three children from the cabin and fell prey to a wyvern. Wyvern rider Ess Tenet and his life mate took the children in and eventually Locum, Encompy, and Dioressa took Ess's name and followed in his steps to become wyvern riders. Dioressa the youngest took the moniker Dee and developed skills greater than her older brothers, who fell in conflict with the Drelves. Kirrie had smote Dee Tenet in the cavern behind Alluring Falls. Dee's blood father, the unpredictable Dream Master, witnessed his daughter's death. The mysterious Sandman saved Kirrie from the Dream Master's wrath. This culminated in her current situation. Ostracized by Drelvedom and the Tree Shepherd in Green Vale the erstwhile Teacher had followed the Dreamraider Amica to this austere cabin. Kirrie moved stealthily among the flora and fauna. The forest and particularly mobile plants did not consider her a "Fire Wizard." Kirrie supplemented her store of food in the cabin with fresh fruits of the forest. The cabin's earlier inhabitant had placed Create Food and Water dweomers on the cabin's supplies. Kirrie carried a stash of enhancing root tubers in her pack, but the fruit so vital to Drelvish life lost its appealing taste. She thirsted more for the smoky waters within the esyuphee hide sack and enjoyed her daily drink. The erstwhile Teacher followed the Dreamraider's instructions and awaited the return of the chalice. After an interval of 832040 minute minuteman heartbeats the ornate cup reappeared. Kirrie followed directions to the "t."

Imbibing the smoky fluid warmed and replenished her.

Kirrie changed.

Ǿ ∞ Ǿ

Travels…
The First Wandmaker Yannuvia and 232 companions traveled in the blue light.

Ǿ ∞ Ǿ

Alms Glen noted the thirteenth anniversary of their departure from Lost Sons.

Ǿ ∞ Ǿ

CHAPTER 6

Outlaws in Lost Sons

At thirteen, Spellweaver Yannuvia went into the wild woods to seek the power hidden behind the waterfalls. His walkabouts had lasted eight years in the time of Alms Glen and the World of the Three Suns. Instead of eight years, Yannuvia had sensed the passage of less than a single dark period, about sixteen days. Yet he appeared to have aged sixty years. The Spellweaver had faced a series of difficult choices. In just fourteen changes of seasons Yannuvia had walked in the grayness of Andreas, traveled in the red and blue light, and drank from the Cup of Dark Knowledge. Mender's blood touched him.

Now 230 souls looked to Yannuvia for guidance. The fourteen-year-old, greenish-grayish, pointed-eared, seventy-ish-appearing, Menderish, Drelvish, Spellweaverish, and wand-wielder Yannuvia didn't relish the role. The Spellweaver and those loyal to him gathered in the Drelvish community Lost Sons. Many events predated the gathering in the community splintered from Alms Glen.

His twin brother and fellow Spellweaver Gaelyss had betrayed him. Yannuvia suffered humiliation and defeat at the River Ornash. The battle resulted in the deaths of noble Ranger Banderas, Diana Maceda, Old Clarke Maceda, and the Water Sprites Condee, Illarie, and Elspeth. Yannuvia deceptively obtained the red and blue tipped wand and escaped Saligia's clutches through *Translocation* to Lost Sons from the River Ornash by traveling in its red and blue light. Each thinking the other unscrupulously possessed it, Gaelyss and General Saligia of Aulgmoor would fight over the missing artifact.

Yannuvia's followers including Menderish Clouse gathered in Lost Sons. Yannuvia and the folk of Lost Sons defied the orders of the council. Missing were his mother Carinne, Banderas, Clarke Maceda, Diana Maceda, Vioss, Bystar, little Deirdre, and Balewyn, all killed by enemies of Drelvedom. Yannuvia's conflict with his brother and the Council of Alms Glen widened after the Drelves' ancestral enemies Drolls killed the Spellweavers' mother Carinne in an ambush at Sylvan Lake. Yannuvia retaliated by destroying the Kiennish fortress Fort Melphat with a devastating Fire Spell. Over a thousand Drolls and Kiennites died. Before Yannuvia's collusion with the Dreamraiders, Fire Magick was alien to Drelvedom's Spellweavers. The ancient Tree Shepherd in Green Vale labeled Yannuvia "Fire Wizard."

231 persons stood among the great trees and dense red, yellow, and orange foliage in the cozy common area of the hamlet Lost Sons. Yannuvia, Klunkus, and Beaux hailed from Alms Glen. Klunkus and Beaux had worked closely with Lost Sons Rangers Lodi, Buck, and Owings. All had seen duty in the battles against Drolls and Kiennites.

Yannuvia's father's friend and the young Spellweaver's mentor Banderas died in the battle at the Ornash River. Banderas's daughters Joulie and Jonna had been stalwart friends and traveling companions for Yannuvia. The sisters accompanied Yannuvia on the Mender Fisher's quest for confinement. Their travels prematurely aged both sisters. Fisher had lived among the Drelves' enemies the Kiennites at Aulgmoor for many years and arrived in Lost Sons while on his quest to accomplish a tribulation necessary to continue his ilk. Too cold, rocky, and exposed, the area around Aulgmoor didn't meet the requirements for Fisher's confinement. He headed south to the plain beyond the Doombringers, crossed the Ornash River by bribing the ferryman with ale, made his way across the plain, and reached the vicinity of the once red meadow. Drelves easily noted the pale healer in the woods and observed his travels. Pain from his enlarging nodule overwhelmed the Mender. The Drelves Buck and Owings carried the prostrate Mender to the common area of Lost Sons and summoned Dienas, Banderas, and Yannuvia. Joulie joined them. Elder Dienas chastised the guards for bringing Fisher to Lost Sons.

Owings defended his actions, saying, "He's in pain, elder. We heard him suffering in the woods. He has no discernible wounds, but he keeps clutching his swollen left hand. Though swollen, it's not discolored. Nothing of him shows color! He's colorless! Only something green outside of Green Vale is harder to find in these woods."

Fisher groaned incoherently. Yannuvia took the Mender's left hand. The area between the fifth and sixth digits stretched the pale skin taut. Beads of milky sweat oozed from the pale person's skin. A drop of thicker liquid oozed from his parched lips at the corner of his mouth. The fluid exuding from the Mender's lip was as white as milkweed juice. Milkweed was a beneficial plant that grew to the size of a Droll and produced a sweet nutritious juice that was high in calcium and vitamins. Yannuvia muttered several phrases in old Drelvish and tightly grasped the suffering pastel chap's swollen left hand. Yannuvia's Empathy Spell intensified the gray light of the approaching sun that fell on the Mender. The Spellweaver absorbed a bit of the Mender's pain and winced. *Yannuvia felt comforted!* Yannuvia then released Fisher's hand. The Spellweaver uttered more arcane phrases, extended his fingers, and touched Fisher's brow. Red sparks flew from the Spellweaver's extended digits and struck Fisher, then returned to Yannuvia. Two small cuts on the Spellweaver's hand closed. Sparks struck Banderas and Joulie and also healed scratches on their bodies. The Mender stopped grimacing, smiled wryly, and entered a deep sleep. Fisher, like all Menders, was a *Reflector.*

Yannuvia, Jonna, and Joulie accompanied him on his journey seeking confinement. Fisher required darkness and potting soil. The arduous journey brought them into many conflicts. Fisher was mortally wounded during a battle with the dreaded tandem of Baxcat and Leicat. His *reflector* status stopped Yannuvia from using Magick to attend the pale healer's wounds. In extremis Yannuvia, Jonna, and Joulie used their xanthochromic rich blood to save Fisher. In the process Mender's milky ichors entered Yannuvia's veins and tainted his essence. Fisher survived, and the small party made their way to dark caverns near Alluring Falls and more misadventures. Yannuvia prepared the dark ground with Dig and Rock to Mud Spells. The Mender Fisher filled the defect in the cavern floor with potting soil. The Mender knelt, crawled onto the soft potting soil, curled into a fetal position, pushed his left forearm deeply into the softened soil, and buried the painful swollen area of his left hand. Fisher closed his eyes. Slowly twig-like structures sprang from the Mender's entire body and grew outward and away from his trunk.

Over a period of three hours, the twigs grew into a dome. Then thin wafer-like structures extended from each twig and grew together. Three cycles of Meries passed. By then a dome of pale green tissue covered the Mender's body. The cocoon grew over the entire area excavated by Yannuvia's Dig Spell and obscured Fisher. Yannuvia carefully extended his left hand and gently touched the hardened cocoon. Fisher's cocoon was harder than the granite-like walls of the cavern.

Yannuvia changed. As he turned to exit the cavern the Spellweaver felt a sharp twinge at the base of the fifth finger of his left hand. He rubbed the area and felt a small tender nodule at the base of his fifth finger and...unquestionably a sixth digit erupted just beyond the nodule. His ears itched. The Spellweaver rubbed them. Small points grew from his ears.

Pointed! Never had a Drelve sported pointed ears!

Yannuvia and the sisters left the Mender in a pharate state inside the chrysalis and returned to the grotto beyond Alluring Falls. To seek respite and encountered the Dreamraider Good Witch. The trio traveled in red and blue light and encountered the Dream Master. They returned to the World of the Three Suns and found Andreas again in Approximation. Traveling in the red and blue light aged the lovely daughters of Banderas. Yannuvia, Jonna, and Joulie hurried back to Fisher's chrysalis. The greenish shell scintillated through colors of the spectrum and then all shades of gray. As the colors changed, the shell contracted and expanded. Each time the shell expanded, it filled more of the cavern.

"It's almost like it's breathing," Jonna remarked.

Then the shell expanded further. A subtle ripping sound filled the cavern, and the covering slipped away and revealed Fisher and a fully-grown, green, pointed-eared, Drelvish-Menderish fellow, a younger lime green version of Yannuvia. The large protuberance had disappeared from Fisher's left hand. The distinctly green second figure resembled a pointed-eared Drelve. Its facial features mimicked the Spellweaver Yannuvia.

Fisher sighed and said, "It is done. Finding an area of darkness in our world where I could plant my seed was not an easy task. The underground caverns near the Alluring Falls provided a site. We encountered zombies, cave bats, and other unpleasant denizens of the dark in the caverns."

Yannuvia quizzically gazed at the two figures standing before him in the gray light and asked, "Is this your spawn?"

Fisher stared back at the Spellweaver and nonchalantly answered, "No, this is *our* spawn. Spellweaver, nothing in the collective consciousness of my ilk explains him. He shares *our* traits. He is a new ilk, I suppose."

Clouse was the product of Fisher's confinement and emerged with Fisher from the chrysalis a greenish nigh spitting image of the Spellweaver Yannuvia. The Spellweaver stared the *new* Mender eye-to-eye and compared their appearance. Same height, nose, lips, pointed ears, facial features, wrinkles, physique...different color. Yannuvia's browning hair was a subtle but telltale sign of aging. His opposite's hair was green. Yannuvia hazarded a glance at the green guy's hands. Another difference...both shared the little nodule at the base of the left sixth digit, but the greener Fisher's spawn had a fully developed sixth digit on *both* hands.

Fisher's path led him back to Aulgmoor.

Clouse stuck with the Spellweaver Yannuvia. Clouse shared Yannuvia's Magick and Fisher's connection to the cumulative knowledge of Menders. Clouse was Menderish, Spellweaverish, and Drelvish. Yannuvia was a bit Menderish and greenish. He developed pointed ears and a small nodule on his left hand. The greenish younger Spellweaverish Clouse came to Lost Sons when Yannuvia, Fisher, and the daughters of Banderas returned from their three year sojourn. The journey seemed only a few days to the travelers but aged Jonna, Joulie, and Yannuvia decades.

All other sojourners were from the splintered community of Lost Sons. Dienas and Yiuryna formed the community after the deaths of the neophytes Bystar and Vioss. Drelves' ancestral enemies the Drolls attacked and killed Bystar and Vioss, who were returning from the harvest of the enhancing root at Green Vale. The Council of Alms Glen refused to take action. The elders Dienas and Yiuryna disagreed with the Council and founded Lost Sons. Many members of the Alms Glen community sympathized with Dienas, Yiuryna, and their followers. Bereavement over the loss of his beloved Diana Maceda overwhelmed noble Klunkus. Klunkus defied the orders of the elders of Alms Glen and pursued the enemies north of the former red meadow and ultimately cast lots with Yannuvia. His friend Beaux followed him. Yannuvia brought down the Kiennish Fort Melphat with a massive Fire Spell.

Yannuvia, Klunkus, Beaux, and the rest of their party became outlaws.

CHAPTER 7

Visions of a New Home

Time was fickle.

The Dreamraiders promised a new realm and averred drinking Seventh Nectar from translucent vessel decreased time's fickleness.

Yannuvia and his friends gathered in the common area of Lost Sons and shared their last moments in the hamlet. The threat from Alms Glen and Gaelyss was imminent. The Spellweaver risked treating with the tall man with the cherry red heart-shaped birthmark on his face and Good Witch. The Spellweaver had accepted the Dream Master's proposal. The Dreamraiders promised a new realm and safe passage though the red and blue light for the Spellweaver and his followers. The Dream Master prepared a demonstration in the common area of Lost Sons.

The Dream Master appeared a Dark Sorcerer with a heart-shaped red birthmark on his face. The ersatz Dark Sorcerer supinated his right hand and summoned a gray sphere six feet in diameter. The sphere appeared, levitated, and rotated slowly in front of the bedazzled Drelves and Clouse. The Dream Master called the orb "The Central Sphere" and deemed it a source of grayness for "the underworld."

The Dream Master waved his left arm and revealed *images* of an ornate edifice in a large cavern. The building was a geodesic dome that contained one massive blue vat, one tiny transparent vessel, and five identical maroon vats. Flames erupted beneath and surrounded the bases of the misty structures. The Dream Master referred to the blue vat as "The Vessel of Life," the five identical maroon vats as "Vessels of Definition," and the tiny transparent vessel as 'the Seventh Vessel." The blue vat was 89-fold larger than the five maroon vats, which were in turn 89-fold larger than the tiny clear vessel. The ersatz Dark Sorcerer produced images of a small lavender rounded pit that was roughly the size, shape, and color of a mature enhancing root tuber, and then translucent uncolored, yellow, red, and green fruits. The Dream Master called the lavender pit and four fruits "the fruits of life." Many exotic spices appeared and fell into the large blue vat. Violet fumes escaped from the towering vessel. Invisible forces filled the five Vessels of Definition with violet liquid taken from the great vat. Lavender pits were added to the Vessel of Definition adjacent to the Vessel of Life. Uncolored translucent fruits, Zirconium, iron, and Aloe Vera went into the second. Yellow fruits, sulfur, and gold, rarity in some worlds and nuisance in others, went into the third. Red fruits, rubies, onyx, lapis lazuli, and other stones went into the fourth. Green fruits, leaves of the enhancing plant, green grasses, emeralds, and mint leaves were added to the fifth Vessel of Definition. Smoke of differing colors billowed from the Vessels of Definition… multihued from the first, colorless from the second, yellow from the third, red from the fourth, and green from the fifth. The minuscule seventh vessel about the size of a tavern mug hovered over a tiny flame near the fifth Vessel of definition. The flickering little flame fashioned a myriad of colors. Little rivulets of gray smoke rising from the tiny vat produced light similar to the rays of the gray sun.

Small equal amounts of liquid from each of the five Vessels of Definition were added to the Seventh Vessel in the order lavender, uncolored, yellow, red, and green. Fluid in the little vat effervesced with the addition of the nectars. After the five nectars were added, a ripened enhancing root tuber was dropped into the mixture. White, then yellow, red, green, and finally gray smoke briefly rose from the Seventh Vessel. When the gray smoke cleared, the nectar within the Seventh Vessel was perfectly clear. The Dream Master referred to this fluid as "Seventh Nectar."

Grayness bathed the hazy images.

The Dream Master muttered arcane phrases, the images faded, and the Seventh Vessel *appeared* in his hand. Clear liquid filled the translucent vessel. The Gray Sphere rotated about six feet above the forest floor and bathed the group with gray light. When the sphere's gray light struck small pebbles and a baby pink elephant, the little rocks and pachyderm flew through the air!

The Dream Master extended the Seventh Vessel to Yannuvia. The Spellweaver Yannuvia took the cup from the Dream Master and drank the Seventh Nectar. Colorless smoky liquid passed beyond his orange lips and shuffled the very fabric of his essence.

First coldness...

Then nothingness...

The Spellweaver fleetingly disappeared then reappeared and changed in color in the order translucent, brilliant yellow, red, green, snow-white, gray, and finally back to his ever so faintly green tinged yellow-orange self. In just fourteen changes of seasons Yannuvia had walked in the grayness of Andreas, traveled in the red and blue light, drank from the Cup of Dark Knowledge, and had now tasted the Seventh Nectar in Lost Sons.

The little chalice refilled with clear nectar. One by one the folk gathered at Lost Sons followed Yannuvia in drinking the contents of the small vessel. The little chalice refilled after each person drank.

The dryad Lexie Glitch arrived with gifts from Green Vale. Lexie carried a small green-leaved tree. A burlap sack filled with rich soil from the hillock in Green Vale surrounded the plant's roots. The little green tree appeared out of place in the common area of Lost Sons. Its trunk bore thirteen branches, gifts donated by the Thirttene Friends and grafted to the trunk by the Tree Shepherd. The Dryad also carried two enhancing plants tenderly wrapped in purplanana leaves and moistened with the waters of the geyser fountain in Green Vale. Lexie also carried two bottles of the geyser fountain's water. The Tree Shepherd instructed the tree and enhancing plants be planted in potting soil.

The Mender Fisher arrived from Aulgmoor, entered the area unnoticed, and said, "And there is a field of potting soil in the underground realm. My ilk has taken from its stock."

Yannuvia looked to the pale healer and said, "Why are you here? General Saligia of Aulgmoor will have your head!"

Fisher replied, "I also came to deliver gifts. Twice after Elfdreams, nightmares, or whatever one prefers to call the interruptions of peaceful sleep, I received odd stones. Out of fairness I presented one to the guard of the entrance to Alms Glen. Now I have two gifts for you and a single gift for Clouse."

Elder Yiuryna said, "We are grateful for any help you give us."

Fisher continued, "Then receive this Locating Stone. I'm told it has the power to give the location of someone or something separated from its holder."

"You said two gifts. What is the other?" Yannuvia asked.

"Me," Fisher answered succinctly.

Fisher approached Clouse and whispered, "Please receive this Mender's Stone. Unlike the gray spheroidal stones, it did not come to me after a visit from the Dreamraiders. I've possessed it a long time and used its greatest power to restore the small tree the Spellweaver Yannuvia destroyed in anger at Alms Glen. Each holder only has a single access to this power of the ashen rock. It bears the same symbols as the gray stones the Drelves carry. Those stones are identical. Note the relative paleness of the Mender's Stone. Now it'll benefit you more than any other, including me."

Fisher extended the pale gray stone to Clouse.

Clouse accepted the stone and added. "I've seen the great field of potting soil in my mind's eye but didn't know what I beheld."

The Teacher of the Drelves Morganne entered the Lost Sons common area and offered, "I'll serve more than teach." Morganne hailed from Meadowsweet, tended Green Vale for seven seasons, and gained valuable experience in caring for the precious plants. She also had the responsibility of guiding the Spellweaver Gaelyss, who was five years younger. She resided in the Old Orange Spruce in Alms Glen after receiving the Stone of Knowledge and succeeding beloved Teacher Edkim.

Still bereft of his beloved Diana Maceda the Ranger Klunkus angrily challenged Morganne, "Where are your mates? Your loyalty lies with Alms Glen!"

Morganne declared her loyalty to Yannuvia and Lost Sons. The erstwhile Teacher presented the gray Stone of Knowledge and explained, "I left all effects of the Teacher of the Drelves in the Old Orange Spruce save one. I cannot leave the Stone of Knowledge. At the time of my death, it would pass my memories."

The tall *Dark Sorcerer* rubbed the heart shaped birthmark and nodded to his sultry companion. The Good Witch gave the Seventh Vessel to Fisher and then Morganne. The Mender and former Teacher drank from the cup. The Good Witch then took the Tree of Thirttene, enhancing plants, and mature fruits and disappeared in a blue flash. In a moment she returned and kissed Clouse on the cheek.

Lexie Glitch scurried up a tall red oak, and called back, "Many voices fill the air. A large group comes from Alms Glen."

"It's time," the Dream Master suggested.

"It's time," Yannuvia agreed.

The Good Witch added, "The cavern in the images is as real as the Seventh Vessel. You may use the wand to reach the cavern. Do not tarry. Your enemies are too many. The vats, seeds, tubers, and mature enhancing plants await you. The command to activate the wand is, '**Hairy true man**.' We'll say farewell, *Wandmaker*."

The Good Witch placed blue fabric on the ground. She and the Dream Master disappeared in a flash of blue. The large gray stone the Dream Master had called the Central Sphere and the little vat remained.

CHAPTER 8

Traveling in Red and Blue Light Arrival

Yannuvia ordered Klunkus, Beaux, Dienas, Yiuryna, Morganne, Fisher, Clouse, Joulie, Jonna, and the gathered community of Lost Sons to draw together into a circle and join hands.

The Spellweaver and neophyte wand wielder said emphatically, "Everyone must hold tightly to those on both sides of him or her. Fisher, please stand between Morganne and Klunkus, hold them, and don't let go! Morganne and Klunkus, hold him securely! Clouse, stand between Jonna and Joulie. Sisters, please keep a tight grip on him! Everyone take a deep breath."

Yannuvia gripped the odd red and blue tipped wand at its midpoint, and said, "**Hairy true man.**"

Blue light surrounded the Spellweaver and his companions. In an instant the group disappeared from common area of the hamlet Lost Sons.

Absolute darkness…

Cold…

Void…

Then colors, energies…

Their feelings spun violently out of control. The Spellweaver and his companions passed through vortex after vortex of color and energy. Pain coursed through very nerve ending and unnatural forces sucked the air out of their lungs. Then, grayness…

Had death taken them?

No…

The young greenish grayish old-appearing Menderish Drelvish Spellweaverish wand-wielder Yannuvia and the folk of Lost Sons fell onto hard stone and arrived on the rocky shore of a great underworld sea in a massive underground expanse. 233 travelers escaped from Lost Sons. The red and blue tipped wand had gotten them to this barren place.

The exhausting journey lasted only a few heartbeats and felt half a life-time. Eerie luminescence filled the area and rendered light roughly equivalent to the Dark Period. The peculiar light came mostly from glowing growths on the distant ceiling and walls of the expanse. The sojourners gathered their humble packs and clustered together. Yannuvia's spells provided enough nourishment to satisfy their hunger for food. Every Drelve longed for a comfortable tree to call his home.

Most of the exhausted refugees from Lost Sons quickly fell asleep. The Spellweaver sighed and leaned against Morganne's willing back. Yannuvia recalled his greeting to Morganne when he returned from his first walkabout,

"Morganne of Meadowsweet, Teacher of the Drelves, I must say you are pleasant to look upon. I spoke to Sergeant Major Rumsie during the celebration. You underestimated the value of your contribution to the defense of the realm. You are a worthy replacement for Edkim."

Yannuvia's dull headache lingered. The Spellweaver closed his eyes and enjoyed Morganne's closeness. The orange-haired she-Drelve's slow deep breathing, pleasant delicate scent, and warmness relaxed the Spellweaver. Yannuvia could no longer fend off exhaustion and fell asleep.

Once Morganne realized Yannuvia was asleep, she stopped her guise. She remained awake until the Spellweaver slept. To practice saying… something she had not found the strength to tell him. Morganne questioned Spellweaver Gaelyss's mistrust of his twin brother Yannuvia. Gaelyss was convinced a secret alliance existed between Yannuvia and the Kiennish General Saligia. Yannuvia and Gaelyss were victims of an elaborate scheme fomented by the liege of Aulgmoor and the nefarious Dream Master. The conflict between the brothers escalated. Gaelyss drew closer to the she-Drelve Kirrie. The Teacher Morganne made the difficult decision to leave Alms Glen and join Yannuvia's group at Lost Sons. In a whisper the she-Drelve tenderly uttered, "I love you, Yannuvia. If you would have me, Spellweaver, I'd give you everything of my being."

Relieved to have muttered the words, Morganne found sleep.

Yannuvia's dreams retraced the history of his life. He dreamed of his youth and time with the beloved Teacher Edkim. His mind revisited youthful days playing with his twin brother Gaelyss under the loving supervision of his mother Carinne, sneaking with his childhood friend Kirrie to see the great Lone Oak, and using infamous invisimoss to evade Sergeant Major Rumsie and Drelvish guards. The Spellweaver dreamt of leaving Alms Glen on the eve of his neophyte group's trek to Meadowsweet and Green Vale, meeting the water sprites, and journeying to Alluring Falls. What Yannuvia sensed as the passing of only a few cycles of Meries appeared to have aged him nigh sixty seasons. Dreams…had robbed him of his youth.

Presently the Spellweaver dreamed of the Gray Wanderer Andreas filling the amber skies of Parallan. Yannuvia had witnessed the rare Approximation four times. The beauty of Green Vale reentered his memory. The Thirttene Friends…the Tree Shepherd…

Redness filled the picture in his sleeping mind.

Wisps…
Threads…
Threads of Magick…
Threads of fate…
Threads of time…
Threads connecting worlds …
Dreams connecting worlds …
Dreams of Magick…
The Magick of Dreams…
Magick connecting dreams…
Magick connecting worlds…
Dream raiders…
Elf pressure…
Albtraum…
Albträume, elf dreams, nightmares…

The Dreamraider Amica appeared as the Good Witch in Yannuvia's dream. A heartbeat earlier she had chatted with Kirrie in the cabin at the foothills of the Doombringers. The beautiful matronly female with smooth, lovely fair skin, deep blue eyes, and soft blonde hair that fell gently down the length of her back wore a soft white dress made of cottony fabric, which stopped alluringly several inches above her knees and exposed her smooth long legs. Her silky hands ended in long fingers with well-groomed nails. She smiled coyly at the dreaming Spellweaver. During the invasion of Yannuvia's first sleep in the new realm, the Dreamraider relayed nothing about events in Alms Glen and claimed no knowledge of the numerous onyum plants that grew in the expansive field of potting soil. She informed Yannuvia of another power of the red and blue tipped wand. The red and blue tipped wand enabled its bearer to summon her three times. To activate the power the bearer must touch the red end of the wand once, the blue end once, the red end twice, the blue end thrice, the red end five times, the blue end eight times, the red end thirteen times, and the blue end twenty-one times. Then simultaneously grip the red and blue tipped wand at both ends, squeeze the colored portions of the rod, and mutter the wand's command, '**hairy true man**.' Amica summarized, "Reserve the three summonsing. If you are in need, or just lonely, handsome Wandmaker, I'll come to do your bidding and serve you. Anything you desire."

The Dreamraider told Yannuvia that three changes of season had passed in the World of the Three Sons. In fact thirteen changes of seasons passed in the World of the Three Suns whilst the First Wandmaker and his 232 companions traveled in the blue light.

Fisher and Clouse had an innate sense of time. In the new realm the Drelves lacked the consistency of the Light, Amber, and Dark Periods. The Dreamraider addressed the issue through the Wandmaker's dream, "Your friend the Mender has an innate sense of time. I don't know about your greenish replica. I can't…read him. Flustering…But Fisher shan't always be around. Menders oft take walkabouts. You'll need… certainly! A time piece!"

A nebulous image hovered before the Good Witch gradually took form. A narrow glassy tube connected two glass bulbs framed by odd blue wood. Shimmering sandy granules of all imaginable colors filled the bottom bulb. The device mysteriously inverted and the granules flowed from the filled bulb into the empty bulb.

"The sands in the glass will always flow at the same pace. In precisely the length of one light and amber period, or 'day' as you like to call it, all the granules will flow into the lower bulb. At that time, the Day

Glass will invert and start the process all over. In terms of the minute minuteman's unvarying pulse rate, the process repeats after 57,600 heartbeats. My Master has constructed many such devices. In another world, the sands have a nominal running time of one hour and the device is oft called an hourglass. That'd be 3600 minuteman heartbeats. Factors affecting the amount of time the device measures include the volume of the sand, the size and angle of the bulbs, the width of the neck, and the type and quality of the sandy granules," the female Dream Raider explained.

"I've traveled widely throughout the World of the Three Suns and never seen such sand," Yannuvia remarked.

"In the World of the Three Suns, such sand does not exist. The sands are made from a single Prismatic Dragon scale. They aren't easy to come by, even for my Master," Amica proudly declared.

"I have never seen a Prismatic Dragon. Theses colors mimic the waters of the rainbow geyser in the Green Vale. Our Teachers spoke of devices to measure the passage of time," Yannuvia conceded.

"The frame of the day glass is made of petrified bluewood. A red diamond won't scratch it," Amica smugly added.

"Surely you can't think the paltry onyum plants you gave us will sustain us! Have you committed us to a lingering death?" the Spellweaver again charged.

"Onyum? Oh, yes, the odd green trees. Wasn't me…uh, us. Those plants predated my visit. They're an unexpected boon," Amica replied.

Unbeknownst to the travelers and Dreamraiders the onyums were planted and cultivated by native denizens of the subterranean cavern, the Duoths. The marshmallow men in turn were preyed upon by Carcharians, Shellies, and Bugwullies.

CHAPTER 9

Early Days in Vydaelia

All 233 members of the group had survived the journey and stood together in the strange new realm. The sojourners had reached the area they had seen in the images revealed by the Dream Master. But, where and *when* were they?

Pleasant breezes massaged their faces and eerie luminescence produced unvarying light roughly equivalent to the Dark Period. Gradually Yannuvia and his followers oriented to the area. Groups of armed Rangers quickly explored the immediate surroundings. Adjacent to the sea and just beyond where the group stood, a massive field of exposed soil covered a gentle slope. Small streams flowed from the rocky wall of the cavern and eventually fed into the great sea. Beyond the field of soil the seashore flattened and changed to stone. A number of trees were scattered throughout the huge field. A *pair* tree brought back memories of Yannuvia's travels with Joulie, Jonna, and Fisher. The tree bore both round red and oblong yellow fruits, thus the name *pair* tree. Unlike pair trees native to Parallan, the tree's leaves were green. A *venous* flytrap plant with green leaves grew at the base of the pair tree. A bamboo tree also with green leaves grew a few feet to the left of the pair tree. Near the pair tree was a cluster of five trees, each five feet tall and bearing five different translucent fruits. Each tree bore one multicolored, uncolored, yellow, red, and green fruit. The diverse fruits appeared in the Dream Master's images.

Eight green-leaved tetra berry bushes with distinct translucent, red, yellow, and green fruits, twenty-one blooming enhancing plants, and a small spring thirteen feet across also occupied the proximal area of the fertile field.

The gift donated by the Thirttene Friends was conspicuously located at the very edge of the field of soil. The unusual small tree bore thirteen branches, and each and every limb differed from its fellows. According to the tree sprite Lexie Glitch, the aged Tree Shepherd created the Tree of the Thirttene. The Tree Shepherd had melded a piece of his heartwood and root system to a sturdy enhancing plant. The ancient Tree Herder had then grafted onto the little tree a twig from each of the thirteen exceptional residents of the grassy knoll in Green Vale. This included twigs from the Apple Tree, *Pear* Tree, Snowberry Bush, Purplanana Bush, Great Green Oak, Rainbow Luck or Cherry Bomb Bush, the Tree Shepherd, Speckled Berry or Jellybean Bush, Gem Bush, Silver Maple, l'orange tree, Sick Amore, and "toot and see scroll" tree. The Tree of Thirttene bore one apple, one pear, thirteen snowberries, one purplanana fruit with accompanying spider web, one Great Green Oak twig, one red, green, blue, black, white, and chromatic berry from the cherry bomb bush, a twig from the Tree Shepherd, thirteen speckled berries, thirteen gems of different color, one silver maple leaf, one giant l'orange fruit complete with blue ice-encrusted leaves, one heart shaped sick amore fruit, and finally a single "toot and see scroll" fruit. The same sort of sparkling rainbow waters of the spring that sat in the center of the knoll in Green Vale filled the diminutive spring situated near the Tree of the Thirttene. Two enhancing plants tenderly wrapped in purplanana leaves and moistened with the waters of the geyser fountain in Green Vale sat on the ground near the tiny spring. A tiny geyser erupted from the little spring. Fine mist from the minuscule geyser traversed the large field and bathed the ground with multicolored waters. Clouse scanned the field and counted thirty-four other bushy trees. Other areas had clusters of green straight leaves standing thickly together. The nearest tree had no flowers. Instead the tree had clusters of bulblets. The clusters of bulblets weighted the tree down and drew its branches toward the soil.

Faint gray light struck the wand wielder Yannuvia, Drelves, Mender Fisher, and green Drelvish, Menderish, Spellweaverish Clouse. The large six-foot diameter gray Central Sphere hovered near the edge of a steep cliff about two hundred paces from the water's edge.

Further to their right the Spellweaver and his followers saw the massive blue "Vessel of Life", tiny transparent "Seventh Vessel", and five identical "Vessels of Definition." Flames erupted beneath and surrounded the bases of the structures. The massive deep blue Vessel of Life towered over the vats to its left. In order from the left, multihued, colorless, yellow, red, and green smoke billowed from the five maroon Vessels of Definition. Little rivulets of gray smoke rose from the tiny vat. Gray light flowed from the Seventh Vessel and Central Sphere. Klunkus and Beaux cautiously approached the seven vats, but Magick formed a barrier around the artifacts and some force stopped them from getting nearer than 34 paces of the "Vessel of Life."

Yannuvia asked the Mender, "Fisher, do you know the odd trees that bear clusters of bulblets?"

Fisher stared at the wide expanse of earth and replied, "And to think how I labored to find enough soil to plant my seed and fulfill my confinement! Plants with green leaves are unusual. I've seen many yellow, orange, and red onyum bushes. Usually spherical with concentric rings, onyums may be grown from seed, or more commonly from sets started from the preceding season's growth. Sowing seeds very thickly one year, resulting in starting plants that produce very small bulbs, produces onyum sets. These small bulbs are very easy to set out and grow into full bulbs the next year. But they have a reputation of producing a less durable bulb than onyums grown directly from seeds. Obviously someone has created sets where we see the thick green parts of the plants above the ground."

Joulie grumpily interrupted, "The Spellweaver didn't ask for a lecture in horticulture, Mender. Why don't you go inspect the onyum tree?"

Fisher wore a quizzical look and responded, "I'll check the tree."

Joulie added, "I'll go with you." Fisher added, "Usually onyums require the light of Meries. The bulbs stop maturing in the Dark Period. Onyums differ from enhancing plants. Enhancing plants bloom and their tubers mature in the Dark Period. I'm not an expert on your enhancing plants. But I know a lot about onyums. Well, most onyums. I can't explain why these plants have green leaves and grow in this sunless underworld. Some grow on trees and some in the soil. The thirty-four shrubs are tree onyums. In my travels I've seen many tree onyums with red, orange, and yellow leaves. Other than the color of the leaves, these are typical."

The red and blue tipped wand *Translocated* 233 people and affected folk who resist Magick, the *reflectors* Clouse and Fisher! Clouse not only traveled from the hill overlooking the Ornash to Lost Sons but also from Lost Sons to the new realm. The Mender traveled from Lost Sons to the new realm.

No spell was specifically directed toward Fisher. The Mender suffered no ill effects from passing through the void. The wand affected his location, not him! Fisher grasped Morganne and Klunkus's hands. Nothing in the cumulative knowledge of Menders explained the functioning of the wand. It was Magick… not Menderish.

Magick touched Clouse through his lineage to Yannuvia. Clouse shared the knowledge of Menders through Fisher. When they left the hill with fallen friends, Clouse clutched the Spellweaver's raiment. When the group left Lost Sons, the Menderish bloke held tightly to the sisters Joulie and Jonna. Did direct contact with them enable the spell to carry him, much as raiment and packs came with the 233 travelers? Maybe *Translocation* treated the Mender and Menderish fellow like sacks of trail mix. The wand's *effects* didn't *affect* them personally. On both occasions, Clouse *wanted* the spell to work. The Central Sphere arrived in the cavern without anyone touching it. It was, after all, Magick.

The gathering of the 88 stones…

Rays from the Central Sphere steadily poured toward the great vat and then splintered to the smaller containers. Yannuvia had seen similar splaying of grayness around the common area of Alms Glen when Andreas the Gray Wanderer drew near and sent its light to the Drelves. Another odd parallel that further convinced the Wandmaker he remained *within* the World of the Three Suns.

Yannuvia approached the sphere. Tentatively the others followed. Yannuvia held the red and blue tipped wand in his left hand. Soon he stood an arm's length from the eerily glowing gray sphere.

When the Spellweaver moved to the left, the Gray Sphere followed.

Yannuvia clutched the little red and blue tipped wand, tentatively touched the wand to the hovering stone, and said "**Hairy true man.**" Silently the six-foot diameter sphere rose to a height of 34 feet. Without warning the Firestone, Cold Stone, and Silence Stone moved from his raiment into orbits around the hovering giant. Runes appeared on the surface of the large sphere and three stones.

The Healing Stone appeared and accompanied the Silence Stone in the third orbit. The stones assumed orbits of progressively increasing diameters, with each increment equal to the six-foot diameter of the Central Gray Sphere. The Firestone assumed an orbit of diameter of 12 feet. The Cold Stone orbited at 18 feet, and the Silence Stone and Healing Stone orbited together at 24 feet. The Stone of Knowledge left Morganne's raiment, two other stones appeared, and the trio moved into rotation around the Central Sphere at a diameter of 30 feet. Intense auras of Magick filled the massive cavern. Altogether eighty-eight outwardly identical stones buzzed into the cavern and circled the Central Sphere in groups of one, one, two, three, five, eight, thirteen, twenty-one, and thirty-four in progressively larger orbits of diameters 12, 18, 24, 30, 36, 42, 48, 54, and 60 feet.

Fisher and Clouse determined the volume of the Central Sphere equaled the combined volumes of the 88 smaller stones. Three runes appeared on the Central Sphere and all eighty-eight smaller stones.

$$Ø ∞ Ø$$

Creation of the first wand...
The Drelves' nodules appear.

The Central Sphere silently left its position, and the 88 smaller stones froze in place. The six-foot diameter sphere approached Yannuvia and stopped with its center four feet off the floor and four feet from the Spellweaver. Slowly the triumvirate of runes on the surface of the Central Sphere faded. The surface of the sphere briefly changed to a brilliant surface and reflected Yannuvia's face. Then the small stones also reflected the Spellweaver's befuddled face. Yannuvia's face disappeared, and the runes reappeared on all 89 stones. When the runes reappeared another wand appeared in Yannuvia's right hand.

At that moment every Drelve noted an itch and found a small nodule at the base of the fifth digit of his or her left hand.

Yannuvia removed *the Gifts of Andreas to the People of the Forest* from his Bag of Holding and placed the spell book on the stone floor near the hovering central sphere. Three runes brightened on the large stone.

$$Ø ∞ Ø$$

The runes etched on the surface of the tome emitted a gray glow.

ΛΑΡΛΣ
A&Ω

Yannuvia remembered his brother Gaelyss's words, *"When the stones come within thirteen paces of the spell book, the runes on the spell book glow. Runes appear on the stone and fade. Always happens. Doesn't matter which stone is used."*

The runes on the spell book always produced deep gray hues whenever the Gray Wanderer drew near. Now, in the presence of the Central Sphere, the runes of the spell book glowed gray. After thirteen heartbeats the runes on the spell book faded and the triumvirate of runes on the Central Sphere persisted. Opposite effect...before the spell book's runes glow persisted and the stone's etchings faded.

Yannuvia left the spell book lying on the floor of the cavern.

The runes persisted on all eighty-eight smaller stones. A stone eerily floated from its orbit. The little stone, one of eight from the orbit of 42 foot diameter, moved to the proximity of Yannuvia's right hand, where he held the new wand. Yannuvia placed the wand in his pocket, extended his hand, and grasped the small spherical stone. The stone softened and meld to the shape of his hand. The Spellweaver knew he held a Stone of Opening, or Knock Stone. Yannuvia released the stone, which regained its spherical shape and eerily hovered near his right hand. Next he removed the wand from his pocket and held it in his right hand. Very small runes appeared on the second wand.

Ǿ ∞ Ǿ

The surface of the Central Sphere again changed. The runes faded, Yannuvia's image briefly reappeared and faded, and then a phrase written in Old Drelvish appeared on the surface of the Central Sphere.

"Cow vine cool ledge."

The Knock Stone wobbled back to its original position in an orbit of twenty-one foot radius with seven other stones.

Then another aura of Magick followed. The Central Sphere returned to its earlier position thirty-four feet above the floor. The eighty-eight small stones resumed their rotations around the Central Sphere. Intense grating sounds filled the air.

Ø ∞ Ø

The formation of the four domes…
The first dome…

Eighty-eight outwardly identical stones resumed their orbits around the Central Sphere. A lattice shell made of gray stone and based on a network of great circles lying on the surface of a sphere (geodesics) formed over the area containing the sphere and stones. The radius of the geodesic dome was 89 feet. The geodesics intersected to form triangular elements that had local triangular rigidity and distributed stress across the entire structure. The Gray Sphere rotated in the precise center of the hemisphere. The northeast section of the geodesic dome contained a single closed door.

Morganne rushed to the door and reported, "There's no obvious opening mechanism, Spellweaver. We're trapped inside!"

The Spellweaver Yannuvia approached, touched the door with the wand that he held in his right hand, and whispered, "**Cow vine cool ledge.**"

The door opened.

Yannuvia returned to the center of the now enclosed structure and retrieved *the Gifts of Andreas to the People of the Forest*. The Wandmaker opened the tome, turned to the first empty page, slowly moved the red and blue tipped wand over the vellum, and painstakingly etched the words "Knock Wand" and the command phrase "**Cow vine cool ledge.**" He then etched *I-one*. Yannuvia again placed the tome directly beneath the slowly rotating Central Sphere.

The second dome…
The Day Glass enclosure…

Lodi waved to the group as they exited and pointed toward a second smaller half-dome. This structure sat 34 feet from the door on the northeast quadrant of the large geodesic dome. Again a closed door prevented access to the odd hemi-sphere. The area of the small dome covered an area of 13-foot radius. Its height in its center was also 13 feet. Yannuvia approached the door, muttered "**cow vine cool ledge**" and touched the door with the second wand. The command activated the wand's Knock Spell and opened the door. Within the dome, suspended at precisely the center of the half-dome, the Day Glass filled with the multicolored sand silently documented the passage of time.

Yannuvia said, "The sands of the glass will always flow at the same pace. In precisely the length of one light and amber period, or day, all the granules will flow into the lower bulb. At that time, the Day Glass will invert and start the process all over. This will enable us to measure time. *Sergeant Major Klunkus*, assign one of our numbers to the Day Glass chamber to record the rotations. For reference and, in fact, this is the first day of the Dark Period. From this point forward, please refer to me as '*Wandmaker*'."

The elder Dienas quizzically asked, "Yannuvia, we have been here at most a day. When we left Lost Sons, the Dark Period had just ended. We must be more than fifty days from the next. Why do you say this is the first day of the Dark period?"

Yannuvia matter-of-factly repeated, "This is the first day of the Dark Period."

Yannuvia was born in the light of the Gray Wanderer Andreas. The erstwhile Spellweaver had drunk from the Cup of Dark Knowledge and tasted the Seventh Nectar. Mender's blood had touched him.

The Drelvish… Menderish…Spellweaverish… Pointed-eared, ever so slightly greenish… First Wandmaker…

Lower levels of the Day Glass enclosure later served as the Wandmaker's quarters.

The third dome…

The Quartermaster's chamber…

When the door of the Day Glass enclosure opened, another aura of Magick heralded the formation of an identical small dome that was thirty-four feet southeast of the Day Glass enclosure and also of thirteen-foot radius. Yannuvia approached the second small dome, touched it with the Knock Wand, muttered, "**cow vine cool ledge**," and touched the structure. A door formed. Yannuvia opened the door and entered the second smaller dome. Interestingly the floor of this dome was potting soil, identical to the large field where the onyums grew. In the center of the chamber, a staircase spiraled downward. Light as bright as the Light Period filled the dome. The source of illumination was not readily apparent. Yannuvia approached and descended the stairs. About thirty feet beneath the earthen floor, the stairs opened into a thirty-four foot diameter circular room with the five-foot wide staircase in its center. Shelves lined the chamber's walls. Yannuvia found several containers filled with purple fruits, which were the size, shape, and color of enhancing root tubers. Many containers of exotic spices filled the shelves. Four cabinets made of blue wood with doors of different colored glass sat against the wall that sat furthest from the sea. Clear glass formed the doors of the first cabinet, which held Zirconium, iron ore, and Aloe Vera. The second cabinet's yellow glass enclosed stores of sulfur and gold. Red glass of the third cabinet surrounded containers of rubies, onyx, lapis lazuli, and other stones. Green glass doors of the fourth cabinet surrounded containers with dried enhancing plant leaves, green grasses, emeralds, and mint leaves. The plethora of ingredients had been added to the five maroon vessels in the Dream Master's presentation at Lost Sons.

Yannuvia asked of Fisher, "Mender, are you familiar with the myriad of spices and complements in this chamber?"

Fisher analytically replied, "Yes."

Yannuvia followed, "Then, this becomes the Quartermaster's chamber, and you are now Quartermaster."

Fisher replied, "I'm the logical choice."

Clouse cleared his throat.

The fourth dome…

The Seven Vessels…

A fourth geodesic dome appeared and enclosed the seven vessels. The observers clearly saw the vats within the eerie translucent shell of this geodesic dome. Wisps of colored smoke rose from the seven vessels, wafted to the porous covering, and escaped into the cavern. The translucent hemisphere surrounding the Vessel of Life, the Vessels of Definition, and the Seventh Vessel had the same dimensions as the gray dome over the 89 stones.

Ø ∞ Ø

Beginning construction…

The transplanted Drelves lacked the protection of their beloved forests. The Mender Fisher had long lived in the fortress Aulgmoor. Yannuvia sought Fisher's counsel. Fisher suggested the construction of a defensive wall to encompass the area around the gray geodesic dome, Day Glass enclosure, Quartermaster's dome, translucent dome covering the seven vessels, bathing stream and lagoon.

Yannuvia reached into his Bag of Holding and took out a rope. The rope obediently extended twenty feet into the air. Next the Spellweaver removed a little piece of hemp canvas and threw the fabric into the air. The durable cloth expanded and formed a tent at the end of the rope. Then the Spellweaver took an ornately woven carpet from the bag. The carpet hovered about waist high. Rangers placed in turn the young, gravid, and elderly on the plush carpet. The rug floated upward and dutifully carried each Drelve-Vydaelian to the hovering tent and formed a floor for the small tent once everyone was in the tent. The tent grew larger on the inside with each new occupant and provided ample room. It remained the same size on the outside. Yannuvia's *high hide* provided a secure resting place for the very young, she-Drelves with child, and elders. The group took a needed rest.

After the rest period the Wandmaker surveyed the area. Four domes sat back from the shoreline and now dominated the landscape. A rockslide occurred during the rest period and produced a large quantity of stones that now rested to the east. No one had heard any commotion. The notched interlocking stones were nigh uniform in size. Clouse and Yannuvia detected for Magick, but the stones were just building blocks. Thousands of building blocks…

Clouse placed Hallucinatory Terrain Spells both to the left and right of the four domes. Seeing red, yellow, and orange lifted their spirits. The Hallucinatory Terrain hid them from voracious unintelligent predators and made more intelligent beasts hesitate. Yannuvia swore to work until the first wall was finished. Buoyed by the Wandmaker's enthusiasm, the Drelves went about their tasks.

The *Wandmaker* surveyed his realm. His strong support included the steadfast loyalty of Banderas's daughters Joulie and Jonna, Klunkus and Beaux to lead his defenses, veterans like Lodi, Owings, and Buck, committed youths like Carmen, Gheya, Tawyna, and Knightsbridge, knowledgeable elders Dienas and Yiuryna, Fisher and Clouse to work with healing and horticulture, the former Teacher Morganne's extensive knowledge of the enhancing plants, the odd flora of the field of potting soil, the power of the Central Sphere, the 89 stones, and the diminutive Seventh Vessel, the red and blue-tipped wand, the four domes, and the promised benefits one day of the Vessel of Life, the Vessels of Definition, and the Dreamraider's help. Would *she* come if he called?

A new beginning… but a life separated from the invigorating rays of the Gray Wanderer. But how different were they from most of their ilk? Generations of Drelves lived out their lives and never beheld an

Approximations of Andreas. The thought popped into Yannuvia's suspicious mind. Were they no longer *in* the World of the Three Suns? Surely Fisher, Clouse, and he should have sensed movement beyond their world, and no one appeared to have aged. They had to be *within* Parallan! Or did the Seventh Nectar protect them while they traveled in the red and blue light?

The Dream Raider said three years had passed in Alms Glen and Lost Sons and that this was the first day of the Dark Period. The Dark Period had always comforted Yannuvia. The eerie light that surrounded the wondering, wandering Wandmaker came mostly from luminescent growths on the ceiling and walls of the expanse and approximated the Dark Period. The hovering gray sphere contributed a bit of grayness. Faint rays eerily similar to Andreas's beams of grayness emanated from the Central Sphere and escaped through the dome of stone.

Blue, green, and gray surrounded them.

Clouse's Hallucinatory Terrain Spells at least created the illusion of familiar red, yellow, and orange foliage. The greenish Drelvish Menderish Spellweaverish Yannuvish Clouse had masterfully utilized Hallucinatory Terrain spells on the knoll overlooking the River Ornash and saved some of Yannuvia's ill-fated group. Yannuvia's younger greener look alike cast similar spells that created the illusion of thick undergrowth to the east and west of the group's location. Another spell disguised the domes containing the Central Sphere and the Seven Vessels as grassy knolls. The red, yellow, and orange illusory plants appeared quite real in the reduced light provided by the lichen overhead.

Yannuvia had not slept beyond short catnaps. Both his mind and body ached. The Wandmaker misspoke a spell and created tofu. His eyes felt like he had just been through a sandstorm and every muscle down to his pointed ears ached. He still was reluctant to close his eyes.

Morganne, Jonna, and Joulie insisted he rest. The Spellweaver-Wandmaker answered, "I shan't find nature's gentle nurse, sleep. If I do, my tormentor's will likely visit me."

Yannuvia reached for another lump of clay to prepare another spell.

Clouse humbly suggested a sleep spell.

Yannuvia declined, "No thanks, Clouse. I'd probably just resist such Magick."

Fisher offered, "I might have something in my pack that could help you sleep?"

The Mender's acquired faint grayish green tint helped him blend a bit into the odd dim light of the underworld, but the pale healer still stood out.

At about the same time the three she-Drelves asked, "What might you do?"

"I offer you a bit of sleep poultice. It always worked for General Saligia," Fisher suggested.

Menders commanded great knowledge of natural and herbal remedies. For instance, Fisher's sleep poultice contained thirteen herbs and spices. Specifically, valerian root, dream fruit, passionless fruit, booderries, byneberries, melon toning, butter fly, slumber berry, nodding ham, kava kava, lavender, rose petals, and a live cricket. Most of the ingredients were commonplace. Only Menders knew the secret of mixing the ingredients and creating the cataplasm. Each Mender had variations of the recipe. The variety of cricket affected the potency.

"Where are you going to find crickets?" Joulie incredulously asked.

Fisher platonically continued, "I have a batch of sleep poultice made up. But I also have a few crickets in my...never mind. That's Mender stuff. Are you interested, Spellweaver-Wandmaker?"

The Mender produced a little jar filled with a dark red sticky unguent.

"Am I supposed to eat this stuff?" Yannuvia skeptically responded.

"No, it's a poultice. I'll apply the unguent to your temples," Fisher answered matter-of-factly.

Yannuvia sighed and leaned against the wall of the cavern. Fisher applied the thick maroon goop to the spell caster's temples. The substance had a rather pleasant aroma. The three she-Drelves yawned when they smelled the sleep poultice. Yannuvia's mind reluctantly drifted from the stony floor to soft fluffy clouds and he slept.

CHAPTER 10

The Wandmaker's Burden

The novice Wandmaker slept fitfully.
A telltale red flash entered his slumber…

Wisps…
Threads…
Threads of Magick…
Threads of fate…
Threads of time…
Threads connecting worlds …
Dreams connecting worlds …
Dreams of Magick…
The Magick of Dreams…
Magick connecting dreams…
Magick connecting worlds…
Dream raiders…
Elf pressure…
Albtraum…
Albträume, elf dreams, nightmares…

A flash of red light surrounded the Wandmaker Yannuvia.
"Am I not allowed even a moment's rest?" his sleeping mind fumed.
The red auras faded.
Where was she? Instead of the Good Witch, Yannuvia looked upon his image. He stood alone within the geodesic dome that housed the 89 stones. The six-foot diameter Central Sphere slowly rotated 34 feet above the exact center of the floor and dominated the chamber. Eighty-eight

identical smaller stones now revolved around the massive gray stone. The fourscore and eight smaller stones moved counterclockwise at precisely the same speed. The stones assumed orbits of progressively increasing diameters, with each increment equal to the six-foot diameter of the Central Gray Stone. The Firestone orbited in a diameter of 12 feet. The Cold Stone orbited at 18 feet, and the Silence Stone and Healing Stone orbited together at 24 feet. The Stone of Knowledge and two other stones rotated around the Central Sphere at a diameter of 30 feet.

Groups of one, one, two, three, five, eight, thirteen, twenty-one, and thirty-four stones orbited the Central Sphere in progressively larger orbits of diameters 12, 18, 24, 30, 36, 42, 48, 54, and 60 feet.

Each small stone was 1/88th the size of the large central stone. Gray rocks that shared orbital paths moved in the same plane, maintained the same speed, maintained a constant distance from the central stone, and kept a constant separation. The outermost small stones circled at a constant speed in an orbit of thirty feet radius. The big stone maintained its position precisely in the center of the chamber. The little stones maintained their orbits without striking the floor.

The eighty-nine stones bore identical symbols.

$$Ø \infty Ø$$

The symbols weren't engraved. The runes were more part of the stones and emitted grayness. The array of grayness fascinated the First Wandmaker. The Central Gray Stone ominously left its middle location, eerily wobbled downward, and approached the lone figure in the chamber. The small stones froze in position. The symbols and grayness faded from the little stones. The Central Sphere's grayness also faded until only very faint symbols remained. The chamber became hot, and then cold and the Wandmaker labored to breathe. The six-foot diameter sphere stopped precisely three feet from his face. The faint symbols disappeared and an image formed in the usually smooth gray surface of the slowly rotating sphere. He wanted to close his eyes, but Yannuvia could not turn his gaze from the horrific face that filled the surface of the sphere. Instinct told the First Wandmaker to flee, but he felt his feet were fixed to the floor. Chills coursed down his spine. He recognized the face from the knoll overlooking the River Ornash, when Saligia and his brother Gaelyss betrayed him. The fiery red bipedal beast had four arms and a long tail and stood the height of three Drelves. Crackling flames encircled the entire demonic body. Two great horns rose from its large head. Rows of dagger-like teeth filled its maw. Sparks flew from the beast's huge red eyes. Yannuvia now looked into those eyes.

The beast's fell voice rose from the image and permeated the air, "Welcome to your workroom, Wandmaker. I trust you are feeling well. Nice work on your first wand! You and your ilk are an industrious lot. I've entrusted my legacy to good stock. You bear the red and blue wand. You must treasure and keep it safe. Note well the grayness of the Central Sphere. It imparts gray light to this underworld. You have seen no variation in that light since you have lived in this place. However, you will learn the grayness will vary. When the gray sun draws near the world above, the Central Sphere will emit greater grayness. That special time in the world above will also be a special time in your domain. Know this, Wandmaker. Mark time well. Sixty rotations of the Day Glass herald the arrival of the Dark Period in the land above. The Dark Period lasts fifteen rotations. You will have the power to create a single wand on the first and last days of the Dark Period. Those wands will have power unbeknownst to all but you. However, the Magick will be finite. Wands created on the first day of the Dark Period will have unlimited charges in the hands of a spell caster. For non-spell casters, each wand so created will have either thirteen uses or uses equal to the seasons since the last Approximation of the Gray Sun. A wand created 21 years after the last Approximation on the first day of the Dark Period will have 21 uses. If it's created a year after an Approximation, it'll have thirteen charges. A wand created on the final or fifteenth day of the Dark Period will always have thirteen charges. Every wand you create will have a specific activating command. The Master Wand uses '**Hairy true man**' and the Knock Wand uses '**Cow vine cool ledge**.' After its charges are used, a wand becomes a simple piece of wood. It's exceptional kindling. You may recharge the device when the grayness of the Central Sphere intensifies. Wandmaker, your greatest power in this realm will coincide with the arrival of the gray sun. Approximations bring you additional power and responsibility. During an Approximation, the light of our father the gray sun amplifies the grayness of the Central Sphere and its four score and eight satellites. During each Approximation, you will be able to create a single additional and very exceptional wand. When a wand is created during the Approximation, that device will have unlimited usages for any user. Each small stone imparts a different power. The Approximation of the Gray Sun is unpredictable. Such is the way of Magick. You and I, Wandmaker, are children of the gray light. Finally, my *Wandmaker-Spellweaver-brother…*

"One day my image will form and relay another message. Your forebears will see their image and that of every Wandmaker to live before them. The final image they will see will be yours, Yannuvia. My message *will* be…

"The time has come today. You must repay the debt of your forebears. The fading of the Central Stone and activation of this dweomer mean the implausible has happened and I have been vanquished. If I have diminished, you will diminish. Your people will suffer and eventually perish. You can restore the Magick of the sphere and the greatness of your people. You must take the treasured Central Stone to the surface world when the gray sun draws near. Only the gray light will restore its power… and your power to create. You cannot restore me, but you can continue my legacy! Carry the Central Sphere to the light of the gray sun Andreas!"'

Yannuvia managed to speak, "I have many questions. The seven vats are not accessible. Why?"

The Dream Master answered, "Go about mastering your realm. In time you will gain access. As we speak, the fourth dome is filled with implements you'll need. You must find ways to replenish what you use, my brother. Remember my gifts and *her* promise, three summonsing with the Master Wand. You held and sipped from the Cup of Dark Knowledge in the grotto behind the Alluring Falls, traveled in the blue and red light, and imbibed the Seventh Nectar. The power of the 89 stones is yours. But remember … The Central Sphere…

"Guard well this orb. Fading of the sphere's light means…it's time to repay the debt you've incurred. Whether by you or the hundredth generation removed, yours is a debt that must be repaid…

"Placing the Central Sphere in the light of the Gray Wanderer will restore the orb's grayness.

"You bear the Wandmaker's burden."

Following a guttural laugh, the image faded from the Central Sphere, and Yannuvia briefly saw his bewildered reflection. Slowly his image faded and the triumvirate of runes returned. The Central Sphere reassumed its central position and the smaller stones resumed their orbits. Blueness surrounded the images and Yannuvia's mind entered deep dreamless sleep.

The Spellweaver-Wandmaker slept for two rotations of the Day Glass. Joulie, Jonna, Morganne, and Clouse scarcely left his side.

Yannuvia awakened refreshed.

Child of the gray light...

The first Wandmaker...

Wisps...

Threads...

Threads of Magick...

Threads of fate...

Threads of time...

Threads connecting worlds ...

Dreams connecting worlds ...

Dreams of Magick...

The Magick of Dreams...

Magick connecting dreams...

Magick connecting worlds...

Dream raiders...

Elf pressure...

Albtraum...

Albträume, elf dreams, nightmares...

Ø ∞ Ø

CHAPTER 11

Denizens of the Underworld

Carcharians were fishy humanoids with scaly skin, webbed feet and hands, gills, finned tails, claws, and fin-like crests on their backs. In other realms, the Amphibimen were called Sahuagin, Sharkmen, Sahagin, Sea Devils, Silurians, or Frogmen. Carcharian were usually green skinned, darker on the back and lighter on the belly. Their coloration rendered them tremendous disadvantage in the surface lands of the World of the Three Suns, where greenness was rare. Adult male Carcharians were over six feet tall and weighed about 200 pounds. Additional webbing appeared down the back, at the elbows, and notably where Drelves developed ears.

Carcharians dealt very harshly with puny, passive offspring. Compulsory fighting to the death eliminated weaker young Amphibimen. Carcharians seemed fixated on all aspects of consumption, and eager to weed out anything they saw as weak or unworthy to compete for resources. Brutal fighters, Carcharians fought savagely, asked for and gave no quarter, and, when swimming, tore at opponents with their sharp feet. The Sharkmen also used nets to entangle prey. Spears and tridents were their favorite weapons. One in 216 specimens was a mutation with four useable arms instead of two. The four-armed mutations were usually black, fading to gray in color.

Carcharians had inhabited grottos in and around the underworld sea for ages. Doug-less was the largest conurbation in the propinquity of the great sea. Long ago Doug, the four-armed son of Carcharian King Stanley had no luck in slaying Duoths in the Onyum Patch. Rather than going back to face his father empty-handed, Doug and his party entered the Endless Fen. Eleven Carcharians, two Shellies, and a Mountain

Giant entered the swamp. Only the Shellie Crunch survived and made it back to King Stanley. Crunch reported the group encountered a pride of sea lions in the muck. The terrain was fit for neither swimming nor running. Fighting sea lions in their domain was ill work. Doug's death devastated old Stanley. When he became King, Emmit, the grandfather of the commune's current monarch Lunniedale, renamed their home Doug-less. Prominent Amphibimen combined jewels, teeth, bones, and fabrics into bling that signified their position in their community.

Once a Mender, a pale surface dweller named Lou Nester lived among the Sharkmen. The odd being journeyed to the underworld of Parallan to seek new materials for his potions and unguents and accomplish the continuation of his kind through a process called confinement. Emmit and Lunniedale's forebears captured the bloke and planned to have him for dinner, not as a guest but as the main course. The pale wanderer saved his hide by caring for and saving a Carcharian princess. The grateful Carcharian King granted the healer permission to live among the Sharkmen. Older Carcharians passed down stories of the healer to younger Amphibimen like Gruusch, a young two-armed guard of the Circle of Willis.

Gruusch was larger than most two-armed Carcharians, dark green, seven feet tall, and well over 200 pounds. He inherited great strength from his four-armed father Phederal and received an atypical sensitive side from his mother Viada, a captive sea elf. Amphibimen and sea elves warred constantly, and the unfortunate Viada was a spoil of war and died during Gruusch's birth. The motherless Gruusch lived in the nursery pond in Doug-less, where he struggled against other minners. Young Carcharians were oft called minnows, or minners. As the young matured, they moved to adolescent pools where battles for survival often resulted in deaths of weaker minners. The term "minnered" or "minnowed" came to mean "death in battle" in the Amphibimen's vernacular. Gruusch seldom suffered injuries because of his strength and usually quickly dispatched any foolish foes that challenged him. As a result he was seldom challenged. However, after defeating opponents, the young Carcharian compassionately allowed vanquished foes to survive and creep away. This resulted in Gruusch's incurring the wrath of his mentors and receiving frequent punishment. Gruusch's benevolence irked his austere father Phederal. Adversity made Gruusch stronger. When he matured, he suffered King Lunniedale's disfavor and was assigned the rather mundane responsibility of watching the breeding pools.

King Lunniedale enjoyed many consorts and sired many spawn. His spawn received special consideration regardless of their maternal lineage. Lunniedale's favorite daughter Starra was borne to a sea elf mother. Like Gruusch's mother Viada, Starra's mother Piara was taken after a successful Carcharian raid against her people. Though very young Piara arrived in Doug-less with the ability to speak and understand the Carcharian language. The unusual trait earned her special consideration and she became the consort of the new monarch Lunniedale. Unlike Viada, the resourceful Piara survived her daughter's birth, made the best of her predicament, ultimately became King Lunniedale's favorite consort, enjoyed a prominent position in the King's court, and earned the title of Queen. Many envious Carcharians referred to the sea elf as the "Queen-Witch."

Piara adjusted to the community and spent time in the birthing rooms assisting Carcharian mothers-to-be. Her skills of midwifery and knowledge of painkilling sea herbs led to her gradual acceptance by the Carcharian females. Truth be known, Piara didn't understand her command of the Amphibimen's language and innate knowledge of herbs, medicines, and alchemy. The she-sea elf was too young when she was taken. Piara had very little memory of her mother, father, grandmother, and other relatives. Interestingly, in quiet times of reflection, Piara recalled many things about her great, great, great grandmother, who was long dead when Piara was born.

Ø ∞ Ø

Shellies…
Shellies frequently allied with other ilks and served as warriors and guards. Shellies were dark green, decapod crustaceans. Thick exoskeleton covered their thorax and head. Two extremities served as legs and enabled the creatures to stand upright. Two upper extremities served as normal appearing arms and provided Shellies very good dexterity. Two upper extremities were modified into large clawed arms with great pincers. The other four extremities were just small protrusions. Crustaceamen's eyes protruded eerily from their thorny heads and moved about on hardened stalks. Shellies had a native tongue, but also communicated

with Carcharians. Their thick exoskeletons were imperious to most projectile weapons and made Shellies good allies in a fight.

Ø ∞ Ø

Bugwullies…

Rather than being killed and eaten on the spot, unfortunate Bugwullies were, on the odd occasion, captured and brought to the Sahaugin lair to perform menial tasks. Ultimately, most Bugwullies found their way to the Amphibimen's dinner tables. In fact, Bugwully legs were one of King Lunniedale's favorite dishes. Smooth mottled olive green tough hide covered Bugwullies. Most were smaller than Carcharians and nearer the size of sea elves, about 4 ½ to 5 feet tall. Bugwullies' faces resembled enormous frogs, with wide mouths and large, bulbous eyes. Their hands and feet were webbed. Bugwullies disdained clothing, but all used weapons, armor, and shields if available. Bugwullies lived in somewhat organized groups and cooperated for the purpose of hunting and survival, particularly in conflicts with the bigger and meaner Carcharians. The frog-faced humanoids were adept hunters and fishermen and skilled in construction of snares and nets. Bugwullies had a male dominated society, with females given largely only the task of laying eggs. The ilk respected only their leader and totally lacked higher emotions and feelings. Bugwullies inefficiently dealt with incursions into their loosely organized territories, but didn't hesitate to kill and devour any interlopers they were able to catch. Members of a given group of Bugwullies seldom fought among themselves unless it was time to choose a new leader. Bugwullies were rapid swimmers and attacked with a hopping charge and impaling weapons. A chameleon-like ability altered their skin coloration to different shades of gray, green, and brown and enabled Bugwullies to attack with surprise. Camouflage helped little against the efficient Carcharians, and Bugwullies usually tried to avoid the larger Amphibimen. Bugwullies' mean streaks led to their aggressiveness against weaker creatures, including Pollywoddles and sea elves.

Pollywoddles...

Pollywoddles bore great resemblance to Bugwullies. However, females dominated Pollywoddle society. The peaceful blue-green Pollywoddles enjoyed wiling away hours by the seashore drawing little pictures in the sand. Carcharians and Bugwullies chortled about Pollywoddles doodling all day. The sand inscriptions actually served as written communication, albeit transient. Through their communiqués, Pollywoddles kept one another abreast of enemy movements and food supplies. Male Pollywoddles served mainly a role of tending the young, which were born alive. Female Pollywoddles served as leaders and did most of the hunting and gathering. Female Pollywoddles had a poisonous spur of their rear left leg. Ill-tempered Bugwullies and malevolent Carcharian killed simply for the pleasure of ending a life. Pollywoddles killed only to satisfy their hunger and needs and never for sport. However, female Pollywoddles tenaciously defended their well-concealed lairs, which were often constructed in marshy and shallow waters near the edges of lakes and seas. Pollywoddles were much more intelligent than Bugwullies and Carcharians, equally adept at swimming and hopping, and usually evaded capture. On rare occasions, a Pollywoddle fell into an enemy's net and ended up on the dinner table. Even more rarely Pollywoddles were conscripted to provide entertainment in enemies' lairs. Rarely Carcharian removed the poisonous defensive spurs, crossbred with captive female Pollywoddles, and produced aberrations of Nature. Even greater aberrations occurred when Carcharians crossbred with captive Bugwullies. Oddly the offspring hatched from eggs. If the Bugwully mother became a dinner item, Carcharian midwives attended the eggs in birthing arenas. Carcharian features dominated both half-Pollywoddles and half-Bugwullies. In all cases of crossbreeding, the Carcharian genome was dominant. Half-breeds usually performed mundane tasks in Carcharian communities, but intelligent half-Pollywoddles found ways to survive.

$$Ø \infty Ø$$

Carcharian society was not kind and gentle! Her young spawn Starra frequently accompanied Piara. Fearing retribution from spurned consorts and denizens of Doug-less that might be overwhelmed by hunger, King Lunniedale ordered veteran defenders to stay with Piara.

Sea elves were, in the final analysis, *prey*. Whenever possible, at least one four-arm remained with the sea elf.

The Giant Amebus...

Giant Amebus was forty-feet long and left a mucous trail along the ground as it gobbled up large quantities of sea debris, plank tons, tons of planks, and unwary land and sea beasts. The mammoth blob of goop benefited the environment; the creature was in some ways a mobile living garbage disposal. The omnivorous Giant Amebus telepathically communicated with the three foot tall rotund Duoths. *Dialogue* with the beast was a bit tricky. Oft the Cane Bisque Bay area bomber ate first and *thought* later. The amoeboid monster shared another trait with Duoths. The big glob of protoplasm produced excrement in the same manner; only Giant Amebus droppings were much larger. When dried, Giant Amebus droppings also exploded. Whereas Duoth dropping could be thrown or hurled with a sling, throwing the three-foot diameter rounded excrement of the Giant Amebus required the use of a trebuchet or the power of the Amebus! Like Duoths the great unicellular monster extended parts of its forty-foot long body and hurled its rounded projectiles over distances of five hundred paces. The effects of such explosions were the stuff of legend. Thus, the Giant Amebus earned the moniker, the Cane Bisque Bay Bomber.

$$Ø \infty Ø$$

Sea lions...

Sea lions hunted in prides. They were powerful swimmers and surprisingly agile on land. Long flowing manes, finned rear legs, huge canine teeth, powerful jaws, and clawed forelegs made sea lions formidable opponents. Males and females looked different. Sea lionesses lacked the big manes, but this made females faster. A male sea lion could be twice the weight of a four-armed Carcharian and a foot longer. Sea lions exhibited sexual dimorphism. Males and females looked different.

$$Ø \infty Ø$$

Duoths...

Duoths were three feet tall, stood on two legs, and resembled biscuit dough. The quickly moving beasts looked like white spheres with two pointed ears, no apparent eyes, no mouths, and two short stubby legs with large three-toed feet. Duoths were Carcharians' favorite prey.

Ø ∞ Ø

The triskaidekapod...

The emirp's body was ten feet wide, and half of the width was mouth. Row upon row of 31 dagger-like teeth lined the creature's jaws. Its eleven flailing tentacles were 31 feet long and each bore 31 suckers. Its teeth, suckers, and tentacles immobilized, inflicted horrific wounds, and squeezed the life out of victims. The beast expectorated huge volumes of thick mucoid goop. The spittle contained digestive juices and sulfuric acid. On land the triskaidekapod moved on two legs and lumbered with surprising speed.

Ø ∞ Ø

Dawgfish...

Dawgfish inhabited deeper waters, smelled very badly, were inedible, and oft swam to the surface of the waters and barked incessantly when they encountered swimmers and sailors. Dawgfish's loud barking drew predators to the location of swimmers and boaters.

Ø ∞ Ø

Jellyfish...

Jellyfish were both formidable opponents and tasty prey. The jellyfish's 24 eyes were arranged in sets of six around the belly of the beast and allowed the creature to see its world right side up regardless of its position. Avoiding detection by the Jellyfish's eyes and evading its many stinging tentacles were substantial challenges. The domes of the gelatinous beasts contained thick syrupy substances of different flavor, which surrounded the jellyfish's four brains. The jellyfish's color predicted its flavor. The purple ones were grape flavored. Golden jellyfish contained a honey-like substance. Yellow jellyfish had a lemony citrus flavor and complimented other seafood well. Yellow jellyfish were a valued condiment to the Carcharians' seafood-based diet. Jellyfish were far more dangerous to sea elves, because the green marine elves lacked the thick hide of Carcharians, Shellies, Bugwullies, and Pollywoddles.

Because of their thinner sensitive skin, sea elves oft died after being stung.

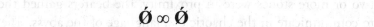

Irukandji...

Very small jellyfish, called Irukandji or *Carukio barnesi*, were a threat to all swimmers because of their small size and deadly venomous stingers. The power of the stinger remained intact after separation from the thumbnail sized creatures. The venom injected from the tip of the Irukandji stinger, making it more deadly. Over time several Carcharians had died after swallowing one of the little beasts while swimming.

Ǿ ∞ Ǿ

Boxjellies...

In contrast to Jellyfish, the rare Boxjelly was a bipedal creature with the head of a large jellyfish, tentacles as upper extremities, and two clawed upper arms. Like Jellyfish, Boxjellies had 24 eyes arranged in sets of six around its belly, many stinging tentacles, and four brains. The intelligent Boxjelly lacked the flavored jelly-like substance. Nasty Boxjellies had the ability to walk outside of water for very brief periods of time, but had to keep their gelatinous cube-shaped heads moist so they rarely came out of the water. Boxjellies roamed the sea in search of a myriad of prey animals.

Ǿ ∞ Ǿ

CHAPTER 12

Omega Stones

Omega Stones were indistinguishable outwardly and the size of 13 graparbles. Yannuvia, Jonna the daughter of Banderas, young Carcharian Gruusch, and Carcharian Princess Starra came into possession of the mysterious stones. Grasping activated the stones. Youthful Yannuvia had gripped the roughly kidney shaped artifact and only felt warmth from the stone. The single rune appeared on its surface during the Approximation of Andreas. Each stone gave its bearer a false impression. Without the presence of another stone, the only effect was this false feeling. Yannuvia thought he possessed a "luck stone." Gruusch thought he held a "charming stone." Starra's performance enhanced the deception. Jonna felt her stone bestowed strength. Queen Piara took Starra's stone, and felt an uncomfortable sense of power. When two or more stones were in proximity, the bearers gained the ability to communicate in the chaotic evil language of the abyss. The bearers became aware of the other stones and who carried them. When three stones came together, the bearers saw into one another's thoughts. Jonna, Gruusch, and Yannuvia first experienced the mind reading effect. This effect superseded the reflecting abilities of Fisher, Clouse, and Piara.

Yannuvia's Omega Stone...
Yannuvia received an Omega Stone when he traveled in the red and blue light to meet with the Dream Master while Fisher was in pharate state in the chrysalis.

The Dream Master's Dark Sorcerer persona commented to Yannuvia, "You see. It's hard to find good help. One day I may call on you, Spellweaver. When you return to *our home world*, you'll be stronger.

You'll find a gift where you left the Mender. By the way, he'll awaken when you return."

"How do you know this?" Yannuvia asked suspiciously.

"The Mender and I are children of the gray light. We...we share certain awareness," the Dark Sorcerer replied.

"The Mender never mentioned Dark Sorcerers," Yannuvia continued.

"Knowing Menders, he said little of anything," the tall man quipped.

"I don't think the Mender knew how long he'd be dormant. Wait... why am I telling *you*?" Yannuvia protested.

"Menders...the gray light heralds and ends their procreation. That time nears," the tall man replied.

Amica carried Yannuvia and the older Joulie and Jonna back to the grotto behind Alluring Falls and returned to the Dream Master.

"They have returned to the World of the Three Suns. Did you speak truthfully?" Amica asked.

The tall man laughed, his voice deepened, and he gutturally answered, "Yes, for the most part."

"What gift have you bestowed upon the ingrates?" Arachnis asked.

"A necklace, with a Luckstone," the tall man answered.

"Why did you give him a Luckstone, Master?" Amica asked.

"I never said what *kind of luck* he'd receive," the tall red-haired chap answered wryly.

Yannuvia sensed he carried a "Luckstone."

The only time Yannuvia had felt warmth from the odd crescent-shaped gray stone and noted the runes had been when the gray sun had drawn near in Approximation.

Gruusch's Omega Stone...

The Carcharian Gruusch received an Omega Stone. The Dreamraider visited the young two-armed Carcharian's dream and gave him the impression the stone had the ability to charm. Gruusch used the artifact in encounters with Princess Starra. The feminine Dreamraider told the youthful warrior that the device was a Charming Stone. Starra initially feigned affection but developed feelings for Gruusch. King Lunniedale learned of Starra's infatuation with the two-armed guard and assigned Gruusch perilous duty, specifically to accompany a scouting party across the sea to scout the Duoths' onyum patch.

Starra's red scarf and Omega Stone…

Carcharian Princess Starra received an Omega Stone.

Starra's dreams were interrupted. The Dreamraider visited Princess Starra's dreams twice. On the first occasion she left a red scarf and told the young Carcharian to accept the amorous advances of a young male and to feign she was charmed. Acceptance of his advances was allegedly critical to Starra's people. The exquisite scarf detected the presence of the stones and "activated" the artifacts, at least producing warmth and the appearance of the single rune. The scarf identified Gruusch as her "suitor." On the second occasion she left an Omega Stone and told Starra that Gruusch still lived.

Amica said, "Pinch your leg, Starra of the Carcharian. You will find you are quite *awake*. This night, your mother also experiences this very dream. *Your* words have been *her* words. Take this Omega Stone. You can see the runes on your scarf brighten when it is near. Your mother will awaken soon. Listen to her counsel. Do not tarry. I can't guarantee Gruusch's safety."

The Dream Raider produced a flattened blue stone, placed it on the floor, muttered a guttural command, and disappeared in a flash of blue light.

Starra picked up the little rock. It warmed in her hand. The red scarf emitted gray light. A single rune appeared on the stone and scarf.

$$\Omega$$

The rune persisted for thirteen heartbeats and then faded. Three runes appeared on the surface of the rock.

$$Ø \infty Ø$$

After 21 heartbeats the three runes faded and the single figure reappeared.

The pattern on the red scarf mimicked the stone. After three repetitions, all runes faded, the stone cooled in Starra's hand, and Piara awakened with a scream.

Starra confided to her mother and revealed the red scarf and Omega Stone.

Mesmerized Piara said, "For untold generations my people the sea elves have felt the yokes of Carcharians, Shellies, and Bugwullies. With devices such as I hold in my hands, I might make them invulnerable to attacks."

"The Dream Raider said we should give these devices to the newcomers," Starra countered.

"What does the scarf tell you?" Piara asked.

Starra honestly answered, "It's more a decoration Mother. Randomly it emits little hums and glows. It always reacted whenever Gruusch was around. It's feels nice to touch, keeps me warm, and in some way told me Gruusch was still alive, even before *her* visit."

Starra's scarf and Gruusch's stone...

Gruusch and Starra reunited at Vydaelia.

When Gruusch reached an area twenty or so feet from Starra, the Omega Stone tucked beneath Gruusch's shoulder blade warmed and hummed. The mere pressure of his skin and clothing against the rock activated its power. Starra's red scarf hummed softly and the single rune appeared on the raiment.

Ø ∞ Ø

Jonna's Omega Stone...

The Dreamraider invaded Jonna's dream and bantered, "I'm leaving you a gift. Touch the green guy with the gray rock. It'll accomplish two things. First, he will find the strength he needs to establish your community. Secondly, he'll melt in your arms. He's not a bad looking bloke."

Jonna demanded, "You are crude, Good Witch. Now, if you'll be on your way, I'll get some sleep."

The Dreamraider quipped, "I've enjoyed our visit, pretty Jonna. If you ever want to throw down, get down, or lie down beside me, let me know. It'd nigh be worth the Master's wrath. He gets over things in a few centuries. Remember what I said."

The Dream Raider *not so good witch* gave a facetious wave, blew a kiss toward Jonna, and faded into blueness. Jonna felt another twinge of warmth and wetness on her cheek. She slept a little longer.

Joulie tapped Jonna's shoulder and awakened her.

Jonna experienced a mild headache but felt rested and ready to resume her many tasks. She found a small gray crescent-shaped stone beneath her left thigh. The stone was a bit smaller than the array of gray stones orbiting the large sphere within the geodesic dome. The 88 stones were 1.61803399887498948482 times larger than Jonna's stone. Initially the little rock felt cold. When Jonna touched its surface, the stone warmed. When she gripped the gray rock, it conformed to fit her hand.

A single rune appeared on the little stone.

$$\Omega$$

After 13 heartbeats the rune faded and the triumvirate appeared.

$$\acute{\text{Ø}} \infty \acute{\text{Ø}}$$

The trio of runes persisted for 21 heartbeats. Thrice the pattern repeated…13 heartbeats, 21 heartbeats…then the surface became featureless.

Other than feeling the warmth in her hand, she felt no different when she grasped the stone. When Jonna released the gray rock, it returned to its crescent shape.

Jonna and Joulie joined a refreshed Yannuvia, Morganne, Klunkus, Clouse, Fisher, Merry Bodkin, and Tariana for a bit of breakfast before starting their work. Jonna sat about three paces from Yannuvia. Morganne sat by the Wandmaker's side.

Jonna felt a vibration and heard a low-pitched buzz emanating from her raiment. With subtleness she eased the buzzing stone from her pocket. She covertly removed the stone and saw a single rune.

$$\Omega$$

Thirteen heartbeats later it faded and the triumvirate of runes appeared.

$$\acute{\text{Ø}} \infty \acute{\text{Ø}}$$

The trio of runes persisted for 21 heartbeats. Thrice the pattern repeated…13 heartbeats, 21 heartbeats. Jonna's eyes were drawn to the Wandmaker.

The stone in the Wandmaker's raiment buzzed for the first time since he walked in the gray light of an Approximation. The Wandmaker glanced around the circle of his staunchest supporters. Jonna's eyes stared directly toward him. He stared back. Jonna turned away from the Wandmaker's gaze and looked toward his green look alike. Clouse seemed lost in thought. Jonna's stone still buzzed. Questions filled her mind. What should she do? What drew her eyes to the Spellweaver-Wandmaker? Should she approach Clouse as the not-so-Good Witch suggested? What activated the little stone? Did the not-so-Good Witch's speak truthfully?

Jonna received her assignments and walked away.

When Jonna walked away, the humming in both stones stopped. Yannuvia's little rock cooled in his hand. Jonna's arrival activated his stone. The veteran she-Drelve Ranger had stared at him with the fervor of a vixen.

Four stones…
Gruusch, Jonna, Yannuvia, and Piara…

CHAPTER 13

Contacts and Conflicts in the New Realm

The Drelves made contact with Duoths, who were three feet tall, stood on two legs, and resembled biscuit dough. The quickly moving beasts looked like white spheres with two pointed ears, no apparent eyes, no mouths, and two short stubby legs with large three-toed feet. Ranger Merry Bodkin discovered a perfectly round brown ball with white specks on its surface. Fisher recognized the Duoth dropping. It was material the Duoth could not metabolize mixed with some of the creature's essence.

Hostilities with the Duoths escalated. Whilst pursuing Duoths and exploring a passageway near their new home the Vydaelians suffered their first losses when a lurker beast fell upon them and smote two Rangers. Yannuvia's Fire Magick ended the battle.

Carcharians monitoring Duoths feeding on Onyums discovered Yannuvia's group. Scouts reported to Carcharian King Lunniedale of Doug-less. The newcomers interrupted the Duoths' onyum activities and therefore the Carcharians' predation of the Duoths. Duoths and inconsequential vampires attempted to breach Vydaelia's defenses. King Lunniedale dispatched a scouting party led by his favorite commander Slurdup. The force included the young Carcharian Gruusch.

An emirp attacked King Lunniedale's scouting party as they approached Vydaelia. Veteran Pincher knocked young Gruusch aside and saved him from the triskaidekapod's flailing tentacles. The emirp's body was ten feet wide, and half of the width was mouth. Row upon row of 31 dagger-like teeth lined the creature's jaws. Its tentacles were 31 feet long and each bore 31 suckers. Its teeth, suckers, and tentacles immobilized, inflicted horrific wounds, and squeezed the life out of victims. The beast expectorated huge volumes of thick mucoid goop. The spittle contained digestive juices and sulfuric acid. The triskaidekapod rose from the water, moved from the millpond, and lumbered with surprising speed toward the fleeing scouting party. The defenders of Vydaelia heard the fleeing creatures' terrified screams.

A four armed Carcharian shouted, "It's amphibious! You said it had thirteen tentacles! You didn't say anything about legs!"

His large clawed companion retorted, "I said it had thirteen extremities. I never said they were all tentacles! It's as comfortable out of water as we are!"

The enormous bloated purplish-pink creature was mostly tentacles and mouth, ran on two stubby tree-trunk-like legs, and pulled its body along the ground with suction cups on its 31-foot long tentacles. Seven of the beast's eleven tentacles were injured. The hideous creature's thick hide undulated as it wobbled with remarkable quickness. The lumbering triskaidekapod spat globs of thick black mucoid material toward the fleeing scaly creatures. The emirp violently disposed of the Carcharian and Shellie and then closed on the Drelves. Yannuvia's Wall of Force spell for a time kept the beast at bay. Many spells, bolts from the Wand of Lightning, and countless arrows failed to bring down the beast. In desperation Yannuvia employed the summoning power of the Master Wand. The Dreamraider answered the call and destroyed the 13-limbed horror. She was wounded by the beast's spittle. The Drelves discovered young Gruusch lying unconscious and a dying Shellie named Cracker.

Yannuvia, Clouse, and others interrogated Gruusch. Gruusch's Omega Stone interacted with those of Yannuvia and Jonna. The Wandmaker placed a dweomer of Gruusch and inferred any straying from a straight and narrow course would activate the spell and result in a painful demise. Purple auras surrounded Gruusch. The supposed Death Magick was actually only a False Aura.

CHAPTER 14

Life Time Commitment

Yannuvia's commitment to Morganne...

In the aftermath of the battle with the emirp Morganne walked with Yannuvia away from the pyres honoring the lost Vydaelians. She asked him to sit by a small fire far from the common area and gave him an enhancing root tuber.

She said, "Rest a while. I'll be right back."

Every muscle in his body, fiber in his brain, and pore in his skin ached. The Wandmaker enjoyed every morsel of the luscious purplish enhancing root. In only a few hundred heartbeats Morganne returned and sat down by Yannuvia. The she-Drelve left no space between them, and reached over, and took the spell caster's left hand. Yannuvia marveled that her freshness and beauty persisted in the face of the ordeals they had suffered though the past three turns of the Day Glass.

Slowly she began, "Ok…how do I say this? Uh…Wandmaker…no, Yannuvia, like Klunkus, I was beneath the Lurker. My sword fell from my hand when the creature fell upon us. Every breath became more difficult. Slowly the creature pressed life from me. I've faced death many times. On the field of the Battle of the Red Meadow when the Lone Oak, Old Yellow, Edkim, and so many others fell, I stood against the enemy many times. But I never felt helpless! A Droll's axe, Kiennite's arrow, Ballista bolt, trebuchet boulder, or shaman's spell may quickly end one's life. But as the Lurker beast was taking my life a bit at a time, my days flashed before me. This also happened when I stood in the Old Orange Spruce and made the decision to leave Alms Glen and follow you. It happened again when you and I stood in the shallow waters after Owings and Miclove were killed. While we worked this past cycle of the Day Glass, I thought about many things, Wandmaker. Just as I mustered strength, the emirp attacked. I thought again I'd missed my chance to tell you…"

Yannuvia responded, "To tell me what?"

Morganne continued, "Many things I've never said…to you. I followed *you* to this place. If it's my role simply to support you and this community, then so be it. But I have to say…I want to be more than…I have never…I want…I've always…"

"I love you, too, Morganne," Yannuvia blurted. "I just never knew how to say it. Remember, in many ways, a fourteen-year-old mind is locked in this seventy-year-old body."

Morganne blushed. Even in the dim light of the Vydaelian Cavern, her pale orange skin briefly burned purplish red. She helped Yannuvia to his feet and led him toward the small structure that housed the Day Glass. Knightsbridge alone stood by the door, dutifully stepped aside when they approached, and allowed them to enter. When he and Morganne entered the room, Yannuvia saw the elder Yiuryna. Knightsbridge followed them into the room.

Morganne sighed and then said awkwardly, "I…I offer lifetime commitment to you, Yannuvia. I want to stay by your side as long as I draw breath."

The Wandmaker just as awkwardly replied, "I offer my commitment and accept yours, Morganne. But in this place…in this time…lifetime commitment may…"

"It doesn't matter. We have this moment. The elder is here to seal our bond and Knightsbridge is our witness," Morganne said with resolution.

Yiuryna queried, "Are you sure you don't want to share your ceremony with the entire community? All of us will be happy about your union."

Morganne briefly recalled Yannuvia's tryst with Joulie and Jonna. Perhaps not everyone would be happy…

Yannuvia answered the elder, "No. This is just right."

The elder Yiuryna took a length of ribbon that his mother had created from the silk of glowing worms. The little ribbon fluoresced prismatic colors. The elder sang an ancient ballad in Old Drelvish and gently wrapped the ribbon around first Morganne and then Yannuvia's forearm. Yiuryna bowed his head silently, then slowly looked up, and smiled at the couple.

Yiuryna extended his left hand and offered a small item to Morganne. The elder said, "I want you to have this as a memento of this day. My mother gave me this before my journey to Meadowsweet and Green Vale as a neophyte. She encased it in Old Yellow's sap, which hardened around the clover but preserved the original red color. The Teacher Alnord told my group of neophytes that only one in ten thousand red clover plants have three leaves. The plants usually have four leaves. A three-leaved red clover is said to bring good luck. I've always carried this with me."

Morganne took the small piece of amber. The delicate three-leaved clover was spread smoothly in the sap. "Thank you, elder. This means a lot to me, to us."

Yannuvia added, "Yes, elder. I'm grateful for having something of Old Yellow in our new home. We'll always appreciate the gift of your heirloom."

Yiuryna answered, "Leaving Alms Glen was the most difficult decision I ever had to make. That decision severed many ties. Building Lost Sons and seeing the community grow was rewarding, but we never found peace. The Drolls and Kiennites posed constant threats. The elders and Council of Alms Glen never fully recognized our autonomy. Seven of our sons and daughters died at the Battle of Lone Oak Meadow, including my daughter by lifetime commitment Jensie. Even our peoples' treks to gather the enhancing root placed them in jeopardy. The decision to leave the world above and follow you was, for me, an easy one. My life mate Ulla, my son and Bystar's father Rickie, and Bystar's mother Jensie have passed on. Rickie fell to a wyvern. My dear friend Dienas still has his son Lodi, though his granddaughter Deirdre shared the fate of Banderas' son Vioss and my grandson Bystar. Our life mates were sisters. My Ulla and Dienas's Petra were equally lovely. After the death of Bystar at the hands of Drolls, you became about the closest thing to family that I have left and always been like a grandson to me, Spellweaver. Excuse me; I'm an old Drelve. I'll try to learn to address you as Wandmaker. You, Bystar, and Vioss were such friends. Excuse an old person for rambling. I...want our new community to thrive. I'll continue to support you with all my energies and help Dienas teach our young. What I'd give for one more precious moment with Ulla... I'll take my leave."

"As will I, Wandmaker, and I assure no one will disturb you," Knightsbridge declared.

Morganne brushed back her orange hair, walked the three paces to Knightsbridge, gently kissed his cheek, and said, "Thank you."

Knightsbridge blushed deep orange red.

The Wandmaker Yannuvia extended his left arm, clutched Knightsbridge's left hand, and said, "I'm honored that you stood as witness to our ceremony."

Knightsbridge stood proudly and said, "The honor was mine, Wandmaker."

The young Ranger turned briskly and exited the little chamber. Yannuvia walked to the door, paused, and produced the Knock Wand. The first Wandmaker touched the door and said, "**Cow vine cool ledge.**" The area around the door glowed briefly.

Yannuvia looked at Morganne, winked, and said, "Wizard locked."

Morganne returned a coy smile and said, "Why ever would you do that? Knightsbridge said he'd guard the door."

"I want to assure we aren't disturbed," Yannuvia said bashfully and blushed.

"Why?" Morganne asked again demurely.

"You know *why*," Yannuvia answered and blushed deeply again.

Now Morganne also blushed. An awkward moment of silence passed.

Morganne walked over to Yannuvia, took his hand, and said, "Aren't you tired?"

The Wandmaker sighed, appreciated her beauty, and answered, "I'm not *that* tired."

Morganne blushed again.

Yannuvia gently kissed her. A bit taller, Morganne slowly wrapped her arms around him, placed her head on his shoulder, and then snugly hugged him. She lifted her head from his shoulder and looked into his eyes.

"OK…" she said softly.

"OK?" Yannuvia asked.

"I'm ready, I think," she uncomfortably answered.

"I'm not quite sure what I should do next. Do you know…?" Yannuvia awkwardly asked.

"No…not really, my love! Let's sit by the Day Glass. Just hold me for a moment. We'll wait a while and see what happens," Morganne replied.

Between the two of them, the Wandmaker and his betrothed had faced Drolls, Kiennites, Generals, Baxcats, Leicats, wyverns, noir skats, fire snakes, dragons, emirps, Duoths, and all manner of beasts.

Now…finally… nothing was between them.

CHAPTER 15

Reflector

The only other survivor of the emirp's attack thought Gruusch dead. The big Shellie Pincher made his way back to Doug-less and reported the deaths of his fourteen comrades to King Lunniedale. News of Gruusch's supposed death reached Starra's ears. The daughter of King Lunniedale and his sea elf consort Piara refused to accept that Gruusch was dead. Piara had an innate knowledge of herbs, medicinal plants, and potables and arrived at Doug-less with knowledge of Carcharian, Shellie, Bugwully, and Pollywoddle dialects. When Piara concentrated, she *recollected* her great, great, great grandmother, who died long before Piara was born. Piara was too young when she was taken to remember things her mother might have told her. It's was more like... she saw through her great, great, great grandmother's eyes. Her great, great, great grandmother was *different*.

The Dreamraider visited Princess Starra's dreams twice. On the first occasion she left a red scarf and told the young Carcharian to accept Gruusch's amorous advances and feign she was charmed. Starra developed true feelings for Gruusch. On the second occasion the Dreamraider left an Omega Stone and told Starra that Gruusch still lived. Starra confided to her mother and revealed the red scarf and Omega Stone. Piara felt strength when she held the stone. Starra relayed the Dream Raider's suggestion to give the stone to the newcomers across the lake. Starra was convinced that Gruusch was still alive. She described the scarf, "It's more a decoration Mother. Randomly it emits little hums and glows. It always reacted whenever Gruusch was around. It's feels nice to touch, keeps me warm, and in some way told me Gruusch was still alive, even before *her* visit."

The sea elf Piara made safe the little stone and made ready. She gathered misfits and those loyal to her to form a party of eight made up of Piara, Starra, Urquhart, Bluuch, Yathle, Loogie, Quunsch, and Sharchrina. Piara's two-armed daughter Starra inherited few of her sea elfish mother's traits, Had she four arms, she'd have every feature thought favorable for a female Carcharian. Four-armed Carcharians enjoyed preferential treatment in all segments of their society. Starra's four-armed guard Urquhart was a trusted soldier of King Lunniedale. His sea elf mother Paige died giving birth. Having four arms overshadowed Urquhart's maternal sea elfish lineage. Bluuch was the four-armed son of another sea elfish mother. Two-armed Yathle's mother was also a sea elf. Loogie was a two-armed half-Pollywoddle with dominant Carcharian features. Two-armed Quunsch was half-Bugwully with a mean streak. Quunsch got all the bad features of both his Carcharian father and Bugwully mother. Starra's very pretty two-armed cousin Sharchrina was betrothed to King Lunniedale's particularly insalubrious lieutenant Gurgla.

Piara wore a skintight suit of waterproof squid bladder. The suit revealed the mature sea elf's comeliness and stretched and extended over the watertight pouch on her back. Powerful four-armed Urquhart stood with heavily scarred four-arm Bluuch, very quiet two-armed fine-featured Carcharian Yathle, two-armed and round-faced half-Pollywoddle Loogie, and two-armed half-Bugwully Quunsch, who was simply the most ugly Carcharian Piara had seen. Carcharian features usually dominated when crossbreeding occurred, but rare instances of hybridizing between Carcharians and Bugwullies produced offspring, well…offspring like Quunsch. He was big, strong, and undefeated in competition, but scorned by most of Doug-less.

Quunsch crudely commented under his breath, "I'd pay good money to watch her put on that suit."

Urquhart elbowed the half-Bugwully and scolded, "That's your Queen, fool. Show some respect."

Quunsch rubbed his side and answered back, "If we get caught, she'll be like us, up **** creek without a paddle."

Piara looked directly at Quunsch and said, "The only thing sharper than my curves is my hearing, young Quunsch. I'm far too hot for you to handle! You wouldn't know where to begin with me, so concentrate on your tasks."

Piara gathered the small party of misfits and led them away from Doug-less. The octet followed the course of Gruusch's ill-fated scouting party, approached Vydaelia, and arrived after the Vydaelians' titanic battle with the triskaidekapod. Sea elf Piara had long green hair, emerald green eyes, and a striking resemblance to Clouse. Her smooth ears lacked the points on Clouse's ears. Piara's sweat had the consistency and fragrance of lime juice. She shared Fisher and Clouse's trait of Spell Reflection. The queen understood every dialect that Clouse and Fisher challenged her with, and Menders spoke 17711 dialects. Both Fisher and Piara had exceptional midwifery skills. Clouse, Fisher, and Piara shared the uncanny ability to estimate the relative sizes of objects. Piara possessed a graparble which was a gift of the Dreamraider Amica. The graparble had been taken from the derriere of an unfortunate dryad. Erstwhile Queen Piara carried Starra's Omega Stone. After a tense interrogation Piara's party entered Vydaelia. The Wandmaker Yannuvia demanded dweomers be placed on each refuge from Doug-less. Urquhart went first. Yannuvia uttered an incantation, and touched Urquhart's shoulder, and duplicated the ersatz *Death Spell* he placed on Gruusch. Purple auras surrounded the big four-armed warrior. The Wandmaker then placed the supposed Death Spell on Bluuch, Starra, Sharchrina, Loogie, Quunsch, and Yathle. Then Queen Piara's turn came.

Yannuvia said, "I'd better finish this. Are you ready, Queen Piara? At least I won't have to reach up to touch your shoulder."

"Proceed, please. I f you want, you may put your arms around me," Piara answered alluringly.

Yannuvia conjured, muttered the phrases, extended his left hand, and touched Piara's shoulder. Auras of Magick filled the area. Purple haze filtered from Yannuvia's extended fingers, briefly surrounded the sea elf, and then suddenly fled from her, moved quickly around the Wandmaker, and surrounded Yannuvia.

Queen Piara reflected the aura back to the Spellweaver. The False Aura Spell encircled its caster! The bewildered Spellweaver-Wandmaker, Drelve-Vydaelians, Carcharians, Mender, Clouse, and beautiful sea elf Piara huffed in disbelief.

Yannuvia puffed, "*Reflector!*"

Clouse marveled, "First, she exhibits knowledge of many languages, and now she reflects the Wandmaker's spell. She's Mender."

Piara smirked demurely and softly said, "I guess you'll just have to trust me."

Piara's group received the same conditional asylum as that given Gruusch. Gruusch and Starra enjoyed a reunion.

In Doug-less King Lunniedale discovered Piara's absence and vowed retribution.

CHAPTER 16

USA

The Wandmaker Yannuvia had created six wands. On the beginning of the fourth Dark Period since their arrival in Vydaelia he walked alone to the hemisphere containing the 89 stones, produced the Knock Wand, pronounced the command, **"Cow Vine Cool Ledge"**, allowed the hidden door to open, and entered the chamber. Yannuvia felt powerful. The erstwhile Spellweaver had not experienced such feelings since he had last stood in the light of Andreas. Intense grayness flowed from the large Central Sphere. Four stones left their positions and approached the Wandmaker. One stone of eight orbiting together 21 feet from the center of the Central Sphere, another of thirteen circling 24 feet from the center, a third from twenty-one moving around 27 feet from the center of the big stone, and a fourth from the thirty-four stones circling thirty feet from the sphere's center. The four stones wobbled toward the Wandmaker, stopped 3.14 feet above Yannuvia's head, and froze in position.

Four stones...

Was he to create four wands?

Faint humming sounds filled the great geodesic dome. Yannuvia anticipated one of the nearby stones coming to his awaiting right hand.

Then...

Redness flashed through the deepening gray light.

Wisps...

Threads...

Threads of Magick...

Threads of fate...

Threads of time…
Threads connecting worlds …
Dreams connecting worlds …
Dreams of Magick…
The Magick of Dreams…
Magick connecting dreams…
Magick connecting worlds…
Dream raiders…
Elf pressure…
Albtraum…
Albträume, elf dreams, nightmares…

Yannuvia tensed.

The Dream Raider appeared as he saw her the first time in his sleep. Amica wore a blazing red dress and appeared very tall and alluring with creamy skin, soft blue eyes, and coal black hair that fell gracefully down her back and chest.

Yannuvia responded coolly, "I didn't summon you, and I'm not asleep. Why are you here? What's up?"

She coyly replied, "Are you sure that you aren't dreaming? Do you want me to kiss you and wake you up?"

Yannuvia glanced at the Central Sphere and four stones that had drawn near. The large stone rotated quicker by the heartbeat and the 84 stones that still surrounded it moved more rapidly, becoming blurs. However, the four stones near him floated in position. Amica abandoned her visage and changed to green hair and a tight exceedingly short white skirt. She ran her hands through her long green tresses and created the disheveled look she preferred.

The Wandmaker impatiently asked, "Why have the stones changed?"

Amica answered spiritedly, "It's the Approximation. Aren't you excited? Let's celebrate together!"

Yannuvia continued, "You told me that three years passed in the World of the Three Suns while our *translocation* occurred. This is the fourth Dark Period by the Day Glass's measurement. History has taught us Approximations never occur four years apart."

Amica sheepishly answered, "I may have stretched the truth a bit. It was the first day of *a* Dark Period when you arrived in this realm. *It was actually the fifth Dark Period of the twelfth year since the gray light bathed the lands above us.* So this is actually the first Dark Period of the thirteenth year since Andreas last appeared. As we speak, the gray sun fills the sky of the World of the Three Suns. As the master promised, you have special powers in times like these. And, you get an unexpected visit from me. Now, give me just a little kiss."

Yannuvia scowled and replied, "So I must tell my followers they have been away for thirteen years. Quit stalling! Let's finish our business so I can get on with informing them."

Amica briefly sulked and then followed, "You're no fun."

Yannuvia kept the red and blue tipped Master Wand in his left hand. The Dream Raider produced and grasped a two-foot long vorpal blade in her right hand. Yannuvia marveled at the thinness and sharpness of the implement. A length of odd blue-black wood appeared in his right hand. Amica reached for the odd wood with her left hand. As she accepted it, she tantalizingly stroked the tips of Yannuvia's fingers and smiled sweetly. Yannuvia relished the feel of her touch and delayed releasing the wooden implement. Once Amica held the blue-black length of wood, the four stones that had left their orbits started moving around the Wandmaker and his svelte companion. One of the four dropped down and hovered by Yannuvia's empty right hand. The Wandmaker reached out and held the stone. Predictably the perfectly spherical stone warmed, softened, and meld to the shape of his hand. Yannuvia's mind identified the artifact as a Stone of Enchantment. The device enabled its user with a power similar to the legendary dweomer *Enchant an Item.* Amica brought the odd length of dark wood and incredibly sharp narrow blade together. Yannuvia extended the softened stone and touched it to the joined objects. Intense red light filtered through the grayness. When Yannuvia pulled the Enchanting Stone away from the objects Amica held, blueness briefly surrounded the artifacts. The Enchanting Stone produced red and blue effects independent of the red and blue tipped Master Wand. The Dream Raider removed her hand from the vorpal blade and revealed the objects were now joined together. Yannuvia released the Enchanting Stone. The artifact reassumed its spherical shape, wobbled briefly, and then resumed its orbit with twenty other stones.

Another of the three remaining nearby stones moved to Yannuvia's right hand and he reflexively took the artifact. Melding to his grip, the stone revealed it was a Stone of Magick Missiles. Yannuvia released the stone, and it hovered briefly. Amica extended the newly created scepter and Yannuvia accepted the device with his right hand. The Wandmaker touched the scepter with the red tip of the Master Wand, and redness surrounded them. Then he touched the scepter with the blue tip of the Master Wand. Blueness enveloped them. The blueness faded into the intense grayness, and the Stone of Magick Missiles retreated to its previous orbit with 33 other stones. Then one of the two remaining nearby stones moved to Yannuvia's hand. He gave the scepter to Amica, grasped the stone, and received a small innocuous shock that told him he held a Shocking Stone, which empowered the Jolt Spell. Yannuvia released the stone and it stayed by his hand. Amica again gave him the scepter. He touched the implement with the red tip of the Master Wand and predictably redness surrounded them. Next he dutifully touched the scepter with the blue tip and produced blueness. When the blueness faded into the increasing grayness, the Shocking Stone resumed its position with seven other stones in a 42-foot diameter orbit. The last nearby stone moved near Yannuvia's hand.

Amica cautioned, "Careful Wandmaker. Give me the scepter. Place the Master Wand in your pocket before you grasp this stone. In fact, I'd remove everything you think valuable. If you remove your robe, I won't object."

Before grasping the last stone, Yannuvia placed his gear on the ground. He did not remove his clothes. Tentatively Yannuvia touched the hovering stone. No shock followed. He wrapped his finger around the artifact and knew he held a Cursed Stone.

Amica said, "I'm probably not supposed to tell you, but this stone instills a curse on the weapon if someone tries to use it without first using the proper command. Go ahead and release the Curse Stone."

Yannuvia answered, "Good advice. Now, what is the command?"

Yannuvia released the stone, and it returned to its orbit with twelve other stones.

The Central Sphere wobbled from its position and the eighty-eight little stones froze in place. The big sphere approached Yannuvia, developed its reflective surface, and reflected the Wandmaker's face. Then his image faded and odd lettering appeared. The writing was *not* in the Old Drelvish he had seen before. Yannuvia could not interpret the runes.

The frustrated Wandmaker muttered, "I can't read this! What language is written on the sphere?"

The Dreamraider Amica giggled and followed, "See, you do need me. It's Foreskorr, a variant of hobgoblinese. Many elfish folks speak the language. It says, '**Abe Linkin**.' Saying '**Abe Linkin**' and touching the scepter activates the curse."

Yannuvia fired questions, "What curse will it impart?"

Amica snickered again and answered, "Give me a kiss and I'll tell you."

The Wandmaker frowned.

The Dream Raider noted her companion's irritation and chirped, "Magick, and feminine intuition, told me. Once you've held the Cursed Stone, you'll sense its aura when it comes within seven feet. You must free yourself of all things Magick before you grasp the artifact. But, I confess, I also knew the Cursed Stone had a role in this weapon's creation. It's a great ally. Powerful devices created during times of grayness require fail-safes."

Yannuvia impatiently asked, "What curse will it impart?"

She replied seriously, "That will be pronounced by your lips, Wandmaker. What curse would you like?"

Yannuvia pondered for a moment and replied, "Let's say, slow the offender's attacks by twenty-five per cent, cut his defenses in half, and give a fifty-fifty chance of the Jolt Spell shocking the abuser."

Amica cooed, "Good, very innovative, Wandmaker. You show promise. Now pronounce the command and touch the scepter."

Yannuvia said, "**Abe Linkin**."

Then he picked up the Master Wand, touched the scepter with the red tip, noted brief redness, touched the weapon with the blue tip, enjoyed the brief pretty blue color, and grasped the Scepter of Power in his right hand. The two-foot long adamantine blade extended from the similar length of rare wood. Grasping the hilt of the weapon, rotating it counterclockwise, and uttering the command "**Abe Linkin**" produced a distinct click and retracted the extremely sharp blade into the length of wood. This did not produce an aura of Magick. Now the scepter was a blunt weapon thirty-four inches long and 3.14 inches in diameter. Turning the handle clockwise and uttering the command "**Abe Linkin**" extended the ominous blade. Extending the blade neither expended

Magick and nor affected the spell powers of the *United Scepter of the Approximation.*

USA!

The Central Sphere produced grayness equal to an Approximation. Intense grayness bathed the artifact during its creation. The powerful weapon enabled its user to employ both Magick Missiles and Jolt Spells. Activating the Jolt Spell required touching the victim. Created on the first day of the Dark Period, the scepter had unlimited uses in its creator's hands. The *USA* differed from other wands. If they knew the command, individuals touched and untouched by Magick enjoyed thirteen uses. The "United Scepter of the Approximation" was a formidable vorpal weapon, blunt weapon, and preserved a union of Nature and Magick. An inexperienced spell caster would think the artifact only a *cursed* weapon.

The Central Sphere returned to its position 34 feet above the center of the floor. Its 88 satellites resumed their usual orientations. The trios of runes on all were intensely brilliant in the deep gray light.

Ø ∞ Ø

Yannuvia approached *the Gifts of Andreas to the People of the Forest.* The runes etched on the surface of the tome dazzled with gray light.

ΛΑΡΛΣ
A&Ω

The Wandmaker opened the tome and etched United Scepter of the Approximation...USA... **"Abe Linkin"** and *I-seven.*

The Dream Raider inched closer and gently stroked the Wandmaker's shoulders. She deftly pushed her chest against him and cooed, "Work is done. There's only the two of us. I'll say anything you want to hear. I'll do anything you want."

Yannuvia enjoyed the warmth and softness of her touch. The deep gray light enhanced her beauty. Her fragrant pheromones further assaulted the Wandmaker's senses. Amica enticingly exhaled onto his left cheek and delivered a soft kiss.

Blue flames flickered in the Dream Raider's eyes.

Why resist?

CHAPTER 16

Wand Making

The Dream Master appeared to Yannuvia and issued the Wandmaker's burden and defined **wand creation guidelines.** The novive Wandmaker had already created his first wand and witnessed the formation of the four domes.

Yannuvia created his second wand, the Wand of Lightning, *I-two*. The wand's command was "**grow veer cleave land.**"

Construction of Vydaelia's walls continued. Rotations of the Day Glass served as a record of passing light, amber, and dark periods. Fisher and Clouse confirmed the Dreamraider's timekeeping device's accuracy. The light in the expansive cavern did not change. Young *translocated* Drelves matured quickly.

On the first day of the next dark period Yannuvia created his third wand, a solid black artifact, the Wand of Masonry, *I-three*. The device had the power to change rock to mud. Its command was "**wood row will son.**" With the power of the Floating Stone, Yannuvia next created his fourth wand, the Wand of Levitation, *I-four*, with the command "**rich herd nicks son.**" The Stone of Speed facilitated the creation of the Haste Wand, *I-five*, with the command, "**jar old ford.**" The Stone of Flying helped create the Wand of Flight. *I-six*, with the command "**run nailed ray gun.**" With the creation of each wand, Yannuvia's nodule increased by a factor of 1.6180339887498948482. The fabulous USA the United Scepter of the Approximation was his seventh wand, *I-seven*.

Work continued.

The Good Witch visited Jonna's dreams and left an Omega Stone. The Good Witch's visit and the stone influenced Jonna to pursue her feelings for Clouse. The relationship flourished. Elder Dienas performed the ceremony of life-time commitment for Jonna and Clouse. Duoths attacked near the conclusion of the ceremony and hurled Duoth bombs into the wall. Piara saved the veteran guard Willifron. Willifron's nodule left his hand whilst he was prostrate. The attack left a gaping hole in the outer wall. Quunsch smote one of the offenders. The Duoths' seemingly unprovoked attacks perturbed the Wandmaker, and Yannuvia allowed the Carcharians to consume their kill. Fisher joined in the feast. Drelve-Vydaelians disdained eating flesh of any sort, save fish. Carcharians were more like Drolls and Kiennites than Drelves.

Piara's party was present for the creation of Yannuvia's eighth wand, the Wand of Languages. Its command was the phrase **"Yule less says grant."** At the moment powerful auras filled the chamber, other than Piara, Clouse, and Fisher, everyone present noted itching at the base of the fifth digit of their left hands. In the cases of Urquhart and Bluuch, it was their lower left hands. The nodules in the hands of each Drelve-Vydaelian doubled in size and the nodule at the base of Yannuvia's sixth left finger increased by the size of a single graparble. Urquhart, Bluuch, Yathle, Quunsch, Loogie, Starra, Gruusch, and Sharchrina developed little nodules the size of a graparble. The nymphs Buckaroo, Kellianne, Leyden, Megynne, and Kimberleigh developed tiny nodules. Rangers Ringway, Peter, Blair, Dennis, Bernard, Noone, Alistair, Gordon, Lethbridge, Stewart, and Liammie stood guard duty and did not witness the ceremony. Their nodules remained the same. Ranger Willifron did not develop another nodule. Piara, Clouse, and Fisher did not develop nodules.

Yannuvia created the Wand of Languages on the last day of the Dark Period. Regardless of who held the device, the Wand of Languages had thirteen charges. Fortuitously, every person in the dome exposed to grayness and the Stone of Languages gained the ability to communicate in the language of the others. Excepting the eleven guards on the walls and Willifron, the remaining 219 Drelves and eight Carcharians no longer had to worry about communication, which was one less thing.

Duoths attacked again with Duoth bombs and an odd sword which released filmy bubbles. Bursting bubbles' residue burned the defenders' eyes. The attackers were repelled and one Duoth was captured alive. Efforts to communicate failed.

The swelling in Yannuvia's left hand was now twelve times larger than its initial size and large enough to impede the movement of the Wandmaker's wrist. The swelling increased in size when he traveled in the red and blue light with Jonna and Joulie, when he traveled in the red and blue light to Alms Glen with the Dream Master and Amica, when he traveled to Lost Sons with the bodies of his slain friends Diana Maceda, Clarke Maceda, and Banderas, when he traveled to Vydaelia, and when he created *I-one, I-two, I-three, I-four, I-five, and I-six*. When Yannuvia created the *I-seven* United Scepter of the Approximation his nodule did not change. It had grown another increment when he created *I-eight* the Wand of Languages.

Sergeant Major Klunkus and Joulie grew closer.

CHAPTER 18

Trysts, Twists, and Turns
Vydaelian Potpourri

Yannuvia and Piara's tryst…
Forbidden fruit…

The Duoths persisted in their attacks on Vydaelia and created another hole in the wall. One again Rangers and their allies from Dougless fought back the attack. Ranger Willifron was wounded seriously in the barrage of Duoth bombs. Piara saved him. Quunsch captured a Duoth. Yannuvia and others failed to communicate with the beast. The Carcharians prepared a feast. The captured Duoth was the main course. Yannuvia ignored Morganne's protests and joined Fisher and the Carcharians. One by one the sated partakers headed off to rest. Only Yannuvia and Piara remained. Yannuvia stared into the dying embers. Visions of Fort Melphat and the screams of a thousand dying Drolls and Kiennites entered his mind. Then he was aware of the warm touch upon his shoulder.

"Why don't you walk with me, Wandmaker?" Piara purred.

Yannuvia stood and accompanied the sea-elf to the small mossy area by the bathing pool. The pair stood alone by the gently flowing stream. Like Morganne, all those not on duty used this time to rest.

Piara softly touched the tips of Yannuvia's fingers and demurely whispered, "I don't need the power of a Magick rock to see your mind is troubled, my Wandmaker."

Yannuvia replied, "Much ado."

The sea elf seductively asked, "Why don't you allow me to comfort you?"

Piara purred and softly kissed his brow, and slipped both arms around Yannuvia. Her pheromones overwhelmed his fatigued senses.

Why resist?

Disagreement...

Later Yannuvia and Fisher met Morganne by the Day Glass enclosure.

Morganne asked derisively, "How was your meal?"

Fisher replied, "Why are you berating us? It's just meat. The creatures are prey animals. Look at the damage they foment. For your information, the Duoth was indescribably delicious."

Morganne dryly commented, "I'd say the Wandmaker is making some questionable choices of late."

Yannuvia's pointed ears burned, but he remained silent.

Morganne prodded, "Are you well, Wandmaker?"

Yannuvia replied, "If you are wondering whether I regret partaking of the beast, I don't. I've tried every conceivable way to communicate with these creatures. Morganne, four of our folk are dead because of these beasts."

Morganne replied, "Have you considered that we may have cut off their food supply?"

Yannuvia disagreed, "These pudgy beasts couldn't subsist on a few onyums. To my eye, they are a malevolent lot. And, by the way, the Duoth *was* delicious."

Morganne fumed.

Duoth dropping soup...

Sergeant Major Klunkus was injured during a battle with the Duoths and favored his injured ankle. Morganne assumed command of the Rangers.

Quunsch suggested, "Take this Duoth dropping. It's fresh. If you make soup of it, it'll hustle the healing of your broken foot."

Morganne asked, "Doesn't it require special preparation?"

Urquhart entered, "The Duoth dropping is the key ingredient. It doesn't really matter what you mix with it."

Fisher examined the round smooth scybala and commented, "Duoth oil in soap bubbles burns you, while the beast's excrement provides healing. That's illogical. The Duoth dropping is quite sterile and pleasant smelling."

Fisher studied the Duoth dropping.

The Duoths' latest attack necessitated rebuilding of the eastern wall of Vydaelia for a second time. The Wandmaker's Aura Spells maintained purple auras around the Carcharians. Nevertheless Piara's "purple gang" helped Rangers bolstered the eastern wall. Because of persistent attacks Yannuvia ordered the construction of a second wall between the passageway leading to the Duoths' domain and their home. Morganne, Clouse, Rangers Merry Bodkin, Lodi, Tariana and their Carcharian allies Urquhart, Loogie, Yathle, Bluuch, and Quunsch explored the areas to the east and approached the Endless Fen. The party encountered Duoths and after a struggle captured stand by *Long206*. The group returned to Vydaelia with their captive. Time and Fisher's remedies, and Duoth dropping soup healed Klunkus's leg and he resumed command. Construction on the walls continued. The Day Glass rotated to the first day of the fifth Dark Period since they arrived in Vydaelia. Yannuvia entered the geodesic dome alone per usual and created the Wand of Healing, *I-nine*. The wand's command was **"rut fir ford bee haze."**

On the 15th day of the fifth Dark Period Yannuvia gathered the community in the geodesic dome and created his tenth wand, *I-ten*, the Wand of Water Breathing. Its command was **"herb art hoof ear."**

A formidable outer curtain now surrounded all of Vydaelia. With the walls reinforced Yannuvia allowed further exploration of the east. A party of eight led by Klunkus and Clouse and including the six male Carcharians Urquhart, Bluuch, Loogie, Quunsch, Yathle, and Gruusch encountered sea lions and retreated back to Vydaelia. The Rangers beat back the sea lions attack.

Duoth leader *Mose14* tired of his folk's lack of success and recruited the *Cane Bisque Bay Bomber* and sea lion allies. The allied forces brought a massive assault on the eastern walls of Vydaelia. The Giant Amebus oozed over the wall and helped Duoths raid the onyum patch. The creature hurled its massive dung bombs into Vydaelia. The first Amebus bomb exploded on the geodesic dome of stones. A ray of grayness flowed from the dome and slammed into the Amebus. Undaunted the Cane Bisque Bay Bomber hurled another bomb. The Amebus Bomb arced ominously downward and zeroed in on the Day Glass enclosure. An enormous disembodied hand formed in midair, caught the three-foot diameter sphere, and broke its fall. Clouse fomented the Grasping Hand Spell. The titan-sized Grasping Hand remained between Clouse and the Amebus Bomb, eerily floated above the green guy, and held the Dung Bomb tightly. Clouse directed the hand toward the charred ground near the Day Glass enclosure and placed the three-foot diameter spheroid lump harmlessly on the ground. The disembodied hand faded away. Exhausted from the rigors of casting the sixth level spell, Clouse collapsed. The Wandmaker threw everything at his disposal at the massive glob and caused little damage. Duoths scooped up onyums and made off with their bounty. The Amebus oozed back toward the Endless Fen. Chaos and terror gripped the inner ward of Vydaelia. Shrapnel from the first bomb wounded Sharchrina and killed a four year old Drelvling. The elder Dienas described Clouse's conjuration and the disembodied hand that stopped the airborne projectile and allowed Clouse saved at least fifty lives.

The unresponsive green guy was in a bad way. Yannuvia recognized the sixth level spell from his reading in *the Gifts of Andreas to the People of the Forest* and somberly commented, "Clouse knew *of the spell*. The spell was too powerful. He should have never attempted the dweomer."

The Wandmaker, Fisher, and Piara worked with Clouse and the injured. Clouse's *reflector* status complicated the matter. He remained in a deep sleep.

Jonna sobbed, "He won't wake up. Will he be OK?"

Yannuvia solemnly replied, 'I don't know."

Word of the casualties came to the eastern wall.

Urquhart arrived in the inner ward, went to Yannuvia, and said, "Do you now believe what we say about Duoths?"

"Every word of it," Yannuvia answered.

The Wandmaker removed the purple auras from the Carcharians. The false aura spells only feigned Death Magick. The Day Glass rotated and Clouse remained unresponsive. Attacks continued. Mountain Giant Guppie and his cave warg Fenrir went on a recon mission for King Lunniedale of Doug-less and hassled the western wall. The Giant and cave warg caused no casualties, but the Giant Amebus reappeared and hurled another bomb. The bomb exploded in the inner ward, demolished two buildings, and injured several Vydaelians including Fisher. Matron Chryssie and young Nauryl died of their wounds. Fisher ignored his injured left arm and assisted the injured. Rangers gathered graparbles from their dead comrades and brought them to Fisher.

Fisher used his uninjured right arm to remove the small mooler hide pouch that contained eight merged and three single stones. When he added the stones passed from Chryssie and Nauryl, deep gray auras filled the area. When the light faded, a single stone remained. The stone was thirteen times larger than a single graparble and outwardly identical to the Omega Stones carried by Piara, Gruusch, Yannuvia, and Jonna.

Fisher held the stone in his hand.

A single rune appeared on the rock and persisted for thirteen heartbeats.

$$\Omega$$

Then the single letter faded, and three runes appeared on the surface of the rock, which briefly emitted gray light.

$$Ø \infty Ø$$

The runes faded after 21 heartbeats and the single rune reappeared. The pattern repeated three times.

The thirteen graparbles had merged into an Omega Stone. Jonna sat with Clouse in the Day Glass enclosure and felt a buzz in her raiment.

Yannuvia felt a buzz in his raiment.

Though he stood guard on the eastern wall, Gruusch felt a buzz in the natural pocket under his shoulder blade.

Piara felt a buzz from the stone in her garment.

Starra's scarf grew warm and the three runes appeared.

The runes faded after repeating thrice on Jonna and Gruusch's stones. However, Yannuvia, Piara, and the new stone in Fisher's hand were within twenty-one paces of one another. The runes persisted.

The *Three Stones Effect* occurred, and Fisher, Piara, and Yannuvia saw into one another's minds.

The artifact affected Fisher and Piara!

Fisher gasped, released his grip on the stone, and tossed it across the chamber. The artifact landed on the far side of the geodesic dome.

The *Two Stones Effect* appeared and affected the Wandmaker and sea-elf. The Omega Stones held by Yannuvia and Piara exerted their "true-speaking" power. Piara's *Menderish* nature did not prevent the effect. Yannuvia and Piara began to speak the unnerving language of the Omega Stones.

Piara immediately looked at Yannuvia and said in the Chaotic Evil tongue, "I have been deceptive. I have held a graparble the entire time I've been in Vydaelia. I am sorry."

Yannuvia answered in the strangely lyrical language, "I also was deceptive. The Spells I placed upon your comrades and the dweomer that reflected to me were nothing more than Aura Spells."

No one else understood the Chaotic Evil conversation.

Piara added, "I must speak the truth. Why does this Magick affect me when others did not? Oh, my, I *do* want to be with you again. But I see, you've been *busy*, Wandmaker."

Yannuvia anxiously replied, "I also must speak truthfully. I enjoyed being with you. I've had other indiscretions."

Piara followed, "I'm *late*."

Yannuvia replied, "What do you mean?"

Piara reiterated, "Late. In *that* way..."

Yannuvia stammered, "I didn't know...what now?"

Piara languidly replied, "I want you again."

Yannuvia cryptically answered, "I want you, too."

Piara coyly whispered, "If it ever gets quiet...by the wading stream."

Though she could not understand Yannuvia and Piara's words, Morganne's face flushed.

Yannuvia and Piara stared silently at each other.

Joulie retrieved and gripped the Fifth Omega Stone, returned to the Wandmaker's side, cast a look of disdain toward Piara, and said in the garbled language, "I see many things I don't want to see, Wandmaker and *elder Piara*! I'd rather forego the knowledge!"

Joulie returned the artifact to Fisher.

Fisher again gripped the stone. The paleness of his hand accentuated the grayness of the rock. Fisher closed his hand and the malleable artefact spread between his six fingers. The uncharacteristically perplexed Mender thought out loud, in the Chaotic Evil language of the Omega Stone, "Why does this device affect me? I already see much of your mind Wandmaker. We have walked the same path. My, you have been *busy*, Wandmaker! You are a naughty girl, Piara, but I understand you no better than you interpret my innermost thinking. We stare at paintings and only see colors. You and Yannuvia are *Menderish*, not truly Mender."

Piara answered quite *honestly*, "I don't understand what I see in the Wandmaker's mind. I don't understand you at all, Fisher. Why are you too stubborn to admit that your arm hurts?"

Fisher matter-of-factly replied, "It hurts."

Yannuvia cleared his throat and suggested, "Let's release the stones and concentrate on our situation. We have two more dead and a score injured by the Duoth's big shapeless ally. Clouse remains unresponsive. Altogether thirteen of our numbers have died. The size of their nodules in their hands varied at the time of their deaths, but after being expelled from their bodies the stones reverted to the size of one little pebble." He then released the Omega Stone and spoke in Drelvish, "Piara, do you have something to tell the others?"

Piara ashamedly retrieved the graparble from her clinging skirt's pocket and said, "Starra and I received this whilst we were in Doug-less."

Morganne asked angrily, "Why didn't you tell us of this?"

Piara answered, "I revealed Starra's scarf and my Omega Stone. I didn't think the little rock mattered. It's never done anything!"

Fisher had placed the Fifth Omega Stone in his raiment and accepted the graparble in his uninjured right hand. He carefully studied the little rock carefully and then asked, "Piara, have you held one of the stones that extruded from our fallen comrades?"

Piara answered, "No."

Fisher continued, "Too bad they've merged into the Omega Stone. Although the stone you gave me has exactly the same outer dimensions as the stones that emerge from our fallen, this stone is denser. In fact it weighs precisely 1.6180339887498948482… times more."

Menders had an uncanny ability to measure things.

Piara wore a quizzical look.

Yannuvia queried, "Are you saying this is a different kind of stone?"

Fisher platonically answered, "Altogether."

Yannuvia muttered two Old Drelvish phrases. A pale blue aura covered the little rock. The Wandmaker noted, "Strong auras of Magick. What say you, Piara? You've carried it."

Piara said, "Holding the larger stone and scarf together gives me an uncomfortable sense of power. The little rock has done nothing that I can ascertain. Still…I'd like to keep it."

Morganne objected, but Yannuvia returned the graparble-sized rock to Piara.

The Wandmaker ascended one of the gate towers at the bathing stream's egress from Vydaelia and scanned the outer curtain. Nearing exhaustion, Yannuvia pondered. Clouse grew weaker by the moment. The Rangers were tired. Giants appeared in the west. Giant Duoth-like beasts, feline predators, and Duoths attacked from the east. The Carcharians reported hostile Amphibimen in the waters. Piara's *condition* now concerned him. Fatigue flawed his judgment and affected his spell casting. What was he to do?

Soon the Duoths' forces and the Giant Amebus began an all-out assault. The Rangers abandoned the easternmost section of the wall. Soon thereafter the Amebus reached and pummeled the structure.

Strong arms grasped both sides of Yannuvia's raiment. The four-armed Carcharians Urquhart and Bluuch followed Morganne and Piara's directions, grabbed the Wandmaker, and carried him to the rear.

Smoke and unsavory odors filled the air.

Casualties mounted.

There was nothing left for it.

Yannuvia took the Master Wand in his left hand.

The Wandmaker touched the red end of the wand once, the blue end once, the red end twice, the blue end thrice, the red end five times, the blue end eight times, the red end thirteen times, and the blue end twenty-one times. He then simultaneously gripped the red and blue tipped wand at both ends, squeezed the colored portions of the rod, and muttered the wand's command, "**hairy true man**."

Redness flashed through quadrangle. A red blur flew over and went into the inner ward. The Dream Raider Amica landed by Yannuvia and wryly said, "Long time, no see. Guess you guys must be in trouble."

At that moment another Amebus bomb sailed over their heads, slammed into the inner curtain, exploded, and sent stone fragments and three unfortunate Vydaelians sailing through the air. The Dreamraider furiously battled the Giant Amebus and finally prevailed. Clouse remained unresponsive. Yannuvia turned to the Dreamraider for help. The not-so-Good Witch tossed her green hair over her shoulder, leaned forward, muttered some arcane phrases, threw both arms around the green guy, and planted a firm kiss on Clouse's lips.

Clouse awakened, reflexively threw his arms around Amica, and stuttered, "Jonna...no...what the..."

Jonna sighed. Clouse drew back from Amica.

The Dream Raider gloated, "Almost as good as new, and almost as good as you, Wandmaker!"

Yannuvia blushed purplish red.

Morganne flushed in anger.

Jonna cried joyously, threw both arms around Clouse, and steadfastly clutched the green guy. Yannuvia, Morganne, Piara, and Amica exited the Day Glass chamber.

Amica again taunted, "Looks like I saved your sorry ***** again!"

Yannuvia swallowed his pride. He had many questions. The Wandmaker asked, "What will you tell me about graparbles?"

Amica flashed a smile and wryly asked, "What do you know of the little rocks?"

Yannuvia replied, "The little stone Piara carried differs from the graparbles that extrude from our dead comrades. You left the artifact with Starra in Doug-less. The stones enlarge with each wandmaking ceremony and shrink to their original size after leaving their host's body. Sometimes they merge, other times they do not. Why?"

Amica retorted, "Don't always place them together, Wandmaker. Try planting them."

Yannuvia quizzically followed, "Planting them?"

Amica cooed, "Yes. You've an entire field of potting soil."

Yannuvia asked, "The Omega Stones perplex me. How do they affect Fisher and Piara?"

The Dream Raider grew a bit impatient and replied, "So many questions! Fisher has the emotions of a knot on a log, and Piara's a ****! I don't have all the answers. Fisher should search the common knowledge of Menders and recall the first Mender Seffa Lexin. Menders...Menderish folk...Fisher...Piara... Clouse... like you and I, Wandmaker, belong to the gray light. The gray stones are extensions of the gray light."

Yannuvia stood quietly. Morganne hung her head.

Amica teased several Rangers and then approached the Wandmaker, drew him aside, and said, "I have a little secret to tell you."

The Dream Raider leaned forward, whispered in Yannuvia's ear, laughed mischievously, and disappeared in a flash of blue.

A forlorn expression covered the beleaguered Wandmaker's face. The Wandmaker worked with Klunkus and Urquhart for a full rotation of the Day Glass and shored up the defenses. Morganne was noticeably absent. Yannuvia wearily made his way to the Day Glass chamber. The Wandmaker acknowledged Xavi, the young guard. Xavi stepped aside, and the Wandmaker entered his living chamber.

Morganne sat on the edge of the bed with her face in her hands. An iridescent tear made its way down her cheek, fell to the floor, and splashed into an array of colors.

Yannuvia sternly asked, "Where have you been? We needed you at the eastern wall."

Morganne silently raised her eyes and stared at her life mate.

Yannuvia harshly continued, "Morganne! Show some strength! Act like a leader of your people! What's your problem?"

Morganne sobbed, "I'm carrying your child!"

CHAPTER 19

Nodules, Graparbles, and Wands

Menders had an uncanny ability to measure things, including time. Piara and Clouse shared this ability. Fisher, Clouse, and Piara confirmed the accuracy of the Day Glass. The Dreamraider's gift of the Day Glass enabled the folk of Vydaelia to determine the beginning of the Dark Period in the unchanging light of the underworld sea. The Wandmaker Yannuvia entered the chamber of the stones in the geodesic dome on the first and last day of each Dark Period. The citizenry entered with him on the last day of the period.

Nodules...

The first Mender Seffa Lexin developed a nodule at the time of his transformation. Mender Lou Nester arrived in the underworld realm with a large nodule on his left hand. The Mender Fisher had a progressively enlarging nodule at the base of his fifth left finger. The Menders' enlarging nodule grew ever more painful. Menders sensed the upcoming Approximation of Andreas and impending confinement. The collective knowledge of Menders gave some insight, but the ordeal was unique for each Mender. The collective knowledge documented no other instances of Mender's contamination by Drelves' blood. Yannuvia, Jonna, and Joulie had shared their xanthochromic rich ichors with the badly injured Fisher. Confinement required potting soil and darkness, both rare commodities in the night less World of the Three Suns. Fisher began confinement in the caverns near Alluring Falls. The caverns provided darkness, the Mender provided potting soil, and Yannuvia's Magick softened the stony floor to create a pit and augmented the Mender's paltry supply of potting soil. Fisher planted his swollen left hand into the soil and the chrysalis surrounded and hardened around him. Confinement began. Yannuvia and the sisters left him and went to the grotto behind Alluring Falls. A trip in the red and blue light followed. Yannuvia received his Omega Stone and the sisters aged. They returned to find the gray light had returned. Gray rays meandered into the caverns and bathed the chrysalis surrounding the Mender. Fisher's confinement ended. He emerged from his pharate state without a nodule. Clouse emerged with Fisher. Three years had passed.

Spellweaver Yannuvia developed a nodule and rudimentary left sixth digit, pointed ears, and a greenish tinge after Mender's blood touched him. Yannuvia's nodule increased in size whenever gray light touched him and he traveled in the red and blue light. When Yannuvia created his first wand, a small nodule appeared at the base of the fifth digit of every person in attendance's left hand. Later nodules appeared when anyone first witnessed a ceremony of wand creation. Fisher, Clouse, and Piara attended wand making ceremonies and never developed nodules. Other attendees' nodules increased by one increment of original size each time they attended such a ceremony. Ranger Willifron lost his nodule after being critically injured whilst battling Duoths. Heroic efforts by sea elf Piara saved him. Another nodule developed when Willifron witnessed a wand creation after his near death experience. Other members of the erstwhile queen of Doug-less's party developed nodules. Four-armed Urquhart and Bluuch developed nodules on their lower left hand. The Carcharians' little nodules were the same size and behaved like the Drelve-Vydaelians' bumps.

Graparbles...

Graparbles extruded from nodules at death and once after the veteran Ranger Willifron suffered a critical injury. The leaders of Vydaelia studied the little graparbles, which extruded from their folk at their demise or in one case from the Ranger Willifron during extremis. Queen Piara arrived with a graparble. She revealed this artifact after a time. Piara's graparble differed slightly from those extruded from Vydaelians. The stone had exactly the same outer dimensions as the stones that emerge from fallen Drelve-Vydaelians, but it was denser and weighed precisely 1.6180339887498948482 times more. Drelves lost their lives battling denizens of the underworld. Once extruded from bodies the stones shrank to the size of the little stone Piara carried. The little rocks reacted to one another. When 2, 3, 5, 8, or 13 came together they merged into a single stone. Willifron's graparble did not merge with others.

One and one became one.

Two and one became one.

Three and one remained three and one.

Three and two became one.

Five and one, five and two remained five and one and five, one, and one. The sixth and seventh did not merge.

Five and three became one.

Four little stones remained solo when added to eight merged graparbles.

Eight and five became one. The stone made of 13 graparbles became an Omega Stone. The Omega rune formed on the new stone and it shared its fellows' characteristics. Omega Stones were smaller than the exceptional stones that revolved around the Central Sphere in the geodesic dome. The 88 stones were 1.6180339887498948482 larger and heavier than Omega Stones.

Piara's graparble...

Piara received her stone from her daughter Starra, who had received the relic after a visit from the Dreamraider. No one in Vydaelia knew the origins of the little stone Piara carried and the leaders thought it prudent to keep it separate from the others. The difference in weight had to be more than coincidental. Only the Dreamraider knew the rock came from a distressed Dryad's butt.

Planted graparbles...

The Dreamraider suggested planting nodules in the field of potting soil. Fisher planted Willifron's contrary nodule. The field of potting soil's little geyser erupted and sprayed rainbow waters from the little pool and bathed the planted nodule. A little purple tree sprouted. Purple pits like those shown in images by the Dream Master in Lost Sons grew from the little bush. If planted, the pits produced another plant. The purple pits made all the fruits shown by the Dream Master available to the folk of Vydaelia. In the Dream Master's images purple pits were added to the first vessel of Definition. To this point the seven vessels remained inaccessible to the Vydaelians. Over time Fisher and Clouse planted additional nodules that did not merge, and little purple bushes sprouted. The bush that grew from Willifron's extruded nodule grew faster than others, but produced similar yield.

Conflicts with Duoths and Carcharians led to more casualties and consequently more graparbles. Fisher was given the task of planting the little stones. Graparbles planted in the potting soil and bathed by the rainbow waters of the spring sprouted into little bushes which in one dark period's time, and these plants bore purple pits like that seen with the Dream Master in Lost Sons before their journey. These pits could be added to the first vat in the geodesic dome or replanted to produce another bush. The purple pitted fruits were precisely the size of 13 merged graparbles. The pits did not instantly replenish once picked, as did the fruits of the Tree of Thirttene, the gift of the Tree Shepherd. If harvested when mature, the little tree's exceptional fruits reappeared as those of their parent lineage in Green Vale. In Green Vale, when a fruit was harvested, a new nubbin appeared in its place. Drelves harvested the fruits singularly and practiced ultimate conservatism. The Annals of Drelvedom detailed the Tree Shepherd's instructions from antiquity. The fruits were to be removed one at a time and only when matured. Maturity coincided with the harvesting of the enhancing plant roots, which occurred every eight dark periods. The Annals did not detail the origins of the Thirttene Friends, the circle of iconic flora that stool at the crest of the hillock in the center of Green Vale. The Dryad Lexie Glitch delivered the little tree just prior to departure from Lost Sons and the Dreamraider carried it to the field of potting soil where it now flourished. The plants bearing translucent fruits grew whenever another graparble was planted in the potting soil. The gifts of the Tree Shepherd including the Tree of Thirttene and enhancing plants flourished.

Wands and the Wandmaker...

The Wandmaker Yannuvia created devices per instructions he had received from the Drelves' benefactors. The chaotic Dream Master's motives remained unclear. Yannuvia remained suspicious, but the old-appearing yet still young Wandmaker-Spellweaver remained unique in the history of Drelvedom. The Grayness of Andreas had touched Yannuvia four times. Never had Approximations of the wandering sun occurred in such short order. He had traveled in the red and blue light. Menders blood had entered his veins when he saved the enigmatic pale healed after the encounter with the Baxcat and Leicat. The First Wandmaker had drunk from the Cup of Dark Knowledge and the Seventh Vessel. He bore the Wandmaker's Burden. The Tree Shepherd ostracized the Lost Spellweaver and termed him "Fire Wizard." Bereft of his mother Yannuvia had immolated thousands of Drolls and Kiennites in a single powerful fire spell. His twin brother Gaelyss had betrayed Yannuvia. The young Spellweaver's childhood love Kirrie had cast lots with Gaelyss, and the council of Alms Glen had set against him. Friends fell before his eyes on the hill overlooking the River Ornash. Lost friends and loved ones included the Teacher Edkim, his mother Carinne, Banderas, Clarke Maceda, Diana Maceda, the water sprites Illarie, Condee, and Ellspeth, Meryt, Bryce, Zack, Debery, the Lone Oak, the Red Meadow, the Tree Herder Old Yellow, Vioss and Bystar, and scores of his people.

Betrayals by his brother Gaelyss, Kirrie, the nefarious Saligia embittered the Drelvish, Menderish, Spellweaverish, pointed-eared, ever so slightly greenish, First Wandmaker. In Clouse, the greenish product of the Mender Fisher's confinement, Yannuvia saw a reflection of much of himself. A complicated life... even for a Spellweaver! Now he found himself and his followers in this strange locale, where the visions presented by the Dream Master in Lost Sons had become manifest. True and steadfast allies counterbalanced the influence of the Dreamraider and her enigmatic Master. Morganne professed her love for him, and he saw the labors of his folk bear fruit.

Over time Yannuvia had created several wands. The red and blue tipped wand which facilitated their travel to the underworld became known as the Master Wand, and it was involved in the creation of all subsequent wands. The little nodule in his hand progressed with each creation. The parallel with Fisher's course leading to the Mender's confinement was striking.

Yannuvia recorded each wand in *the Gifts of Andreas to the People of the Forest*, the Spellbook entrusted to all Spellweavers at the time of their nymph hood. Each Spellweaver added new spells and personal experiences to his Spellbook during his life's journey. The notation began with the Old Drelvish numeral I, indicating his being the first Wandmaker. Then the number of the wand in order of its creation was written in script rather than numeral. The wand's name and the unique command to activate its power followed. At the time of the Giant Amebus's attack on Vydaelia, Yannuvia had created 10 wands.

I. (one) Knock Wand with the command "**Cow vine cool ledge.**"

II. (two) Wand of Lightning with the command "**Grove veer cleave land.**"

III. (three) Wand of Masonry with the command "**Wood row will son.**"

IV. (four) Wand of Levitation with the command "**Rich herd nicks son.**"

V. (five) Haste Wand, Wand of Speed, with the command "**Jar old ford.**"

VI. (six) Wand of Flight, Wand of Flying with "**Run nailed ray gun.**"

VII. (seven) The United Scepter of the Approximation, an exceptional artifact with command "**Abe Linkin**"

VIII. (eight) Wand of languages with "**yule less says grant**"

IX. (nine) Wand of Healing with "**rut fir ford bee haze**"

X. (ten) Wand of water breathing with "**herb art hoof ear**"

CHAPTER 20

King Lunniedale's Anger

King Lunniedale of Doug-less dispatched many search parties to look for his prodigal spouse and daughter. The King's Viceroy, old four-armed Carcharian Phederal, Commander Gurgla, Sergeant Tapasbar, *three*-armed Heraldo and his espoused Reefa, Top Guard Clootch, recently promoted Brace and Phoodle, the Mountain Giant Guppie, and other members of the King's court sat around the table. Phederal and Gurgla were particularly dreading telling the king they had no luck in tracking down his missing consort and her party. Phederal informed the irate King that Commander Gurgla led a group eastward as far as the catacombs. Phoodle even swam down to the underwater conduit to the eastern ocean. Phederal followed the shoreline to the west, looped around the great lake, went as far as the river that feeds the lake, and found no signs of the lecherous Queen. Lunniedale was predictably displeased. His words burned Phederal and Gurgla's ears.

King Lunniedale grumpily responded, "Poltroons! You lot make it ill work to besiege a hencoop! That's not what I wanted to hear, Viceroy Phederal."

The hulking four-armed Carcharian King toyed with his favorite trident as he spoke.

Gurgla gulped and said timidly, "Tracking along the stone and in water is impossible. My King, I…"

Top Guard Clootch suggested, "It's possible they swam out to sea."

Everlie added, "Piara, Starra, and Sharchrina are not strong swimmers."

Without speaking King Lunniedale tensed his grip on the trident, hurled it violently across the wide room, and struck the unfortunate

Everlie in the chest. Everlie groaned and fell to the floor. Uttering the queen's name was a fatal mistake.

Lunniedale growled, "I said *her* name was not to be uttered in this realm. Does anyone else have any doubt about my resolve in the matter?"

Old Phederal wisely answered, "No, my King. We get your drift! Everlie was no better than his brother Donphil! As I said, I found no signs of Pi...uh, the ***** who abandoned you! But I did detect Bugwully scent along the trail to the west and south. I lost the scent at the river. I'd surmise the traitors sought refuge with the newcomers. Shall we prepare for an assault?"

Enthusiastically Tapasbar added, "My King, as your warriors return, we have kept them in Doug-less. Free swimmers that hear of the treachery against you swim to support our ranks. A four-arm and two-arm joined us this day."

Lunniedale raised his thick brows and muttered sourly, "Free swimmers are allowed into my dominion! Who guards the Circle of Willis to assure shape changers and other scum doesn't invade our inner realm?"

Top Guard Clootch quickly added, "The most experienced two-armed warriors now guard the Circle of Willis. Double shifts stand at all times, my King. Tippie, Caanno, Tilertoo, Ambroo, Nuttin, Hunnie, Ruutchie, Draacks, and Fraaid are watching the circle as we speak."

Lunniedale commented, "The devious Queen victimized many of this group when she escaped. Why, why, why, do my guards have such woefully bad names?"

Phederal now gulped and reminded the King, "My King, the Queen, I mean, the *****, could be quite persuasive. And my liege, it was you that named most of my guards, usually after celebrating their births by drinking sea elf's mead with their fathers."

The old four-armed Carcharian Viceroy cringed and prepared for the worse.

Instead of hurling his trident Lunniedale conceded, "Their names... they can't all be gems. It's unusual for you to say anything contrary to me, Phederal. You're normally a passive hunk of ****. Are you sick? Are you developing a backbone in your old age?"

Leaving well enough alone, Phederal opted to change the subject and queried, "Again it's my best guess the erstwhile Queen fled toward the newcomers. When shall we attack them?"

King Lunniedale sat back in his big chair, pondered for a moment, and then continued, "There are too many pretty sea elves in the sea for me to opine about my devious former Queen. The Cane Bisque Bay Bomber protects the Duoth settlements along Cane Bisque Bay, but my grandfather told me of good Duoth hunting in the Hills of Lithonia to the north and Doubling to the east beyond Cane Bisque Bay. Tapasbar, you are a simple ****! Do you think you could organize the free swimmers and try your luck in Lithonia?"

Tapasbar cleared his throat and gurgled, "Yes, My King. It will be done."

Gurgla obediently bowed and then tentatively asked, "No disrespect intended, my King, but what about those who betrayed you...us? I no longer desire your niece. She was influenced by the Queen-Witch."

King Lunniedale, "No offense taken, Commander Gurgla. Fifteen of the strongest members of this community trekked westward. Only one returned alive, and only long enough to tell the tale. If the traitors are not already dead, we'll get to them in time. Why should the newcomers suffer a devious whorish sea elf and a motley crew of Carcharians? If they meet my erstwhile consort, the sorcerers will think all feminine sea elves are harlots! I have to think of Doug-less and defending my people. Many Carcharian warlords and others are beholding to me. It's time for me to collect on some of the many favors due me. Phederal, send surveillance teams to monitor events on the far side of the lake and strong swimmers to my allies. Before I attack the newcomers, I want to shore up my forces and attack from a position of strength. Why do we care what happens on the other side of the lake? Only the harvesting of Duoths interests me. I don't like onyums! Duoths! Other sources of Duoth flesh are available in Lithonia and Doubling. As far as my former Queen, two-armed daughter, immature two-armed niece, and five traitorous warriors are concerned; it's a matter of mind over matter, Commander Gurgla. I don't mind because they no longer matter. Now someone bring me some mead."

Viceroy Phederal stood and stridently ordered, "You heard the King! Clootch, make sure any free swimmers that enter Doug-less are screened. I want everyone tested! Brace, you're in charge of organizing surveillance teams. I'd prefer four-arms be emissaries to the allies. Heraldo, you've traveled more to the east than I. You should lead our expedition to the areas north and east of Cane Bisque Bay."

Heraldo stammered, "I...I don't know if the King can do without me. I'm important as..."

King Lunniedale interrupted, "I can do without you, Heraldo. I'm missing Duoth flesh! Make haste!"

Heraldo acknowledged the assignment, took his espoused Reefa and younger brother Craig, and exited the meeting room. Craig also had four arms. No current resident of Doug-less remembered another couple having two four-armed sons. Craig had been very successful in competitions, but the young Carcharian was about to head out on his first adventure outside the friendly confines of Doug-less.

Brace chose Phoodle and a large two-arm named Taktaki to accompany him in scouting the newcomers. The other parties left Doug-less. Emissaries set out to collect favors owed King Lunniedale. Brace, Phoodle, and Taktaki made their way to the shoals outside the newcomers growing stronghold. They encountered few predators in the dark waters. The trio witnessed the battle between the newcomers and the allied forces of Duoths, sea lions, and the Giant Amebus. The trio tentatively watched the fight with the Giant Amebus, horrific explosions ripping through the walled structure, and the massive beast's destruction in a dreadful explosion. The walls of the fortress sustained damage. The scouts from Doug-less could not see the extent of the newcomers' casualties, but the explosions and waves of sea lion and Duoth attackers had to take a toll. Brace languished over the thought of wasted Duoth... and the King's table was empty! Brace sent two-arm Taktaki closer to shore. Taktaki abruptly submerged. Brace and Phoodle followed his lead. Quunsch's unmistakable wide Bugwullyish face appeared on the allure. His keen sense of smell picked up the Carcharians. The threesome sped back to Doug-less to give news of the battle to their king.

On the allure facing the great sea, watch duty was bestowed on skeletal crews. Quunsch stared intently at the dark waters and sniffed repeatedly. Ranger Tawyna stood on battle-weary legs by the half-Bugwully.

Tawyna asked, "What are you sensing, Quunsch?"

"Quunsch frowned and replied, "Unmistakably the stench of Doug-less! Carcharian!"

Taktaki hustled back to his comrades.

Tawyna followed, "Stench? You are of Doug-less and part Carcharian. I don't understand."

Quunsch continued to stare across the gentle lapping waves and muttered, "You don't know belittlement until you've lived in Doug-less with Bugwully lineage and two arms."

Tawyna asked, "Aren't most Carcharians two-armed?"

Quunsch continued to concentrate and muttered, "But most aren't half-Bugwully. I held my own physically, but I caught every s**t duty the king could think up."

Tawyna said, "Sorry! I can't see any intruders."

Quunsch replied, "I can't see them either, but I can smell them. They are about fifty paces out. At least two of 'em! Spies from Doug-less, I'd suspect. I could swim out and kill them."

Tawyna discouragingly said, "Our orders are to stay on the wall. The last attack weakened our defenses and we suffered many casualties. The green guy Clouse is down and out. The Wandmaker Yannuvia is exhausted. Even the winged Dreamraider took a beating from the big glob. Besides… you don't know how many foes you'd face."

Quunsch muttered, "I'm not sure I can hold back. I've a lot of pay back to give Doug-less and old King Lunniedale."

Tawyna insisted, "Best follow your orders! Sergeant Major Klunkus specifically wanted this area watched. We are vulnerable from the sea. We… I need you here!"

Quunsch blushed as much as Bugwullies might and beamed, "You need me! Really?"

Tawyna starred across the gently lapping waves and answered, "Yes!"

Quunsch suppressed his urge to plow into the water and seek out the interlopers and stood by his tough little companion.

Brace, Phoodle, and Taktaki beat a hasty retreat to Doug-less.

Squaddie Frayn of Graywood also watched the goings on around Vydaelia. The gray-green sea elf kept a safe distance from the Carcharians and stuck close to his trained pottyhippomus. The plesiohawg's generous bottom, floppy ears, and rounded belly earned it the moniker pottyhippomus. Plesiohawgs had thick seal-like hair and scurried along the surfaces of bodies of water much faster than a sea elf might swim. Sea elves oft employed the playful creatures to travel large distances or escape predators quickly. Frayn's folk recruited the sea steeds with promise of sea oats, the pottyhippomuses' favorite food and a grain cultivated in land locked patties. Frayn's mission was to monitor activities of Doug-less but he had shadowed Slurdup's ill-fated lot and tagged along a safe distance behind Brace, Phoodle, and Taktaki. Frayn'd ascertained little of the strange newcomers, but any enemy of the Carcharians benefitted his folk.

The veteran Squaddie of Graywood followed Brace and his colleagues away from Vydaelia.

Tawyna queried, "Gruusch, I still see nothing in the water. I only smell the lingering stench of battle. What do you, uh, smell?"

Quunsch sniffed and reported, "Nothing now! They're gone. Probably saw us on the wall. I caught a glimpse of a pottyhippomus. Wish it was closer. They are pretty good eating!"

Tawyna said, "We should report this to the Wandmaker. Perhaps your people are planning an attack."

Quunsch snorted, "They're not my people. It was just a scouting party. The King wants the onyum patch monitored. It's the best place to catch Duoths. It's like hunting in a baited field, though. The dough-boys can't resist the fruits of the onyum trees. Carcharians fight well in the water, but they do better with weapons on land. If King Lunniedale is going to attack, he'll send forces from the route we followed."

Tawyna questioned, "Why? Earlier forces encountered the triskaidekapod. Everyone but Gruusch was lost."

Quunsch said, "One Shellie, an oldster named Pincher, got back to Doug-less with grievous wounds. He returned to the sea to die after he reported to the King. As to the kraken spawn, there's probably not another one in these parts. I'd only heard stories of them. Now King Lunniedale knows we are here. He yearns to skewer the Queen and talks a mean talk. Bottom line is that he's sea chicken s**t. He'll attack only with superior numbers and then in absentia. There's nothing in the water now."

Tawyna continued, "Just the same, we should report to the Wandmaker."

Quunsch shrugged and pointed his trident toward the dark waters. The half-Bugwully said, "When I last saw the Wandmaker, he was overwhelmed. When the scouting party reports the destruction of the Giant Amebus, the King won't want any part of you guys. But I'll stand watch. Mind you I'd rather be chasing Duoths. They're tasty!"

Tawyna said, "The Dreamraider destroyed the Amebus. For that matter she bested the triskaidekapod, too. She's gone now."

Quunsch rubbed his thick skinned chin and answered, "The King of Doug-less doesn't know that. Besides, we softened them up for her!"

Tawyna anxiously replied, "I am going to report to our superiors."

Tawyna made her way to the quadrangle. The inner ward of Vydaelia bustled with activity. The Wandmaker's life-mate Morganne was notably absent. The Wandmaker Yannuvia, Mender Fisher, Sergeant Major Klunkus, and others gathered around the green guy Clouse. Jonna held Yannuvia's greenish look-alike tightly. Smoke wafted through the air and intermingled with the unchanging light of the massive cavern. Tawyna reported Quunsch's observations. Sergeant Major Klunkus warned the greatest threat came from the direction of the Duoth's passageway where the wall was compromised, but he also instructed Rangers to maintain vigilance on the walls facing the sea and the west. Urquhart supported Quunsch's opinion that an attack from Doug-less was more likely to come from the west. Both Yannuvia and Klunkus discouraged following the retreating Duoths and sea lions and ordered every available person to assist in repairing the defects in the wall. Quunsch grumbled most loudly but acquiesced and lent his strength to placing boulders in the holes in the eastern wall.

Brace, Phoodle, and Taktaki passed through the circle of Willis and entered Doug-less proper.

Frayn treaded water a while and then sneaked to a rendezvous point in the reeds to the east of Doug-less. There a stream promised clean water and fresh water crustaceans provided ample nourishment for the veteran scout. The spot gave a good vantage point to monitor the approach to Doug-less, though entry to the stronghold proper required passing through many underwater checkpoints. Frayn had not ventured beyond the first two checkpoints. Someone approached.

Frayn smiled. He had trained young Bryni well. He'd scarcely heard the youth's approach.

Bryni asked. "How goes the watch?"

Frayn answered, "Can't say. I've been away. I followed Carcharian scouts across the sea. Rumors are correct. There is a stronghold under construction at the site of the large onyum patch."

Bryni said, "The Duoths won't accept intrusion on their onyum patch."

Frayn said, "You know they wouldn't! I witnessed a furious battle. The newcomers were up against sea lions and Duoths. The liege of Ty Ty summoned an Amebus from Cane Bisque Bay. The big glob hurled exploding bombs into the newcomers' stronghold and fomented great damage. The newcomers fought tenaciously and smote many sea lions. Still the Duoths breached their walls. The battle culminated with the explosion of the Giant Amebus."

Bryni said, "Impossible!"

Frayn said, "Impossible by natural means, but the newcomers fomented Magick. They occupy the Carcharians' hunting grounds. Return to Graywood and tell Commandant Inyra of my findings."

Bryni cautioned, "Squaddie Frayn, you have long served Graywood. Why do you risk life and limb by lingering in the shadow of Doug-less?"

Frayn said, "I follow my orders. It's my business to know our enemies' movements. Now go!"

Taktaki returned to the barracks and rejoined two-armed comrades. Brace and Phoodle sought out Phederal and joined the viceroy in King Lunniedale's council room.

King Lunniedale bellowed, "It's painfully obvious that you've returned without Duoth flesh. I hope for your sakes that you've knowledge that's worth my time."

Brace tentatively addressed the monarch, "We witnessed a furious battle. The newcomers were up against sea lions, Duoths, and a giant jiggly glob. The big glob hurled exploding bombs into the newcomers' stronghold and fomented great damage. The newcomers fought tenaciously and smote many sea lions. Still the Duoths breached their walls."

Lunniedale surmised, "The liege of Ty Ty summoned an Amebus from Cane Bisque Bay. That should have been all for the newcomers. Why didn't you go in and scoop up Duoth remnants for my table?"

Brace shuddered and replied, "My liege, the Duoths breached the wall but the newcomers rallied. The Giant Amebus threw bombs into the center of the stronghold and shook the very foundation of the fortress. The beast oozed over the wall. I too thought it was all she wrote for the newcomers. Then there was a series of flashing red lights. Flames ripped into the Amebus, but the big critter still oozed onward. Then the beast blew up. It must have choked on one of its bombs."

Lunniedale queried, "Are you saying these folk destroyed a Giant Amebus? Amebus bombs only explode if thrown. Add this to Cracker's report that they smote a kraken spawn! Who are these guys?"

Phederal huffed, "Let's put them to the spear and trident, my king! Mindless beasts can't compare to the courage and might of well-armed Carcharians! Our envoys are mustering allies as we speak. We should strike the newcomers in force before they grow stronger."

Lunniedale smirked and replied, "Why, Phederal, for a moment I'd swear I sensed you had a backbone. It doesn't sound like the newcomers need to get much stronger. I'm sure my nefarious queen has filled their ears with knowledge about our folk. We'll be lucky if they don't storm the Circle of Willis. The ***** queen got by the guards easily enough to escape Doug-less, so she'd just as easily get back in."

Brace interjected, "My liege, we saw no signs of Pi... I, mean, the ***** that deserted you! We saw the hideous Bugwully on the wall. He's allied with the newcomers."

Lunniedale spun his trident in his huge left upper hand and acknowledged, "Quick thinking, scumbag! Had you muttered either of their names you'd have shared old Everlie's fate. Too bad! I could have used some throwing practice. Needless to say if that half-a**ed Bugwully has joined forces with them, my **** of a queen has done so as well."

Phederal added, "Maybe she was killed by an Amebus bomb."

Lunniedale's eyes widened and he moaned, "I'm not that lucky!'

Phederal persisted, "My liege, the Amebus, sea lions, and Duoths have weakened them. We should attack as soon as possible."

Lunniedale growled, "When I want your opinion, I'll ask for it, Viceroy Phederal, but in this case you have a point. Gather a company and lead them to the billabong area. Send probing forces. Just keep them busy until our allies arrive. The Duoths can't stay away from those cursed onyums. I suspect they'll continue to aggravate the newcomers. Why are you still standing before me! Get going!"

CHAPTER 21

Aftermath of the Giant Amebus in Vydaelia

For the second time Yannuvia used the special power of the Master Wand to summon the Dreamraider. After a touch and go battle the Dreamraider prevailed. The combined forces of Duoths, Sea lions, and massive Amebus stretched the Vydaelians defenses to the limit. Clouse fell exhausted after casting a Grasping Hand Spell which halted one of the Amebus's explosive projectiles. The greenish Spellweaverish Clouse's effort saved many lives in the quadrangle of Vydaelia. Once again the Drelves relied on the Dreamraider's skills to resuscitate the green guy. Sergeant Major Klunkus mustered the Rangers to shore up defenses. Half-Bugwully Quunsch boisterously urged pursuit of the fleeing Duoths, but the battle had stressed the Vydaelians to the point of exhaustion. Klunkus and his tired charges stacked broken pieces of the wall to fill in holes created by the attackers. Tending the wounded required much attention. Klunkus used all the resources at his disposal. The folk of Doug-less proved valuable. Urquhart insisted on staying in the quadrangle with Piara and Starra. Gruusch remained with the Rangers at the wall. Bluuch and Loogie maintained vigilance. Quunsch's exceptional sense of smell helped screen for Duoths, but the defenders had to hold the big fellow back from pursuing the marshmallow men. Sea lions barked in the distance. All defenders feared the arrival of another Amebus. Vydaelians were not privy to the rarity of the big beasts and hoped the unlikely demise of the Duoth's big ally left the marshmallow blokes without such reinforcement. No one really knew how the Amebus propagated. Were there *little* Giant Amebuses?

Klunkus spared only a few Rangers to watch the sea and the area toward the billabong from which the triskaidekapod and Piara's group came. With Vydaelia's defenses compromised, an attack from the Carcharians would be devastating. The intact walls enabled the Sergeant Major to bolster forces to the east in the direction of the Duoths' lairs. Half-Bugwully Quunsch and Tawyna stood watch toward the sea. Quunsch grumbled all the while about wasted Duoth flesh.

Massive clean-up continued. The Giant Amebus hurled three bombs into Vydaelia. The first exploded on the geodesic dome that housed the Central Sphere and 88 rotating stones. The dome sustained no damage and sent a countermeasure that rocked the Amebus. Unfortunately debris from the explosion cost the Vydaelians lives and injuries. Clouse intercepted the second bomb. A third exploded in the inner ward and destroyed two buildings and injured many including Fisher. Rangers busily rebuilt the houses and cleared wreckage.

The Wandmaker Yannuvia, Sergeant Major Klunkus, Fisher, Joulie, Merry Bodkin, Dienas, Yiuryna, Tanteras, Willifron, Carcharian Princess Starra, two-armed Carcharian Gruusch, and four-armed Urquhart met in council in the outer ward of the quadrangle of Vydaelia. The sea elf Piara attended the wounded, including her niece Sharchrina. Jonna stayed with Clouse, who suffered lingering effects from casting the sixth level spell that saved many lives by stopping the Amebus' bomb. The Dreamraider revived Clouse with a kiss and spell and then departed after giving whispered news to the Wandmaker. Quunsch remained at his station on the allure facing the sea. Two-armed round-faced half-Pollywoddle Loogie stood guard on the western wall with Drelve-Vydaelians Alistair, Gordon, Leftbridge, and Stewart. Four-armed half sea elf Bluuch lent his massive frame to the defense of the breached eastern wall. The Carcharian stood outside the wall with two tridents and two spears in hands and stared intently at the passage leading to the Duoths domain. Two-armed half sea elf Yathle stood within the breach with Peter, Blair, Dennis, Bernard, and Noone. Sea elf Queen Piara returned to the outer ward from the inner ward of the quadrangle. Her niece's condition had stabilized. Morganne remained in the Day Glass enclosure that doubled as her and Yannuvia's home.

Piara, Gruusch, Yannuvia, Jonna, and Fisher carried Omega Stones. Omega stones were 13 times larger than graparbles and 0.61904762 the size of one of the 88 stones revolving around the central sphere. Starra's red scarf detected the presence of the stones. Grasping the stones and exposing them to the gray light of the wandering sun Andreas and its surrogate the Central Sphere activated the devices. The stones sensed the presence of their fellows. Whenever two bearers were in proximity the little rocks buzzed and runes formed on their surfaces. Individual stones gave their bearer delusions. Two or more stones empowered their bearers with the ability to speak the chaotic evil language of the abyss and forced the truth, the *two stones effect*. Three stones produced windows into the bearers" minds, the *three stones effect*. Four stones had been presented to Yannuvia, who felt "luck", Gruusch "charming", Jonna "strength", and Piara "power." The presence of a fourth stone had produced no discernible effect. A fifth stone formed when 13 graparbles merged. Joulie gripped the Fifth Omega Stone, saw into Yannuvia and Piara's thoughts, and discovered their secret. Joulie cast a look of disdain toward Piara, and said in the garbled language, "I see many things I don't want to see, Wandmaker and *elder Piara*! I'd rather forego the knowledge!"

Joulie returned the artifact to Fisher.

Fisher gripped the stone. The paleness of his hand accentuated the grayness of the gray rock. Fisher closed his hand and the stone spread between his six fingers. The uncharacteristically perplexed Mender thought out loud, in the Chaotic Evil language of the Omega Stones, "Why does this device affect me? I already see much of your mind Wandmaker, and we have taken the same steps for many years. My, you have been *busy*, Wandmaker! You are a naughty girl, Piara, but I understand you no better than you interpret my innermost thinking. We stare at paintings and only see colors. You and Yannuvia are *Menderish*, not truly Mender."

Fisher felt the stone defined the workings of the odd artifacts and gave "meaning."

The Wandmaker's mind bore many complexities that barred access to those not touched by Magick, but the stones revealed his painful secrets. Jonna, Fisher, Joulie, the unpredictable Dreamraider, and Piara shared his secret and knew his angst. Morganne revealed her expectant status but had not experienced the *Three Stones Effect* and was not privy to the Wandmaker's trysts.

Was there a *Five Stones Effect*? Five stones being in proximity produced no discernible additional effect. Fisher's impressions of the fifth stone were akin to Gruusch's feeling of "charming" and Yannuvia's sense of "luck."

Fisher was Mender. Piara was Menderish. Clouse was both Menderish and Spellweaverish. The Wandmaker was Spellweaver and Fire Wizardish with a hint of Mender.

Lifelong friends and co-adventurers now also bore Yannuvia's secrets. Bearing these secrets would be a heavy load. The beleaguered Wandmaker advised the stone bearers refrain from activating the devices.

Yannuvia mustered strength and walked to the damaged walls near the onyum patch. Klunkus's charges had done yeoman's work in filling in the defects. Two-armed Yathle and powerful four-armed Bluuch now stood atop the assembled rubble to maintain better vantage points toward the Duoths' passage. The sea lion barking had disappeared and now only the busy sounds of the transplanted Drelves' work filled the air. The Wandmaker produced the Wand of Masonry, approached the wall, and muttered **"Wood row will son."** The wand combined Rock to Mud and Mud to Rock effects. Initially the broken boulders transformed to soft clay. Workers smoothed the clay into smooth walls and the Wandmaker repeatedly touched the new walls with the wand and repeated the command. In an instant the new wall hardened and painstakingly repaired the damage fomented by the Duoths and Giant Amebus.

Mighty Bluuch gave a shout and hurled a spear toward the passageway. A soft thud communicated a Duoth scout's demise. *Pierce 178* stayed behind to monitor activities in the aftermath of the battle. His curiosity left him vulnerable and in view of the Carcharians and range of powerful Bluuch's throwing spear. Bluuch and Yathle bounded down from the wall and retrieved the victim. Drelvish bows created by renowned bowyer BJ Aires covered the Carcharians, but Bluuch and Yathle returned without incident and reported no other activity in the area.

Pierce178's stand-by clan mourned him, and his replacement took the moniker *Pierce179*. Other than leader of Ty Ty, Duoths' highest statuses were Onyum Growers and Stand-byes. Onyum growers were named *Wheeler, Montgomery, Toombs, Tattnall, Candler, Evans, Bacon, Emanuel, Telfair, Jeff Davis, Appling, Treutlen, and Bulloch.* Stand-byes were named *Laurens, Jenkins, Wayne, Dodge, Screven, Pierce, and Long.* Numbers after the names depicted the number of predecessors that had passed, usually in pursuit of onyums and at the hands of Carcharians and other predators. 178 *"Pierces"* had now fallen whilst serving in the role of Stand-by.

The Wandmaker ignored the pleas of Klunkus, Dienas, Yiuryna, and others and worked through two rotations of the Day Glass. Piara joined the work and reported Sharchrina had made progress. Near the end of the second period Clouse arrived. Jonna stood close by his side and chastised him for leaving the inner ward. Clouse was unable to cast spells but used his Menderish skills of measurement to help Fisher and Piara assure the walls were smooth and even. Occasionally the erstwhile sea elfish queen of Doug-less descended from the wall and walked about the quadrangle. The beautiful light green tint to her smooth skin took on a more bluish tint and beads of her lime juice colored perspiration poured from her brow. She refused food and declined Fisher's offer of aid. Morganne remained absent.

Drelves scurried about the quadrangle and removed debris. All the while Rangers remained vigilant on the allures.

CHAPTER 22

Piara's Decision

The Vydaelians repaired the breach in the outer curtain. Exhaustion fell over the Wandmaker and he returned to his dwelling. Facing his life-mate Morganne added to his angst, but the orange-haired she-Drelve did not question him. Yannuvia did not answer questions about his life-mate's absence from the repair efforts. Through the Omega Stones' *Three Stones effect* Piara, Gruusch, Jonna, Joulie, and Fisher shared his knowledge of Morganne's gestation. Piara watched Yannuvia return to his dwelling and dejectedly returned to the bartizan that housed the outcasts from Doug-less. Urquhart followed the queen and joined her.

The massive four-armed Carcharian's thoughts lingered with Starra, who had headed to the allure with Gruusch to relieve Quunsch and Tawyna.

Piara removed her outer raiment. Her green hair cascaded down her back. Tension ripped through her well-defined muscles and fatigue distorted her fine features. Urquhart politely requested entry to her chamber.

Urquhart asked, "Are you ill, my queen?"

Piara answered, "Just tired, Urquhart."

Her loyal guard persisted, "Your look belies your words, my queen. You seem worried, or preoccupied."

Piara replied, "I might say the same thing about you, Urquhart."

Urquhart said, "I assure you, your highness, that I'm fully alert and will give my all to protect you."

Piara continued, "Thank you. I must rest, Urquhart. I can't think clearly."

Urquhart said, "Take your rest, my lady. You have served these people well. I am available if you need me."

Piara answered, "If you want to serve me, take rest yourself. You fought well. Many sea lions fell before your weapons."

Urquhart bowed respectfully and left Piara alone. She sighed deeply and fought off a bit of queasiness. Chewing a bit of ginger helped. She stretched and lay down on the soft bedding. Sleep came soon. Unsettling dreams of Doug-less and Lunniedale's tyranny gave way to dreamless slumber for a while. Then… redness entered her sleep.

Wisps…
Threads…
Threads of Magick…
Threads of fate…
Threads of time…
Threads connecting worlds …
Dreams connecting worlds …
Dreams of Magick…
The Magick of Dreams…
Magick connecting dreams…
Magick connecting worlds…
Dream raiders…
Elf pressure…
Albtraum…
Albträume, elf dreams, nightmares…

Ø ∞ Ø

When the redness cleared, Piara looked upon the familiar visage of an older sea elf. The visage appeared often in her deepest thoughts. Long ago her great-great-great grandmother had looked upon her reflection in a clear stream. Piara saw the reflection through her ancestor's eyes. Her great-great-great grandmother appeared an older version of Piara. Features were remarkably similar; only the older sea elf's skin grayed a bit and lacked Piara's brilliant greenness. Piara thought her great-great-great grandmother's reflection dulled her skin. In quiet times as a captive young Piara concentrated and beheld the visage. It comforted her in the unfriendly environs of Doug-less. Now the image of her great-great-great grandmother appeared in her dream and ended painful dreams of Doug-less, but redness heralded its arrival.

Piara addressed the image, "You've peered into my inner thoughts, Dreamraider, and chosen a visage that comforts me, but it doesn't allay my questions of your motives."

The ersatz elderly sea elf replied, "That's not nice. I thought you'd appreciate my taking your mind off your condition. You've made a thorny bed in which you must lie."

Piara said, "I'm indebted to you for helping fight off threats to my daughter and niece. In saving the Vydaelians, you also saved us. But you are as reprehensible as I am. I've looked inside the Wandmaker's mind."

The visage replied, "I'm not staying around and making like a princess. How do you think you're going to fit in after Morganne, the Wandmaker's squeeze, finds out about your condition? She'll throw your green a** out of Vydaelia!"

Piara said, "I regret my impulsiveness. I was lonely and found the Wandmaker quite appealing. I've put myself in a difficult position, but I must persevere and watch after my daughter and niece. I'll accept censure."

The visage taunted, "Don't you want to find out more about me?"

Piara scoffed, "You are a visage in my dream, not my great-great-great grandmother. You've only fabricated an image you have taken from my mind. It might not be correct. I don't understand the images I see. Fisher says I'm Menderish. I never saw my great-great-great grandmother's face, only a reflection in a pool. She left my home long before I was born. I have seen images of her destination, but I don't really know where she went after she left her people. I just… see a dark room."

The Dreamraider said, "I know where she went. Her legacy awaits you. You need only seek it."

Piara said, "I do have an intuitive sense of her home. But it's not in the propinquity of Vydaelia. I'd never find my way."

The Dreamraider replied, "You know my way with gifts. I've leave you a little something." She maintained the visage of Piara's ancestor and produced a small stone and a strand of purple rawhide in her left hand. She continued, "Marvelous little device! It has an identical sister. It'll lead you to its twin. Keep it safe and hold it close. It'll both guide and protect you. Pay heed to the *twin speak* when the sisters are together.

The sisters are the keys to unlocking many doors, dissuading Magick, and saving time. You'll discover many secrets about your ancestor. You don't want to stay in Vydaelia. You will only make things more difficult for your spawn. The folk of Vydaelia already think you a whore. I must say they have you pegged!"

Piara snipped, "There's no shortage of harlots in this dream. You're nefarious, Dreamraider. I shan't trust you. I know you have designs on the Wandmaker!"

Amica maintained her guise and said, "You don't have to trust me. Hold the amulet in your hand. You'll know I speak the truth. I'll let you sleep, since you are sleeping for two. Your big guard personifies loyalty. You're lucky to have such an ally."

Blueness surrounded the image and it faded from Piara's dream. She slept fitfully for a few moments and then awakened. She found a small dark gray stone about twice the size of a graparble and a strand of purple rawhide. She hesitated for a moment, but then held the small stone. The rawhide wrapped around the stone and created an amulet. It warmed, softened in her hand, buzzed gently, and pulled her fingers toward the sea. The erstwhile queen of Doug-less placed the fiber around her neck. The device faded from view. Piara sensed its slight weight as it hung imperceptive and comfortably around her neck. Piara's uncanny sense of timing told her she had slept for about 4 hours. She peeked into the hallway. Quunsch snored loudly and no one was in the hall. She tiptoed down the hall and checked Urquhart's room. The massive four-arm sat on the edge of his bed and stared silently at the floor.

Piara whispered, "Urquhart?"

Urquhart said, "My lady, are you unable to sleep?"

Piara said, "I've rested some. May I speak with you?"

Urquhart replied, "I'm always at your service. I'll do whatever I can to assist you."

Piara said, "I do not doubt that at all. You have long protected my daughter Starra. I also know your feelings for Starra are strong."

Urquhart said, "My queen, that matters little now. Starra's eyes are fixed on the two-arm Gruusch. That I'd be second best to a two-arm would chagrin my father, but it matters little to me. If Gruusch is what makes Starra happy, so be it. Gruusch fought well. My travels with my two-armed friends have taught me that one's value can't be determined simply by the number of his arms. My purpose is, and has always been, to give my all for your and the princess's safety."

Piara extended her left hand, softly stroked the massive four-armed warrior's brow, and softly answered, "Noble Urquhart, your loyalty is unquestionable. Remember I'm no longer queen. In this place I'm merely another elder. You are honest with me, and I must be so with you. I'm afraid I've shown some indiscretion."

Urquhart asked, "Regarding what, my... elder Piara?"

Piara blushed and said, "In regard to my relationship with the Wandmaker, Urquhart. I've gotten myself into a situation."

Urquhart sighed and stoically said, "You are with child."

Piara blushed again and said, "How'd you know."

Urquhart answered, "I've spent many shifts guarding you and Starra. You oft spend time in the birthing area. The look... the perspiration... I sensed... your situation."

Piara asked, "How many gravid sea elves have you encountered? Your mother died bringing you into the world, a sad but common occurrence."

Urquhart answered, "My queen, or, Elder Piara, as you prefer, I served in the king's royal guard. I am privy to his activities. Sea elfish females are oft spoils of raids and brought back as consorts. It's how you came to Doug-less. Of my mother, I only know what I've been told. I doubt she shared your beauty."

Piara replied, "All Doug-less spoke of your mother's beauty. That I appeal to your eyes compliments me, noble Urquhart. Your Carcharian features and four arms would have placed you in great favor. That you followed us to this place speaks highly of your loyalty. I find you appealing and, if circumstances were different, could easily see my body in your four powerful arms. But now is not the time for mutual admiration. My indiscretion has compromised my daughter's safety. I have a difficult decision before me."

Urquhart shrugged, "You carry the Wandmaker's spawn. The spawn will be beautiful and touched by Magick. This should increase your import in Vydaelia."

Piara replied, "Urquhart, the Wandmaker is espoused. I have taken liberty with his affection. I don't understand the ways of Magick and how the Wandmaker was chosen. In the time we've been here, I've heard the newcomers speak of Spellweavers. Their world shares the light of three suns. The third appears irregularly and brings wondrous things with its gray light. Among those wondrous things are the births of new Spellweavers. New Spellweavers appear only when the land is bathed by the Gray Light of the wandering sun Andreas. The sphere in the large geodesic dome is surrogate for their gray light. It's not the father of my child that determines its relation to Magick. It's the timing of its birth."

Urquhart noted her pause and broke the brief awkward silence, "The light of one sun perplexes me, my lady, let alone three. I understand the spear and trident, not Magick. Still seems that carrying their leader's spawn will raise your stature."

Piara sighed and continued, "Urquhart, the ways of Magick perplex everyone. I have always pondered my ties to my great-great-great grandmother. How does it seem I oft see the world through her eyes? How do I bear so much resemblance to Clouse and share so many features with the Mender Fisher?"

Urquhart disagreed, "Beg pardon, my lady, but the greenish Vydaelian Clouse does not shine a candle to your beauty. He also has pointed ears, which you lack."

Piara smiled and replied, "Again, thank you, Urquhart, but Clouse and my similarities lie more inward. Most Magick does not affect Clouse, Fisher, and me. I *reflected* the Wandmaker's Aura Spell. However, the Omega Stones affect me, Fisher, and Clouse. I've experienced the *Three Stones Effect* and looked into the Wandmaker's complex mind. Most of what lies there befuddles me, but I can read his feelings and desires. Though I'm amongst his desires I also see his feeling for the she-Vydaelian Morganne. They have shared many paths, though someone named Kirrie fills more of his heart. The shadows of the Dreamraider Amica and her Master lurk in his thoughts and Yannuvia thinks of fire and grayness." Piara stopped short of revealing the Wandmaker's tryst with the Dreamraider.

Urquhart said, "There's none called Kirrie with us, and you carry his seed. I've witnessed negative interaction between the Wandmaker and his consort. She disapproved of his partaking of Duoth flesh and has been noticeably absent from reconstruction. Such action would not be tolerated in Doug-less."

Piara followed, "These folks look at things differently and take commitments more seriously, Urquhart, but there's more to it. As I said, I've seen into the Wandmaker's thoughts. He knows that Morganne also carries a child. When her status becomes known, the folk will rally to support her. My status is tenuous already. Many she-Vydaelians show hostility toward me. If my tryst with the Wandmaker becomes known, given his gravid mate… you see what I mean. Resentment toward me could extend to Starra and Sharchrina. My pursuit of pleasure has compromised our welcome in Vydaelia."

Urquhart countered, "You have contributed to their well-being, my lady. Any male should be glad to procreate with you."

Piara managed another smile and said, "You're full of compliments. Bearing your child would honor me, but that's not a point of discussion. The Wandmaker and his followers have bested the greatest foes in this realm. I can think of no place safer for Starra and Sharchrina. My being here compromises their safety."

Urquhart offered, "What of your people, the sea elves?"

Piara answered, "There's always the threat of a Carcharian raid. Capture means certain return to Doug-less and King Lunniedale. I am willing to take this risk, but not for my daughter and niece."

Urquhart said, "I don't like where this is going."

Piara answered, "I can't stay in Vydaelia. I must leave… and soon. My condition is already known to Fisher, Clouse, and the sisters Joulie and Jonna. You figured it out, and without a truth stone. I am a strong swimmer. I'll leave by the sea and make my way through the swamps to Cane Bisque Bay."

Urquhart replied matter-of-factly, "You are not a strong swimmer. Morganne led a party of us beyond the Duoth passageways and we met great resistance. The sea lions will be in particularly bad moods after the beating they took in the recent battle. You'd best stay here and take whatever consequences follow your actions."

Piara shook her head negatively and persisted, "No. I must leave Vydaelia. I want you to watch over Sharchrina and Starra. Promise me you'll stand by them."

Urquhart answered, "Starra has found Gruusch. He is the love of her life. He has proven worthy. The Wandmaker has powerful allies. The flying wench has come to his aid. We saw her battle with the Giant Amebus and Rangers have relayed stories of her battle with the triskaidekapod. If he gets in trouble the Wandmaker simply will summon her again. I'm not needed here. I shall cast my lot with you."

Piara protested, "No! I want you watching Starra! The Dreamraider's assistance is bought at high cost and limited. I don't trust her and fear her motives. She is more a rival than friend. The Wandmaker's relationship with her is complex. The Wandmaker has a complex bond with the Good Witch, a bond that goes beyond Fire Magick. The bond creates a curtain in his mind. Still, I think Starra and Sharchrina are best off in Vydaelia."

The erstwhile queen did not elaborate. She had seen into the Wandmaker's thoughts and knew of his tête-à-tête with the Dreamraider. The Dreamraider's intrusion into her sleep had further stirred Piara's suspicions. Was it wise to wear the little now invisible amulet? Should she tell Urquhart of the artifact?

Urquhart said, "The fiery Dreamraider has provided assistance. I neither understand Magick nor her relationship to the Wandmaker's folk. One four-armed warrior will not be the difference between winning and losing against a full blown assault from Doug-less. However, I might defend you against a solitary predator in the sea or swamp. I still think you should remain in this stronghold, but if you insist on leaving I shall accompany you."

Piara took a deep breath and said, "I'm not ruling out returning. I was taken from my people as a youth and carried to the stronghold Doug-less. I fared better than most of my folks, who were killed and oft eaten. I have few memories of my mother and father. Another young sea elf named Viada was taken from my village. Viada was Gruusch's mother. I was espoused to the King of Doug-less and bore him the child Starra. In Doug-less I have made the best of my situation and served as midwife, alchemist, and healer. I have an innate knowledge of herbs, medicinal plants, and potables. I arrived at Doug-less with knowledge of Carcharian, Shellie, Bugwully, and Pollywoddle dialects. They just come to me."

Urquhart said, "I know all those things. You can't return to Doug-less, even though you'd benefit from the midwifery skills of the matrons in the birthing rooms. Where would you go?"

Piara answered, "To a place I've never been. There is a secluded cove a short journey from my childhood home."

Urquhart warned, "My lady, the trials of battle and stresses of expectancy have warped your reasoning. Why go to a place you've never been? How'd you know of its existence, let alone location?"

Piara explained, "When I concentrate, I *see* the memories of my great, great, great grandmother. She left my home settlement and died long before I was born. I don't remember *stories* of her. When the Carcharians took me, I was too young to remember stories my mother might have told me. It's more like...I see through my great, great, great grandmother's eyes. She visited the cove that I visualize and lived there when she was exiled. Beyond the inlet there is... maybe a valley. Odd trees, stony areas, and rich soil fill the area. Maybe there's a cave... or an odd building. Though I've never stepped on the stony floor of the alcove's cave, my mind's eye sees it well. I... I just know the way. It's a hazardous trek and will require either swimming across the lake or navigating through the swamp, the Endless Fen. Carcharians, Shellies, and Bugwullies had not discovered this hidden area."

Urquhart solemnly responded, "The Endless Fen... Doug's bane! My lady, this exceeds my warrior's comprehension. I've seen many things in Vydaelia I didn't think possible. I don't understand your resemblance to the Mender and Clouse and your bond to your long dead ancestor. I can't allow you to leave alone, but can I allow us to travel to a place neither of us has ever seen? The destination is likely moot. I doubt we'd survive the journey!"

Piara said, "Well spoken, my loyal guardian. I'd rather you stay, but my survival chances increase when I'm with you."

Urquhart asked, "When do you plan to leave?"

Piara answered, "Now."

Urquhart said, "Now! We must make preparations! I should inform the others!"

Piara followed, "No. Starra will protest my leaving. I... we'll tell only Bluuch and have him only inform the others after we are well on our way. We'll travel light. The bounty of the sea will sustain us. I'll leave everything I brought from Doug-less."

Urquhart asked, "Are you leaving the Omega Stone?

Piara answered, "Most definitely."

Urquhart looked about the comfortable quarters in the bartizan and gathered weaponry and a few provisions. Piara slipped into the same garb she wore when she left Doug-less. She placed the Omega Stone on the bed. Urquhart returned after a moment. Piara told him she planned to surreptitiously carry the Omega Stone to Bluuch and instruct the four-arm to entrust the artifact to either Fisher or the Wandmaker. Piara and Urquhart slipped out of the bartizan.

Massive Bluuch stood guard on the newly repaired allure on the wall facing the Duoths' domain. Piara and Urquhart made their way across the outer ward of Vydaelia. Rangers and matrons scurried about and performed needed tasks. Most Rangers rested to recover from the recent battles. The Wandmaker had retreated to his abode in the inner ward. Fisher studied plants in the onyum patch. To observers the former queen of Doug-less and her loyal guardian were simply taking a constitutional. Their small packs contained only essentials. Piara wore a skintight suit of waterproof squid bladder. The suit revealed the mature sea elf's comeliness and stretched and extended over the watertight pouch on her back. The sea elf and Carcharian crossed over the first wall and passed through the illusory terrain. Few Rangers lingered in the area. Bluuch's imposing form standing watch on the allure of the second outermost wall by the tower facing the passageway leading toward the Duoths' realm reassured the weary defenders. The stalwart warrior did not turn to face Piara and Urquhart as they approached. His keen senses recognized their footsteps and he addressed them respectfully. Rangers on the wall allowed the Carcharians privacy. Piara informed the warrior that she'd be leaving Vydaelia to attend to personal matters and Urquhart was accompanying her. Piara gave Bluuch little details. Little knowledge meant he had few answers to give when questioned. Piara gave Bluuch the Omega Stone and asked him to deliver it to Starra. She warned him to avoid grasping the artifact. Piara and Urquhart did not tarry and descended the wall walk and passed through the second wall via one of Yannuvia's expertly hidden secret one-way doors. They sneaked past the empty passageway that led toward the Duoths' realm and moved in the direction of the Endless Fen, taking the route of Morganne's party, of which Urquhart had been a member. They entered the waters of the sea and disappeared.

Bluuch stared across the waters. Slowly he slipped his lower left hand into his pack and grasped the Omega Stone. Bluuch felt powerful. Strange words appeared in his mind. Bluuch tentatively inspected the smooth crescent-shaped stone. A single rune appeared.

$$\Omega$$

The rune persisted for thirteen heartbeats. Then the single letter faded, and three runes appeared on the surface of the rock, which briefly emitted gray light.

$$Ø \infty Ø$$

The runes faded after 21 heartbeats and the single rune reappeared. The pattern repeated three times. The thoughts of power persisted in the big four-armed Carcharian's mind. Piara had said to give the stone to Starra. Why should he? The rock was safe in his four hands. Bluuch noted the approach of his relief. Drelvish Rangers Fexa and Fenideen ascended the wall stairs. Bluuch stuffed the little rock in his pouch and greeted his relief. He descended the stairs and made for the bartizan.

CHAPTER 23

Hazardous Journey

Piara and Urquhart encountered sea moolers, sea goats, Shellies, Bugwullies, Pollywoddles, dawgfish, jellyfish, and a dangerous boxjelly. They searched in vain for sea horses or pottyhippomuses, which might have helped carry them across the water's surface. Pottyhippomuses or plesiohawgs were even faster. Carcharians considered sea horses and plesiohawgs prey, but sea elves had a way with the aquatic steeds. Dawgfish were a nuisance and placed the traveling duo at risk with their loud barking.

Piara and Urquhart glanced back. Bluuch stood on the allure until his relief arrived. He towered over the Drelve-Vydaelians, who had to stand on stones behind the merlons to peer over the wall. Bluuch then descended the stairs. The duo then scurried along the cavern wall. Urquhart took the lead. Piara hustled to keep up, kept an eye toward the sea, and brought up the rear. The Carcharian's presence diminished threats from the sea. Boxjellies were solitary hunters and seldom came ashore. Few of the sea's predators were amphibious, and fewer still were inclined to tangle with a four-armed Carcharian. Abominations like the emirp and Giant Amebus were quite rare.

The cavern wall meandered in a gentle northeasterly direction for two hundred Yardley paces. The distance from the shoreline to the cavern wall ranged from thirty to seventy feet. To their right the sheer wall of the great cavern rose several hundred feet to the ceiling covered with luminescent algae. Piara and Urquhart stayed near the wall and stopped at the verge of the second passageway, listened, and heard nothing. Piara peaked around the corner, rushed across the twenty-foot wide corridor, and signaled all clear. Urquhart followed.

The big four-armed Carcharian sniffed longingly and paused near the passage opening.

Piara whispered, "Urquhart, what's the problem?"

Urquhart sighed, "My lady, I smell Duoth and it's so hard not to seek out the pudgy blighters. They are so delicious!"

Piara anxiously followed, "I gather that from my time in Doug-less and my consort's compulsion to obtain Duoth flesh. In Vydaelia even the Mender Fisher and Wandmaker partook of the feast. My daughter and niece participated in the roasting of the captured Duoth. I abstained. I prefer the fruits of the sea and marshes. My taste parallels more closely the majority of the newcomers."

Urquhart answered, "The Wandmaker leads the newcomers and he enjoyed Duoth with the rest of us."

Piara flatly replied, "The Wandmaker's different."

Urquhart moved away from the rocky opening and joined the erstwhile queen of Doug-less and said, "Sure he's different. He's the reason we're on this journey."

The first passage leading from the Duoth's home Ty Ty to the onyum patch was hopelessly closed by the newcomer's Magick. The second passage was damaged when Morganne's party captured the ill-fated Duoth *Long206*. Standing guard in the cubicles on either side of the second passageway to the east of the Onyum Patch was the responsibility of Stand-byes, Duoths who were subordinate to onyum growers and stood ready to step up should an onyum grower fall. Numbered Stand-byes were next in line to become Onyum Growers. Unnumbered members of a numbered Stand-by's pod assisted the numbered member. After the arrival of the newcomers, Duoth leader *Mose14* dictated numbered Stand-byes stand guard. *Long207* and *Dodge191* drew the duty of watching the cavern. It was young *Dodge191*'s first important assignment. The cubicles were only five feet wide and a similar height. A narrow archway above the passageway connected the two observation posts. A passage connected the western observation post to the northern wall of the great central cavern of Ty-Ty east of the huge tater patch. The entrance to the passageway that led from Ty-Ty to the cubicles was revealed only to Onyum Growers and Stand-byes. Secret sliding stone doors enabled the occupant of the western cubicle to both exit to the sea and retreat toward Ty-Ty. The secret doors were imperceptible to all but the most discerning creature. The eastern cubicle connected to the western cubicle via an archway over the major passageway. In both small cubicles, small slits cut in the stone allowed the Duoths inside to peer out toward the sea. The narrow slits were smaller than murder holes that archers fired through in drum towers and bartizans. Duoths couldn't squeeze through the slit. When the Duoth guards were in position, their bodies filled the openings and made the apertures imperceptible to passersby in the outside cavern. The cubicles and passages had been damaged in a battle with Morganne's party. The skirmish had cost the Duoths *Long206*. Duoths had labored to reconstruct the guard posts and clear the passageways. Efforts to hide the secret doors were redoubled.

Long207 sat in the cubicle to the west of the passage and *Dodge 191* watched from the other.

Their predecessors *Long206* and *Dodge190* had detected the exploration party lead by Morganne. *Long207* and *Dodge191* heard accounts of the fateful encounter between their predecessors and the party from Vydaelia and heard Long206's report.

"Ten separate thought patterns…five Carcharians and five sea elfish creatures…uh, no…four sea elfish and another quite different…the lot meanders along the wall of the cavern," Long206 concentrated and silently *relayed to Dodge190, who was situated about twenty feet away.*

Dodge190 silently answered, "They've crossed over to my side. Animalistic thoughts…then again, I don't understand what I'm sensing, Long206. I thought sea elves were simple creatures. You're right! One of these is very different. Is it my inexperience?"

Long206 thought in return, "No. I can't interpret his complex thoughts. Actually, I see little of his mind. Sea elves appear in these waters fairly often. These aren't sea elves. What are they doing?"

Dodge190 silently replied, "Most are waiting near the passageway. They refer to the unusual elfish bloke as 'green guy.' The green elfish creature has sent a Light Spell into the passage. He's a sorcerer! It's good none of our folk was watching. Should I join you? Do we attack?" Dodge190 replied silently.

Long206 mutely answered, "No, let's wait. Perhaps a sea lion pride will take care of the problem. Many are nearby. Besides the ten beasts aren't entering the passageway and pose no immediate threats."

Dodge190 replied noiselessly, "I await your instructions."

The more experienced *Long206* mutely thought back, "I've stood guard many times and never seen Carcharians advancing this far. I've only heard of sorcerers in my pod's legends. The only sea elves I've encountered were green. Only the sorcerer among this lot is green. It's ominous that Carcharians, Sorcerers, and strange sea elves are in cahoots."

Dodge190 shuddered silently. His veteran companion *Long206* sensed the youth's trepidation. Had Duothdom truly fallen on black days?

Now *Dodge191* and *Long207* sensed one Carcharian and one sea elf. Urquhart joined Piara on the far side of the second passage beyond the Onyum Patch.

From this point and to their right the massive cavern's wall extended to the northeast for fifty paces, and the shore was consistently thirty feet wide. At fifty feet, the cavern's wall turned abruptly to the east, while the shoreline continued to the northeast. This resulted in a wider beach. The second passage beyond the Onyum Patch remained ten feet wide, extended to the southeast thirty feet, and then turned due east. Few lichen lined the top of the corridor so the area was rather dark.

Piara stared into the dim light and saw no movement. Urquhart moved forward and looked around the cavern wall. The big Carcharian made the fifty-foot walk in few steps. Urquhart peeked around the corner. The cavern wall extended 130 Yardley paces to the east. At that point the landscape changed dramatically to a marshy area covered by odd green undergrowth. The shoreline continued the general northeasterly 45-degree direction for another 130 paces and then turned sharply to the north. Where the shoreline turned to the north, the sheer cavern wall resumed and the width of the shore was only twenty paces. The marsh extended to the east...for a long way!

Piara and Urquhart edged up. The waters lapped gently against the shore, and many sounds came from the marshy land.

The fen reminded the Wandmaker's espoused Morganne of a swamp or rain forest and found its greenness unnatural. Greenness was typical in the underworld.

Piara asked, "Are you familiar with this area? I never heard hunters speak of it."

Urquhart replied, "I told the Wandmaker what I could. Other than the Onyum Patch that now resides within the walls of your citadel, our hunting grounds lie on the other side of the great lake and in the sea to the east. We look upon the Endless Fen. I only know its reputation. Hazard fills this area. King Lunniedale forbade our hunting parties going beyond the first passage past the Onyum Patch. In fact, for three generations our leaders have forbidden entry."

Piara queried, "It looks like a good place to find prey. Natural place..."

Urquhart turned his head quickly, looked all around, and sniffed the air before he answered, "If natural means fraught with danger, then you are looking upon a natural place. Even Duoth flesh doesn't give one's immune system the power to fend off diseases he might catch within those grounds. Marshy soil, quicksand, giant leeches, carnivorous plants, and likely worse horrors lurk in the thick underbrush. Poor footing prevents successful hunt and pursuit. Swimming isn't possible. At least, I'm told these things. I've not entered the Fen. I looked upon it for the first time with Morganne."

Piara said, "I understand your concern. To the casual observer the marsh appears less foreboding than the sea and dark passages. I'm more comfortable with the sea. An event that occurred three generations ago led Doug-less's leaders to forbid hunting in the Endless Fen. King Lunniedale lamented many times. Doug, the four-armed son of King Stanley had no luck in slaying Duoths in the Onyum Patch. Rather than going back to face his father empty-handed, Doug and his party entered the Endless Fen. Eleven Carcharians, two Shellies, and a Mountain Giant entered the swamp. Only the Shellie Crunch survived and made it back to King Stanley. Crunch reported the group encountered a pride of sea lions in the muck. The terrain was fit for neither swimming nor running. Fighting sea lions in their domain is ill work. Crunch sired Pincher's grandfather. It's a bit ironic that both Crunch and his great-grandson Pincher were sole survivors of an ill-fated mission. Doug's death devastated old Stanley. When he became King, Emmit, the grandfather of our commune's current monarch Lunniedale, renamed the conurbation Doug-less."

Urquhart commented, "I relayed the story to Morganne."

Urquhart pointed his left lower arm toward the sea and suggested, "Just as I did with Morganne, I feel we're watched. We are only two. I can give any foe a scrap; I think its best we get moving. Sea lions hunt in prides. They are powerful swimmers and surprisingly agile on land.

Long flowing manes, finned rear legs, huge canine teeth, powerful jaws, and clawed forelegs make sea lions formidable opponents. Males and females look different. Sea lionesses lack the big manes, but this makes females faster. A male sea lion can be twice the weight of a four-armed Carcharian and a foot longer. The sea lions suffered substantial losses in their battle with the newcomers. They are likely licking their wounds, but they still watch for easy prey, like a sumptuous sea elf. This is as far as I've come this way. Are we now traveling blind?"

Piara curiously answered, "Not exactly. I... I see my ancestor's sanctuary, but she never walked these shores. Still... it's not entirely unfamiliar to me."

Urquhart noted, "That's sort of a triple negative, my lady. Not... entirely... unfamiliar... are you saying you know which way to go?"

Piara answered, "More or less... I received a gift from the Dreamraider. She appeared to me as my ancestor while I slept just before we departed and left this amulet."

Urquhart said, "I see nothing, my lady."

Piara said, "Oops! I forgot. It became invisible when I placed it around my neck. Extend your hand... uh, your left lower hand and touch my chest. You'll feel it."

Urquhart blushed and said, "My, lady... would it be proper?"

Piara replied, "Urquhart, we are standing on the verge of a dangerous swamp. I want you to be aware of the amulet."

Urquhart gingerly extended his left lower hand and discovered the small stone which was suspended around the sea elf's neck. The Carcharian said, "My lady, should we place any trust in this gift from the Dreamraider? It may be cursed. What can a necklace tell you?"

Piara replied, "It's very hard to explain, Urquhart. Magick befuddles me. I'd never heard the languages the Wandmaker and Fisher challenged me with when reached Vydaelia. Still I understood every word. I thought it had something to do with the little rocks we carried and the encounter in my dreams. But I'm not carrying them now and I'm most definitely awake. The Dreamraider said the stone in the pendant has a twin that it will seek. She implied the stone would lead to answers to my questions. The Dreamraider's guidance led Starra to Gruusch."

Urquhart interrupted, "A fact that doesn't particularly please me."

Piara said, "Understood! She also came to our aid against the Duoths, sea lions, and oozing monstrosity they called Giant Amebus.

The amulet doesn't speak to me. It directs me to follow the shore along the Endless Fen. But something within my mind… tells me to do the same thing. I trust my inner feeling more than the rock."

Urquhart looked around and added, "Not to be disrespectful, my lady, but following the shoreline is rather our only option, unless you want to swim across the sea. That would lead us to Doug-less. From there I know direction to the last known homes of the sea elves, including the village from which you were taken. It's required training and wasn't an easy task to learn tactics to attack my mother's and your people. Doubtlessly King Lunniedale will have the paths watched. His scouts remain in contact with Vydaelia. I wonder how safe Starra and Sharchrina are."

Piara answered, "They are as safe as we could make them, Urquhart. The newcomers will lay down their lives to defend their new home. Gruusch, Bluuch, Loogie, and Quunsch will fight to the death. But I hope it doesn't come to it. You're right. Two more… you and I… would not have swayed any outcome. At least I'll keep telling myself so. My continued presence in Vydaelia worsened my daughter and niece's situation… we've already been through this."

Urquhart said, "Then we'll proceed. I'll follow your lead."

Piara and Urquhart traveled quickly. The Carcharian brandished weapons in his upper arms and a walking stick in his lower right arm. Piara carried a short staff made from a reed chopped by Urquhart's spear. They followed the marsh edge. Urquhart speared a sea chicken and offered Piara a share. She declined and instead munched on abundant cibbage and dew berries. They came upon a wide stream flowing into the sea. The waters came from an opening in the rocky wall.

Urquhart transferred his weapons to his lower arms and used his powerful upper arms to glide through the water. Piara wrapped her arms around his upper body. The stream teemed with life. Singing shrimp scattered as they swam though their schools and informed other aquatic creatures of the duo's approach. For the better part of a Day Glass rotation they traveled through the marshy soil. A sea lion growled from within the thick mangroves. Urquhart ushered Piara behind him and threateningly brandished his weapon. The sea lion bounded from the brush, took a brief look at the Carcharian, and beat a hasty retreat. Fearing the sea lion would summon his fellows the pair moved quickly to the water and swam near the shore. This exposed them to aquatic beasts but enabled them to travel faster and separate from the sea lion. Urquhart skewered a yellow jellyfish as it wandered past them and kept it secured on his trident. Small islands provided resting points. They went onto a twenty pace wide rocky island. Urquhart quickly determined they were alone and set up a subsistence shelter. He squashed a dried fire ant to ignite a spark and create a small fire to warm Piara. He left his short spear with her and splashed into the waters, and came out with an *eclectic* eel. The eclectic eel got its name from the variable coloration of its skin and very diverse flavor. The odd thin fish tasted very much like what it had most recently eaten. In the case of the example pulled from the sea by Urquhart, the flavor was booderry clam. The eclectic eel had been feeding in dark clam beds at the bottom of the lake. The clams munched on aquatic booderries. The eclectic eel munched on the clams. Piara gathered sea weed and fallen leaves and fashioned bedding. She prepared the eel and the duo settled into the austere accommodation. The lichen maintained constant illumination in the massive underworld cavern and mists from the waters kept the humidity constant. The little island made an effective resting spot. Piara slept. Urquhart remained vigilant.

CHAPTER 24

Amica's Angst

Amica Carmisino, the Good Witch moaned. Her ilk was not immune to the nausea that oft accompanied gestation. Neither the familiar confines of her favorite grotto near Fire Lake nor the healing smoky waters quelled the tumult in her tummy. Nature prevailed over Magick. The she-demon labored to keep her condition hidden from the Master and her cohorts and underlings. Her Deceiver moniker was well earned and to this point she had succeeded. Her malady did not relieve the Good Witch of her responsibility in monitoring goings on in the underworld cavern. She'd mustered enough strength to pay the sea elf Piara a visit and deliver one of a set of "twin stones." The second stone sat with the possessions of a contact she'd made long ago. The Dreamraider had long toyed with the sea elves. Piara was her latest target. She'd planted seeds in Piara's thoughts that she hoped would sprout into the idea of the sea elf's leaving Vydaelia. It was a self-centered task and not directed by the Dream Master. Now Amica's thoughts returned to her directed tasks and monitoring events in Vydaelia.

Maintaining her deception precluded turning to one of her chaotic colleagues and their "look after number one first" philosophy. She clutched a Locating Stone in her left hand and Omega Stone in her right. The Omega Stone meld to her hand, but she could just as easily have changed her hand to fit the malleable stone. Grayness surrounded her and briefly eased the queasiness that plagued her. Amica gripped the stones and concentrated. Her mind flowed to the underworld cavern. She sought the thoughts of the ******* sea elf. Something had gone awry. The Omega Stone… did not rest in the hands of the former queen of Doug-less. Another hand gripped the device. The Good Witch sighed.

She had enough energy for one small trip… maybe. Needed… rest! Cursed condition! This meant an unscheduled trip and the acceleration of a possible ally's skills… perhaps too much of an acceleration.

Kirrie returned to the mountainside cabin after a foray into the forest. She enjoyed time in the forest less and sipping smoky waters from the thick leathery pouch more. Four Dark Periods had come and passed since the Dreamraider left her alone at the foothills of the Doombringer Peaks. In about 400000 minute minuteman heartbeats the chalice should return. The former Teacher gave in to curiosity and checked the woods around Alms Glen. The keen senses of the Drelvish Rangers were not alerted by detecting another Drelve's presence. Sergeant Major Rumsie continued to run a tight ship and maintained close scrutiny of goings on in the propinquity of Alms Glen. Kirrie used her skills to sneak into the few Droll and Kiennites' camps and kept up with her old enemies' activities. Drolls talked mainly of hunting and adventure: Kiennites talked of trickery and subversion. All camps muttered about General Saligia's tenuous position.

This had been an uneventful Amber Period. Kirrie had gathered some berries and some delicious kale grubs. The she-Drelve fought the urge to take prey from her longstanding friends among the fauna and mobile flora. Fighting such desires became more difficult but she had succeeded this day. Now she settled in to gaze toward the yellow skies as Meries reestablished dominance and heralded the beginning of the Light Period. Then… red light flashed in the room. The Good Witch returned and appeared less than jovial.

Kirrie said, "I wasn't expecting you. You look like death warmed over. Why are you here?"

The Good Witch answered, "I am a bit under the weather and could use your help."

Kirrie marveled, "You need my help! That's a good one. What's ailing you?"

Amica answered, "I'd rather not talk about it. I need you to take a little trip for me."

Kirrie said, "Why? You can go most anywhere, and anytime."

Amica answered, "I need backup. You are my best bet. It just requires a little trip in the red and blue light."

Kirrie protested, "Whoa! Last time I did that it aged me quite a bit, and put me in debt to your Master. Besides, I don't have a red and blue tipped wand, unless you brought one along."

Amica said, "There's only one such device, but you don't need it to do what I ask. It's just a short trip and your body isn't taking the trip. I want you to invade a simple bloke's mind."

Kirrie said, "That makes even less sense! I'm no Dreamraider."

Amica followed, "Actually, you are… to an extent. Grayness touches you. Granted your powers are limited and you'd need a focal point, but I can give you one."

Kirrie snapped her fingers and watched little sparks of blue fire flicker with each repetition. She added, "I have seen many things I never thought possible. Not much going on here. General Saligia cowers in Aulgmoor. Drolls retreat north into the Doombringers. The big visitors from the south have not appeared in numbers. I only saw a few of them. The Drelves rebuild around Alms Glen. Gaelyss grovels with the harlot he chose to replace me. During the last Approximation no Spellweavers came and I was glad. I'm not a Spellweaver. I'm called a Fire Wizard. I don't know what I am. Are you saying now that I'm a half-***ed Dreamraider?"

Amica answered, "That's one way of putting it. The subject of your invasion lives in a place I'd rather not be right now and I'm not feeling well."

Kirrie asked, "Don't you have other Dreamraiders to stand in for you?"

Amice said, "Would you trust another Dreamraider?"

Kirrie asked, "I don't trust you, but I don't have anyone else. What the heck! I'd give me purpose. What exactly am I to do?"

Amica said, "I want you to visit a four armed sharkman. It's a very short trip, not even to another world, just to the innards of this one. The Carcharian, as he's called, has activated one of these. I don't know how he came into possession of the artifact and I must have this information."

Amica revealed a gray stone. She grasped the artifact. A single rune appeared.

Ω

The rune persisted for thirteen heartbeats. Then the single letter faded, and three runes appeared on the surface of the rock, which briefly emitted gray light.

$$Ø \infty Ø$$

The runes faded after 21 heartbeats and the single rune reappeared. The pattern repeated three times.

Amica said, "This is an Omega Stone. It finds its fellows. It'll enable you to contact the bloke. You'll project your image and awareness into his dreams."

Kirrie said, "I thought Translocation required the use of the wand, a nigh impossible spell, or your innate ability. I've held stones. There are lots of exceptional stones. This one is smaller than the Summoning Stones and others I've seen. You say it seeks its fellows. How can you be sure it'll find the right one?"

Amica added, "It's hard to explain. It's Magick. It's Grayness. You concentrate on your intended victim. You are observant. This stone is 0.61904762 the size of the Fire Stone. Look! It's malleable! It bends to the shape of your hand."

Kirrie scoffed, "Big deal! Most of them do! Let me have it! I'll do it!"

Amica held back the stone and said, "Wait! Take this as well. This is a Locating Stone. It'll direct you thoughts. Also! You can't look like that! You've got to look like a Dreamraider. Here! An Illusion Spell. You'll project this image."

Kirrie asked, "Why can't I look like myself? A four-armed sharkman likely has never seen Drelves."

Amica followed, "Well, actually, he has. I should tell you. He is allied to your Lost Spellweaver and First Wandmaker Yannuvia. Your Fire Wizard predecessor. I hope that's not a problem. Besides! We try to avoid showing our natural form… and especially our names."

Kirrie noted, "Yannuvia also chose a ***** from Meadowsweet over me. Seems a trend in my life. We've certainly seen many of your forms. What do you really look like?"

Amica answered, "Let's not get into that. Here's what you need to know. You'll see his thoughts. Reinforce them. Give him a false name. Tell him you'll be watching him. The Master deems the lot he's with important."

Kirrie said, "Deceiving! Maybe I am becoming you."

Amica said, "A bit at a time, Kirrie, a bit at a time."

The Good Witch gave Kirrie the Omega Stone and Locating Stone. Kirrie gripped the artifacts. The predictable series of runes appeared. Kirrie felt wise. She spoke to Amica in the Chaotic Evil language of the abyss, "Feels good. Now tell me what to do."

Amica answered, "Think about your task, grasp the stones, and relax. It'll be like dreaming, only you'll be in charge."

CHAPTER 25

Kirrie's Initiation: Bluuch's Dream

In Vydaelia Bluuch made his way back to the bartizan. Activities in the quadrangle's outer ward resumed and the watch changed on the walls. Bluuch ate food prepared for him by Drelvish matrons and fresh fish Quunsch had harvested the preceding day. Bluuch spoke to Yathle and Loogie but adhered to Piara's wishes and did not make them aware of the Queen's departure. He then went to his rest chamber. Bluuch grasped the little gray stone in his massive left lower hand. The rock softened and expanded to fill the expanse of the Carcharian's hand. Bluuch inspected the smooth crescent-shaped stone. A single rune appeared.

$$\Omega$$

The rune persisted for thirteen heartbeats. Then the single letter faded, and three runes appeared on the surface of the rock, which briefly emitted gray light.

$$Ǿ \infty Ǿ$$

The runes faded after 21 heartbeats and the single rune reappeared. The pattern repeated three times. Bluuch felt powerful. He heard Quunsch telling Yathle and Loogie about his encounter with the scouts from Doug-less and stuffed the little rock in his pack. Bluuch removed his armaments. It'd taken awhile for the seasoned warrior to feel comfortable enough to leave himself vulnerable in Vydaelia. As he lay in his comfortable bed Bluuch's thoughts went to his former queen

Piara. If he'd had his druthers, it'd be him accompanying her to who knows where instead of his lifelong friend Urquhart, but Bluuch knew Urquhart had given his heart to Princess Starra long ago. Starra loved Gruusch. Urquhart could focus his energies on protecting the queen. In his mind Bluuch felt he had seen his friend and Piara for the last time. At least Yathle and Loogie remained. Even the loud and brash Quunsch had proven a friend. There was little in Doug-less for Bluuch, and now with Piara's departure, little more in Vydaelia. Having four arms and performing well in competitions had outweighed his sea elfish lineage and gained him favor with Viceroy Phederal and King Lunniedale. Though Bluuch took considerable teasing over his green eyes, which directly tied to his sea elfish lineage and broke through the Carcharian dominant traits, Bluuch joined Urquhart with Protector Status and stood guard in King Lunniedale's court. He watched Piara daily.

Grasping the little stone gave him feelings of strength. He reached into his pack and again gripped the stone. The rune appeared. The same sequence followed. Faint grayness bathed the massive Carcharian. Bluuch felt snug. Soon sleep came. He dreamed of the queen's flowing green hair and friendly competition with Urquhart and Loogie. Once he almost bettered Quunsch, but the half-Bugwully's strength always helped him prevail. In Bluuch's dram he secured victory over Quunsch! Then...

Redness filled his mind and obscured the dreamy images.

Wisps...
Threads...
Threads of Magick...
Threads of fate...
Threads of time...
Threads connecting worlds ...
Dreams connecting worlds ...
Dreams of Magick...
The Magick of Dreams...
Magick connecting dreams...
Magick connecting worlds...
Dream raiders...
Elf pressure...

Albtraum…

Albträume, elf dreams, nightmares…

Slowly an image appeared in the four-armed Carcharian's mind. Was it Piara, who'd entered his dreams many times? Another sea elf? No…

The curvaceous lines were much more pronounced…and rather pleasant. A face of a beautiful female appeared.

She was not Carcharian, Bugwully, Pollywoddle, Shellie, or Boxjelly?

The alluring female in his dream had smooth reddened skin, fiery red eyes, and wore a deep purple dress. Long purple hair fell provocatively across her back and chest and produced a disheveled look. The female walked proudly back and forth across a field of green grab grass with purplish flowers. Bluuch had seen varieties of the dangerous plants in the marshes where sea elves, Pollywoddles, and Bugwullies dwelled. Stone and Mountain Giants told of seeing red grab grass in the upper world. The blades of the thick grass tenaciously held to any poor creature that stumbled upon it, and the grab grass's victim usually starved or fell to a predator. This green grab grass tantalizingly grasped and released the female's powerful lower legs. Tiny sparks of blue flame burst from the talons on the female's strong hands as she rubbed them together. The sleeping four-armed Carcharian beheld her beauty and *felt* her hot breath. Vibrant black and red flower petals showered the beautiful female. She pursed her lips, emitted small bursts of hot breath, and burned petals that neared her.

Bluuch spoke first, "Visitor, you now invade my dreams as you have those of Gruusch, Starra, and my Queen Piara. You are beautiful! But you look different than when you battled the big blob. I thought you'd be healing."

The visitor answered, "Simpleton! Speak when you are spoken to! Do you think there's only one of us? You gripped the rock! I'm here in *her* stead and at *his* insistence! But you are a rather impressive brute! I was expecting the winsome wench the Deceiver spoke to me about."

Kirrie studied his thoughts. Piara's departure and instructions were predictably at the lead of his feelings. The big four-armed sharkman had picked up the task of guarding his princess and responsibility for the Omega Stone.

The sleeping Bluuch was taken aback.

Speaking in a dream…
Interacting with one's dream…
Hearing one's dreams and responding…
Speaking and hearing one's dreams respond…

The visitor continued, "Where is your queen? The rock is with you."

Bluuch timidly answered, "Queen Piara, she now prefers Elder Piara, has left Vydaelia to attend business that is her own. She entrusted the stone to me. Don't you know these things?"

She replied indignantly, "I've more important things to do than keep up with the comings and goings of your lot! I'm not tied to the red and blue tipped wand as *she* is! But back to business! Bearing an Omega Stone carries with it responsibility. Your Elder trusts you. I'd fancy going a few rounds with you, in battle or otherwise. You must guard the stone and pay heed to its will. You felt it, did you not?"

Bluuch subserviently muttered, "I felt its strength. It bonds with its fellows. The Vydaelians will know I carry the stone. If she wears her red scarf, Princess Starra will as well."

The Dreamraider allowed, "From what I've heard, they are naïve but not stupid! Of course bearers of the rocks will know when another is near, as will the princess when she wears the red scarf. It's up to you what to do then. You are Carcharian."

Bluuch answered, "In this realm, I can be proud of my sea elfish lineage. I'm valued for more than just having four arms. These folk are not enemies. I'm not so sure of your intent. Have you a name, Dreamraider?"

The female smiled wryly and continued, "I've found an optimist. Talk about naïve! I'm going to have to pay you some more visits! For now, you should honor your Queen's wishes and protect your princess to the best of your abilities. The Master has great expectations for these folk and your path now intertwines with theirs. Grayness has now touched you, Bluuch of the sea elves and Carcharians. I've a name but you wouldn't be able to say it. You may think, or dream, of me as Constance, because I'm constantly watching your sorry ***!"

Bluuch resolutely said, "I don't have to be told to guard Princess Starra. My loyalty is unquestioned. Elder Piara asked me to hold the stone. I'd prefer dreaming of her. Can you do anything to help Piara?"

Constance muttered, "She is, at this point, not my concern. Keep focused! Don't let your guard down!"

Blueness surrounded her and she disappeared from Bluuch's dream. The big warrior slept fitfully for a few hours and awakened to face another guard shift. He would have to face Starra and his colleagues from Doug-less.

. Kirrie relaxed her grip on the Omega Stone and the blueness that had surrounded her disappeared. She rolled the little Locating Stone in her left hand. She was seated at the bluewood table in the cabin at the base of the Doombringers and felt no worse for the wear.

The Dreamraider Amica sat with her head in her hands in her Good Witch guise. Her face had a bit of a greenish tinge and little beads of sweat trickled down her cheeks. She looked up and murmured, "Now that wasn't so bad, was it? Congratulations, Dreamraider! What have you learned?"

Kirrie glanced at the Omega Stone and answered, "It's as you supposed. The four-armed warrior is as big as a Droll, though not nearly as handsome. His loyalties lie with his princess and few colleagues in this place Vydaelia, and he does think highly of the Wandmaker and his folk. He has great feelings for his former queen. I'd call it amore. His warrior's mind is easy to read. His loyalty is steadfast. His sense of duty will prevent his expressing his feeling for the queen. The folk in the fortress have faced many battles. It'd seem the Lost Spellweaver has jumped from the frying pan into the fire. That sums up what I learned. I think he enjoyed your purple-haired illusion. Is that what you're looking for?"

Amica said, "You did well. It's not what I was expecting. I'm hoping their conflicts diminish. It's taking a toll on me."

Kirrie looked at the Good Witch and observed, "It'd seem you've been busy. Your symptoms betray you. You're gravid, aren't you? Who's the lucky father? Your Master?"

Amica took a sip of herbal essence, a remedy the Mender had concocted, and answered, "You don't want to know."

Kirrie smirked, "I think I do know. Serves Morganne right! I can only hope Fadra gets to experience the same betrayal. When may I visit her? I'd love to ravage her sleep. In fact, I'd like to pay her a visit and kick her ***!"

Amica said, "If I didn't feel so rough, I'd laugh. You are getting more like me, a true sister of grayness. What you are asking requires physical corporal transfer, in other words, *Translocation*. That's what ages folk not of my ilk. The red and blue rod accomplishes the task. You won't age if you travel within the same realm. It's complicated. You have gained abilities. *Projection* into dreams is nothing to sneeze at. How much more you'll gain... who knows? It's Magick. You certainly saw through me. I may as well drop the illusion. I'm going to crash here awhile."

Amica stretched out on a cot in the cabin and revealed a telltale bump on her tummy. Kirrie grumbled under her breath but allowed the queasy Good Witch a respite.

To the north reports reached Aulgmoor and General Saligia of disappearances of Kiennites, Drolls, and stone ponies that tried to cross the River Ornash. Survivors spoke of a dark shadow in the water. High in the Doombringer Peaks wyvern riders reported seeing a misty form among the clouds. Saligia's paranoia grew. Support grew for warren leader Henery the Ninth.

CHAPTER 26

Missing

Starra awakened upbeat. She had spent considerable time with Gruusch on the allure facing the sea. Closeness to her beloved lessened the sting of recent battles and being ripped from the only home she'd known. Starra had only two arms and a sea elfish mother, but being the king's daughter outweighed these disadvantages. Other than two-arm status, she had every other physical trait considered desirable in a female Carcharian. Now she lived in the newcomers' settlement Vydaelia with seven other refugees from her home Doug-less, over 200 Drelves, people from another land, and some exceptional blokes, including the Wandmaker Yannuvia, Mender Fisher, and green guy Clouse. Help had come to the settlement in the form of a winged female who had destroyed a Giant Amebus in a battle with Duoths and sea lions. Starra shared a bartizan on the westernmost wall of the fortress with her mother sea elfish Piara, guardian four-armed Urquhart, four-armed Bluuch, half-Bugwully Quunsch, half-Pollywoddle Loogie, cousin two-arm Sharchrina, and two-armed Yathle. Spending time with Gruusch the guard shift past buoyed her spirits. The displaced Carcharian princess hoped to see much of Gruusch during the next period. Rotations of the Day Glass marked the passing of periods. The Drelves had told her of changing light in their native land. The concept was foreign to Starra and the others from Doug-less. The unchanging light in the underworld cavern did not present to quantifying segments of time. In Doug-less, one ate when hungry, rested when tired, and worked when ordered by the King or his court. The industrious Vydaelians who had called themselves Drelves were much more regimented. Starra stretched and then dressed. Starra chose her favorite sea mooler armor and the pretty red scarf she had discovered in her chamber after a visit from the Dreamraider. The bartizan was unusually quiet. Even Quunsch's boisterous voice was subdued. The princess made her way to the common eating area.

Heavily scarred four-arm Bluuch, her very pretty two-armed cousin Sharchrina, very quiet two-armed fine-featured Carcharian Yathle, two-armed and round-faced half-Pollywoddle Loogie, and two-armed half-Bugwully Quunsch sat around the breakfast table and munched on fruits of the sea. Urquhart and her mother Piara were not there.

Starra asked, "Where is my mother?"

Silence greeted her.

She queried, "And Urquhart? Are they summoned by the Wandmaker?"

Loogie answered, "They weren't here when I awakened. I assumed they were summoned."

Quunsch gulped down a large portion of eclectic eel and chased it with purple jellyfish ichor. The half-Bugwully wiped his mouth and gleefully said, "Delicious! Sea almond flavored eclectic ell with grapple flavored jellyfish. Caught them myself! Only thing better would be fresh Duoth! Have some, Princess Starra."

Starra replied, "Just call me Starra, Quunsch. I'm not a princess in Vydaelia, nor do I want to be. Again, has anyone seen my mother Piara?"

Yathle said, "I came in very late. I was listening to my relief, the Rangers Merry Bodkin and Willifron telling stories of their red, orange, and yellow world. Sounds like a pretty strange place. I saw neither Elder Piara nor Urquhart."

Starra turned to Bluuch and asked, "How about you, Bluuch. I saw you come in late."

Bluuch shook his head negatively.

Then Starra noted her scarf.

A single rune appeared on the wrap.

$$\Omega$$

The rune persisted for thirteen thumps. Then the single letter faded and three runes replaced it.

$$\emptyset \infty \emptyset$$

The runes persisted twenty-one times. The three runes faded and the single lettering replaced them. The pattern repeated thrice.

Starra rubbed the silken wrap between her fingers and looked around the table. Bluuch hung his head.

Starra said, "Bluuch?"

The Omega Stone in Bluuch's pack activated with the proximity of Starra's scarf. A single rune appeared on the smooth crescent shaped stone.

$$\Omega$$

The rune persisted for thirteen heartbeats. Then the single letter faded, and three runes appeared on the surface of the rock, which briefly emitted gray light.

$$\varnothing \infty \varnothing$$

The runes faded after 21 heartbeats and the single rune reappeared. The pattern repeated three times.

Starra again addressed the scarred four-armed Carcharian, "Bluuch, are you holding my mother's stone?"

Bluuch looked up and said, "Elder Piara entrusted the stone to me. It is the stone she carried from Doug-less. The Elder and Urquhart have left Vydaelia."

Starra cried, "What? When?"

Sharchrina asked, "Why didn't you tell us, Bluuch?"

Bluuch stammered, "The queen, uh, elder, departed about a period ago. She did not tell me her business. She asked that I hold the stone and protect you to the best of my abilities."

Starra said, "Which way did they go? What are you waiting for? We must follow her!"

Bluuch answered, "No, Princess. We cannot."

Starra wailed, "Bluuch, I order you to tell me where my mother went, and give me the stone!"

Bluuch shook his head negatively and answered, "No, Princess Starra, Urquhart entrusted me with your stewardship. Your mother said I was to hold onto the Omega Stone. I will follow their orders, even if it means not obeying yours. Elder Piara left in the direction of the Endless Fen, but I lost sight of them. She's in four good hands with Urquhart."

Starra disagreed, "She's traipsing off into the wilds of the Endless Fen to who knows where with a single guardian. I'm going to the Wandmaker. Bluuch, come with me and bring that cursed rock!"

Bluuch stood and followed Starra from the bartizan. Yathle, Loogie, Sharchrina, and Quunsch followed close behind. Starra proceeded directly to Gruusch's quarters and knocked impatiently on his door.

Starra said, "Gruusch! Gruusch! Gruusch!"

Gruusch quickly opened the door and said, "Starra, I was not expecting to see you until later. You are upset!"

Starra said, "Get your Omega Stone. I want you to interrogate Bluuch!"

Bluuch's prowess as a warrior was legend in Doug-less. Stories of his deeds filtered down to Gruusch and his comrades who served as Circle guards. There were three stories for every scar on the big four-armed warrior's body. Young Gruusch replied, "Starra, I love you very much, but I respect Bluuch. Besides, the stones give me access only to other stone bearers. Your mother, the Wandmaker, Mender Fisher, and Ranger Jonna carry the other stones. What should I ask Bluuch?"

Starra sobbed, "My mother has left Vydaelia with Urquhart. Bluuch now holds the stone that she carried. He won't tell us where she went."

Gruusch and Bluuch exchanged contemptuous glances. Then the Princess's young two-armed suitor went into his quarters and retrieved the crescent shaped Omega Stone, which was on the surface indistinguishable from its fellow. Gruusch grasped the stone and Bluuch reached into his pack and gripped in his left lower hand the rock he'd stored within. The stones meld to the Carcharians' large hands. Starra's scarf and both stones passed through the sequence of runes. The *Two Stones effect* occurred.

Gruusch looked at Bluuch and said in the guttural chaotic evil tongue, "No offense and nothing personal Bluuch. I have greatest respect for you."

Bluuch answered in the same tongue, "None taken Gruusch."

The Carcharians conversed in the guttural tongue. Starra became more impatient by the moment. The *Two Stones Effect* facilitated the odd communication and forced truthful answers. Plaintive expressions covered Starra and Gruusch's faces, but Bluuch remained unemotional. Gruusch's final statement to his four-armed colleague in the unnerving dialect was, "I'm going to release my grip on the stone and report to Starra."

Bluuch released his stone and stood staunchly by the Princess.

Gruusch said, "Bluuch is a noble warrior who stands steadfast by his queen, princess, and word. He does not know Piara and Urquhart's plans and destination. He intends to hold the stone because Piara gave it to him. Elder Piara insisted that he not inform us of her departure and we remain in Vydaelia. She thinks you are safer in Vydaelia than anywhere in the realm."

Quunsch noted, "This place has been attacked by 13-limbed terrors, Duoth bombs, the Giant Amebus, and sea lion hordes. I've seen scouts from Doug-less offshore. King Lunniedale knows we are here and plots against us. How can this be safe?"

Loogie asked, "Where'd be safer?"

Yathle added, "Nowhere that I'd know."

Quunsch rubbed his chin and found to his delight a morsel of eclectic eel. He gobbled it down and followed, "What if King Lunniedale knew the queen had departed?"

Bluuch said, "It's one factor that affected her leaving."

Starra angrily said, "My father's spies don't know she is gone. The king of Doug-less will not rest until he gains revenge against all of us. I still say we should follow my mother. I'm not that confident in the infallibility of these stupid rocks!"

Bluuch adamantly replied, "I will stand against the king's forces till I no longer draw breath. King Lunniedale has many allies, some through giving favors and more through inciting fear. These walls and the newcomers provide the greatest deterrent to his forces and wide reach. The Wandmaker and his people have thrown back everything thrown against them, including a triskaidekapod and Amebus. Before he died Old Pincher gave witness to our warriors' futile struggle against the triskaidekapod. Only Gruusch survived."

Starra opined, "The winged Dreamraider helped the Wandmaker's people, Bluuch! She isn't always around. My mother, Gruusch, and I faced her in our dreams. We can't trust her! She is manipulative and lacks conscience."

Gruusch interrupted, "Without her efforts, my love, we'd not be together. The road has been difficult, but I'd rather be in jeopardy in

Vydaelia with you and these people than groveling in Doug-less whilst you are betrothed to one of your father's cronies."

Bluuch added, "Another Dreamraider visited me and urged me to follow the Queen's orders and guard you, Princess Starra. That, I will do."

Starra grumbled, "Gruusch, do I stand alone? Will you help me find my mother?"

Gruusch tenderly rubbed a blue-green tear from Starra's cheek and answered, "You do not stand alone, my love. We will never forsake you. But you are safest in Vydaelia. You must remain within these walls. We must inform the Wandmaker of Piara's departure."

Quunsch added, "Princess, your beauty heightens all our spirits. Urquhart will protect your mother. Every waking time period the Drelves make this place stronger. We'll be ready for old King Lunniedale!"

Starra cried.

Gruusch said, "Your mother's wisdom far exceeds mine, my love. We must trust she knew best and hope she remains safe. We are left with the lot we have. Let's report to the Wandmaker. Bluuch, you should come with me. Starra, if you don't feel up to it, please return to the bartizan. Sharchrina will accompany you."

Starra wiped another blue-green tear, sniffed, and declared, "I'll not whine in my boudoir! I can kick *** too. I'll accept my mother's decision, though I disagree with it and prefer to follow her. We'll all see the Wandmaker. Bluuch, will you give me the Omega Stone?"

Bluuch without hesitation said, "No, my lady, the stone is mine to hold."

The refugees from Doug-less found the Wandmaker in council with Sergeant Major Klunkus, Fisher, Clouse, Jonna, and Joulie. Bluuch informed the group of Piara and Urquhart's departure and revealed his possession of the stone. The four-armed warrior offered to share his thoughts with other stone bearers through the *three stones effect*.

The Wandmaker declined.

Starra requested the leaders of Vydaelia send scouting parties to seek out Piara and Urquhart and bring them back to the fortress. Loogie, Quunsch, and Yathle volunteered to join such a party, but Yannuvia and Klunkus, and Bluuch were disinclined to acquiesce to their request.

Sergeant Major Klunkus said, "We are down two able bodies. Urquhart's strength and Piara's Menderish skills have been boons for us, but we cannot pine over their departure. Repairs are almost completed, but we must endeavor to make the walls stronger lest the marshmallow men throw greater adversaries against us."

CHAPTER 27

Journey continues...Boxjelly

Piara awakened after dreamless sleep. She found her long green hair wrapped around Urquhart's powerful upper left arm. She stood and straightened her raiment. Urquhart also stood and looked toward the marsh and the sea to assure they were alone. The duo did not have the advantage of the Day Glass to measure passage of time, but Piara had innate sense of timing, quite similar to Fisher and Clouse. She was, after all, *Menderish*. She was also susceptible to waves of nausea common just after awakening. The sea elf had little appetite, but attempted to consume the fruits of the sea that Urquhart quickly obtained. The Carcharian found sea biscuits and a small golden jellyfish. He removed the tentacles from the jellyfish and opened its thick head to expose the thick sweet nectar. Sea biscuits were doughy floating plants that grew in warm waters and browned and became crunchy when exposed to a flame. Seabee honey was a good accompaniment to sea biscuits, but honey flavored jellyfish made a good substitute. The small honey flavored jellyfish topped off the meal and helped ease some of Piara's nausea.

Whilst consuming their victuals the pair laid out plans for their travel. Both Piara's intuition and the odd amulet bade them to continue to follow the shoreline and bear northwest.

Urquhart asked, "We have traversed unfamiliar waters. I've neither personal nor collective knowledge of this area. What does your memory of your great-great-great-grandmother tell you?"

Piara answered, "Urquhart, it's not a memory. I "see" what she saw. She lived among the sea elfish brethren who suffered raids from Doug-less. You'd know more of navigating to the area than her or me."

Urquhart replied, "I know better the way from Doug-less. We have long crossed the great sea between Doug-less and the land surrounding the onyum patch which is now the Wandmaker's people's homestead. I'm familiar with landmarks and stone outcroppings along this route. Though it's a substantial distance our mappers record this to be the narrowest part of the great sea. While searching for food, I swam out about three hundred body lengths and noted the Endless Fen does in fact curve toward the west and the sea widens against rocky walls. Ahead I saw only great expanse of water. If we follow the water's edge along the cliffs we'll eventually circumnavigate the great sea, but I have no knowledge of its expanse. You have a sense of direction superior to mine. What does the amulet indicate?"

Piara answered, "Intuitively I feel we should continue on this general heading. My ability only extends to maintaining course. Fisher and Clouse relayed the same ability. The little rock buzzes when we follow this course. It becomes silent if I deviate a few paces in another direction. What we seek will be hidden. Sea elves seek reclusive abodes and form loosely knit communities, lest they fall victim to raids from Carcharians. Our journey will be arduous. Food won't be a problem. Becoming something's meal might be. But fatigue will be my greatest enemy. If I only had your strength! We need help."

Urquhart said, "Help is going to be hard to find. There was little to be found when we lived in Doug-less. I was forced to lay aside my sea elfish lineage. Yathle, Loogie, and I met privately and discussed our feelings for our mothers. Isolation pushed Quunsch into our group. We endured chastisement from the King's court, Quunsch more than the rest of us. I feel sorrow over the misdeeds carried out against your people by Carcharians. Though I'm outwardly like my father, I'm proud that my inner feelings mirror my mother, a sea elf like you my Queen, I mean Elder Piara. I yearn to one day make some measure of amends with sea elves. When you asked me about leaving Doug-less, it was one of the easiest decisions I've ever had to make. I'll give my all for you… and Starra. Rest a bit longer, my…Elder. I'll scout around."

Piara's aching muscles overrode her desire to push forward and she sat down in some soft marsh and munched on a bit more jellyfish honey. Her queasiness waned. Barking dawgfish and predatory growls in the distance pierced the silence. Splashing sounds overrode the gentle waves flapping up against the little island. High overhead clusters of luminescent algae provided light. In some areas the ceiling of the great cavern dipped and brought the source of light closer, making the ground brighter. Some areas of the ceiling had denser clusters of lichen and also produced light that would have exceeded the light period on Parallan.

Urquhart's skills with throwing nets paid off! The big Carcharian captured a young plesiohawg, sometimes called a pottyhippomus. Piara skillfully soothed the anxious flippered equine and eased onto its back. Piara whispered into the beast's large floppy ear and then effortlessly sat upon its wide back. The plesiohawg's generous bottom and rounded belly earned it the moniker pottyhippomus. Plesiohawgs had thick seal-like hair and scurried along the surfaces of bodies of water much faster than a sea elf might swim. Sea elves oft employed the playful creatures to travel large distances or escape predators quickly. Piara's folk recruited the sea steeds with promise of sea oats, the pottyhippomuses' favorite food and a grain cultivated in land locked patties. Urquhart didn't have any sea oats but he had his trusty net and nabbed the blue-green plesiohawg as it ran across the water. He brought the terrified beast to Piara who carried sea elfish trail mix in her skin tight squid bladder pack. Piara sang and rubbed the captive plesiohawg's thick fur. She extended her hand and offered the six foot long equine a nibble. Urquhart loosened the noose and allowed the beast to extend its neck and take the nutritious snack. The pottyhippomus emitted a low pitched squeal and sought more.

Piara said, "There's plenty more in the oat patties, big fella. I have a bit for later. Urquhart, did you see others?"

Urquhart answered, "No, but he's a fine specimen. He'd just grace King Lunniedale's table in Doug-less. The king is fond of their side meat. He'll serve a better purpose than breakfast. He's strong enough to carry you and pull me along. In my scouting I saw no other land masses. The rocky wall turns away from Vydaelia and Doug-less and extends westward. We face a trek across the open sea. The waters are odd. Few creatures scamper about the surface. I dove deeply and found fewer than normal fish and prey animals."

Piara answered, "There's been a lot of activity. Not long ago the triskaidekapod made its way into the area and the tussle between the Giant Amebus and newcomers disrupted the sea. Urquhart, there is at least one large predator in the area."

Urquhart snapped his head around quickly, looked in all directions, and then said, "My lady?"

Piara smiled wryly and said, "You, Urquhart. A four-armed Carcharian!"

Urquhart replied, "We've traveled far from Vydaelia but who knows how much further we have to go. The pottyhippomus will help us."

Piara sat upon the bulky plesiohawg. Urquhart gingerly removed the net and grabbed hold of the plesiohawg's thick hide. Gleefully the flippered porcine beast bounded into the water and scurried across the surface. Piara held tightly and Urquhart aided his grip by looping his noose loosely around the big steed's left front leg. Dawgfish rushed toward the odd trio but the plesiohawg easily outrun the yipping fish. After half a period of travel Piara saw a Seabee flying eastward. She guided the steed after the bee and followed to an area of raised marsh. The islet gave them a spot to respite and an unexpected treat of Seabee honey. Piara took a deep breath and exhaled over the beehive. The sea elf's breath calmed the bees and enabled her to secure a big scoop of honey and cone. The islet was little more than a clump of marsh grass and a few bushes. The omnivorous plesiohawg munched on grasses and unfortunate insects that found their way into its eager maw. After resting a bit they were on their way. After a few minutes Urquhart winced.

The Carcharian said, "Something just stung me! Stop! I'm going below!"

Piara whispered to the steed and the plesiohawg came to a stop Urquhart took a deep breath and rotated all four arms inward. He exhaled into his chest. His powerful breath expanded his chest. He then inhaled deeply and dove beneath the surface. Being Amphibiman had its advantages. The Carcharians had air bladders beneath their skin that they filled with air. This gave them a limited supply of surface area and allowed longer dives. The Sharkmen also had limited ability to extract oxygen and nitrogen from sea water. Under the water Urquhart studied the area. His powerful leg was stinging. He saw a dislodged tentacle dangling from his thick skin. Though broken off from its owner's body, the tentacles barbs still reflexively fired and pumped more venom into the Carcharian. Urquhart ripped the tentacle away and peered into the murky water. A glance ahead confirmed his fears.

A boxjelly blocked their way.

Urquhart swam between Piara and the boxjelly. The bipedal boxjelly had the domed head of a large jellyfish with both two tentacles and two clawed arms as upper extremities. Like jellyfish the Boxjelly had 24 eyes arranged in sets of six around its belly. It had many small stinging tentacles and four brains. Boxjellies lacked the sweet flavored jelly-like substance that made jellyfish in demand. Boxjellies had the ability to walk outside water for brief periods, but didn't like to get on land because they had to keep their domes moist. Four upper extremities and many flailing tentacles made the Boxjelly a formidable foe for Urquhart. The Carcharian brandished a spear in his left upper arm and trident in left lower arm. The big four-arm was double-left handed. Urquhart used his right arms to steady in the water and kept his throwing net in his right lower arm. With the battle under the water throwing was not an option, but he might use the net to entangle his opponent should they come close or break the surface. The Boxjelly circled menacingly and extended its eight foot long gripping tentacles. Its flowing stinging tentacles drifted toward Urquhart. Urquhart urged Piara to ride away on the Plesiohawg, but she was reluctant to leave and the boxjelly reacted to any movement of the steed. Urquhart labored to remain between the predator and Piara. The Carcharian winched when one of the stinging tentacle brushed against his left leg. Urquhart's thick skin stopped some of the stingers but the attack still had its effect. The Boxjelly lunged forward and threw its gripping tentacles toward Urquhart. One tentacle wrapped around his right lower arm and squeezed tightly. The other maneuvered toward his left upper or spear arm and disrupted the Carcharian's attempt to stab his opponent. Urquhart's pole weapons were serving him poorly. Still he managed to move his hand up the shaft of his trident and grip the weapon just below its three prongs. He did a sawing motion and dug the outer prong into the tentacle wrapped around his upper arm and cut the Boxjelly's flesh. Thick yellow blood oozed from the wound. The Boxjelly held on tenaciously all the while zapping Urquhart with more stinging tentacles. The predator anticipated a sea elf feast. The Carcharian felt dizzy and numbness in his legs as the venom inched through his thick skin. Urquhart gave a powerful ripping motion with his trident and hewed through the gripping tentacle wrapped around his upper arm. The desperate maneuver freed the spear arm and he stabbed the Boxjelly's trunk. The attacker recoiled from the blow and pulled its injured tentacle away. Several stinging tentacles ripped away from the Boxjelly and remained attached to Urquhart's throbbing legs. Urquhart motioned to Piara and she guided the plesiohawg further away on the surface. The Boxjelly moved toward Piara. Urquhart extended his spear and stabbed the beast through its previously uninjured gripping tentacle. The Carcharian used the spear with the impaled tentacle to pull the boxjelly toward him. He then thrust his trident powerfully into the Boxjelly's dome. The points on Carcharians' tridents were the stuff of legend and pierced the thick hide, which created a painful and grievous wound. The Boxjelly threw its stinging tentacles into Urquhart and wrapped its shortened tentacle around the left power arm which held the trident. Pain ripped through the four-armed warrior, but he persevered and pushed the trident further into the Boxjelly. The beast's four brains pondered a course of action. Urquhart twisted the spear and further injured the impaled tentacle. The part of the appendage distal to the spear's entry point fell limply. Urquhart used his bare right upper arm to rip stinging tentacles from his body. He pulled his numbing legs inward and delivered a kick to the Boxjelly's midsection. The blow incapacitated at least one of the beast's four brains. Urquhart withdrew and jabbed with the trident thrice in rapid succession. Now copious fluids escaped from the Boxjelly's dome. Urquhart pulled the trident from the beast's dome and then thrust it deeply into its midsection and luckily impaled another brain.

The Boxjelly floated lifelessly away.

Urquhart broke to the surface and gasped for air. Piara drew near and dismounted from the Plesiohawg. The sea elf gingerly pulled sting tentacles from Urquhart.

There was nothing for it.

She wrapped Urquhart's right arms in his net and sling and secured them to the Plesiohawg's flippers. She urged the steed forward in the same general direction. Piara scanned the waters for raised areas. After a painfully long time she spotted a small island and guided the pottyhippomus to it. She and the beast dragged Urquhart ashore. The Carcharian was in a bad way. Hundreds of stings cumulatively added venom to his system. The boxjelly depended on its venom to weaken foes and lessen their resistance to its grapping tentacles. Once weakened the grippers had they prey in place whilst the boxjelly began to feast on its unfortunate victim. Piara painstakingly removed pieces of tentacle from Urquhart. Sea elf removed containers from her squid bladder pack.

She applied unguents to sucker wounds on Urquhart's arms and gave the big four-arm a thick tarry goop.

Urquhart battled spasms from the neurotoxins but managed, "That tastes awful! What is it?"

Piara answered, "Something I was saving for extremis. It's a small piece of my legacy, a sea elfish variant of Mender's Panacea."

Urquhart noted his spasms diminishing. He asked, "How can you know sea elfish concoctions, my lady. You were so young when taken."

Piara answered, "Save your strength. How do I know languages the first time I hear them? I arrived in Doug-less with little knowledge of my people. There was few of my folk held captive to teach me. I just see in my mind's eye. Fisher said I'm Menderish. I suppose it's a gift from my ancestor. My unguents differed from those Fisher carried. I can't duplicate what he does, but I can make antitoxins for boxjelly and other venom! Your resistance is remarkable. The number of stings the creature inflicted upon you would have been fatal to any of my ilk."

Urquhart felt better. The big four-arm gratefully responded, "Thank you, my lady. My size gives me some advantage. My thick skin blocked some stingers. My people are sworn enemies of Boxjellies. They don't tarry around Doug-less or anywhere we live in numbers. They don't attack us when we are in groups and they always travel solitary. Don't suppose they can get along. Don't know how they make little Boxjellies, and don't want to know. I don't suppose you mind's eye has seen the location of your great-great-great grandmother's sanctuary?"

Piara sighed, "I thought I'd lost you. I know this general direction should take us to her domicile. I don't have any more Panaceas. We'd best avoid further goes with Boxjellies."

Urquhart answered, "I'm down with that. Are you ready?"

Piara asked, "Are you?"

Urquhart answered, "Let me look around first."

The big Carcharian took another dive and soon resurfaced and reported no immediate threats. They headed again in the general direction northwest from Vydaelia. They traveled uneventfully for another half-rotation of the Day Glass in Piara's accurate estimation. The pottyhippomus tired and they searched for another site for respite but saw nothing.

Urquhart suggested, "Let me lead us."

Piara whispered to the plesiohawg and loosened her hold. The weary porcine turned its head and snorted a few times. It swam due east and in a while a small rocky island appeared. They crawled ashore. Urquhart quickly inspected the ground and searched through the marsh grass. He found a couple quick snacks in some swamp rats. The plesiohawg chewed on marsh grass and a few bits of sea oats Piara gave him, and the sea elf found some tasty booderries and reeds.

CHAPTER 28

Fisher's Proposal

In Vydaelia Gruusch labored to calm distraught Starra. Sharchrina shared her cousin's angst and Loogie stood by her. Quunsch was itching for action and also wanted to pursue Piara and Urquhart. Bluuch held the Omega Stone within his sea mooler-hide vest. Sergeant Major Klunkus continued defensive measures. Rangers maintained vigilance toward the Duoth passageway to the west and toward the billabong to the east from whence the triskaidekapod, Gruusch's party, and Piara's group had come. Yathle watched the sea but had not seen scouts that Quunsch had noted.

The Wandmaker stared at the 13-graparble sized nodule on his left hand. The lesion impaired movement of his wrist a bit and throbbed at times. Yannuvia used the time to produce building blocks for the wall. The Wand of Masonry made the task much easier than casting the Rock-to-Mud and its reverse Mud-to-Stone spells. Saying **"Wood row will son"** and using the wand was much less labor intensive than casting the spells. Clouse slowly regained his energies. Jonna remained with him. Fisher spent the period in the Onyum Patch studying the plants and the soil. Morganne remained in the Wandmaker's abode.

Yannuvia finished his work. He'd produced more building blocks than his followers could lie in place. The refugees from Doug-less had been preoccupied with Piara and Urquhart's departures and worked less productively. To the Wandmaker's knowledge only he, Piara, the Dreamraider, Fisher, Jonna, Joulie, and maybe Clouse knew of his tryst with Piara. He'd been reluctant to risk the *Two Stones effect* with the big Carcharian Bluuch. How would Bluuch react to knowing Yannuvia had taken liberties with his erstwhile queen? Four stones in proximity had not shown any additional effect. Five stones had not been grasped together. At this time Yannuvia, Bluuch, Fisher, Gruusch, and Jonna carried the odd rocks. Princess Starra's red scarf detected the presence of the stones but again to the Wandmaker's knowledge the scarf did not give the Princess privy to the stone bearer's thoughts. Yannuvia disliked talking to Morganne about Piara. Morganne had not held an Omega Stone and thus never experienced the *Two Stones and Three Stones* effects. Did his life-mate know of his tryst or was it just his guilty conscience weighing on him? Was there to be a Forgetting Wand? There was nothing for it. It was time for the Wandmaker to go to his abode and tell Morganne of the day's news.

Young Ranger Knightsbridge dutifully stood outside the Day Glass chamber. Knightsbridge stood witness to Yannuvia and Morganne's ceremony of life time commitment performed by the elder Yiuryna. He nodded politely as Yannuvia the chamber that housed the timekeeping artifact and served as the Wandmaker's quarters. He entered the chamber. Morganne sat in the rest area. Her long red-orange hair fell disheveled across her chest. The protuberance on her belly told of her gravity. Her nausea slowly abated but she had participated little in the working of the community. She did not look up when Yannuvia entered.

The Wandmaker asked, "Are you feeling better?"

Morganne answered, "I've taken nourishment and slept. My energies are returning. I attended many of my friends and relatives in Meadowsweet when they were with child. I don't remember seeing many with my symptoms. Probably they kept it to themselves."

Yannuvia responded, "I admire your perseverance."

Morganne asked, "You spend little time here. Are you without tasks to perform or *elders* to attend?"

Yannuvia sensed sarcasm, blushed, and mechanically answered, "I've compiled large quantities of building stones. Klunkus is reinforcing the walls to the east. I wanted to check on you... and update you."

Morganne answered coolly, "I've been of little value to the community of late. In fact I'm more a liability. It's not important to keep me informed."

Yannuvia said, "Nothing could be further from the truth. You have ever served out people. Your efforts are legend. Your condition now... is my doing. You carry my child and I'm honored."

Morganne looked up and into his eyes. She said, "Then tell me of the day's events."

Yannuvia cleared his throat and said, "Our ranks are reduced. Last period Elder Piara and Urquhart left Vydaelia."

Morganne smiled wryly and asked, "Why did they leave? I thought they had nowhere to go."

Yannuvia answered, "Their business is their own."

Morganne replied, "Interesting! What of the stone she carried?"

Yannuvia said, "She left the Omega Stone with Bluuch."

Morganne continued, "I've wanted to hold one of the stones. Perhaps I might take it from Bluuch."

Yannuvia answered, "She left instruction for the big Carcharian to hold possession of the artifact. He is reluctant to part with it."

Morganne asked, "Did you pry into his mind?"

Yannuvia answered, "No. I did not want him privy to my thoughts."

Morganne said, "I'd think the thoughts of a Wandmaker would be too complex for a fish-man to understand."

Yannuvia said, "Morganne, you have seen Gruusch's contribution to our community. They are not simpletons. It was a security issue."

Morganne again looked into his eyes and said, "I'm sure."

The Wandmaker asked, "Are you in need of anything?"

Morganne answered, "Yes. I'd like an enhancing root tuber. I have some in my pack. We'll miss Urquhart's strength. He smote many sea lions and Duoths."

Yannuvia queried, "What of Piara? She saved Willifron?"

Morganne said, "I'm sure you'll miss her company. Your bond is obvious. We'll be better off without her."

Yannuvia retrieved an enhancing root tuber from Morganne's pack and gave it to her. She peeled the fruit and consumed the purplish center.

Morganne said, "You should sleep Wandmaker."

CHAPTER 29

Kirrie's Second Dream Journey

The Good Witch gulped and won a minor victory over her queasiness. She sat up. Kirrie sat at the bluewood table and stared out toward the Doombringers.

Kirrie said, "You're not very good company."

The Dreamraider replied, "What? Suppose you'd rather be out blowing up some fortresses and killing a few thousand Drolls."

Kirrie replied, "It wouldn't hurt. I'd rather singe a whore from Meadowsweet. Fadra lies in a bed that should be mine."

Amica answered, "In time you get used to such things. Most of the time I'm the fomenter instead of the victim."

Kirrie replied, "I'd say you're more the victim now. One of your trysts backfired on you."

The Good Witch answered, "We'll see. I can break up your boredom. I have another little trip for you."

Kirrie asked, "Are you saying you want me to invade someone's dreams? I hope it's better than a Fishman!"

The Good Witch replied, "You'll enjoy this one. You need to deliver a message. You remember the Mender Fisher?"

Kirrie answered, "The epitome of bland!"

Amica answered, "Don't sell him short. Menders are complex."

Kirrie answered, "Menders are also very resistant to Magick. They reflect even beneficial spells. I can't imagine his dreams would be very interesting."

Amica replied, "Relax. I don't want you to visit the Mender. The point I was making regards the knot he had on his hand. Are you familiar with it?"

179

Kirrie replied, "I never spent much time with him. I notice it when he was in Alms Glen. He revived a small tree the Lost Spellweaver Yannuvia destroyed in a fit of anger."

Amica replied, "The knot only gets so big. In fact it gets 13 times its original size and then gets no larger. The knot ties the Mender to grayness. My message is not for the Mender. It's for your Lost Spellweaver, or First Wandmaker. He's blessed with a nodule too."

Kirrie said, "I know that."

Amica said, "It gets larger when he uses certain gifts. When it reaches a certain size, specifically 13-fold larger, his benefits become limited. He needs to know this."

Kirrie asked, "Won't he figure it out?"

Amica asked, "Wouldn't you like to spend some time in his head? You already guessed my bond to him."

Kirrie followed, "Yannuvia is another who dropped me in favor of a harlot from Meadowsweet. I'd like to have seen her inner feelings when she learned about you."

Amica answered, "I'm not sure she knows about my tête-à-tête with the Wandmaker. You'll get lots of surprises when you look into his thoughts."

Kirrie said, "I'm intrigued. I've little else to do. Let's do it. What do you want me to tell him?"

Amica said, "That's the spirit. He sleeps as we speak. Take the Omega and Locating Stones. Concentrate your thoughts on him. Give him this message."

Kirrie asked, "I disguised my appearance to the sharkman. Should I do it again?"

Amica asked, "Don't you want him to see what he is missing?"

Kirrie gripped the stone. Grayness filled the cabin.

Yannuvia tossed. Morganne lay quietly by him. The Wandmaker dreamed of the battle with the Duoths and his nearly losing Clouse.
Then...
Redness entered his dreams.

Wisps...
Threads...
Threads of Magick...

Threads of fate…
Threads of time…
Threads connecting worlds …
Dreams connecting worlds …
Dreams of Magick…
The Magick of Dreams…
Magick connecting dreams…
Magick connecting worlds…
Dream raiders…
Elf pressure…
Albtraum…
Albträume, elf dreams, nightmares…

Ó ∞ Ó

The Wandmaker muttered, "Oh. no! Not you! The smoke has barely cleared from the battle! Why have you returned?"

The redness cleared and the Wandmaker's mind saw Kirrie sitting upon a wyvern.

Yannuvia muttered, "Drop the illusion. That ship sailed long ago. Kirrie chose my brother Gaelyss over me. Are you going to press guilt upon me over our venture?"

Kirrie spoke, "My… you have been busy, Wandmaker? Do you like the title? Are you a big fish in a small pond? Are you enjoying your whore from Meadowsweet? Think of the Lone Oak, The Invisimoss, Sergeant Major Rumsie, cleaning boots, and Old Yellow. We shared many childhood memories, Fire Wizard. Now we share that moniker too. If it makes you feel any better the tree shepherd has labeled me the same. I have now killed more Drolls than you. I am not welcome in Alms Glen and Meadowsweet. Green Vale allows me entry, but the Tree Shepherd shuns me. Sound familiar?"

Yannuvia replied, "Good Witch, you'd know these things. Just appear as your Good Witch persona. At least on the surface it's appealing to the eye."

Kirrie answered, "I come as I am. I don't have the ability to change my look once I have appeared. I appeared differently when I spoke to your fish-man comrade Bluuch. He knows little of your escapades Wandmaker, but now I know a lot. I'd love to let your whorish life-mate

181

know the whole story. The Good Witch sends me in her stead. You fixed her up pretty well. It appears it's something you're good at. Oh, my! The sea elf too! I'd love to tell Morganne about it! But I'm here to give you a message. I don't know what all this means but here goes. You have created new wands with each dark period. During the Approximation you created the exceptional USA Wand. Your nodule can get no larger. When the Dark Periods arrive you will be able to create wands, but they will be of the same power and that power will be limited to Magick Missile Spells. When the grayness returns you'll be able to create another exceptional wand. The Central Sphere and the 88 stones will direct you. Your nodule will then *tell* you what to do. Grayness will recharge the wands."

Yannuvia said, "Kirrie? Fire Wizard? Are you now a Dreamraider? Have you mastered *translocation*? If so, come to us. You can help us."

Kirrie replied, "I am a sister of Grayness and only a messenger. You've made your bed, Yannuvia. Now you must lie in it."

The Wandmaker answered the visage in his dream, "We've chosen similar beds, Kirrie."

Kirrie answered, "I don't share mine with another."

Yannuvia said, "Perhaps no longer... but before with my brother Gaelyss!"

Kirrie said, "Touché! I got mine! Your brother shares his bed with a whore from Meadowsweet, just as you do."

Red lights flashed around the image. The dreaming Wandmaker watched her eyes. Kirrie's image did not speak again. Blueness surrounded her and she faded from Yannuvia's mind's eye.

Kirrie opened her eyes. The Dreamraider Amica slept in the cabin. An iridescent tear cascaded down the erstwhile Teacher's cheek and dropped to the floor where it burst into a rainbow of colors. Words entered Kirrie's thoughts.

"I give you my blood through which you will receive all you seek. You in turn give to me your all."

Ó ∞ Ó

Yannuvia awakened. Morganne snoozed by his side. Words entered his mind.

"I give you my blood through which you will receive all you seek. You in turn give to me your all."

Ǿ ∞ Ǿ

The Wandmaker pondered his dream. Had Kirrie truthfully aligned with the Dreamraiders?

Since it formed, Yannuvia's nodule had increased in size 13 times. Each time it grew by a factor of 1.6180339887498948482... When it formed, the Wandmaker's nodule was precisely the size of one graparble. It increased in size when he traveled in the red and blue light with Jonna and Joulie, when he traveled in the red and blue light to Alms Glen with the Dream Master and Amica, when he traveled to Lost Sons with the bodies of his slain friends Diana Maceda, Clarke Maceda, and Banderas, when he traveled to Vydaelia, and when he created *I-one, I-two, I-three, I-four, I-five, and I-six.* The exceptional *I-seven* was created during an Approximation and did not result in expansion of the peculiar nodule. The Dreamraider assisted in the creation and confessed the Drelves had been away from Lost Sons longer. They had arrived during the fourth dark period of the twelfth year *since the gray light bathed the lands above us.* The Dark Period when I-seven was created was actually the first Dark Period of the thirteenth year since Andreas last appeared. The gray sun again filled the sky of the World of the Three Suns. *I-eight* and *I-nine* resulted in incremental increases in the nodule's size. It was now 13-fold larger than when it formed. The creation of *I-ten* did not produce an increase in size.

The great battle with Duoths, sea lions, and Giant Amebus occurred after the 5th Dark period in Vydaelia. Yannuvia's nodule throbbed and interfered with his dexterity. The outer dimensions of the nodule mimicked those of an omega stone. Fisher estimated the size was precisely the same.

Yannuvia recalled Fisher's state when he had been captured outside Lost Sons and the eventful journey with the Wandmaker to complete Fisher's confinement. Clouse came to be. Yannuvia was not Mender. Mender's blood had touched him.

CHAPTER 30

A Journey Ends

Piara and Urquhart resumed their journey. The sea elf trusted her intuition more, and the pendant directed her along the same path. A bit of numbness persisted in the big four-arm's left foot but Piara's concoction had stopped the muscle spasms that ripped through his body after the encounter with the boxjelly. Boxjellies were solitary and territorial so the duo hoped they'd not encounter another. The well-rested pottyhippomus sped along on the water's surface. Urquhart assisted with leg kicks and Piara held on tightly. Piara directed the plesiohawg in a general northwest direction. Encouragingly more sea life meandered and scattered in front of them. They crossed over expanses of shallow water where stands of sea grasses flourished. The sea flora provided much needed snacks. They traveled for the better part of a Day Glass rotation and saw another island rising from the water. It was a more substantial raised area and showed signs of cultivation. Rows of sea peas and cibbage glistened in the ever-present illumination. Constant light and rich water resulted in healthy robust plants. Finely made tools were scattered about the ground and a basket made of intertwined fibers of blue wood with spilled harvested sea peas lay near the third row of sea pea plants.

Urquhart surmised, "Looks like we might have surprised somebody."

Piara agreed, "No matter! They've left us a feast."

Urquhart sighed, "Doesn't define a feast to my way of looking at it."

Piara picked up a small rake and commented, "These gardening tools are not unlike what I remember of my people's tools. We have found cultivated areas. We are near settlements."

Urquhart held his throwing spear and trident in his left hands and looked all about. He said, "And they know we are here."

Piara said, "Bugwullies and Carcharians aren't farmers. We have nothing to fear from Pollywoddles and sea elves. Let's eat and rest up."

Urquhart said, "I'd dive and seek some fish, but I don't want to leave you."

Piara replied, "Have some cibbage and sea peas. You should eat more veggies, Urquhart. You'll get lots of vitamins and nutrients."

Urquhart answered, "The creatures I consume have eaten plenty of fruits and veggies. That's how I prefer to get my vitamins and nutrients."

Urquhart placed his net around the pottyhippomus and bent down to pick a cibbage. An arrow streaked by his left shoulder. Reflexively the veteran four-armed warrior pulled a shuriken from his belt and hurled the throwing star in the direction from whence the arrow flew. A soft thud followed by a moan told the Carcharian that his weapon found its mark. Urquhart then pushed Piara to the ground, carried his spear and trident in his left hands, held another shuriken in his upper right hand, and quickly pillaged through the bushes and plants on the forty by sixty pace island. His shuriken had menacingly lodged in a sea elf's chest. Some faint splashing in the water to the north broke the silence. The dead sea elf carried a bow and quiver with several finely made arrows. A thick gummy substance covered the arrowheads, which were sharpened pieces of bone and flint. The victim wore squid bladder suit quite similar to Piara's.

Piara scurried to Urquhart's side and checked the fallen sea elf. She relayed, "He's dead."

Urquhart said, "Good thing! He attacked us. He looks like you, but at the same time his coloration is a bit… grayish-green. Look! He has a little nodule on his left hand, there, at the base of his, yes… his sixth finger! He has six fingers like the Wandmaker! Has he been spying on the Wandmaker's ceremonies? It sure looks the same size."

Piara answered, "He attacked you! He saw a Carcharian trespassing on this island and in control of another sea elf … me!"

Urquhart checked the quiver and allowed, "Did he think he'd hurt me with these arrows? It'd sting, but little more."

Piara jerked an arrow from his hand and said, "Careful! Something covers the tip! Until we know its properties, we should avoid contact with the tarry unguent."

Urquhart replied, "Thanks! Foolish of me to pick it up! I've heard old Phederal's troopers talk of painful injuries received from battles with your and my mother's ilk. I should say mine lineage, too. I killed him, but he attacked first. It's… my training."

Piara reassuringly said, "I do not fault you for defending us. You reacted appropriately. He couldn't have known you were my guardian. His garb is typical and rather well made."

Urquhart noted, "He is about your size. His outfit should work as a spare for you, provided you can repair the hole created by the shuriken. Let's take his things and be on our way."

Piara said, "I agree this should not be wasted but we can't leave him like this."

Urquhart said, "My lady, there will be more of them. As you said we don't know the effects of the unguent coating the arrowheads. I can match many of them hand-to hand but I can't defend against a host of archers. They tend and obviously defend this island. Let's grab and go."

Piara said, "He did try to shoot you, but he's my kind. Every creature deserves respect. I can't leave him as carrion for the scavengers. Let his tissues nourish the plants he loved. Bury him among the cibbage."

Urquhart opined, "My lady, his fellows could arrive at any time. I implore you. Let's leave now."

Piara insisted, "I cannot leave him exposed to the scavengers."

Urquhart saw the futility of arguing and used the tip of his spear to dig among the cibbage plants. The tilled soil separated easily at the surface but required more effort as the Carcharian dug deeper. Having four arms helped. Urquhart used the sea elf tools in both his right hands and soon had a hole six feet deep and large enough to hold the sea elf's corpse. When he lifted the lifeless body, a graparble dropped from the sea elf's left hand. Piara picked up the little rock.

She said, "This is outwardly the same as the little stones that left the Vydaelians. Just as the stone I carried to Vydaelia differed in weight, this also does. In fact it's 0.61818182 the weight of the one I carried."

Urquhart said, "You may carry the little rock."

He placed the sea elf's body in the grave, filled the hole, and asked, "Now may we go?"

Piara gathered sea peas and more cibbage and replied, "Yes. We must be near settlements."

Urquhart allowed, "We'll have to be wary of outcroppings that might hide them."

Piara said, "I'll carry his bow and arrows. The quiver is lined with squid bladder too which should maintain a barrier between the arrows and me. The graparble is in my pocket."

The well fed pottyhippomus took to the water with Piara aboard and Urquhart in tow. The waters were quiet.

Ø ∞ Ø

Inyra had seen many Carcharian raids. He'd heard his sister's screams as she was dragged away and lit the pyres that consumed his father's mauled body. The sea elf Commandant had doubled his efforts to keep his people safe. His scouts bravely patrolled the regions to the west, literally under the shadow of Doug-less and the Reed Creek Delta in Carcharian Lord Crudle's domain. Setting up farms outside the warren was risky, but to this point the farms had not been discovered. That had just ended. Inyra awaited the report from Squad Leader Agarn, who had witnessed an incursion into one of the outermost growing sites. Lieutenant Dain arrived with Agarn.

Inyra rubbed the little nodule at the base of his sixth left finger and inquired, "Tell me of this encounter."

Agarn breathlessly began, "Commandant, Giryn and I were working the cibbage patch in the outer quarter. Dawgfish barking alerted us to intruders. We dropped our tools and took up defensive positions. We beheld a monstrous four-armed Carcharian who held a comely sea elf hostage. They rode a plesiohawg. We hid in the bushes while they came ashore. The heavily armed Carcharian let down his guard and stepped away from the sea elf and gave Giryn a clear shot. Luck smiled on the four-arm for he ducked down just as Giryn fired and the arrow slipped just over his left shoulder. The Carcharian's lightning-like reflexes served him well. He threw a weapon that struck down Giryn. I escaped with my life and little else. I don't think he followed me."

Inyra said, "This is very confusing. Why should a four-armed Carcharian be traveling alone and this far west? Furthermore, you described his arrival from the south. Our enemies oft take our females hostage. This is likely what you witnessed. I am aware of no recent raids on our people by Carcharians. Certainly I'd have heard of abduction. You said this female was mature. We must remain vigilant. The one you encountered must be a scout. Usually four-arms demand two-arms accompany them if for no other reason to do mundane tasks. Carcharians typically attack in force and from the west. They try to block avenues of escape. I have fortified these reeds and made it impossible for them to approach from more than one direction. Our entranceway is well hidden and defended by archers at all times. The entryway is large enough to only admit one Carcharian. We cannot fight them one on one, but we can handle them one at a time. You have served well, Agarn. For now we must abandon the planted areas in the sea. Concentrate efforts to shore up out defenses. An attack is likely coming. Frayn and Bryni are watching Doug-less."

Ó ∞ Ó

Piara and Urquhart saw rocky cliff walls in the distance. To the east the sea extended to the horizon. Urquhart remained apprehensive. They stayed in the shallows and watched both directions up the rocky beach. The area was similar to Vydaelia, but the beach was considerably narrower. Thick marsh grass facilitated their hiding. The lack of activity was unnerving.

Urquhart surmised, "My lady, it would seem your intuition has failed us. We have crossed the sea only to find barren wall. My time in King Lunniedale's guard exposed me to many battle reports. Sea elves inhabit marshes and inlets. The rocky barren walls are too inhospitable, even for a native of Doug-less like me."

Piara responded, "I have so few personal memories of my people, but I visualize many things through my connection to my ancestor. I see more clearly now. Perhaps being in this place… Now it's as though I was there with her."

Urquhart asked, "Were you taken from this place?"

Piara replied, "No. I've never physically been on this shore. My home was… I know… it was far to the west."

Urquhart asked, "If you and your great-great-great grandmother lived so far away, then why are we here?"

Piara glanced in both directions down the beach and then at the sheer stone wall about thirty Yardley steps from the water's edge. The wall rose about the height of its fellow in Vydaelia. She said, "Four clicks… four clicks to the west… That'd be about 4181 Yardley paces in the measure the Vydaelians use. I can feel every step."

Urquhart replied, "My lady, many in Doug-less called you 'witch-queen.' I was not one of them, but your knack for defining distance and other measures perplexes me. 'Clicks' and 'Yardley paces' are meaningless terms in Doug-less. I heard the Vydaelians use the term Yardley pace. Never Click."

Piara said, "I've always been able… in Vydaelia Fisher and Clouse share the ability. Fisher said I was Menderish. I just know I lived as a child about four clicks from where we now stand."

Urquhart answered, "I accept what you say. That'd take us in the general direction of Doug-less and the sea elfish warrens that King Lunniedale's forces… uh… we raided. Participating in raids was a requirement of our training. Phederal and Gurgla enjoyed forcing those of us with mixed blood to participate in the raids. But the bottom line is that it's on me. I performed well… to advance in the ranks. My work earned me the right to guard you and Starra. When the raid ended we carried the spoils back to Doug-less. I'm not proud of my deeds. Walking on that ground will bring back painful memories but we'd best get going."

Piara said, "Our path does not lead to my childhood home. We have reached our destination."

Urquhart said, "My lady, it's just a rock wall. I have neither seen nor smelled sea elves…uh other than you. No crops… no stockades… their wooden and grass constructions never kept us out."

Piara continued, "My great-great-great grandmother was exiled from the community. I now see… for loving an outsider. She walked this ground."

Urquhart said, "Then there's nothing for it. Let's explore a bit."

The Carcharian and sea elf cautiously exited the reeds and shallow water and stepped onto the rocky shore. Urquhart carried shuriken in both right hands and his trident in his left upper hand. He kept his left lower hand free and on Piara's shoulder. Piara knelt down and touched the coarse sand on the shore. The rocks glistened in the ever-present luminescence from the lichen growths far overhead. The rocky wall extended to the west about a hundred paces and then extended outward toward the sea which blocked their view. To the east the wall actually extended to the horizon and separated from the sea to provide a clear view of the shore. Nothing stirred. Then they heard a deep croak from up the rocky beach around the corner. Urquhart readied his spear and throwing star.

Ø ∞ Ø

Sea Elf Commandant Inyra and his Lieutenant Liani watched the shapely sea elf female and hulking four-armed Carcharian walk ashore through murder holes in the rocky wall. Young Bryni had brought word from veteran Squaddie Frayn. Frayn had seen no forces leaving Dougless but had given unsettling information about newcomers on the far side of the sea. At the moment Inyra had a four-armed Carcharian and rogue sea elf as his concerns. A dozen finely made bows honed in on the encroachers through other holes.

Liana said, "How can we attack the Carcharian and not endanger his captive? Wait! She is not restrained and walks by the side of the Carcharian."

Inyra agreed, "Very observant! Our eyes deceive us. The Carcharian king has many allies. Shape changers number among them. This female sea elf is beyond beautiful! Mesmerizing, in fact! She is meant to deceive us."

Liani asked, "Should we not attack them now, Commandant?"

Inyra answered, "No! Let's see what they are up to? Send the general alarm. This must be a probing attack."

Ø ∞ Ø

The Carcharian said studied the beach and said, "Nothing here. That's worth investigating."

Piara agreed and they moved across the beach and edged along the wall. The croaking sound intensified. Urquhart moved ahead and quickened his pace. Soon they stood at the corner.

Piara peek around and commented, "This is … our destination. It's eerily familiar. Our path leads to the north along this billabong."

The rocky wall bent back sharply and extended several hundred paces to the north. The sea ended and gave way to a billabong, quite similar to the area west of Vydaelia. The marshy area surrounding the billabong tapered as it went away from the sea. Where they stood across its beginning the marsh and billabong were a hundred Yardley paces wide. Gradually it narrowed. The ceiling remained very high and difficult to estimate. The lichen maintained the light, though the alcove darkened in the distance and the duo could not see to its end. About two hundred paces to the north, the eastern and western walls looked about twenty paces apart. On either side of the central marshy area there was a narrow strip of rocky soil next to the walls. Loud croaking sounds came from the billabong and reverberated from the walls.

Urquhart muttered, "I hope that's neither a triskaidekapod nor dinosaur!"

Piara answered, "It's not a dinosaur, Urquhart. It's a fawagy! It's not a dinosaur!"

Urquhart readied his weapon and asked, "What's a fawagy?"

Piara replied, "Fawagies are giant amphibians which sometimes serve as watchers for sea elf communities."

Urquhart said matter-of-factly, "I'm a large amphibian and certainly wouldn't make an appropriate guard for sea elves. Though I've never faced a fawagy, I've heard stories of the big beasts in the king's council room. They've taken down a fair number of warriors over time. Your inner thoughts tell you we have arrived. If we are to explore this marsh, we can't leave an enemy behind us."

The fawagy was also known as giant frog. A giant frog basically resembled a regular frog though it actually more closely resembled a toad. The creature had a greatly increased size, growing up to 4 feet long and three feet high. Urquhart looked upon a beast nearer the larger end of the size spectrum. It was the typical dark green in color and it was covered in warts and boils. Foul smelling ooze covered its skin. Giant frogs, for the most part, dwelled solitary in deep marshes and swamp with habits fairly similar to normal frogs and feasted on giant insects. They attacked by applying their poison ooze to their tongue and then whipping prey with it. They used the method to gain prey and fight off poaching humanoids. The poison caused skin irritation and infection and killed if injected into the blood. Bugwullies tamed Fawagies and used them as attack-beasts and even mounts. It was common knowledge in Doug-less that sea elves used them as guardians.

Piara managed a slight smile at the big four-arm's attempt at humor and said, "Fawagies have some intelligence. Sea elves train them to be guards. The giant frog-like critters can be quite aggressive and have ravenous appetites. They'd easily be capable of eating one of our Vydaelian colleagues or a sea elf, but Fawagies prefer giant insects and smaller denizens of the sea. Suffice it to say, our presence has been announced to any sea elves or anyone else that might be around."

The fawagy's bellowing drowned out insect calls and most every other sound. Urquhart scanned the area and answered, "Seems a moot point, my lady. This marsh appears uninhabited… except for the fawagy. It makes dawgfish seem quiet."

Piara said, "My people hide well, but sea elves prefer expansive marshy areas."

Urquhart gripped his trident and spear and said, "I'm going to shut that thing up! He'd make a fine dinner too."

Piara said, "It'd be like killing a pet, but the noise is deafening!"

Urquhart moved toward the high reeds from which the croaking emanated. Piara stayed back. The four-arm extended both his spear and trident before him and parted the tall thick grass. The giant frog leapt toward him. Urquhart deftly jumped aside and Piara scurried toward the sea. Urquhart lashed at the beast with his spear but only nicked its thick hide. A glob of tarry skin oil tarnished the tip of the spear. Urquhart pulled his net from his belt and held it in his lower right hand.

Piara shouted, "You aren't going to try to catch him in that little net?"

Urquhart puffed, "I'm going to try?"

Piara asked, "Aren't you left handed… uh, *handeds*?"

Urquhart moved side to side and awaited the fawagy's next move. He added, "I throw better with my right hands."

The fawagy's tongue protruded menacingly from its maw. In attack position with gaping maw the big green beast gave the visage of a mouth on four legs. The giant frog leaped. Urquhart held his ground until the last split second and then fell to the ground and threw the net toward the beast's legs as it flew by. The net tangled in the critter's hind legs and the fawagy hit the ground with a loud splash. Urquhart's net encumbered the beast and kept it from using its powerful hindlegs to leap upon the Carcharian. Still the fawagy drug its bulky body forward with surprising speed, closed on the four-arm, and snapped at him. Urquhart moved aside and avoided the beast's webbed claws and great maw. The fawagy's lunge put it in spear range and Urquhart managed another jab at the thick hide. The giant toad extended its long sticky tongue and rubbed it across its back coating its tongue with the thick tarry substance that covered most of its body. The fawagy then lunged toward Urquhart, flailed its tongue with lightning-like speed, and smeared a large quantity of goop on the Carcharian's left shoulder. Urquhart yowled in pain. The giant frog rubbed its tongue over its back and coated it with toxic goop. Urquhart thrust his trident into the frog's thorax and followed with his spear. The beast gurgled animalistic groans and wrapped its tongue around the Carcharian's right lower wrist. Urquhart's thick skin sizzled from the digestive juices in the fawagy's toxic saliva. The fawagy then rubbed tarry goop over the injured skin. Urquhart drew a shuriken from his belt with his uninjured right hand and used his spear and trident (both of which remained imbedded in the creature's body) to pull the giant frog toward him. The fawagy stuck out its tongue again, and Urquhart lopped it off with the sharp edge of the throwing star. The Carcharian then pushed the spear and trident with all his remaining strength further into the beast's bloated body. The giant toad let out of load squeak and collapsed. Urquhart fell onto the warty back and amongst the thick tarry goo. Piara ran to the fallen toad and dragged Urquhart off its body. The four-arm had a burned area on his lower right arm that was precariously close to breaking through his thick skin, a large area of his left shoulder covered with tenacious mucoid material, and large quantities of toxic over his broad chest. The most pressing issue was his lower right arm. The poison was dangerously near entering his bloodstream.

Piara urged, "We must remove the poison. It will slowly penetrate your skin, but it could kill you quickly if it enters your blood."

Piara used swamp grass and tore pieces from her squid bladder suit to remove the toxins. Urquhart lapsed in and out. She cleaned his wounds vigorously with sea water and took a phial from her pack and gave Urquhart the last bit of cleansing syrup that she carried. Urquhart sat up with a start, stood, and ran into the water. He thrashed around with all four arms and rubbed his skin vigorously to clear away the fawagy's thick secretions. He placed a seaweed wrap over the open wound on his lower right arm.

Ø ∞ Ø

Inyra and Liani watched the battle unfold.

Liani said, "He smote the fawagy, but it should have cost the Carcharian his life. She helps him battle the poison."

Inyra replied, "If there was any doubt about her allegiance, it is gone. *She* may not even be female, let alone sea elfish. We have two enemies."

Liani added, "The Carcharian is weakened. This is a good time to attack."

Inyra answered, "You saw what he did to the giant frog. The beast had kept every attacker from the sea at bay and ate many of them. I still want to see what they are up to. There's always a chance there's more of them around."

Liani added, "Others would have come to his aid. The female did not fight."

Inyra said, "Mistakes of youth! You don't know our enemies tactics. Shape changers maintain the ruse until they die or choose to revert to normal form. Death prevents maintenance of their deception! Carcharians would certainly sacrifice one of their own to further their plans. The fawagy's poison made him drowsy. He's rapidly regained his prowess when it's removed from his skin. His wounds are not serious. There's plenty of fight left in the four-arm."

Ø ∞ Ø

Urquhart hewed one of the fawagy's legs, skinned it carefully, and chowed down. Piara politely declined his offer to share and cautioned, "Make sure the flesh is not contaminated by its skin. I'm not sure how the poison would affect you if you ingest it."

The four-arm said, "Not to worry! I cleaned it. Tastes like sea chicken."

The Carcharian then used seaweed to clean his weapons. He checked the water and both directions up and down the beach. Piara munched on some cattail, bulrush, and watercress. Urquhart reported lack of activity.

The veteran warrior said, "Sounds of battle draws the curious, opportunistic, and those just itching to join a fight. We'd best get on with our exploration. I'm pessimistic of our finding anything in this alcove my lady."

Piara insisted, "My... this ancestor walked this ground. I don't understand my feelings, Urquhart, but we must push ahead."

The Carcharian muttered, "Stay close to me."

The duo chose the western side of the billabong and moved forward. They reached the end of the blind pond and discovered a small stream feeding it. The stream flowed from the north into narrowing alcove. Two hundred paces into the alcove the distance between the rocky walls had narrowed to twenty paces. After another hundred steps the passage darkened and the ceiling came downward. They were looking into a passage that narrowed to ten paces wide and about ten feet high. Urquhart's frame filled much of the height and he had to carry his spear and trident before him. The little stream filled the center of the passage and the soil changed to more hardened clay then the rocky soil near the sea. Urquhart and Piara followed the stream. The Carcharian grew increasingly apprehensive. They entered a section some eighty paces long. It widened slightly and the ceiling rose to about fifteen feet. Sea elves armed with bows and arrows passed from the rocky walls in front and behind them. Shouts filled the passage.

Urquhart shouted, "Secret doors! Ambush!"

Piara screamed, "Wait! I'm sea elfish!"

Twenty paces ahead gray-green Sea elves formed two ranks of five. The front rank knelt. On command the archers fired. Urquhart stepped in front of Piara. Eight arrows struck the Carcharian, but one sailed past and grazed Piara's left shoulder. The projectiles barely penetrated the Carcharian's thick skin. Urquhart shoved Piara toward the western wall and turned toward the group of sea elves that stood between the duo and the sea. The sea elves fired again and several arrows struck Urquhart.

The four-arm shouted, "Definitely not friendly! Stay low and near the wall and follow along behind me!"

Piara crawled along on her knees. Urquhart brandished his spear and trident in his left arms. As he ran, he threw a shuriken and impaled one of the standing sea elves. He tossed his net over two kneeling sea elves. Arrows struck his back as some of the enemies in the rear risked firing in the direction of their comrades. Urquhart reached the sea elves and tore into them. He stabbed repeatedly. Two sea elves squirmed in the net. Others used their arrows as stabbing weapons but ineffectively jabbed at Urquhart. Soon seven of the rear guard fell. The Carcharian raised his spear to attack his netted prey when he heard Piara's scream. The Carcharian turned and saw an arrow protruding from her back. She slumped against the wall. The four-arm turned and angrily charged the attackers to the north. Bowstrings hummed and more arrows struck him. The wounds were shallow but searing pain ripped through him at each site. The pain was familiar! The sea elves' arrows were coated with the poison from the fawagy's back. The sea elves managed two volleys before Urquhart reached them. The walls spun wildly around him. Numbness spread to his hands as the neurotoxins spread through his body. Drawing his breath became difficult. He stabbed furiously with his weapons. Sea elves drew short swords and fought back. Urquhart's dexterity faltered by the moment. The four-arm threw down his weapons and grabbed four sea elves, one with each arm and gripped with all his remaining strength. He fell forward onto his squirming victims. Numerous blades stabbed at his back. Warmth… Coldness… Darkness…

11 sea elves lay dead. Two others required help from their colleagues to extricate themselves from the Carcharian's net. Inyra and Liani came through a secret door in the rocky eastern wall.

A young sea elf panted, "The four-arm is dead."

Inyra asked, "What of the shape changer? Shape changers must concentrate to maintain their ruse."

Lieutenant Liani joined two sea elves that stood over Piara and, after checking her, said, "She was not a doppelganger! She remains sea elfish."

Inyra said, "What? We've killed one of our own!"

Liani continued, "Commandant! The resemblance… is remarkable."

Inyra said, "Resemblance! What do you mean?"

Liani said, "Her face, Commandant, mimics the Gray Matron. But for her greenness I could be looking at the image on the tomb!"

Inyra approached and looked upon the fallen female and pondered, "She's definitely greener than most of us. My goodness! I agree! This female bears more resemblance to the Gray Matron than does my great Aunt, who is directly descended from the matron. Who is this female? Why'd she ally with a Carcharian? She deserves to share his fate!"

Liani quickly added, "Wait! She still draws breath… but shallowly! And, her stomach! Commandant, she is with child!"

Inyra gasped, "With child! What have we done! Have you got any antidote?"

Liani replied, "Uh…yes, Commandant."

Inyra ordered, "Give her the antidote!"

Liani placed thick syrup in Piara's mouth, pulled the arrow from her shoulder, and applied unguent to the wound. The Lieutenant then said, "It is done. The arrow is removed and bleeding stopped. She's unconscious."

Inyra said, "There's no more we can do. Get her to the infirmary. Have we seen other interlopers?"

Scouts near the water's edge reported the area was clear.

Inyra ordered, "11 of our brethren lie dead. Attend them. Gather the graparbles that left their bodies. Keep them apart and don't let them merge. We need planting stones. Bring the female. Give the Carcharian's carrion to the sea."

Liani said, "About the Carcharian! He had a graparble in his lower left hand. It's lying on the ground by his body. It extruded after his death."

Inyra said, "This scenario gets stranger by the moment. A Carcharian has given his life to protect a sea elf and had a nodule of grayness too. Keep his nodule separated from the others."

Liani added, "I...I'm reluctant to touch it."

Inyra impatiently followed, "Sea chicken s**t! Time is wasting! More Carcharians could arrive at any moment. In case you didn't notice, one four-arm clobbered us. Get the nodule of grayness!"

Liani took a deep breath, grabbed the little gray rock, and added, "I have it. It's the same shape and size as those that left our colleagues. But, Commandant Inyra, it weighs more... a good bit more."

Inyra reiterated, "Keep it separate!"

CHAPTER 31

Captive

Dreamless sleep…

Floating aimlessly and thoughtlessly in shades of purple and gray fading to black…

Was she to enter the blackness?

Lancinating pain in her back and shoulder brought her back to consciousness.

Dry mouth…

Horrific taste…

Piara reluctantly opened her eyes. Moving her shoulder intensified the pain. She was lying on a bed of soft seaweed in a brightly illuminated chamber. The plush thick blue seaweed nestled her bare skin. Nudity exposed her shoulder wound, which was dressed with cottonweed, and her protuberant tummy, which she had managed to conceal before leaving Vydaelia and gently compress with her squid bladder suit. Subtle movement in her tummy reassured her. Gray-green sea elfish matrons hurried about the room and tended the wounds of a seriously injured sea elf, who moaned again and again. A young female sea elf stood at the foot of Piara's bed and relayed to her colleagues, "The *prisoner* is awake."

Piara was unable to move her hands and feet.

The young she-sea elf spoke in a dialect that differed from that used by Piara and other sea elf captives in Doug-less, but she understood every word. It was one of 17711 languages in which she was fluent. The word "prisoner" was most disturbing. Her hands and feet were bound and tied to the bed. An armed guard entered the infirmary and stood by Piara's bed. Another sped away. Piara remained silent and studied her captors. Their grayish-green rather than the emerald green coloration was consistent with the individual she and Urquhart encountered in the sea and battled in the narrowing marsh. The victim of Urquhart's shuriken, her armed guard, and young caregiver had little nodules on their left hands. Otherwise the lot shared traits typical of sea elves. Piara had long green hair, emerald green eyes, and smooth ears. Her ears differentiated her from pointy-eared Clouse in Vydaelia, where she was called "Clousish" and "Menderish." Piara did not develop a nodule on her left hand. All of her followers, called "the purple gang" after the Wandmaker placed False Aura Spells upon them, had developed nodules at the base of their fifth left digit after witnessing the Wandmaker's wand ceremony. Clouse and Fisher did not develop the nodules. Piara shared many traits with the Mender and his greenish spawn. She looked around the infirmary for Urquhart. She did not see the Carcharian and feared the worst. In a little while an entourage arrived.

An older sea elf wore a robe made of purple sea mooler hide and carried an ornate scepter which bore similarities to the Wandmaker's handiwork. He cast a disdainful glance at Piara and said, "I didn't think you'd make it, but you have survived. That's more than I can say for my good friend and loyal squaddie Giryn, who braved the dangers of the sea to grow food for my people only to be killed by you and your Carcharian friend. Who are you?"

Piara understood every word he said but did not respond.

The leader asked the caretakers, "Has she spoken?"

The young caretaker answered, "No, Commandant Inyra. She simply turns her head from side to side."

Inyra impatiently asked, "Who are you? My squaddies heard your conversations with the Carcharian! You spoke a variant of sea elfish. I know you understand me! Answer!"

Piara turned her head and looked directly toward her inquisitor and said, "When you have finished staring at my body, might you have the decency to provide me some cover?"

Inyra answered, "You are in no position to demand anything, and your body does not interest me!"

Piara replied, "Your eyes tell another tale."

Inyra motioned briskly to the sea elf maiden that stood silently at the foot of the bed. The maiden reached under the bed and produced a bedsheet and covered Piara. Soft glowworm fibers of the bedding caressed her body and restored a bit of modesty.

Inyra rubbed his thumb on the scepter he carried and impatiently chided, "Is that better?"

Piara said, "You must think me a dangerous woman. The bonds on my hands and feet are uncomfortable. Might you loosen them?"

Inyra angrily replied, "You carried the bow and quiver that you and the fishman ripped from Giryn's lifeless body. You violated my friend after his death by robbing him of his pebble of grayness. We found it in your squid skin suit's pocket. Your companion killed 12 of my people, 13 if Fytch does not survive." The gray-green leader pointed toward the badly injured sea elf that languished in the nearby bed.

Piara answered, "I am Piara. The one you call Giryn attacked us. We meant no harm. We buried your friend among his plants where in death he might nurture them still. I never fired the arrows from the bow."

Inyra scoffed, "Giryn'll have no legacy without the stone's accompanying his body in interment. It should have been buried with him! At least a graparble tree might have sprouted from his ashes. You are sea elfish, though not of our clan. Where are your mates? I can't imagine you had good intentions. Why did you travel with a Carcharian, our sworn and worst enemy? Carcharians always mean to harm our ilk. I am waiting for answers! Start talking!"

Piara grimaced and asked plaintively, "My back hurts. Might I please sit up?"

Inyra huffed, "No!"

An elderly matron left the gravely injured sea elf's bed and came to Piara's bed. She addressed the leader, "Inyra, she is with child and I'd say more than halfway along! Many of our folk are taken by the Carcharians as children and know no other family or masters. My son Liani said she did not fire the bow in the battle and reported the Carcharian fought to protect her. She is unarmed! You have six armed guards on her. I've examined her. She is of our eastern ilk. She only lacks our grayish hue to reflect the image on the tomb's door. Please loosen her bonds. Allow her nourishment."

Inyra blushed. His face became more purplish than gray-green. He muttered, "Matron Nila, your son and my subordinate Liani speaks too freely of tactics and scouting. Out of respect to you and in deference to her gravid state, I will allow her to sit. Be aware, Carcharian-friend, that our spears are tipped with the same poison that took your friend's life and nigh ended yours!"

Piara gasped, "Did you say… Urquhart is dead?"

Inyra callously answered, "The four-arm feeds the scavengers of the sea. We denied him the accompaniment of his pebble of grayness, just as you denied Giryn. Just rewards for his murderous deeds!"

Piara sighed and belabored said, "Urquhart's was born of sea elf. His mother shared my fate. I was taken from my family as a child and coerced to live with the Carcharians. We were taken from our homes by raiders from Doug-less."

Elderly Nila and young maiden Sabrina carefully loosened the woven grab grass ropes that bound Piara and helped the injured sea elf sit up. Piara's shoulder throbbed and her back ached but she relished being free of the bondage. She took a deep breath and tearfully said, "We meant no harm. Giryn attacked us. My friend and companion Urquhart only defended me. He responded to the attack. We only learned our assailant's identity after the deed was done. We treated your friend with respect but did not know of your tradition of burying the little crescent shaped gray rocks that we call graparbles with their bearer. In Vydaelia the extruded nodules are collected after the deaths of their hosts."

Inyra followed, "Carcharian traits always dominate. The four-arm was Carcharian, not sea elfish. You did not come from the west, from Doug-less, the home of the Carcharians. My most-veteran Squaddie Frayn watches the comings and goings at Doug-less. Sea elfish warrens lie mainly to the west, between here and the Carcharian stronghold Doug-less. We seldom interact with the western warrens and rarely see shark-men in our area. Where is Vydaelia, this Carcharian citadel?"

Piara sobbed and replied, "Outwardly, yes, Urquhart was Carcharian, but he had a good and loyal heart. To our knowledge he was among the first of his kind to bear a graparble. We know little of the pint-sized rocks. The newcomers across the sea bear them. Vydaelia is the newcomers' citadel. We left Doug-less, the Carcharians' stronghold, and traveled to the far side of the sea, where newcomers to the realm befriended us."

Frayn had sent word to Inyra of a stronghold across the sea and a furious battle between newcomers and Duoths and their allies.

Inyra skeptically said, "Duoths inhabit those regions, and they befriend no travelers. So these newcomers also befriend Carcharians. The friend of my enemy must also be my enemy."

Piara asked, "Did you at least keep Urquhart's little rock? If so, I'd like to have it. It'd be something to remind me of my friend and ally."

Inyra replied, "That should be of little concern to you. But it's kept separate and will not be planted in the forest of grayness, where we honored our 12 comrades that the Carcharian killed."

The injured sea elf Fytch groaned loudly and sat up. The matron Nila ran to his side. Fytch fell back onto the bed, gasped, and breathed no more. The nodule on his left hand opened and a small gray crescent shaped rock fell to the floor. The stone was precisely the shape and size of the stone Amica Carmisino had given Piara after visiting the erstwhile Queen of Doug-less in a dream and those stones that extruded from dead or gravely injured Vydaelians.

Nila sadly said, "I'm sorry, Commandant Inyra, Fytch suffered grievous wounds. He joins our forebears."

Inyra gaze hardened and he icily said to Piara, "Now you and your comrade the Carcharian have smote 13 of my people. Nila, prepare Fytch's body for interment. The ceremony will commence when you are ready. Organize a procession. Fytch was young, but he served well and has earned a resting place among the gray trees near the tomb. A strong sapling will spring from his resting place. Piara, if that is your name, Fytch's death has augmented my anger. He adds another increment just as the little stones combine if they are allowed to touch."

Nila said, "Just as merged gray stones will not grow into a fruit-bearing gray tree, Inyra, your anger will not bear fruit. I will prepare Fytch. This woman is in need of care. She carries another life, which is just as precious as those we've lost to the Carcharian. She was taken, ripped from her family. She says the fallen four-arm's mother was as well."

Inyra said, "Get on with your tasks, Nila. She may have been taken but she walked unrestrained with the four-arm. Our observers noted she had many opportunities to escape. I surmise she is a willing whore and likely carries the four-arm's seed."

Nila angrily answered, "Sea chicken s**t, Inyra! She is with child and has fought off grievous injury. You must allow her rest and nourishment before you question her further. Cruelty is not our way... and not your way! I'm going to attend Fytch now. Be the caring and responsible leader I know you to be."

Inyra watched Nila tenderly wrapping Fytch and quietly answered, "Grief overwhelms me. I don't yet trust this female. She'll be allowed rest and food, but must remain under guard."

Inyra left. Four armed guards remained stationed by Piara's bed. Dark poison glistened on the tips of their short finely made spears. The guards and indeed every passing sea elf stared intently at Piara. The erstwhile queen of Doug-less was accustomed to stares in Doug-less. The lustful stares from the Carcharians differed from the reverent mesmerized looks on the faces of the young sea elves. Nila bade the maiden Sabrina give Piara nourishment. Sabrina brought sea bee honey, purplish fruit, and refreshing blue-green tea. Grief gave way to hunger and maternal instinct to gain nourishment for her unborn. Famished Piara snuggled in the soft sheet and accepted the food. Successful beguiling the four guards was unlikely. After eating she sat quietly on the side of the bed and studied her surroundings. The well-lit infirmary was much brighter than most areas of the underworld. Underworld creatures had long since adapted to the dim light. Several rolling pedestals covered by colonies of luminescent lichen were positioned about the chamber. One such pedestal had illuminated her daughter Starra's chamber in Doug-less. Years ago a pale visitor had spent some time with the Carcharians and ingenuously created the rolling pedestal upon which grew a colony of luminescent lichen. Sprinkling ground up sea beetles and lake water upon the pedestal fed the lichen. Rolling the pedestal into and out of the room varied the light in the chamber. The devices lighting the sea elves' infirmary were quite similar to Starra's. Starra released a few fireflies into the chamber and augmented the light further. Many fireflies flew around the infirmary and two flames flickered in giant conch shells. Fragrant sea bee comb provided fuel for candles in the room. All in all the works were quite similar to what Piara had seen in Doug-less and her childhood home, though those vague memories were seen through her great-great-great grandmother's eyes. The walls were stone, but the sea elves had brought in plants and greenery to liven up the place. Gray-green sea elves wrapped Fytch's body in sea weed. Matron Nila placed the little gray rock that fell from his body at the time of his death in soft soil and wrapped it in thick green moss. She placed the moss in a small rucksack and inserted the rucksack within the wrappings with Fytch's body. Under Matron Nila's direction sea elves carried Fytch's wrapped corpse from the infirmary. Sabrina diligently cleaned the bed upon which he had passed away.

Piara felt stronger.

Nila soon returned and bade the four guards give way. Initially they resisted but the persuasive matron managed to get them to step back. From their conversations with Nila, Piara learned the four young guards were named Rory, Turlough, Adric, and Horton. Nila stood by Piara's bed.

Nila said, "Inyra has led us through difficult times. He has been a strong leader and made every effort to keep our home hidden from the outside world and particularly the Carcharians. His scouts constantly watch the routes to Doug-less and Reed Creek Delta. He defended us against the troglodytes' despot Oogum. Troglodytes are a constant threat, but we can fend them off. This is the first attack from a Carcharian we have endured in two generations. Never has Inyra witnessed the loss of so many of our people. Most folk who live here in Graywood give up their pebbles of grayness through dying of old age or accident. Rarely a boxjelly seizes one of our sea goers but we don't recover those stones. Anyway, predation and illness are rare causes of our demises. Please tell Inyra the truth. We don't have one of the Gray Matron's lines to guide us. She was older and barren when she founded Graywood. The few kin that arrived with her are gone. Everyone who witnessed the construction of the tomb is dead. Inyra has our community's best interest in mind. Please tell him the truth."

Piara answered, "Thank you for your kindness. I, too, am bereft. My friend and traveling companion only acted to protect me and responded to aggression. I don't understand much of what you've said. I met folk with nodules on their hands, but those nodules appeared when they witnessed... uh, their nodules were acquired. I traveled with seven companions from the Carcharian stronghold Doug-less, where I'd been held captive. One of Urquhart's ilk traveled before us. All my companions developed the little nodules... I did not. Our acquaintances' nodules increased in size over time. When death occurred, the little rocks left their host and reverted to their initial size. I have no idea how large the nodules might get in life. Different ilks seem to have different types of rocks. They are called graparbles by the newcomers."

Nila said, "I am a simple nurse. I employ methods passed down from the pale healer and Gray Matron. Everyone who witnessed the creation of the Mender's Tomb developed a nodule on their left hand. Since that time the nodules have been passed along and are present at birth. They do not increase in size and leave us at death. Experience taught us that the nodules merge if brought together. Merged nodules are inert. They will not grow if planted. However, if we place extruded gray pebbles with the remains of those who bore the nodules in the forest surrounding the Mender's Tomb, trees sprout from them. These trees produce purple fruits. You just ate one of them. The pits within the fruits are not seeds. Trees only grow from gray pebbles planted with the individual that bore the nodule that burst open in death and expressed the rock. The pits will not produce trees if planted. We use the pits in many remedies. Ground up purple pits was a major ingredient in the mixture that saved you from the Fawagy and Irukandji poison. This knowledge passed down from the Gray Matron and those who witnessed the creation of the tomb. We now have 12 nodules to plant. The Carcharian did have a nodule and lost a gray stone when he passed. But it's heavier than those that passed from our ilk. Inyra fears it. We all fear it. I tell you these things because Inyra seeks the truth. Please tell us everything. Inyra is a good sea elf. Also... I tell you because... I've seen your face before... any times."

Piara befuddled answered, "That's a lot to digest. I've never been to Graywood. All your folk stare at me. I'm accustomed to it. Yet, other than my greener color and the lack of a nodule on my hand I'm little different to you. Where have you seen my face? Were you in Doug-less or near the newcomers' stronghold Vydaelia?"

Nila answered, "I've never left the confines of Graywood. I have many responsibilities and perform roles passed down from my mother. I tend the Forest of Gray Trees and the gardens of the tomb. The tomb's door... bears an image of the Gray Matron. The image has your face... to every minute detail. But for your greenness... you could be the Gray Matron."

Piara replied, "My greenness is typical of sea elves, but not for the folk I've seen here. In fact I'm more like the person Clouse that I met in Vydaelia. I've never been to Graywood, but I've seen this place in my mind. I see images through the eyes of my ancestor. My mind's eye has seen a chamber that was special to my ancestor. I only recall of her that my kin said I looked like her, but she was sent from our home when her daughter, my great-great-grandmother was a child. I was seeking

answers to these visions. That's what drew me here. I followed a path…
I just sensed this was the way. But I didn't know how to gain entry to
Graywood. Otherwise Urquhart and I wouldn't have fallen into Inyra's
ambush. Urquhart was simply assisting me. Could this chamber that I
envision be the tomb of which you speak?"

Nila said, "Your answers may well lie within the tomb. As to its
contents, your guess is as good as mine. None have entered since it was
sealed by the Gray Matron. Legend holds the tomb contains secrets
and is a door to other realms. You should rest for the sake of the child
you carry. When Inyra returns, please tell him everything you have
told more."

Young Sabrina resumed her duties. With Fytch's passing the nurses
had only minor injuries to attend. Piara stretched. After effects of the
sea elves' poison included muscle soreness and fatigue. Had her mind
clouded as well?

For the first time she remembered the pendant she had carried. The
little direction finder had been invisible to Urquhart's eyes after she
placed it around her neck. She had awakened naked and the sea elves had
discovered the graparble she carried. The leader Inyra had chagrinned
over the death of the sea elf Giryn that had given up the little rock at
the time of his death. Her captors had searched her thoroughly. Had her
gravity saved her from molestation? She slapped her hand instinctively
to her chest. The artifact was indeed missing. She had felt its minimal
weight during the tide of the battle. Had she lost what the Dreamraider
had called a key to finding answers to questions about her abilities and
strange connection to her great-great-great grandmother? Had the gray-
green sea elves discovered the amulet? The little stone had reinforced her
innate sense of direction. Had the nefarious Dreamraider given her the
device to insure she'd either be killed on the desperate journey or wind
up in the custody of these oddly pigmented sea elfish blokes? Were these
sea elfish folk really her brethren?

Then her tortured mind's thought turned to Urquhart. He'd been
loyal to the end. He'd left a life of privilege through having four arms,
though his sea elf lineage held him back. Piara languished over her
allowing him to come with her, but knew he'd been right about the
hazards of her journey. Alone she'd never have made it past the sea
lion and boxjelly. Four young guards continued to watch her. She'd

only seen adult female sea elves brought captive to Doug-less. The four young males were quite attractive though not to the standards of the Wandmaker and the greenish Clouse. Piara scanned the room. The four were attentive. Rory's spear was scarcely an arm's length from her chest. There was a single exit from the well-lit room. She wasn't going anywhere. Piara fell back onto the soft covering of the bed and snuggled in the soft bedsheet.

CHAPTER 32

Gray Vale

Inyra watched the procession with Fytch's body exit the common area of the Graywood community and move toward the passageway that led to the area his folk called Gray Vale. 13 of his folk fell to the vicious Carcharian. Why had this green eastern sea elf led the four-armed monster to his home? He'd not experienced this much loss since his mother was taken by Carcharians while harvesting sea urchins and clams. Inyra had been a lad of 11 seasons when the raiders surprised the harvesters. Fortunately the raiders had not found the way to Gray Vale and the community Graywood. Inyra had followed the policies of his forebears and maintained isolation, including separation from their greener sea elfish folk. The Carcharians made off with their ill-gotten bounty. The Commandant at that time ordered the sea urchin and clam beds abandoned and the folk of Graywood never returned to the site of the raid, for the Carcharians were sure to return. The Carcharians had not fled toward the feared stronghold Doug-less. Instead they traveled toward the lesser Carcharian settlements to the north deeper into the underworld rocky recesses, where legend held another sea fed into the great sea. Inyra grew embittered and vowed to keep the way to Gray Vale safe and hidden. His bravest Squaddie Frayn maintained vigilance near the feared Doug-less and others kept vigil along the route to the northern Carcharian settlements and the Reed Creek delta. Inyra expanded the watch rooms in the rock walls and assured animalistic allies occupied the marshy that led from the sea toward his people's homes. The odd artifact that helped him hollow out the rock walls was passed down from the Gray Matron and pale healer. The scepter that he carried designated his leadership and served several functions.

Turning "rock to mud" was most valuable. Inyra did not understand the garbled phrases that activated the scepter's powers. Before he held the scepter for the first time he uttered the phrase **"Win Stone Church Chill."** Without so doing legend held the scepter struck down anyone unfortunate enough to grasp it. **"Wood row will son"** enabled him to soften and excavate stone. The mud so created had many uses in construction of dwellings and edifices. Uttering **"Lend dawn john son"** while holding the scepter produced light that far exceeded the lichen and if focused on an enemy's face blinded him long enough to facilitate escape. The scepter served as a weapon in its own right to deliver both blunt and stabbing blows. Muttering **"Eyes inn hour"** extended the scepter's adamantine blade and in effect changed it to a short sword. Inyra accepted the scepter from his predecessor. Legend held the Gray Matron and pale healer created the ornate scepter in the early days of Gray Vale. The tomb supposedly contained documents that elucidated the artifact's origin, but the edifice had been sealed since the Gray Matron's passing.

Commandant Inyra had to get more information from the invader. Her greenness enhanced her beauty. Her gravidity stood in his way. But safety of the realm took top priority. The greener folk of his ilk had ostracized and sent the Gray Matron away after all. Nurse Nila insisted he treat the prisoner gently. He agreed… for a time. However, if the she-elf didn't cooperate, all bets were off.

The dirge murmured by the folk carrying Fytch reached Inyra's ears, and fueled both his sadness and anger. He'd allowed the winsome wench rest and nourishment. As to her spawn… he doubted it was of benevolent parentage. Now Inyra had to put his anger and personal grief aside and perform his solemn duty as leader of Graywood and assure Fytch received his due honor and chance to live on in the gray forest. He'd been unable to do so for noble Giryn.

******* Carcharian!

Inyra left Liani in charge of the watch and supervising the guards and doubled the number of guards peering through murder holes looking onto the inlet where Urquhart had smote the fawagy. The animal had fended off jellyfish, Boxjellies, Oglethorpes, Chocolights, and many other trespassers. The four-armed Carcharian had proven too much a foe.

Inyra's command center had been painstakingly hewn from the hard stone with the aid of the scepter the Graywood elves called UK. The moniker UK stuck for the device. It was another tidbit passed down from the Gray Matron. Gray-green sea elves always occupied the command area and watched the sea. The outcropping in the stone extended such that Inyra's charges could peer through murder holes and observe 270 degrees. The guards had watched Urquhart and Piara from the time the pair first stepped from the sea. The rear of the chamber curved back from the inlet and allowed view of the main settlement Graywood and its common area.

Nurse Nila had completed preparations.

The Commandant now descended stairs hewn from the stone and passed along a winding narrow corridor intentionally left barely wider than the breadth and height of a mature sea elf. The passage twisted several times. Each turn passed a hidden cubicle that contained an armed sea elf. The passage ended in a dead end. Inyra extended the scepter, touched the wall eight times, and said, **"Lend dawn john son."** The block blocking the passage slid nigh silently aside and allowed the commandant to enter the common area of Graywood. The door closed behind him. An ever-present guard stood near the door, which was hidden in the rock wall. Entering from the Graywood side did not require the scepter, only knowing the location of the door and the key, which was a single stone, set in the gray soil. Each change of the guard carried its instructions to open the door by touching the leaning stone a number of times. As Inyra passed a young relief guard touched the leaning stone eight times and then walked to the imperceptible door and touched it. The youth returned to the leaning stone and touched it once. The door opened and allowed him passage.

Sadness gripped the community. Inyra walked through the common area and joined Nurse Nila. Agarn led the contingent bearing the wrapped remains of Fytch. The ceiling high over the community was yellow from the large concentration of luminescent lichen. Its height was far beyond the reach of a finely made self-bow. Inyra gently touched Fytch's body and walked to the heads of the column. The bearers and followers continued to sing mournfully as the column proceed through the common area and past many little abodes. They traveled onto a rocky path that ended in stairs at the end of the common area and ascended the stairs. Inyra and Nila walked at the head of the procession, followed by the bearers, and the gathered community who walked five abreast. The wide stone path meandered through 200 paces of stone and finally exited onto an open area, which widened before them. Looking above one saw no ceiling, only grayness with occasional points of light. The ground changed from stone to soft gray soil. Green foliage changed to deep gray leaves. Taller trees and bushes rimmed the entire roughly circular area, but a valley filled with gray trees made up the greatest part of Gray Vale. A hill in the center of the valley obscured the far side of the circular vale. Gray plush grass covered a rim that extended several paces. At the edge of the gray moss, the terrain inclined gently at about fifteen degrees for thirty paces and reached the floor. The floor of Gray Vale extended several hundred paces, rose gently in several areas, and circled the central knoll. A grassy upslope began where the floor ended and extended fifty or so paces to the top of the central hill. Many small rivulets coursed through the landscape. A gentle breeze crisscrossed the surprisingly warm valley. Overhead deep blueness intermingled with ever-present gray light. The gray light mimicked the approximation of Andreas. Potting soil filled Gray Vale. Lichen did not provide illumination in Gray Vale, and the overall illumination exceeded the great cavern with the sea.

An edifice sat upon a hillock in the center of Gray Vale. Atop the hillock 13 gray trees circled the eight sided building. Stands of gray trees were scattered about the Vale. 12 soft mounds filled the area at the fringe of the forest. The trees bore purple and gray leaves and purple fruits reminiscent of the fruit served Piara in the infirmary and rather similar to enhancing root tubers, though these fruits grew on the trees.

A Stone Circle rested upon the gray grasses. The circle had five small stones and one large alignment stone. The huge monolith was a rectangular slab and had been arranged radially to the circle and was aligned with the NE-SW circle axis. It totally dominated the site and sat very close to the tiny circle of five stones, and the whole site was perched on a little terrace halfway up the hillside. The five slab-like stones of the ring were tangentially placed.

Inyra and Nila walked to the area with the 12 fresh graves. Sea elves had laboriously opened an area one Yardley pace deep in the gray potting soil. Nila and Inyra climbed into the shallow pit. Bearers gently lowered Fytch's wrapped body into the open grave. Inyra place the little gray stone on Fytch's body, covered the stone with gray leaves, touched the body with the scepter UK, and muttered, **"Lend dawn john son."** Brilliant light filled the grave and enhanced the light in the cavern. A small blue flame erupted in the leaves around the little stone. The flame produced no heat.

Nurse Nila sprinkled ground up pits over Fytch's body. Slowly the blue flame extended over the wrapped corpse. Little rivulets of purple smoke rose from the grave. Inyra and Nila stepped out of the grave. Sea elves gathered around the grave and sang. The blue flames slowly consumed the body and left in its stead purplish gray ashes. Inyra grasped UK and again uttered **"Lend dawn john son."** The light faded and blue flames extinguished. He then said **"Wood row will son"** and pushed a bit of gray soil on the ashes. The little stone emitted intense gray light. The gathered community covered the stone and filled the gray with gray potting soil.

Nila and Inyra left the grave and walked up a winding path toward the octagonal structure on the hill. Halfway up the duo passed the stone circle. Inyra touched each of the five small stones once and the large stone five times. Nila followed his lead. Then they continued on to the crest of the hill. The black stone of the tomb stood out against the grayness of Gray Vale. Inyra looked upon the sealed doors that made up one of the edifice's eight sides. The door faced the large stone and circle of five smaller stones. The sea elfish Commandant said, "Remarkable! But for her youth and the greenness of her skin, the image on the door perfectly reflects the prisoner."

A beautiful sea elf's image occupied much of the door. The strikingly detailed image's eyes stared right through the observer and peered into his essence.

Nila remarked, "The resemblance is uncanny. When the Gray Matron came to Gray Vale and founded Graywood, she was older than the female we have encountered. The likeness is said to represent her youth. We've long separated from our greener ilk. How did this Piara find us? I've examined the items she carried including the unguents and balms in her pack. They'd almost pass for the medicines I use."

Inyra took a deep breath and said, "She carried more than medicine that mimics our goods. There are more similarities. Look at the Gray Matron's neck."

Nila said, "Of course the Gray Matron wears the amulet that stories passed down say she was never without. When she lived it was said it disappeared from sight when she placed it around her neck. I examined Piara. She wore no jewelry when Liani brought her to me. She had no such amulet."

Inyra answered, "In fact she did. Agarn searched the marsh after the battle with the four-armed Carcharian ended and found this amulet. Liani and I watched her walking with the four-arm before the battle. The necklace was not visible."

The Commandant produced the Twin Stone and its purple thread. The Twin Stone changed from gray to deep purple and emitted purple auras. The engraved amulet around the figure's neck also changed to purple and emitted similar purple hues. Auras surrounded Inyra. He felt chilled and the urge to place the amulet around his neck. He resisted the impulse and said, "We should go. I must interrogate Piara."

Nila asked, "Should I carry the amulet? I've tended the gray forest and tomb all my adult life and never seen the amulet in the figure change. Perhaps Piara comes to us for a reason."

Inyra responded, "But what are her reasons for coming to Gray Vale?"

CHAPTER 33

Interrogation

Young Sabrina gently tapped on Piara's shoulder and said, "Wake up! Commandant Inyra will return shortly."

Piara sat up and straightened her green hair. Adric, Turlough, Horton, and Rory remained near her bed with arms at ready. Nurse Nila sat by the door. Soon Commandant Inyra entered with Liana, Agarn, and Lieutenant Dain. Inyra's face maintained its stern look.

The Commandant of Graywood began, "You've enjoyed our kindness, Piara of Elder Ridge, if that is your name. You've had nourishment and time to rest. Now I need answers. More importantly, how'd you come to this place?"

Piara answered, "I seek answers to questions that have vexed me and hope to discover the home of my ancestor."

Inyra followed, "How'd you find us? Does the monarch of Doug-less know of our settlement?"

Piara replied, "The king of Doug-less only wants to see me and all who traveled with me dead."

Inyra persisted, "Hard to believe! Tell me of the Carcharian?"

Piara tentatively asked, "His name is Urquhart, and he is my guardian. Is he really dead?"

Inyra said icily, "Yes. He killed 13 of my people. He feeds the scavengers in the sea."

Piara sobbed, "You just threw him in the sea."

Inyra said, "Yes. You still have many questions to answer and may yet share the Carcharian's fate."

Piara said, "I'll say no more now. Please leave me to grieve."

The gray-green Commandant angrily responded, "That's not going to happen! The fawagy's poison should have killed him! How'd you save him? I need answers!"

Piara stared directly into his yellow-green eyes and returned, "So do I! We showed no aggression on the island. Why'd your Squaddie Giryn attack us?"

Inyra said, "I'd have attacked a Carcharian too. I'm weary of waiting! How did you find this place? Why are you here?"

Piara fought tears and evasively answered, "Urquhart was my loyal friend and defender. I was taken from my family by Carcharians. Urquhart's mother was sea elfish! Physically he was Carcharian, but he had a good heart!"

Inyra scoffed, "I'm aware of Carcharian society. Compassion is not among their traits."

Piara again tangentially said, "Half breeds are treated poorly. Being born with four arms outweighs this to an extent, but he was always an outsider. I lived among them many years. I led a group of outcasts away from Doug-less. Urquhart followed me."

Inyra said, "Where are your mates?"

Piara insisted, "Urquhart and I traveled alone. It's a long story."

Inyra answered, "Tell me!"

Piara remembered Nurse Nila's plea and relented, "All right! I was espoused to the King of Doug-less and bore him a daughter. My daughter found love, but she was betrothed to one of the king's lecherous honchos. The King sent her beloved on a quest and he was thought lost. Opportunity presented itself to leave Doug-less. The small group that accompanied me faced ongoing degradation and ridicule. All were loyal to me. We received word that my daughter's much-loved Gruusch still lived, We sought my daughter's love and in so doing encountered the newcomers."

Inyra asked, "Do you carry another spawn of the King of Doug-less?"

Piara said, "No."

Inyra persisted, "Who sired your spawn? The Carcharian?"

Piara somberly answered, "No."

Inyra asked, "Why'd you leave your 'newcomer' friends?"

Piara answered, "Circumstances dictated that I leave."

Inyra said, "I imagine the lump in your belly had something to do with your leaving."

Piara answered, "I won't lie. It did. But I've long been driven to learn of my heritage. I learned things during my time with the newcomers that spurred me to action."

Inyra said, "You carried medicines nigh indistinguishable from Nurse Nila's creations. You understand our dialect. I'm told these newcomers foment Magick. Are you a sorceress?"

Piara began, "To the contrary... I resist Magick. I've always had gifts with language and alchemy. Creating potions and unguents is second nature for me. I have a connection with my ancestor, my great, great, great grandmother. I've recently encountered a Mender among the newcomers. He's given me some insight, but I think he knew more than he told. The lore of my people speaks of one of the pale folk. Purportedly Duoths had injured the pale wanderer and my great, great, great, great grandparents nursed him back to health...for a time. Through circumstances known only to my *great, great, great, great grandmother* and *great, great, great, great* grandfather, my *great, great, great grandmother* came into the world *different*. Many of the recipes used in my elixirs and unguents are attributed to the pale traveler. I *see* the recipes through her eyes. Unless they fall victim to predation sea elves oft enjoy full long lives, but my *great, great, great grandmother* lived an extraordinarily long life. She was accused of sorcery, witchcraft, and tomfoolery. I see her face in my inner thoughts and bear striking resemblance to her. I remember none of my family save her, and I never met her. She died long before I was born. Fisher postulated my resistance to Magick stems from my great, great, great grandmother. I see ... some of her thoughts. It's as though I've shared some of her experiences. She gave me more than her looks."

Inyra lowered his guard and said, "You imply you are descended from the Gray Matron. You are green! She was grayed! We are grayed! We of Graywood are her progeny. You are clearly of western ilk. Your greenness betrays you."

Piara said, "I readily admit that I was taken from the sea elf village Elder Ridge. My folk lived in the shadow of Doug-less and foolishly thought we could evade the Carcharians. This place... I've seen the gray valley in my mind's eye many times. I've seen it through her eyes, but I don't know her. Tell me of my great, great, great grandmother. Please!"

Inyra sighed and continued, "If you are truly descended from the Gray Matron, you should have announced your arrival. You may still be an elaborate ruse."

Piara said, "All right then! Beyond the area that contains your housing and living areas there is a wide valley with a hillock in its center. Halfway up the hill there is a stone circle with five small stones and a larger stone. An edifice made of coal black stone sits upon the hillock. 13 gray trees encircle the edifice. Gray grass covers the ground and an ever-growing stand of gray trees cover the area. There is no sky over head, only fathomless grayness. From time to time the grayness is accentuated and wondrous things occur. The structure on the hill is the final resting place of one very dear to my ancestor."

Inyra gasped, "How could you know these things? Are you a mind reader?"

Piara answered, "Goodness, no! I see through my great-great-great grandmother's eyes. I came seeking knowledge of her. Do you still doubt my words?"

Inyra grimaced and said, "It's a trick!"

Piara continued, "I'll describe the inner works of the tomb. The tomb is bigger on the inside. Both time and space are distorted. Walls between the doors bear images of my great-great-great grandmother and one who looks remarkably like the fellow Fisher that I met in Vydaelia... only the bloke in the tomb's image is paler... On three walls there are identical doors. These doors are not visible from the outside. Two sarcophagi sit near the wall opposite the three doors. They are made of black stone, like the walls and doors. The sarcophagus on the right had an open lid and was empty long after the one on the left was closed. A simple black rod sits on the sarcophagus on the left. A little piece of black stone sits by the rod. A huge stone called heel stone dominates the area of the tomb opposite the sarcophagi. The heel stone is a single block of sarsen stone. It is sub-rectangular, with a minimum thickness of 2.4 meters. A meter is 39.37 inchworm lengths. It rises to a tapered top 4.7 meters high. A further 1.3 meters is buried in the ground. Gray soil makes up the floor of the tomb. The heel stone sits 77.4 meters from the sarcophagi and is nearly 27 degrees from the vertical. Its overall girth is 7.6 meters. It weighs 35 tons. A ton is... very heavy! The heel stone is the means to exit the tomb. I'm not sure how... it works though."

Intra dumbfounded asked, "How can you know this! *I* don't know this! We can't enter the tomb."

Piara said, "Really? The stone circle on the hillock is the key. The circle has five small stones and one large alignment stone. The huge monolith is a rectangular slab. It has been arranged radially to the circle and is aligned with the NE-SW circle axis. It totally dominates the site and sits very close to the tiny circle of five stones, and the whole site is perched on a little terrace halfway up the hillside. The five slab-like stones of the ring are tangentially placed. To enter the tomb... one stands in the center of the circle. Go and touch the monolith, then one of the little stones. Then go touch the monolith twice. Then touch another stone thrice. Next return to the monolith and touch the big stone five times, followed by touching a third little stone eight times. Next it's back to the monolith to touch it thirteen times. Then it's to the fourth stone twenty-one times. Go the monolith again and touch it thirty-four times. Lastly go to the final stone and touch it fifty-five times. Stand in the center of the stone circle. After eighty-nine heartbeats... you are carried into the tomb and stand on the gray circle within it."

Inyra mumbled, "But... how... we haven't been able... are you sure? Why should I believe you?"

Piara said forcefully, "I've seen this image many times in my thoughts. Does this not describe the inside of the tomb? Do you still doubt my words?"

Inyra stared at Piara and said, "I have never seen the inside of the tomb. In fact, no one had since the Gray Matron's passing. But your description of Gray Vale is spot on! I..."

Piara followed, "Fragmented memories flash through my mind like pieces of a puzzle that I can't assemble...because pieces are missing. I can't tie them together. I mean you no harm. Please trust me."

Inyra said, "I must believe you. You should have let us know you were coming! We almost killed you! If you want to see your great-great-great grandmother, gaze into a looking glass. You bear a striking resemblance to our matriarch. Every story of her paints a picture of the person sitting before me."

Piara said, "I've told you all I know. Please tell me about my ancestor."

Inyra said, "Everyone who knew the Gray Matron is long dead. My parents relayed stories to me that passed down from my grandparents, great-grandparents, and great-great-grandparents. The Gray Matron arrived in Gray Vale touched by grayness. She brought life to the barren valley and founded Graywood. The pale healer named Lou Nester taught her many things. By Magick she created the scepter I now hold. UK became an heirloom of the fledgling community. A small contingent of loyal sea elves arrived with Lou Nester and the Gray Matron, but the Matron left most of her family behind. After her arrival she welcomed homeless sea elves and Graywood grew. Her physical description is common knowledge in this realm. Many sought her healing skills. When you arrived with the Carcharian, I thought you were likely a shape changer. It made sense for a shape changer to mimic The Gray Matron's appearance to gain entry to our home. That's why we suspected you of malfeasance. I'll tell you what I know of the Gray Matron, whose name was Alexandrina. We seldom use her name out of reverence. To all she was the Gray Matron. Her parents aided and befriended Mender Lou Nester, who had traveled to our realm in search of a dark place to continue his line. I know little of Menders, but the stories of the gray lady's parents and the Mender are true. Were they your great-great-great-great grandparents? I don't know. They were green and of the western realm. The Gray Matron's parents found the Mender in a bad way and took him in and helped him fulfill his quest. I can't confirm the Duoths' involvement in his misery. Some say Carcharians put the Mender in a bad way. Others say he ran afoul of a great sea beast. Bottom line was he was in a bad way. A Samaritan dropped him on your ancestors' doorstep. One story holds the gray matron's mother carried her at the time and came into contact with the Mender's essence. By whatever means the Gray Matron came into the world different. She was driven by curiosity and became the Mender's protégé. She had a more subdued color, like greenness diluted by the Mender's paleness. Later she looked upon the surface of the World of the Three Suns and stood in the gray light. This changed her further. She developed a nodule in her left hand and passed this trait to her progeny."

Piara asked, "Surface? On the other side of the sea the settlers talk of a surface world. The Wandmaker is their leader. He creates exceptional wands, one of which is called USA and looks quite like your scepter UK. The settlers have nodules in their hands, at least most do. Theirs appear when exposed to the Wandmaker's ceremonies and get larger in later rituals. Yours are all the same. Don't they get larger?"

Inyra said, "No. We are born with them. They do not change. They are with us until we die."

Piara replied, "That happens to the newcomers as well. Why don't you remove them?"

Inyra said, "We are told to leave them in place. Removing them might be risky. We're also told to keep them apart lest they merge. When they extrude from our bodies at death, we plant them with their bearer in the gray forest in Gray Vale. They produce robust trees that yield edible fruits."

Piara added, "The newcomers are still learning about their realm and traits. They speak of a surface world. Are we indeed beneath their home?"

Inyra said, "I know only these environs. I fear these newcomers, who allow Carcharians to live among them! Are they allied to Doug-less?"

Piara quickly said, "No!"

Inyra continued, "You'll have to tell me more of these settlers. I'm told the Matron's journal says we're more parallel than beneath the surface. I'm not exactly sure what she meant. It's complicated. Legend holds special doors lead to other realms. These doors are not unlocked by keys. It requires special powers to access them. This lore has passed down through our forebears."

Piara asked, "How'd the first Mender get to our realm?"

Inyra responded, "Portals to the World of the Three Suns is accessible when the third sun draws near and bathes the land with its gray light. Beyond that the knowledge is beyond me. Lou Nester arrived during a time when the gray sun drew near the land and must have found such a portal. Alexandrina's parents led the Mender Lou Nester to Gray Vale and built a small stone structure atop the hillock in Gray Vale. Alexandrina was born in Gray Vale. She lacked the greenness of her parents and arrived with a little nodule on her left hand. She and her parents lived with the Mender in Gray Vale for some time. Lou Nester entered the structure and remained secluded within its rocky walls for several seasons. There are no records. The Mender was old and feeble. Legend holds there was even a second Mender for a brief time. The young Gray Matron used things she'd learned from the Menders. Eventually she and her parents returned to their home. Shortly thereafter Carcharians attacked and killed both her parents. Heartbroken she sought and found the portal to the surface world. Grayness opened the portal. Standing in the gray light changed her. Alexandrina returned to her western home, but many feared her. She was accused of many things. She left her home settlement with her two of her children and some loyal to her. Alexandrina's life-mate and older daughter, your great-great grandmother, remained in the settlement. Alexandrina's progeny who lived in her native settlement did not possess little nodules, whilst everyone born here arrives in the world with a nodule. The Gray Matron Alexandrina was my great-great-great grandmother."

Piara tried to digest the wealth of information and managed, "What... what happened to her? My vision only shows me fragments of her life. Alexandrina's life...."

Inyra continued, "She had lived long beyond our usual lifespan. She had lost her parents to Carcharians, her life-mate to peer pressure, and her older daughter to whatever influenced her to stay behind. She told matrons of many of her recipes and recorded others in text. Alexandrina's parents supervised the construction of the eight sided tomb. The black stone that composed the structure is referred to as Stone of Ooranth. The tomb was built around the Mender Lou Nester's resting place. Alexandrina grew weaker and entered the chamber and sealed the door. The Stone Circle sits near the tomb. It's about half way up the hillock."

Piara asked, "Who built the Stone Circle?"

Inyra answered, "Don't know!"

Piara said, "The visions that enter my mind describe the inner tomb. Are they accurate?"

Inyra replied, "Don't know. We've been unable to open the tomb. Those who have tried have met with injury. We can't enter the tomb. Touching the stones in the circle 'awakens' the Gray Matron's image on the door."

Piara said, "I can see much of what you are telling me. It's like... my mind is assembling pieces of a psychic puzzle. Pieces are falling into their proper place. You touch each small stone once and the bigger stone five times to produce the image on the door."

Inyra said, "You're right!"

Piara replied, "I don't make it a habit to guess."

Inyra said, "You must be at least part Mender."

Piara replied, "Fisher used the term Menderish."

Inyra said, "I suppose I'm really just partially sea elfish. Three generations now separate us from the inhabitants of the settlement from which Alexandrina came. We have little contact. That's fine. They live closer to the Carcharians."

Piara asked, "May I see this tomb?"

Inyra answered, "In time. You must recover... and prove your intentions are well-meaning. Defense of Graywood is my first and foremost concern."

Piara said, "I'm gaining strength."

Inyra cautioned, "You were injured by the arrow and subjected to the effects of the poisons."

Piara noted, "You said poisons."

Inyra said, "Well, yes, we combine fawagy oils with ground Irukandji. Our antidote was untested... until you survived. I guess fawagy excrement is effective. The giant frogs eat the little jellyfish and, shall we say, process them."

Piara said, "You gave me Fawagy poop? I shouldn't be surprised. Duoth dropping soup heals many maladies."

Inyra said, "Nila's remedy contains many ingredients. The recipe for the antidote is a modified version of Mender's panacea. The Gray Matron passed the recipe to our nurses. Sabrina will take you to quarters. Mind you, Horton, Rory, Adric, and Turlough will keep watch over you. Don't try anything. You still have to earn my trust."

Piara sighed and agreed. Inyra and his subordinates left the infirmary. Young Sabrina and Nurse Nila gave Piara robes and sandals. Sabrina led Piara to a small abode with pleasant furnishings.

CHAPTER 34

Dreamy Visitor in Graywood

Amica Carmisino in Good Witch guise moaned, "Bugger! I'm not up for a trip."

Kirrie stared toward the forest and watched a rambling bramble bush chase down an unfortunate coati-Tuesday. The ring-tailed possum-like beast tarried too long at the forest edge and the motile bramble bush impaled it with sharp thorns and now enjoyed a leisurely feast. The ex-Teacher said, "What's up? I'd be up for another journey."

The Dreamraider answered, "That's the spirit! Unfortunately I'll have to do this one. I can't give you a focal point. That fool sea elf has gotten in a jam. I just got to wait till she goes to sleep."

Ø ∞ Ø

Piara sat down on the little cot and sank into the soft cushion. A pleasant amount of light filled the room in the cheery little cottage in Graywood. Sabrina placed fresh sea biscuits, Seabee honey, and refreshing aloe juice on a little table by the bed. The nurse's aide pulled shades closed and blocked out a bit of the outside light. Piara marveled at the amount of illumination in Graywood, given that few algae were present in the fathomless gray sky. Young Sabrina left her, but the four guards Adric, Rory, Turlough, and Horton remained positioned outside the little cottage. Piara walked over to the open door and teased, "You must think I'm dangerous. Come inside and chat for a while."

Turlough crisply replied, "No, lady. Our mission is to guard you. Commandant Inyra ordered us to stay by your side. You are beautiful, but we must keep to ourselves."

Piara closed the door and returned to the bed. She munched on the victuals left by Sabrina. She'd walled Urquhart's death from her mind as much and long as she could and lay down and sobbed. She rolled over onto her back. The soreness in her shoulder remained. Her unborn child's kicking reassured her. The displaced queen and elder closed her eyes. After a time sleep came. Immediately she dreamed of times in Doug-less with Starra whilst under the guard of the stalwart four-armed Urquhart. Then redness entered her mind's dreaming eye.

Wisps…
Threads…
Threads of Magick…
Threads of fate…
Threads of time…
Threads connecting worlds …
Dreams connecting worlds …
Dreams of Magick…
The Magick of Dreams…
Magick connecting dreams…
Magick connecting worlds…
Dream raiders…
Elf pressure…
Albtraum…
Albträume, elf dreams, nightmares…

Ǿ ∞ Ǿ

The Good Witch stood before her with her arms crossed and frown on her face.

Piara muttered, "Not again. I left Vydaelia. You're free to pursue the Wandmaker. What more do you want?"

The Dreamraider said, "I'm just checking in. Looks like you've had a spot of trouble."

Piara said, "My friend and ally is dead, you *****! I'm in the hands of these dingy sea elves. I don't know whether they plan to kill me or not. I came here with questions, but I'm answering more than I'm asking."

Amica glibly quipped, "That's usually what happens when you show up unannounced with someone's sworn enemy. I've been through it."

Piara said, "So much for my lot! Why have you invaded my sleep?"

Amica answered, "I'm impressed you made it to Graywood. Sorry about Urquhart. He was a fine specimen. I had more reasons than jealousy to send you away."

Piara said, "Graywood is very familiar to me. I've seen it through another's eyes. I've seen vague visions of the gray valley and stone circle that sits halfway up the hillock in its center. I've visualized the inside of the tomb. I know more about it than the Commandant."

Amica said, "I've not well versed on Menders, but I'd say you have a tangential connection to the collective consciousness they talk about. You had more in common with Fisher and Clouse than any other person in Vydaelia. You are also a ***** and *****, but that's a separate issue! Menders have disrupted my Master's plans before."

Piara asked, "What do you mean? Master?"

Amica said, "My Master has been interested in this sunken sea world for some time. The Mender Lou Nester treated with the Master for potting soil and a dark place. The Master has a knack at paving the way."

Piara interrupted, "Our world is filled with dark places. In fact there are more dark places than light. Why'd you put soil in pots?"

Amica answered, "Potting soil! It's a special kind of dirt Menders need to... you know... do what you and the Wandmaker did."

Piara quickly interjected, "And what you and the Wandmaker did. I've seen into the Wandmaker's mind!"

Amice added, "And while we're at it, what the Wandmaker and his orange-haired ***** did!"

Piara said, "I get it! Menders need potting soil to procreate."

Amica said, "I'm not sure it's that simple. At any rate Gray Vale is filled with the stuff. Just like the Onyum Patch in Vydaelia. The dirt doesn't necessarily have to go in a pot. Lou Nester was to provide a service for the Master after his confinement, but the pale healer was gravely injured. Two sea elves saved his sorry ***. At least for a time... Edward and Victoria nursed the Mender back to health and sheltered him in their abode in your sea elf village Elder Ridge. The sea elves gave something of themselves to save him. Victoria was with child. Lou Nester lived for a time in Elder Ridge, but the nodule he bore on his left hand grew larger and drove him to confinement. Edward and Victoria led him to Gray Vale. Intense grayness enveloped the valley. A circle of gray stone appeared among the five stones of the stone circle that sat on the hillock. A black rod and chuck of black stone appeared in the center of the circle. These were called the rod and stone of Ooranth. While Grayness enveloped the vale Victoria's time to deliver came and her daughter was born in Gray Vale. Lou Nester assisted in the complicated delivery of the child. The Mender saved the child by giving her his breath and repaid his debt to the sea elves. The child drew her first breath in the deep gray light and became a sister of grayness. The babe became a Menderish sea elf. Alexandrina had graying of her skin and a tiny nodule on her little left hand.

"Lou Nester grew weaker. Edward and Victoria used the rod and stone to construct a small structure upon the central hillock."

Piara asked, "How'd they build something from a single stone?"

Amica continued, "Lou Nester directed Edward and Victoria to use the rod and stone of Ooranth to create building blocks. Though growing weaker the Mender attended little Alexandrina while her parents worked. Touching the small stone with the cylindrical rod and saying **"Jams Gar Field"** replicated the block. Running the rod over the newly formed replicate reshaped it. Edward and Victoria used the blocks to create a small structure with a potting soil floor. They left an entryway large enough for the Mender to enter. Lou Nester crawled inside whilst intense grayness still bathed the Vale. The Mender told his helpers the length of his confinement was undefined and ended with the return of the increased grayness. Edward closed the chamber at the Mender's behest. Edward, Victoria, and Alexandrina lived in Gray Vale whilst Lou Nester was confined. After three years intense gray light returned. The structure opened. Lou Nester and a second fully grown Mender emerged. Whilst the gray light concentrated on Gray Vale, a number of Xennic Stones gathered around the Menders and your forebears. Four score and eight Xennic stones now rotate around the central sphere in the geodesic dome in Vydaelia. Little Alexandrina created the scepter UK with the help of four Xennic Stones. The second Mender left after a season and returned to the World of the Three Suns. Menders share collective consciousness. The Mender Fisher who travels with the Wandmaker sees the site of Lou Nester's confinement in his mind, but he is not privy to knowledge of a route to it.

"Lou Nester's earlier injuries and the ordeal of confinement weakened him. Tirelessly Edward and Victoria worked at creating blocks and constructed an octagonal structure on the hillock. When the structure was completed, Lou Nester entered and the others closed the door behind him. Edward, Victoria, and Alexandrina returned to Elder Ridge. Young Alexandrina differed from other youths. She tinkered with potions and unguents. The Master's interest waned after the Mender's death, but I kept an eye on the young sea elf. I visited Alexandrina in her dreams and left her a Twin Stone. I kept its sister. The second Twin Stone still rests with her. You carried its twin. Events brought the Master's attention back to this realm. My ties to your great-great-great grandmother Alexandrina led me to you and your daughter Starra. The Wandmaker's party will need all the help they can get. I selected Gruusch as bait for you through your daughter. Plan was working pretty well. I hadn't counted on the triskaidekapod, Giant Amebus, Duoths, and your tryst with the Wandmaker. You are more of a ***** and ***** than I'd counted on.

"Carcharians raided Elder Ridge and killed Alexandrina's parents. Little Alexandrina's differences isolated her. Her community ostracized and belittled her. She spent more time alone and explored catacombs in the walls beyond Doug-less. She found her way to the World of the Three Suns and stood in the grayness. Shunning in Elder Ridge grew. Alexandrina and those loyal to her returned to Gray Vale. Her life mate Albert and spawn, including your great-great grandmother Helena, stayed in Elder Ridge. Two daughters Alice and Louise accompanied her. Alexandrina used the scepter UK and the rod and stone of Ooranth to create Graywood. Most sea elves are wimps. The folk of Graywood are stronger. The gray soil, trees, and light strengthen the folk who live there. They could be valuable allies for the Wandmaker's troupe."

Piara said, "I have little memory of my mother's touch. My great-great grandmother Helena did not follow her mother Alexandrina to Gray Vale. Were my mother, grandmother, and great grandmother like me?"

The Dreamraider shrugged, "I don't even know their names. The folk of Elder Ridge considered the Menderish traits an affliction. Your mother, grandmother, and great grandmother were not ostracized. It would seem the Menderish traits skipped three generations and then found a home in you."

Piara said, "Why didn't you tell me in Vydaelia?"

Amica answered glibly, "I'm not beholding to you. This knowledge will help you deal with your current situation."

Piara asked, "Why not just get me out of here?"

Amica answered, "Not in the cards. Tell me what you know... or see in your mind."

Piara relayed her visions of the inner tomb, the means of entering it, and Inyra's detailed story of her ancestor.

The Dreamraider said, "Commandant Inyra's story of Graywood is accurate. The Gray Matron, as they called Alexandrina supervised the final construction of the tomb. She sealed the tomb after entering it. The accuracy of your vision impresses me. Your visions of getting in and out... may be correct. The inner tomb does contain a heel stone. It's identical to the one... never mind. I forget you haven't been to Stonehenge. I've given you some pointers, but I've been out of the loop for a long time. I don't know the secrets of the tomb. You've got work to do. Keep safe the Twin Stone."

Piara asked, "What price? I still ponder... why are you telling me these things? Why should you want to help me at all?"

Amica answered, "I am a Samaritan. And... the Wandmaker's crew will need all the help they can get."

Piara said, "I'm afraid I won't be much help to you. I doubt I'll ever be welcomed in Vydaelia."

Odd feelings gripped the Dreamraider. Twinges of pain welled up in her lower abdomen. Fiery red perspiration made its way through her pores and dripped to the ground. She struggled to maintain her Good Witch visage in the dream. Further instruction would have to wait. The sea elf would have to prove worthy.

Amica said, "Might be true for both of us... you have found your ancestor's stamping grounds. I must be going now. There's a soft bed calling my name."

Blueness surrounded the Dreamraider and she faded from Piara's dream.

CHAPTER 35

Inyra and Piara

Sabrina gently awakened Piara. The displaced queen of Doug-less sat up on the bed. Sabrina had brought fresh fruit and dried fish. Outside the door only one unarmed young gray-green sea elf nonchalantly looked around.

Piara asked, "Where are my guards?"

Sabrina answered, "Commandant Inyra dismissed them. He's chosen to trust you."

Piara said, "Suppose I'm not so dangerous now."

Sabrina said, "No other Carcharians have appeared. None of us understand why you'd willingly travel with one. What happens if he gets hungry?"

Piara stopped trying to explain her relationship with Urquhart. Most efforts to do so had been counterproductive. She dismissed Sabrina and munched on her breakfast. Soon Commandant Inyra arrived. Nurse Nila's son Liani was tagging along. After exchanging pleasantries, Inyra and Liani led Piara along a path that ascended the rocky cavern wall to the east. The winding path was indiscernible from the fields below and scarcely wide enough for one sure-footed sea elf to pass. It provided a more direct route to Gray Vale than that taken by the procession for Fytch. The gray valley appeared as it had in her vision. The central hillock was bathed in brighter grayness than the rest of the valley. The stone circle sat exactly as she had envisioned halfway up the hill. The top of the hill was dominated by the eight sided obsidian edifice. Thirteen remarkably similar gray-leaved trees encircled the edifice. Gray grasses flourished in the valley and exposed areas of rich gray soil poked through. Stands of gray trees with gray to purple leaves and purplish fruits grew throughout the area. Overhead she saw no ceiling… just grayness. The air was remarkably fresh and little breezes crisscrossed the valley as they descended along the path. 13 fresh grave mounds were orderly arranged near the fringe of the forest.

Inyra said to Piara, "The elders criticized me for furthering our isolation. My great-great grandfather abandoned our ancestral home in the moors and moved everyone into Gray Vale. How many times did I hear 'sea elves were not meant to live within rocks'? But Carcharians don't look for us in the walls of the cavern. Our numbers have grown. To feed my people we have been forced to pursue farming and fishing outside the confines of Gray Vale. It was my mother's bane. She was taken away by Carcharians whilst tending our people's needs for food. After this devastating raid my father ended our harvesting in the sea beds that she was taken from. Now I send my stalwarts into the wilds of the sea to cultivate. Giryn lost his life while performing assigned tasks. I have your Carcharian friend to thank for his loss as well as the loss of 12 others. The mounds you see in the foreground are Giryn, Fytch, and the others' resting places. In death they will further our community's needs by increasing the growth of the gray forest. The gray trees bear nutritious fruits with pits that have medicinal qualities. You're probably alive because of this medicine and Nurse Nila's skills at concocting antidotes."

Piara said, "The colors in the valley are so subdued, yet it's beautiful. I've seen this in my mind many times. The black tomb sits on the hill exactly as I've seen it with the stone circle halfway up the hillside. The walls are bare. I look forward to looking upon the image of my ancestor."

Inyra reiterated, "Touching the small stones once and the larger stone five times produces the image."

Piara calmly answered, "Yes. So I've seen in my mind's eye."

CHAPTER 36

Fishtrap

The Mountain Giant Guppie and his old cave warg Fenrir entered the realm through a giant-sized secret door at a point halfway between Doug-less and the newcomers' fortress. As did his grandfather and father before him Guppie kept the entry secret. Only the Mountain Giant knew the means to identify and enter through the door. King Lunniedale of Doug-less had requested Guppie petition his ruler for forces to ally with the Carcharians against the newcomers. Truth be known... Guppie could not bring additional Mountain Giants. He kept secrets from his Carcharian ally. It was forbidden for Mountain Giants to possess items of Magick. Guppie's family had long known it was just an old matron's tale. Fenrir wore a collar made of mooler hide and decorated with a pink stone. The stone was an Amulet of Protection which enabled the giant to pass through the gate between their land and the underworld. Giants discovered the door long ago but never successfully traversed it until Guppie's great grandfather took the amulet from a Kiennish noble. The heirloom had allowed Guppie's family access to the Carcharians' realm and they had derived benefits and attained riches through the association. A single Mountain Giant proved a great ally to Doug-less. Guppie's great grandfather Knuckle had been the first to traverse the gate. Doug, the four-armed son of Carcharian King Stanley had no luck in slaying Duoths in the Onyum Patch. Rather than going back to face his father empty-handed, Doug and his party entered the Endless Fen. Eleven Carcharians, two Shellies, and the Mountain Giant Knuckle entered the swamp. Only the Shellie Crunch survived and made it back to King Stanley. Crunch reported the group encountered a pride of sea lions in the muck. The terrain was fit for neither swimming nor running. Fighting sea lions in their domain was ill work. Crunch sired Pincher's grandfather. It's a bit ironic that both Crunch and his great-grandson Pincher were sole survivors of an ill-fated mission. Doug's death devastated old Stanley. When he became King, Emmit, the grandfather of current Carcharian monarch Lunniedale, renamed the Carcharians' home Doug-less. Knuckle had carried the Amulet of Protection into the endless fen. The artifact helped him little against a horde of sea lions. Knuckle's son Tidbit *dreamed* the amulet appeared by his bedside. When he awakened the artifact was wrapped around his night stand. Tidbit knew his father was dead. Tidbit passes the amulet to his son Morsel. Morsel's son Guppie now possessed the amulet of protection. The artifact hung from Fenrir's thick neck. To pass through the portal Guppie grasped Fenrir's collar and they passed together. The Mountain Giant and cave warg made their way along the cavern wall. Guppie did not enter Doug-less through the circle of Willis. He was too big. Fenrir easily sniffed out the secret door on the cavern wall. Mountain Giant strength was required to move the great rock. Guppie and Fenrir entered and the door closed behind them. They followed a wide meandering corridor that ended behind Lunniedale's chamber. The passageway was a last ditch getaway for the liege of Doug-less should difficulties overwhelm the conurbation.

King Lunniedale's hatred festered. Lack of Duoth flesh and information about his missing spouse and daughter fueled the monarch's enmity. He should have never trusted the four-armed son of a sea elf Urquhart. The King surmised the privileges of having four arms would outweigh any lineage to the weak sea elves. Loyal minions had been lost. Commander Slurdup, four-arm Sergeant Phlegg and Yoorin, the Shellies Pincher and ill-tempered Cracker, and two-armed Carcharians Mullums, Jammup, Jellitite, Allen, Wickes, Lowe, Lew, Wooten, and Vallely fell to the emirp on a mission to investigate goings on across the great sea. The only survivor Pincher relayed details of the fight before returning to the sea to join his forebears. Pincher relayed the newcomers had smote the emirp and carried Gruusch, Slurdup, and Cracker's carrion inside their refuge.

The King's spouse Piara took their daughter Starra and the King's niece Sharchrina with her. Sharchrina had been promised to Gurgla, who now moaned over her absence. Old Viceroy Phederal lost his older two-armed son Jellitite in Slurdup's ill-fated party. His son

Gruusch was unaccounted for. If Phederal grieved it was not evident. The Mountain Giant Guppie had returned to his home and promised to return with reinforcements, but the Mountain Giant leaders had traditionally disdained coming to the sea world in numbers. Fact was… they always came one at a time and bearing striking resemblance to their predecessors. Lunniedale really didn't want large numbers of the large hominids running amuck. He feared their undermining his authority. Giants tended to be quite chaotic in their outlook. Guppie for the most part followed orders and had terrorized the newcomers a bit with his canine companion the cave warg Fenrir. Just to be safe Lunniedale made it a point to always reward the mountain giant.

Envoys were slowly returning from missions to the King's allies. Viceroy Phederal supervised the goings on. He was better at supervising than really doing anything. Clootch monitored the defenses and made sure free swimmers that entered Doug-less were screened. Everyone was tasted! Brace was in charge of organizing surveillance teams. Four-arms were sent as emissaries to the king's allies. Heraldo traveled to the areas north and east of Cane Bisque Bay. Heraldo took his espoused Reefa and younger four-armed brother Craig.

King Lunniedale paced in his chamber. Then the guard Ambroo knocked on his door.

The King bellowed, "Enter!"

Ambroo entered and reported, "Guppie has returned, my liege."

Lunniedale excitedly said, "How many giants are with him?"

Ambroo tentatively replied, "Only one, my king, him!

Lunniedale disgruntled said, "Send the big ****** ****** in!"

Guppie entered with his old cave warg Fenrir.

Lunniedale asked, "Where are you mates?"

Guppie answered fallaciously, "My king is at odds with the Draiths and can't spare anybody. I did bring these wyvern hide shields and old Fenrir. That ought to help."

Lunniedale growled, "You promised help! A few shields and mangy cave warg doesn't qualify as help!"

Guppie answered, "Now, now, now, my friend. Fenrir has taken out many foes. My king secured these shields at high cost. They will afford protection against projectiles and most fire and cold attacks."

Lunniedale continued, "From what I've heard the newcomer's sorcerer will easily roast that mutt!"

Guppie said, "Won't happen!"

Lunniedale said, "How can you say such a thing? The only thing I see that's worthwhile about the hound is his collar. I wouldn't mind having his collar as a gift for my next spouse."

Guppie hesitated and replied, "I'm not sure I can part with the collar."

Lunniedale frowned and said, "I think you must."

Guppie said, "It's an heirloom, King Lunniedale. It belonged to my father Morsel. I might loan it to you."

The King said, "Oh. Bother! Assemble my court!"

Lunniedale, Guppie, Fenrir, and Ambroo headed for the council room.

In the meeting hall old four-armed Carcharian Phederal nervously paced and awaited King Lunniedale's arrival. Commander Gurgla, Sergeant Tapasbar, *three*-armed Heraldo and his espoused Reefa, Top Guard Clootch, recently promoted Brace and Phoodle, two-armed Unfirth, Nuttin, Hunnie, Ruutchie, and Clootch's crew, Tilertoo, Agnoow, Cannoo, and Tippee, and other members of the King's court sat around the table. Phederal and Gurgla were particularly dreading again telling the king they had no luck in capturing his prodigal consort and her party.

King Lunniedale entered and all in the chamber stood sharply. Ambroo stayed by the door. Mountain Giant Guppie and Fenrir stood by the king's table with a pile of shields.

One by one the subordinates reported. Everyone was careful not to mention the missing queen by name. Doing so had cost predecessors their lives. Phederal gulped and reported the queen remained at large. Lunniedale fumed silently. Clootch reported the entry circle remained secure and all who entered had been tasted. Free swimming Carcharians had joined the ranks of Doug-less and bolstered the king's forces. Heraldo returned from Cane Bisque Bay with 19 two-armed Carcharians and the four-armed lieutenant Fishtrap, an earned not given name. Sergeant Tapasbar reported training proceeded well for youths and new recruits. Finally Brace reported scouts' findings. Brace's scouts had seen members of Piara's group among the newcomers. Quunsch was unmistakably among the newcomers and he came into the waters unrestrained to pursue scouts. The scouts observed the battle with the emirp and Giant Amebus and sea lions. Mountain Giant Guppie expressed his regret that his sovereign was embroiled in conflict with Draiths and unable to spare any other warriors, but did present the king with a dozen wyvern hide shields. Four-arm Fishtrap joined the group.

Lunniedale growled, "So your scouts were discovered."

Brace shivered and responded tentatively, "My liege, they risked life and limb to get near the newcomers' fortress. They confirmed at least some of the queen… uh, *****'s entourage is allied with the newcomers. They skillfully escaped and got back to you with intelligence and await your commands."

Lunniedale smirked and replied, "Nice a**-kissing, Brace. I like you. So we know the ***** is among the lot that blocks our access to the prime Duoth hunting grounds at the onyum patch. I've two reasons to go to war with them!"

Phederal asked, "Do you want me to send another scouting party, my king?"

Lunniedale said, "Sea chicken ****, no, Phederal! You are a dawg fish t**d! Gurgla, organize a hundred warriors into a phalanx. Send them to the far side of the sea to engage the newcomers. They may leave Doug-less via the dry corridor. That'll get them onto the shoreline well on the way to the interlopers' bastion. Brace, send squads of scouts through the sea. Tease them! Keep them on edge. Make sorties against their wall. I don't care if you inflict casualties or damage. Just worry the ever-loving **** out of them. Gurgla, organize the hundred warriors in phalanx formation. Move along the seashore loudly. Make sure they know you are coming. Make them think it's an all-out attack."

Phederal timidly said, "My king, we can't storm their fortress with a hundred guys. These folk turned back a triskaidekapod and Giant Amebus. Shouldn't we attack in legion force and from all directions?"

Lunniedale said facetiously, "May I be king and command, **** for brains? We will use the teasing from Brace's scouts to keep them occupied from the sea. Phederal, do you have any idea how heavy our losses would be to go through the sea lions' territory in order to attack from the east? Do you not remember Doug and Guppie's great grandfather Knuckle's party? Let the newcomers think we only have a hundred warriors to throw against them. My friend Guppie has provided us a dozen wyvern hide shields to protect our phalanx. Feign attacks, you idiot! Draw their fire! Waste their resources! When they are tired and worn down I'll send in my full forces. Fishtrap, I know your father Crudle. We had good competitions in the arenas. Mind you, I usually kicked his a**, but we have long been friends. You honor me by joining my forces."

Fishtrap stood and stoutly replied, "The honor is mine, King Lunniedale. My father speaks highly of you, though he says he won the battles."

Lunniedale laughed and said, "Will you honor me further by commanding the war phalanx?"

Fishtrap bowed and said, "I'll gladly command your warriors."

Lunniedale stood and said, "So be it."

Guppie sighed and said, "The newcomers encroach on your hunting grounds. I'll help you destroy them."

Lunniedale said, "This is an expeditionary force, Guppie. Since it seems you are the only giant I'm going to have in my forces, I'd rather you stay in reserve in Doug-less."

Guppie said, "Then let me send my trusty companion Fenrir with Captain Fishtrap."

Fishtrap said, "You may keep your warg. I'm only fond of animals I can eat. But his collar fascinates me. I'm drawn to the stone. Might I wear this in battle?"

Guppie said, "Nope, it's an heirloom."

Fishtrap's face hardened and he said, "I said I'd really like to wear it in battle. You got a problem with it?"

Carcharians stood and surrounded Guppie. The Mountain Giant remembered the story of the artifact returning to his line after Knuckle was lost in the fen. He sized up his and Fenrir's chances against a room full of ornery Carcharians and relented, "What the heck! Take it! Keep it close! Keep it safe! I'd like it back after you finish with the newcomers."

Fishtrap extended his lower arms and removed the collar. Guppie steadied the big cave warg whilst the Captain removed the amulet.

King Lunniedale laughed and said, "That's the spirit, Guppie. Now come into my dining room and we'll share some sea biscuits, jellyfish, and Seabee mead."

Gurgla, Phederal, and Fishtrap began the process of choosing well-conditioned warriors to make up the war phalanx. The first 12 chosen eagerly grabbed up the wyvern hide shields before realizing bearing the shields put them in the first rank. Wyvern hide was tough enough to fend off most arrows, resisted normal flame, and purportedly gave some protection against Magick. The light weight shields enabled two-armed Carcharians to more freely use their weapon hand. Once organized the phalanx passed through the King's back rooms and exited through the door into the corridor. Quickly they retraced Guppie's route and reached the hidden door. The front rank opened the door and the warriors filed out in orderly fashion and followed the route taken by Slurdup and Piara's parties. Stealth was not a priority. Fishtrap encouraged war chants and the loud Carcharians scattered all creatures they encountered. Brice personally accompanied three teams of scouts to head directly across the sea toward Vydaelia. For the strong swimmers this direct route was much quicker and quite secure due to frequent Carcharian patrols, unless, of course another triskaidekapod meandered through.

Ø ∞ Ø

Sea elf Squaddie Frayn tarried near the entrance to Doug-less and heard the commotion when the Fishtrap's warriors left the citadel. Frayn had not followed small parties of Carcharians unless they moved in the direction of Graywood. Brace's charges entered the water and began the swim across the lake. Fishtrap led a contingent of a hundred or more loud warriors to the west. Faryn followed Brace from a safe distance.

CHAPTER 37

Two Fronts

Cleanup continued in Vydaelia. Rangers completed repairs on the wall. The Wandmaker got some needed rest and Clouse recovered from his stupor after the last battle. Sergeant Major Klunkus ordered Gruusch to stay with distraught Starra and Sharchrina and monitor them constantly in their bartizan home. Bluuch also remained in the bartizan. Quunsch insisted on assisting in guard duty and constantly sniffed the air on the allure facing the sea. Yathle positioned on the western wall facing the direction from which Piara and Gruusch had traveled. Tawyna watched with Gruusch. Tanteras and Andra shared the seawall shift and Alistair, Gordon, Leftbridge, and Stewart watched on the western wall. Suddenly Quunsch stood perfectly still and pointed to the sea. About twenty paces from the shore and fifty from the wall a brace of Carcharians leaped from the water, charged into the shallows, and hurled spears toward the wall. The first spear clanked harmlessly into the hard stone and the second actually cleared the wall, but from the distance it was thrown the defenders on the wall easily avoided it. The greatest danger was to folk in the quadrangle below the allure but no one was near the impact point. Tanteras and Andra fired arrows and hit the Carcharians but the offenders charged away into the sea. Quunsch wanted to pursue the Carcharians, but Tawyna discouraged him. Ridgway, Thalira, Ringway, Songway, and Breeley ran up the wall stairs to the wall walk to reinforce the watchers.

Ruutchie grumbled loudly about the Drelvish arrow in his rump. Brace removed the arrow and reckoned the greatest injury was to the two-arm's pride. Brace then sent another duo toward the shallows. This pair yelped and threw stones toward the Rangers on the wall. Again the rocks sailed over the guards' heads and landed harmlessly in the quadrangle. Seven Rangers fired arrows at the two Carcharians. The attackers fled into the sea.

Shift leader Merry Bodkin arrived and asked Quunsch, "They have been watching us. Why are they making such meaningless attacks and putting themselves in range of our bows?"

Quunsch extended his muscular left arm and replied, "Pinch my hide! Feel the thickness. Your fine tipped arrows will scarcely penetrate their hides. Carcharians are much tougher than Duoths and sea lions. They are just ******* with us!"

Tawyna chastised, "Watch the language, Quunsch! No one's fornicating!"

Quunsch grumbled and moved to the wall. The big half Bugwully readied his throwing spear and muttered, "Those ******** will feel this!"

Merry Bodkin looked toward Tawyna and said, "He is… who he is! Stay alert! There are at least four of them out there!"

Three more times pairs of Carcharians made moves toward the shoreline and hurled stones. No injuries resulted from the attacks. Rangers fired at them each time. Suddenly a ruckus appeared from the west. Shift leader Willifron shouted, "We are under attack! Sound the general alarm! Alert the Wandmaker!"

Shouting and brandishing swords and shields a large clustered group of Carcharians turned around the corner about 150 paces from the illusory forest and approached the western wall of Vydaelia at a run.

Yathle shouted, "Phalanx formation! A four-arm leads them!"

Quunsch said, "That's a hundred warriors! King Lunniedale is serious about this conflict now!"

The clustered Carcharians were within range of the Drelvish self-bows when they rounded the corner at 150 paces. The well-trained phalanx moved as a unit in precise steps. Fishtrap stood in the center of the phalanx and barked commands. He carried weapons in all four arms. Brace's scouts had informed the Carcharian commander of the illusory forest that appeared and hid the western wall of the newcomers' fortress to the unwary eye. Fishtrap knew enemies were hidden in the convincing illusory foliage. Fishtrap drew an arrow from his quiver with his right upper hand. The four-arm nocked the arrow into his bow. He used his right lower arm to paint unguent on the arrows tip, struck a flintstone, and ignited the oil. The big warrior growled, "My fellow warriors! Oil will burn a tree. Follow the course of my arrow but be ready lest they return fire. Keep the wyvern hide shields raised in the front rank!"

Fishtrap drew the bowstring taut, aimed, and released the flaming arrow. He aimed intentionally at the lower part of the *forest*. The arrow clanked against the stone wall. Most Carcharian warriors now saw through Clouse's illusion.

Willifron remained in command pending the arrival of Klunkus and the Wandmaker and shouted, "Hold your fire."

Rangers mustered on the western wall walk. Reinforcements poured into the outer ward. The Wandmaker Yannuvia rapidly made his way from his home in the Day Glass enclosure. Clouse, Jonna, Joulie, Sergeant Major Klunkus, and Tariana ran with the Wandmaker. Yannuvia ordered Knightsbridge to stand guard at the Day Glass enclosure. Morganne stayed within her bed chamber. Fisher stayed in the inner ward. Gruusch led Starra and Sharchrina into the inner ward. Sergeant Major Klunkus ordered the Carcharian to remain within the inner ward and stand guard by the females. Bluuch charged from the bartizan to the inner ward and stood by Starra. Yathle and Loogie joined Quunsch on the seaward wall walk. The entire community mobilized. Matrons and young prepared the inner ward to receive casualties.

Yannuvia carried the red and blue-tipped Master Wand in his robe and held the Wand of Lightning in his left hand. Yathle, Loogie, and Quunsch impatiently watched Brace's instigators moving in and out of the water. The powerful Carcharians had taken to throwing rocks over the wall. The thrown rocks created greatest danger for the mustering Vydaelians in the outer ward. Rangers on the wall walk shouted when the projectiles were coming and tried to give direction, but the folk in the outer ward had to remain on maximal alert. Merry Bodkin, Tawyna, Ridgway, Thalira, Ringway, Songway, and Breeley stood with the three Carcharians with bows drawn. Geber, Yebek, Rudyard, and Hummitch stationed several paces eastward and watched the sea. A small contingent of Rangers remained on the eastern wall and looked toward the Duoth passageways. Others took preassigned positions along the outer ward. As last resort the elders and youths in the inner ward were armed with bows and positioned on the inner wall. Morganne kept a bow and sword by her bed. If called upon, all Vydaelians would join the fight.

Tawyna remarked, "It'd be a bad time for the marshmallow men to attack. We're occupied on two flanks!"

Quunsch disagreed, "It's never a bad time to get Duoth flesh! But they took a pretty good whipping recently. They usually stay hidden for a while after we attack them. I think they have to train new guys."

Yathle said, "Duoths look pretty much alike."

Quunsch energetically said, "Yeah, but they all taste good!"

Two more two-armed Carcharians emerged from the water, ran forward a few paces, and hurled rocks toward the wall. One smashed into the wall a few feet below the guards, but the second sailed over their heads and Merry Bodkin warned, "Look out below! Incoming!"

The rock fell amongst several Rangers and shattered.

Sergeant Major Klunkus ascended the wall stairs and relieved Willifron. The veteran Willifron descended and went to the eastern wall to assume command of the limited watch remaining there. Klunkus instructed Tanteras, Andra, Alistair, Gordon, Leftbridge, and Stewart to make bows ready.

Fishtrap labored to keep the phalanx in order. The Carcharians were itching for a fight. Many had fought Quunsch and Urquhart in arena battles and lost. Fishtrap ordered, "Keep those shields up! Maintain your ranks! Our intelligence tells us these are formidable foes."

On the allure Yannuvia joined Klunkus.

Klunkus warned, "Wandmaker, I'd prefer you stay under cover. These folk are bigger than Drolls. Their bow reached the wall. Remember how far Quunsch threw his spear toward the Duoths. It's safe to assume that some of these guys are as strong as Quunsch."

Yannuvia said, "I'm as safe here as I would be in the outer ward, Klunkus, and I must know what is afoot. They are showing discipline by keeping their formation. Do all have two arms?"

Tanteras answered, "Wandmaker, their large shields block our view. The arrow flew from the center of their formation."

Klunkus strained to look through the faint light and said, "I'd swear those are wyvern hide shields, Wandmaker. We've seen no wyverns. Have the Carcharians bartered with Kiennites?"

Klunkus summoned Yathle who promptly arrived from the seawall.

Yathle said, "The Kings of Doug-less have traded with Mountain giants for generations. A mountain giant died with Doug in the Endless Fen. I have no knowledge of Kiennites."

Klunkus asked, "Yathle, why don't they attack?"

Yathle answered, "Beg pardon, Sergeant Major, but they *are* attacking from the sea. May we go out there and get them?"

Klunkus answered, "I suspect that's what they want you to do. We'll hold our ground. How many warriors does King Lunniedale command??

Yathle answered, "Urquhart would have had more information than I. The King has fought many battles and depleted his ranks. I can't recognize anyone from this distance. The attackers from the sea are muttering expletives and saying very bad things about Queen... uh, Elder Piara. They've insulted our mothers and have had some rather nasty things to say about your folk."

Klunkus said, "After dealing with Drolls, Kiennites, and wyvern riders, we are accustomed to such insults."

Yathle said, "They are in bow range. Why don't you give them a volley?"

Klunkus answered, "I appreciate your enthusiasm but arrows are valuable. They are clustered together with shields up so we have little chance of inflicting much damage."

Yannuvia listened intently and watched the phalanx moving back and forth about a hundred paces from the wall. He said, "Klunkus, please fire an arrow into the shields. I'm curious as to their make-up. Wyvern hide resists fire and cold Magick."

Klunkus said, "Will do."

The Sergeant Major drew his bow, nocked an arrow, and fired it toward the phalanx. The arrow struck dead center and bounced off the shield. Klunkus surmised, "If it's not wyvern hide, it's something just as tough."

Fishtrap chuckled when the arrow bounced off the shield and he ordered the phalanx to move forward. The Carcharians advanced at a quick step to within fifty paces of Vydaelia's wall.

The first rank of eleven Carcharian warriors interlocked their wyvern-hide shields. The second rank readied throwing spears. Fishtrap kept a spear in his lower left hand, wyvern-hide shield in his right lower hand, and his bow and quiver in his upper hands. He nocked an arrow.

Fishtrap shouted, "Lower shields!"

The shield bearers lowered their shields in unison and gave the second rank a clear field of fire.

Fishtrap yelled, "Throw!"

The four-armed commander fired an arrow over the wall. Eleven Carcharians in the second rank hurled spears.

Fishtrap shouted, "Raise shields!"

The shield bearers raised and interlocked their shields. Carcharians in the rear ranks positioned shields over their heads.

Tariana peered around the merlon and shouted, "Incoming!"

Rangers on the allure squeezed behind the merlons and reserves in the outer ward ran for cover. Eleven large Carcharian spears sailed through the air and cleared the crenellated parapet. Fishtrap's arrow ripped through the air. The spears slammed into the wall or sailed over the merlons and crashed into the outer ward of the quadrangle. The arrow reached almost to the inner ward and stuck into the wall of a utility building. No one was injured by the missiles but a young Ranger named Eustace suffered an ankle injury whilst evading the spear and one of the spears smashed a water vessel.

Yathle remarked, "I'd call that an attack!"

Klunkus agreed and said, "We'll get some arrows through at this range! Fire!"

Jonna, Joulie, Sergeant Major Klunkus, Tariana, Tanteras, Andra, Alistair, Gordon, Leftbridge, and Stewart and thirty other Drelves fired after Klunkus's order. Forty Drelvish arrows sailed into the Carcharians. The shields stopped most, but three passed under the shield and dug into the burly lower legs of three front rank Carcharians. Another passed through the canopy of shields and inflicted a more serious injury to the neck of a third rank warrior. Fishtrap ordered the phalanx to fall back fifty paces to again stand a hundred paces from the wall of Vydaelia. Within the formation the wounded Carcharians were sent to the rear and others took their place in the front ranks. Fishtrap angrily fired another arrow. The missile easily cleared the wall and sailed into the quadrangle. Reserves once again scattered. The arrow narrowly missed Carmen, who waited in reserve with Gheya, Petreccia, Myrna, Bret, and Maverick. Rangers fired another volley of arrows but at the greater distance the missiles did no damage.

Clouse stood by the Wandmaker and asked, "Are you ready to send spells against them?"

Yannuvia deferred to Sergeant Major Klunkus, who had great battle experience from serving with Rumsie in Alms Glen. Klunkus expressed concerns that the Vydaelians were only facing a probing force.

Yannuvia confirmed, "The Carcharians indeed carry wyvern-hide shields, which will protect the enemies from fire, including most Magick fire. Jolt Spells require touching them. Magick Missiles are a good option."

Clouse stepped from behind the merlon, gained a clear line of sight, extended his left hand, and sent mauve rays from his extended hand into the leg of one of the shield bearers. The Magick Missile found its mark and the big warrior yelped. Yannuvia followed with another Magick Missile and sent a ray into the rightmost warrior in the front rank. Another yelp filled the air. The shields briefly dropped and an arrow streaked toward Clouse's position. Jonna pulled him down behind the parapet in the nick of time before Fishtrap's arrow whizzed by. The missile tore through the air and stuck into another storage room's wall.

Yathle watched through a murder hole in one of the merlons and declared, "That was fired by a four-arm!"

Sergeant Major Klunkus asked for one of the errant Carcharian spears. Leftbridge obliged. Klunkus said, "Yathle, might you send this spear back from whence it came?"

Yathle grinned and said, "I thought you'd never ask. I'll try to hit the phalanx where the four-arm was standing."

The big Carcharian stood and towered over the merlon. He gave a mighty heave and sent the spear toward the phalanx. The missile clunked into the shields interlocked over the phalanx and knocked a shield from its bearer's hands. Clouse and Yannuvia sent Magick Missiles into the two previously wounded front rank wyvern hide shield bearers. Another wound opened in their legs. Within the phalanx Fishtrap sent reserves to replace them and the wounded Carcharians hobbled to the back. Fishtrap then moved the phalanx back another 25 paces. Now the Carcharians were stationed only 25 paces from the corner of the outcropping. The seaward wall remained under constant aggravation from Brace's warriors. The Carcharians hurled rocks for the most part, but one innovative attacker hurled a squirming jellyfish toward the wall. Quunsch alertly extended his spear and intercepted the jellyfish before its tentacles did any harm. Quunsch muttered, "Shucks! It's purple! Grape flavored! I'd like some honey flavor with my sea biscuits."

Quunsch hurled the purple jellyfish down to the ground.

Thalira asked, "How many are attacking us?"

Loogie said, "Hard to say! We're only seeing two at a time. I see only two-arms. This sort of duty is below four-arm status."

Quunsch added, "Let's find out. The three of us could go out and engage them!"

Loogie answered, "Yathle is with the Wandmaker and Bluuch and Gruusch are in the inner ward with Starra and Sharchrina. We might best those warriors in the sea two on two, but we'd quickly be outnumbered. Besides we should wait for the Wandmaker's orders."

Quunsch grumbled, "So we just stand up here and watch them chucking **** at us!"

Tawyna quipped, "Yes."

Two more rocks flew past and fell into the quadrangle. Carmen, Gheya, Petreccia, Myrna, Bret, and Maverick bore responsibility watching for and helping others evade the projectiles.

Fishtrap ordered his charges forward and the phalanx closed fifty paces. Klunkus ordered another volley of arrows but the Carcharians' shields fended them off. Seventy-five paces from the wall the front rank again dropped their shields and the second and third ranks fired arrows toward Vydaelia. Four-armed Fishtrap threw a spear toward the wall. The front rank quickly raised their shields, but both Yannuvia and Clouse fired Magick Missiles and hit two archers. Twenty-two arrows streaked over the wall, sprayed the quadrangle, and wounded two Rangers named Vasor and Rettick. Colleagues helped the injured to the inner ward. Injuries were not life-threatening but effectively eliminated them from the fight.

Clouse lamented, "Sometimes a blind squirrel finds a nut."

Sergeant Major Klunkus added, "Lucky shots, but we can't afford attrition. I want three rounds of continuing fire. One shot at a time! Aim for the center of the phalanx. If those shields go up, they'll have a surprise!"

Sergeant Major Klunkus fired first. Then in orderly fashion and one at a time forty archers sent the arrows along the same path. The arrows plunked into the shields. Halfway into the sequential volley, Fishtrap ordered the shields lowered. The shield bearer upon whom the Vydaelians concentrated was hit with three arrows before he got the shield raised. The other shield bearers followed his lead and the

Carcharian's attack was aborted. Fishtrap ordered retreat and the phalanx withdrew to twenty paces from the corner. The wounded Carcharian had more serious injuries and others helped him to the rear.

Klunkus observed, "We inflicted only one casualty with forty arrows, but stopped an attack, and they fell back. Stay alert!"

Three times the adversaries jockeyed back and forth. The net result was another wounded Ranger Byron in Vydaelia and a lot of arrows in the wyvern hide shields. The seaward wall saw constant activity. A brace of Carcharians charged the wall with spears drawn with intent to draw fire from the Rangers. When they received no response the Carcharians hurled spears. Quunsch again snagged a spear from the air and sent it back to its thrower and hit the two-arm in the chest. He fell and his partner scampered back into the sea.

Sergeant Major Klunkus summarized, "It's clear that neither we nor the Carcharians are going to gain an advantage from these encounters. They don't show any interest in scaling the wall, and I am against battling them hand-to-hand. We'd suffer heavy casualties. On the other hand they are not tiring and can be easily reinforced and supplied. Sea lion and Duoth attacks felled none of our Carcharian allies. Now the shoe's on the other foot. We're facing strong opponents. Rocks are constantly falling over the seaward wall. Our reserves are forced to move constantly, so the enemies are tiring them too. Any ideas, Wandmaker?"

Yannuvia said, "At least they aren't blowing holes in the wall. The phalanx has not moved in a while. Yathle and Clouse, follow me to the seaward wall."

Clouse, Yathle, and Yannuvia followed the wall walk toward Quunsch's group. Twice Carcharians rushed from the sea and hurled debris toward the wall. Yannuvia reached Tawyna and Quunsch. Two Carcharians came out of the water and moved toward the shore. Yannuvia directed the Wand of Lightning toward them and said, **"Grove veer cleave land."** A beam of yellow light erupted from the end of the Wand of Lightning and streamed into the brace of Carcharians. The force of the spell knocked them off their feet. The Carcharians floated lifelessly in the water. The number "nine" appeared in Yannuvia's mind.

Brace treaded water about 50 paces from the shore and saw the electrocution of his warriors. To his way of looking at it, the attack had been successful because his scouts' efforts had gotten the sorcerer's attention. Fishtrap saw Yannuvia's attack from within his phalanx formation. The four-arm didn't understand the spell caster's waiting to attack his troops. He'd fully expected to lose most by this time. Instead the Carcharians had a few troops with sore feet and one more seriously wounded veteran. Brace's seaward attacks had now cost three lives. A replacement squad of fourteen had arrived from Doug-less. Fishtrap assign quartermaster duties to the wounded. Restocking, fire starting, and food preparation would keep them busy. The Mountain Giant Guppie and his cave warg Fenrir had agreed to transport weapons for the King. Fishtrap clutched the spear that had been thrown back at his formation. He sent young two-arm Jenta to order Brace to continue assaults and then ordered the phalanx forward. Brace resented Fishtrap's command but nonetheless sent his minions into harm's way.

Clouse stood by the Wandmaker and Loogie and said, "They are coming back for more. Are you going to hit them again?"

Yannuvia watched the Carcharians move into the shallows and launch large stones. Ducking aside was simple. Another pair followed. One threw a dead dawgfish toward the wall. The lifeless beast fell short of the wall, but its stench reached the wall walk.

Quunsch muttered, "That's bad... even by my standards."

Fishtrap's phalanx moved forward fifty paces.

On the wall walk Klunkus said, "More fun and games! Fire an arrow in rotation every 60 counts. Shoot over the front rank. We might get lucky and drop a few in between the shields."

Jonna, Joulie, Tariana, Tanteras, Andra, Alistair, Gordon, Leftbridge, and Stewart and thirty other Drelves fired after Klunkus's order. Most of the shots bounced off shields, but occasionally loud growls indicated an arrow made it through the canopy of shields and hit one of the Carcharians. The Carcharians dropped their shields and archers fired toward Vydaelia. The huge crudely made arrows weren't pretty in flight but sent Rangers scattering in the quadrangle. After firing the warriors raised the shields, but Tariana's arrow found its way into an archer's upper chest and the forces of Doug-less lost another warrior. The phalanx charged toward the wall. The Rangers sent another volley into the well-disciplined group, but Fishtrap's charges maintained their positions. When the front rank came within three paces of the wall, the shield bearers dropped their shields and permitted colleagues in the rear to move forward and throw a large ladder against the wall. The ladder fell between two bulwarks. Klunkus, Jonna, Joulie, Tariana,

Tanteras, Andra, Alistair, Gordon, Leftbridge, and Stewart fired down into the Carcharians and inflicted grievous injuries on three warriors. Two fell dead. Undaunted Carcharians began to ascend the ladder. Yathle, Loogie, and Quunsch charged from their seaward positions. Clouse and Yannuvia followed. Rangers grabbed the ladder and pushed mightily. Below Carcharians strained to keep the ladder in place whilst colleagues attempted to scale the wall. On the wall walk Klunkus, Jonna, and Joulie drew swords and prepared to meet the ascending warriors. The first Carcharian to reach the top found himself in a hopeless situation. Three Drelvish short swords worked against him, and he lost his balance and fell backward onto his colleagues. The fallen warrior crashed into shields and knocked several colleagues down. The phalanx was disrupted. Fishtrap barked commands and hurled his spear toward the wall. From close range the four-arm's powerful throw gained accuracy and slammed into young Ranger Lynnae as she struggled to push the ladder back. Lynnae fell backward off the allure onto the hard ground in the quadrangle. The small nodule opened and a graparble passed from her hand.

Yathle shouted, "Four-arm!"

Yathle, Quunsch, and Loogie reached the ladder just as a second Carcharian stepped onto the allure. Quunsch threw both arms around him and fell onto the allure on top of the struggling two-arm. Yathle and Loogie grabbed the ladder, gave a mighty heave and pushed it back onto the cluster of warriors. Two Carcharians fell off the ladder and onto their colleagues. The ladder fell onto the phalanx and disrupted it further. Quunsch wrapped his powerful arms around the Carcharian on the wall walk and squeezed and pinned both his arms against his side. Quunsch's half-Bugwully thick powerful legs further immobilized the struggling warrior. The phalanx was breaking apart. Quunsch delivered a head butt and mercifully knocked his opponent senseless. A quick stab with his trident ended the battle. Outside the wall Carcharians struggled to get onto their feet. Several limped badly. Fishtrap ordered a retreat. The Carcharians sped back toward the corner. Yathle hurled a spear and dropped a fleeing warrior. Jonna, Joulie, Tariana, Tanteras, Andra, Alistair, Gordon, Leftbridge, and Stewart fired at the retreating Carcharians and scored numerous hits. Brace sent seven pairs of Carcharians from the sea. They hurled rocks toward the wall. Merry Bodkin, Tawyna, Ridgway, Thalira, Ringway, Songway,

Geber, Yebek, Rudyard, Hummitch and Breeley fired a volley toward the instigators. The arrows found their marks but inflicted no serious injuries. Fishtrap stopped about 140 paces from Vydaelia and defiantly fired an arrow toward the wall. His arrow cleared the wall and sailed over Andra's head toward the inner ward and narrowly missed matrons who were attending Lynnae's body. Quunsch yelled loudly, raised the dead Carcharian over his head and hurled the body over the wall, where it fell among other victims. Six Carcharians fell in the assault. Add the two slain by Yannuvia's Lightning Bolt and Doug-less lost eight. Vydaelia mourned Lynnae.

For the next rotation of the Day Glass (eight hours) the Carcharians in the sea unpredictably pelted the wall with stones, debris, and prostrate sea creatures. The phalanx retreated behind the outcropping 150 paces beyond Vydaelia's wall. Fishtrap kept a brace of two-arms posted to monitor the wall and several times groups of three to five Carcharians charged around the corner and fired arrows toward the wall. Most volleys fell short, and Jonna, Joulie, Tariana, Tanteras, Andra, Alistair, Gordon, Leftbridge, and Stewart returned fire and scored frequently. The powerful Carcharians wore thick armor and withstood the Rangers' attacks.

Yathle stood on the allure by Yannuvia and asked, "Just curious, Wandmaker. Why didn't you hit the phalanx with one of those lightning shots like you did the warriors in the sea?"

Yannuvia stared at the pair of two-armed Carcharians standing in the murky light. Both held wyvern hide shields. The Wandmaker said, "I won't discuss tactics with you."

Yathle fumed.

Quunsch added, "This is vexing! I've recognized several of my old tormentors among their ranks! Boggle was among them!"

Sergeant Major Klunkus shared the Carcharians' frustration and said, "They are disrupting us on two fronts. What if the Duoth's attack again?"

Yannuvia sighed and said, "The wyvern hide shields defended them and the wand's beam is focused. Had it passed the shields, the lightning attack would have injured only a few warriors. I want to determine their strength and attack modes. They are stronger than I had expected. The Carcharians attacking from the sea don't enjoy protection of shields. I wanted to see how the Lightning Wand affected them and give them a little taste of our capabilities."

Quunsch commented, "You zapped them! Why don't you just keep hitting them with the wand?"

Clouse said, "The wand has limited uses, Quunsch. We may need it later. I suspect we're looking at the tip of an iceberg. The King of Doug-less is not showing his full strength. The Wandmaker is not showing our full strength. Magick should be reserved and used when necessary."

Quunsch replied, "They'll neither show you quarter nor ask for it! Gruusch, Urquhart, Yathle, Bluuch, Loogie, Starra, Sharchrina and I are not typical residents of Doug-less. Our King is ruthless! He'll stop at nothing to get revenge against Piara and the rest of us. He doesn't like encroachment on his territory, particularly the prime Duoth hunting grounds. He'd fight for the onyum patch even if we weren't involved. Come to think of it… I can't blame him for resenting your occupying the onyum patch."

Klunkus said, "I'd estimate a hundred warriors in the formation that attacked us. It's hard to tell how many are coming from the sea. Have you any idea the number of soldiers he commands?"

Quunsch shrugged.

Yathle said, "Urquhart and Queen Piara were privy to the inner circle of Doug-less. The rest of us were outsiders. Doug-less saw a lot of comings and goings. Usually about five hundred two-arms and a dozen or so four-arms live in the King's stronghold, but King Lunniedale has many allies and many more chieftains indebted to him. No one has prevailed against the Doug-less war machine since before Doug's time. All Carcharian males undergo tactics training. The phalanx is usually used when we are outnumbered and in defensive positions. It was odd to see the phalanx formation used offensively. We truly have told you everything we can about Carcharian society."

Yannuvia said, "I'd like to know what they are up to beyond the stone outcropping."

Quunsch offered, "I'll swim over and check them out."

Yathle said, "Are you crazy? The sea is teeming with the King's troops. They will take notice of you in the water and recognize you in a heartbeat."

Quunsch answered, "I know I have an unforgettable pretty face, but I am a fast swimmer."

Loogie said, "Your Bugwully lineage and powerful legs won't get you past them."

Quunsch said, "I was thinking the Wandmaker might bestow some of his Magick to me. You got their attention with that last blast. Dose me up and keep them busy!"

Yannuvia pondered a moment and said, "I can make you fly, but you'll be discovered. The ceiling of the cavern is lower near the outcropping. You'd easily be in reach of thrown spears and arrows. It's not a good option. Invisibility is a better plan."

Klunkus said, "Should you do one of us?"

Quunsch frowned.

Yannuvia replied, "Invisible creatures still make noise and have scent. Carcharians are predators. We've seen their keen sense of smell in action against the Duoths. They'd sniff us out easily. In Quunsch's case, Carcharians will just smell another of their kind in the water."

Yathle asked, "What about the noise he'd make? Quunsch isn't subtle!"

Yannuvia answered, "I'll keep them busy!"

Quunsch bellowed, "I'm ready to kick some butt!"

Yannuvia said, "Not going to happen right away! Aggressive action betrays your invisibility. My orders are to sneak about among them and learn what you can about their plans. Are you ready, Quunsch?"

Quunsch grunted, "Yes, Wandmaker! I'll do my best!"

Yannuvia said, "We'll proceed. Get undressed."

Quunsch said, "What? There are she-Drelves around!"

Yannuvia continued, "The spell affects you and your belongings, but water that drips from you will be visible. If you drop your weapon, the enemies will be able to both see and hear it. They can hear you breathe, sneeze, pass gas, burp, cough, and other sounds. Your clothing and weapon will increase the amount of noise you make."

Quunsch anxiously said, "You mean I have to go naked and weaponless!"

Yannuvia replied, "It would be best. Are you ready and willing?"

The half-Bugwully said, "There are a lot of people in Doug-less that I'd like to give a comeuppance. Maybe I won't run into any of them. Get on with it. I'm going to leave on my clothes as long as I can. It wouldn't be fair to make these females look at this body too long!"

Tawyna quipped, "Yeah, right!"

Quunsch passed his spear and garb to Yathle.

Yannuvia said, "First let's make you faster."

The Wandmaker produced the Wand of Speed. He said **"Jar old ford"** and touched Quunsch. Yannuvia then took gum Arabic from his pack, plucked an eyelash, and wrapped the eyelash in the gummy substance. He conjured and uttered an incantation. When he finished the lyrical phrases, the Wandmaker touched the big broad shouldered half-Bugwully. Quunsch faded from view.

Tawyna jumped and shouted, "Quunsch! You pinched me!"

The half-Bugwully reappeared and said, "Gosh! I'm sorry, Wandmaker. I couldn't resist."

Yannuvia chastised the big warrior and said, "I told you aggressive action negates the spell."

Quunsch sheepishly replied, "I didn't consider pinching a she-Drelve's derriere aggressive."

Tawyna said, "If you do it again I'll knock a knot on your head!"

Yannuvia added, "So will I. I'm not fond of pulling out my eyelashes. Behave!"

The Wandmaker repeated the spell. Quunsch again faded from sight. Quunsch moved to one of the hidden doors on the seaward wall. Yannuvia remained on the allure. Two Carcharians chose that moment to rise from the waters and run toward the wall. Yannuvia directed the Wand of Lightning toward them and said, **"Grove veer cleave land."** A beam of yellow light erupted from the end of the Wand of Lightning and streamed into the brace of Carcharians. The force of the spell knocked them off their feet. The Carcharians flew backward, splashed loudly into the water, and floated lifelessly away. The number "eight" appeared in Yannuvia's mind. Quunsch opened the door. He and Tawyna slipped through the door. Tawyna shouted and fired an arrow toward the area the last warriors came from. Quunsch slipped into the water and swam quickly away. Tawyna reentered the fortress and closed the door, which was not evident from the sea. Two more Carcharians moved toward the wall. Yannuvia directed the Wand of Lightning toward them and said, **"Grove veer cleave land."** Another beam of yellow light erupted from the end of the Wand of Lightning and streamed into the Carcharians. The force of the spell thumped them. The Carcharians sailed backward, splashed loudly into the water, and drifted motionlessly away. The number "seven" appeared in Yannuvia's mind. Another pair of warriors from Doug-less came out of the water. They had barely moved forward when Yannuvia focused the Wand of Lightning toward them and said, **"Grove veer cleave land."** A beam of yellow light erupted from the end of the Wand of Lightning and flowed into the Carcharians. The force of the spell again smote the Carcharians. The number "six" appeared in Yannuvia's mind.

Carcharian Lieutenant Brace watched eight veteran warriors fall to the newcomers' devilry and for the moment stopped the next pair from going forward. Quunsch used Yannuvia and Tawyna's diversions to swim into deep water and with his enhanced speed easily evaded several pairs of Carcharians who were concentrating on goings on near Brace and awaiting his orders. Most hoped they wouldn't be called next.

Ǿ ∞ Ǿ

Sea elf Squaddie Faryn watched from the sea. His plesiohawg stayed by his side in case he needed a quick getaway.

CHAPTER 38

Quunsch's Mission

Quunsch swam further and made for the tall grasses on the far side of the largest river that fed into the underworld sea. Two Carcharians slowly crossed the turbulent river. Fresh water wasn't as friendly to their physiologies as the sea, but the Amphibimen crossed without much difficulty. Quunsch waited in the tall grass. The grass only extended about ten swimming strokes from the point where the river joined the sea. To the east he faced an open area with very little cover. Wait! He was invisible! Small crustaceans scuttled around. A few Carcharians milled about and adeptly snared the creatures and downed them in one gulp. Chasing the prey brought two Carcharians disturbingly close to Quunsch. A large two-armed Carcharian named Boggle that Quunsch recognized from Doug-less stopped and sniffed loudly a few feet away. Quunsch stood quietly with clenched fists. A colleague called Boggle's name and the big Carcharian headed back toward the shoreline. Quunsch eased forward. Around the corner the wall veered about 45 degrees to the right for 60 paces, then turned 90 degrees, took a northeasterly direction for roughly 100 paces, and then turned back toward the southeast. The shoreline was only twenty feet wide from wall to sea. Where the cavern's wall turned back to the northeast, it widened and a small stream flowed from fifty feet above the floor, cascaded down the wall, and continued as a ten foot wide stream to the sea some 70 feet away. The gentle waterfall obscured most noise and aided the invisible half-Bugwully's advance. The ever-present luminous lichen gave light to the area. In most areas the height of the cavern was such that one only saw a fuzzy glow when he looked upward. The shoreline was only about thirty paces from the cavern's edge and then widened to as much as a hundred paces. An outcropping from the cavern wall about 110 paces ahead gave some cover, but there was little vegetation. Quunsch moved to the extension of the rocky wall. At this point the waters lapped only thirty feet from the wall and the ground was nigh entirely stone, save a few sandy areas. In the area immediately ahead, the height was about a hundred feet, or twice the point of the egress of the stream that created the waterfall. The Amphibimen watched for a while. A squad of eight Carcharians gathered at the seashore. Two others wandered in from the sea carrying large fish, much to the delight of their companions. The group quickly devoured the catch.

Quunsch continued to retrace the steps he'd made with Queen Piara and checked out the stream.

The half-Bugwully went to the stream and waded into the rivulet. The gently flowing water was six inchworm-lengths deep. Crawdads, wiggleworts, shrimp, and many larvae scurried about in the stream. Algae and abundant small plants fed the myriad of small creatures in the little ecosystem and made the stream's bottom slippery. Quunsch followed the narrow strip of seashore. The shoreline retreated almost due south for sixty feet, squared up and went east for forty feet, and then turned northeast for eighty feet. The sea also retreated and widened the beach.

Quunsch took the next turn and extended his thick neck around the corner. The sidewall extended thirty feet to the southeast, turned leftward for 80 feet, and then jutted sharply backward. Quunsch went to the outcropping. The passage turned northeast for thirty feet, bent to the southeast for a hundred feet, curved back northeast for over seventy feet, and then extended due eastward as far as his eyes could see. Two streams flowed from the cavern's wall. The streams formed a millpond of about thirty-foot diameter. A stream exited the millpond and continued some 80 feet to the sea. Many reeds and grasses filled the millpond. Crickets, water bugs, and knight flies flew around the noisy area. Knight flies were particularly aggravating. The pesky critters had hard shells, big stingers, and aggressive natures. On the positive side, if caught, dried, and ground up, knight flies made exceptionally seasoning. Quunsch crawled along the floor of the cavern and carefully entered the reeds by the millpond. The main group of Carcharians seventy strong gathered between the two streams and around the millpond. The precious cache of wyvern-hide shields was stacked against the wall. Warriors stationed at the outcropping facing Vydaelia carried the shields. More elaborately armored two-arms gathered around a massive four-armed Carcharian. Quunsch had not seen him in Doug-less, but quickly learned his name was Fishtrap, the son of four-armed Crudle, one of King Lunniedale's allies. The two-armed half-Bugwully ignored several bites from aggravating knight flies and entered the fresh water of the millpond. Red, green, and yellow water lilies floated on the surface of the pond. The wall of the cavern went forward about 90 feet, then turned northeasterly for 60 feet, made another northeasterly turn, extended 70 feet, and turned around a corner to the southeast. The shoreline remained about 100 to 120 feet from the wall's edge. A few sea birds flew overhead and knight flies feasted on Quunsch. The millpond was about waist deep to him. Quunsch walked out of the reeds, moved around the western side of the pond, approached the first stream, and forded it without difficulty. The water was only about knee high and flowed slowly. He crossed the second stream just as easily and now faced an area of solid stone floor. Quunsch ran sixty feet to the wall of stone and then inched eastward. A gentle bend toward the northeast prevented his seeing fully into the distance but also shielded him a bit. More colonies of the luminescent lichen increased the illumination. Quunsch moved slowly along the cold damp wall and walked 120 feet. The wall straightened and turned due east for 50 feet. At that point both the wall of the cavern and the shoreline turned eastward at about a 60-degree angle. Quunsch warily peered around the corner. Two guards holding wyvern-hide shields stared toward the illusory terrain surrounding Vydaelia. Quunsch stared briefly at the trees and they faded from his mind's eye. The half-Bugwully was no longer affected of the illusory spell.

The wall went southeast for some 90 feet. The seashore paralleled the rocky wall, but it narrowed 110 feet away to a width of only 60 or 70 feet. From the edge of the outcropping it was about 150 paces to the wall of Vydaelia.

Quunsch returned to the billabong. It was big enough to hide a triskaidekapod and should work for an invisible half-Bugwully. Carcharians milled along the rocky shore. Stragglers moved from the direction of Doug-less and carried supplies. Wounded Carcharians hobbled along the rocky shore headed for nursing care in the birthing rooms near the Circle of Willis. Piara's expertise would be sorely missed. Some warriors entered the water to gather fresh snacks. The big four-arm Fishtrap barked orders. The two-arm named Boggle approached the billabong with several other Amphibimen. Whilst they munched on cattails, jellyfish, and sea gars the group grumbled about Fishtrap's authority and recklessness. The smoky sea gars tempted Quunsch, but he hunkered down in the deep reeds and avoided detection.

Boggle said, "The boys who came to Doug-less with his high-a** Fishtrap said he had a 'blood and guts' reputation… his guts and their blood. We can't maneuver in that phalanx formation."

A young warrior named Bradlee replied, "I fought with Fishtrap near Cane Bisque Bay. He'll get in there and mix it up with alongside us. The formation saved us casualties. We must utilize the shields to fend off the sorcerers' spells."

Boggle said, "I'll believe it when I see it. Doug-less boasts good commanders. Brace is relegated to teasing them at the cost of Carcharian lives."

Another newcomer Monty added, "Brace has two arms. The four-arms I saw in Doug-less seem to stay near the King. Others betrayed the King and fled with the ***** Queen! At least Fishtrap is here with us."

Another from Doug-less named Earwin said, "I couldn't believe my eyes when I saw some of our folk on the wall walk with the interlopers!"

Boggle said, "Yes. I saw Quunsch on the wall walk. You'd smell the ugly ******* even if you couldn't see him."

Bradlee asked, "What's his problem?"

Boggle quipped, "Besides being half-Bugwully and the ugliest ****** ****** in Doug-less? I always thought he suffered from Exactly Disease."

Monty chewed on a booderry flavored eclectic eel and asked, "What's Exactly Disease?"

Boggle guffawed, "His face looks exactly like his a**!"

The four Carcharians guffawed.

A few feet away Quunsch hid invisibly in the millpond, heard every word, and fumed.

Boggle continued, "Quunsch is sea chicken ****! He ran away from Doug-less to get away from me! I kicked his a** over and over again in the arena. If he were here right now, I'd throw down with him and throw him down!"

Bradlee, Monty, and Boggle laughed again, but young Earwin asked, "Sergeant Boggle, I just competed in the King's arena, and sadly, didn't do so well. The guards around the Circle of Willis and the judges in the arena said Quunsch was an undefeated champion, and he even bested some four-arms."

Boggle cleared his throat and said, "I fought Quunsch in the informal games. There were no judges. He was afraid to face me in the real games. I'd have made him eat dirt! My father told me Quunsch's mother was the ugliest Bugwully he'd ever seen!"

Suddenly Boggle's head jerked back and the two-armed warrior fell backward. Quunsch stood over him, spat, and said, "Eat that, you a******!"

Bradlee, Monty, and Earwin were taken aback initially, then Monty uttered, "What the ****?"

Quunsch leveled Bradlee with a forearm and landed a kick from his powerful left leg in the middle of Monty's chest and knocked him back onto the hard ground. The half-Bugwully moved with blazing speed. Young Earwin took a swing at Quunsch but the half-Bugwully quickly grabbed his arm, applied a full arm bar, and in seconds had the youngster calling "calf rope"! By then others took notice of the commotion. Fishtrap turned toward the millpond, saw Quunsch leveling the foursome and yelled, "Get him"

Many warriors ran toward the fully visible Quunsch, who muttered, "Uh, oh!"

Quunsch evaded the first arrivals and jumped head first into the millpond. Two Carcharians hurled spears into the water. One of the projectiles came precariously close to Quunsch as he swam toward the deep water. Fishtrap ordered his charges into the water. Quunsch swam to the bottom of the sea and sped toward deep water. He passed several of Brace's lot but made it by them. He saw a cluster of swimmers ahead. Brace's reserves! Quunsch stayed near the bottom. Bugwullies had bigger lung volumes and swim bladders to store oxygen and tolerated deep water better than Carcharians. Quunsch swam deeper, farther, and thanks to the Wandmaker's speed spell faster than pureblood Carcharians. He went well past Brace's lot and then turned east and swam to the surface. A barking dawgfish gave away his position but Quunsch was far beyond Brace's charges. He looped around and came upon the eastern wall of Vydaelia. He'd hoped maybe to run across a Duoth, but no one stirred in the passages to Ty Ty. A small contingent of Rangers remained on the eastern wall and looked toward the Duoth passageways. Peter, Blair, Dennis, Bernard, and Noone now stood guard. Youngsters carried word on goings on in the quadrangle, western wall, and seaward wall. The skeleton crew on the eastern wall maintained vigilance, but all wanted to be in the thick of the action to the west. Still the ever present threat of attack by Duoths required their presence. Quunsch bellowed as he exited the water to alert the guards to his presence. Blair descended the wall stairs and opened one of the hidden doors and allowed Quunsch to enter. The half-Bugwully exchanged pleasantries and made straight for the Wandmaker.

Quunsch reached the western wall and ascended the wall stairs.

Sergeant Major Klunkus said, "We heard quite a commotion in the distance and thought you'd had it."

Quunsch snorted, "Yep, they discovered me, but not before I got a good look around. It helped that I came along the same route with Queen Piara. They are digging in. The wounded guys are heading back to Doug-less. There's a steady stream of traffic to their camp. The four-arm that commands is not a native of Doug-less. He's the son of one of King Lunniedale's friends Crudle. The Mountain Giant ally Guppie is descended from the giant Knuckle that died with Doug in the fen. I didn't see the giant but they spoke of him bringing stuff from Doug-less. There's about two hundred on the shore, and another fifty in the sea. I recognize many of them."

Klunkus asked, "What of the east?"

Quunsch shook his head negatively and reported, "Nothing! They're concentrating on the sea and this wall."

Yannuvia said, "It's an effective ploy. They are creating a nuisance, but also preventing us from harvesting from the sea and going about our tasks. Already we have lost one of our numbers Lynnae."

Klunkus said, "Wandmaker, we lived in the forests of The World of the Three Suns. Our enemies lived in strongholds like Aulgmoor. You destroyed one of their fortresses. Now it's we who are huddled within walls and besieged. I'm not versed in such tactics. Probably twenty of their warriors have fallen in their assault and the sea. Quunsch tells us they are replacing their losses. Perhaps you should summon *her* again."

Yannuvia answered, "We are not yet in duress. We had nothing left to battle the triskaidekapod and Giant Amebus. We have faced great numbers of Drolls and Kiennites. Stay alert. I am grateful for Quunsch's intelligence. We must take shifts and rest. I want everyone to hide behind the merlons on the seaward wall. We'll appear to ignore their attacks from the sea. If they come in numbers we'll respond. Let's wait this out for a few rotations of the Day Glass."

Brace left the water and consulted with Fishtrap. Fishtrap expressed chagrin over Quunsch's escape and ordered Brace to continue to hassle Vydaelia's seaward wall. Brace countered with concerns over his losses but the four-arm insisted on continuing the attacks to deplete the newcomers' Magick. Brace obliged. His friend Phoodle arrived from Doug-less with young Taktaki. The threesome had explored together often. Brace valued their input and kept Phoodle and Taktaki nearby. The sea commander had received fresh troops from Commander Fishtrap. Boggle, Monty, Bradlee, and Earwin joined Brace, the cost of incurring Fishtrap's anger at their allowing the half-Bugwully Quunsch to escape. Quunsch's killing or capture was a major prerogative. Brace reluctantly sent Monty and Bradlee toward the seaward wall. The duo walked closer but elicited no response from the defenders. Monty turned, shrugged his shoulders, and reported seeing no defenders on the wall. Brace sent Boggle and Earwin forward. The foursome edged closer to the wall and reached the edge of the rocky beach. Gentle waves lapped over their exposed ankles. They stood thirty paces from the wall and saw no entryways.

Boggle looked back and shouted, "Looks like nobody's home!"

Brace said, "Go closer."

The four Carcharians stepped onto the rocky beach and inched toward the wall. They still clutched throwing stones. When they were ten paces from the wall Brace ordered them to halt and throw their stones over the wall. Tawyna watched through a murder hole in the parapet and signaled those behind her. The Carcharians hurled four large boulders over the wall. With forewarning the Drelves in the outer ward managed to evade the stones which crashed onto the hard ground. Not getting a response, Boggle, Monty, Bradlee, and Earwin moved toward the wall. The Wandmaker's Magick produced smooth building stones with nigh unappreciable joints. The hidden doors were visible and opened only from the inside. Boggle moved his hardened nails across the stone and barely scratched the surface. The two-arm growled to Monty and Bradlee, who moved together and cupped their hands to allow Boggle to step upon them. They lifted him toward the merlon. He extended his seven foot frame and reached for the edge of the wall. It was just beyond his fingertips. Undaunted he pulled his ever-present net from his pack and with great effort hurled it over the parapet. Monty and Bradlee struggled to keep him balanced. Young Earwin kept his spear ready. Boggle grabbed the net and labored to climb up the wall. He managed to reach the edge and pulled his upper body onto the merlon such that his large head was above the wall. He saw the inner quadrangle and glimpsed the large fist just before it smashed into his face. The force of the blow knocked Boggle backward from the wall and he fell down onto Monty and Bradlee and left the threesome sprawling on the rocky shore.

Quunsch bellowed, "Does that feel familiar? What exactly does it feel like, a******?"

Earwin broke for the sea. Monty and Bradlee helped Boggle retreat from the wall. Tawyna fired an arrow and struck Boggle's backside. The Carcharian wailed. Quunsch gloated, "Now both his face and a** are hurting!"

Tawyna agreed, "It may have injured his brain."

Brace sent pairs of warriors to hurl stones every few minutes, but forbade them approaching the wall. The Rangers did not return fire.

Fishtrap sent six Carcharians toward the western wall in a run. When they reached a point fifty paces from the wall, they hurled spears toward the wall. One cleared the wall, but the Drelves evaded it easily. Rangers did not return fire. The Carcharians yelled insults and taunted Yathle and Loogie and then and ran back to the outcropping, where two of their comrades always stood. About every thirty minutes Fishtrap sent others to repeat the maneuver with the same results. This occurred for a rotation of the Day Glass.

CHAPTER 39

Tactics

To the Wandmaker's knowledge only he, Piara, the Dreamraider, Fisher, Piara, Jonna, and Joulie, and maybe Clouse knew of his tryst with Piara. He'd been reluctant to risk the *Two Stones effect* with the big Carcharian Bluuch. How would Bluuch react to knowing Yannuvia had taken liberties with his erstwhile queen? Four stones in proximity had not shown any additional effect. Five stones had not been grasped together. At this time Yannuvia, Bluuch, Fisher, Gruusch, and Jonna carried the odd rocks. Princess Starra's red scarf detected the presence of the stones but again to the Wandmaker's knowledge the scarf did not give the Princess privy to the stone bearers' thoughts.

In the outer ward of the quadrangle of Vydaelia the Wandmaker Yannuvia, Sergeant Major Klunkus, Fisher, Clouse, Jonna, Joulie, Merry Bodkin, Dienas, Yiuryna, Tanteras, and Willifron met in council. Carcharian Princess Starra insisted on being involved, and two-armed Carcharian Gruusch, four-armed Bluuch, two-armed half sea-elf Loogie, and Sharchrina joined her. Quunsch remained at his station on the allure facing the sea and hoped for another chance to belittle his old nemesis Boggle. Drelve-Vydaelians Alistair, Gordon, Leftbridge, and Stewart remained on the western wall. The Carcharian Bluuch stood by Starra with two tridents and two spears in hands. Peter, Blair, Dennis, Bernard, and Noone still watched the eastern wall. The entire community remained on high alert. To this point the Carcharians' aggression had cost Vydaelia only one life, young Lynnae.

Yannuvia stood and said, "My friends, we move from one conflict to another. Quunsch has given us valuable intelligence. Our enemies are digging in for the long haul. We've inflicted losses, but they replace their losses as I speak. Their supply line to Doug-less is unbroken. We cannot harvest from the sea, our supplies dwindle, and we cannot perform our needed tasks."

A strong female voice said, "And the next turning of the Day Glass heralds the return of the Dark Period. You must perform the wandmaking ceremony in the dome of the spheres."

Morganne arrived from the Day Glass enclosure home she shared with the Wandmaker. She carried her self-bow and quiver of arrows created by bowyer BJ Aires. Knightsbridge walked beside the orange-haired she-Drelve-Vydaelian. Morganne's pregnancy had advanced to the point that it stretched the orange fabric of her walking dress to the limit. She sat by Yannuvia.

The Wandmaker said, "You should not be here. Knightsbridge, I specifically ordered you to keep Morganne in her chamber."

Knightsbridge stammered, "Yes, Wandmaker, but she insisted..."

Morganne said, "Don't chastise him. It's my decision to be with you. We can't allow this aggression. We defended our homes in the central forest against Drolls, Kiennites, and all manner of ilk thrown against us."

Sergeant Major Klunkus said, "Yes, but we weren't locked inside four walls and had the forest as our ally."

Morganne said, "Then we must leave these environs and take the fight to the enemy. Wandmaker, have you considered this option?"

Gruusch said, "I'm glad to see you feeling well enough to be up and about, Lady Morganne. I'm sorry for the circumstances. I worry that our presence among you has triggered King Lunniedale's attack."

Morganne replied, "I'm not royalty! Address me as Morganne. Gruusch, you have been a valuable addition since your arrival. Your former queen has left Vydaelia. I don't miss her. But the rest of you have benefited the community. Our home lies on the onyum patch and therefore the Carcharian King's hunting ground. Conflict was inevitable. We have to address this now while we are strong."

Gruusch said, "Thank you ...uh, Morganne. If only Urquhart was only here! He is far more versed in Carcharian tactics. King Lunniedale will persist."

Fisher added, "The common knowledge of Menders sheds little light on Carcharians, but what I know would support what Gruusch says. And the Dark Period is upon us."

Klunkus said, "We fought Drolls hand-to-hand with the forest to support us. We cannot stand hand to hand against these Sharkmen! We've seen the tenacity of our Carcharian allies in battle."

Yannuvia said, "But we must meet them. I have precious little sulfur, but I'll use some to attack the main group. Klunkus, Morganne, Gruusch, and all of you… I welcome your ideas."

Yathle entered, "Interrupting their supply and reinforcement lines is imperative. Gruusch, Loogie, Quunsch, Bluuch, and I could swim around and attack their rear flank."

Starra demanded, "You are too few. If Gruusch goes, I go too. I can fight!"

Sharchrina said, "Me, too!"

Gruusch and Bluuch immediately protested.

Yannuvia said, "You *are* too few. I can empower thirteen of my folk with water breathing capabilities to bolster your numbers. Merry Bodkin, will you please command them. Clouse, you will stand on the seaward wall and provide Magick support, including the Wand of Lightning. It'll bear six attacks. Klunkus, you'll organize a direct assault from the western wall. Feign an attack, and draw the enemies to within archers on the wall. If they are not in their phalanx formation, we'll score well against them. Morganne, I value your input, but now I want you to go back to the Day Glass enclosure for safety."

Morganne said, "I will not, Wandmaker. Pregnant or not, I'm still the best shot with a bow among you. My place is on that wall with my sisters and brothers."

Yannuvia sighed and said, "So be it. Let's finalize plans."

Fisher said, "Give me the Omega Stones for safe keeping. We don't want them to fall into enemy hands."

Bluuch, Gruusch, Yannuvia, Jonna, and Fisher carried Omega Stones. Gruusch and Jonna gave their stones to the Mender. Bluuch refused. Yannuvia kept his also. Fisher seemed happy enough to hold three. No additional effect had been noted from the presence of the fourth and fifth stone. Any two produced the "*two stones effect*" and any three produced the "*three stones effect*." Two or more stones empowered their bearers with the ability to speak the chaotic evil language of the abyss and forced the truth. Three stones produced windows into the bearers' minds.

Omega Stones were 13 times larger than graparbles and 0.61904762 the size of one of the 88 stones revolving around the central sphere. Starra's red scarf detected the presence of Omega Stones. Grasping the stone activated its effects. Light of the wandering sun Andreas and its surrogate the Central Sphere activated the devices. The stones sensed the presence of their fellows.

Individual stones gave their bearer differing feelings. Yannuvia felt "luck", Gruusch felt "charming", Jonna felt "strength", and Piara felt "power." Bluuch felt the same as Piara.

The presence of a fourth stone had produced no additional effect.

A fifth stone formed when 13 graparbles merged. Joulie retrieved and gripped the Fifth Omega Stone, and discovered the Wandmaker and Piara's secret. Joulie returned the artifact to Fisher.

Fisher again gripped the stone. The paleness of his hand accentuated the grayness of the gray rock. Fisher closed his hand and the stone spread between his six fingers. The uncharacteristically perplexed Mender thought out loud, in the Chaotic Evil language of the Omega Stones, "Why does this device affect me?"

Fisher felt the fifth stone gave "knowledge."

Fisher said, "I'll watch the eastern wall and assist in caring for wounded when the need arises."

The Mender left the area and the others busily prepared.

Merry Bodkin chose twelve Rangers; Breeley, Liammie, Jannette, Scottie, Morris, Goodman, Ridgway, Thalira, Gebek, Yebek, Ringway, and Songway. Yannuvia produced the Wand of Water Breathing and said **"Herb art hoof ear"** and touched Merry Bodkin. The veteran Ranger took a deep breath. The Wandmaker repeated the action for her dozen companions. Each time he uttered the command **"Herb art hoof ear."**

Clouse accepted the Wand of Lightning and took up position on the seaward wall with Carmen, Gheya, Petreccia, Myrna, Bret, and Maverick.

Sergeant Major Klunkus organized veterans into two groups, archers to be stationed on the allure and faster runners to for an assault force. Gruusch, Bluuch, Starra, and Sharchrina joined Klunkus's force.

The Wandmaker produced a glob of gum Arabic and pulled eyelashes. He uttered incantation and placed Invisibility Spells on Yathle, Quunsch, and Loogie. The Wandmaker sacrificed thirteen more eyelashes and repeated the spell on Merry Bodkin and her 12 comrades.

Merry Bodkin tapped the Wandmaker's shoulder and confirmed her charges were lined up against the wall and ready to go. She asked, "When will we know to attack?"

Yannuvia said, "You'll know."

Yannuvia produced the Wand of Flying said **"Run nailed ray gun"** and touched his thigh. The spell empowered him with flight. He pulled an eyelash, wrapped it in gum Arabic, uttered an incantation, touched his chin, and faded from sight. He continued to direct the others. The Wandmaker held the Master Wand in his right hand and a pinch of sulfur in his left. Klunkus reported he was ready. The sixteen invisible characters moved toward the door in the wall. Carmen opened the door ran to the edge of the water, shouted toward Brace's position, and fired an arrow. During the commotion the sixteen invisible characters exited the door and entered the water. There was a bit of stumbling about and one or two took a tumble but once in the water, they submerged and moved uneventfully along the sea floor to a predetermined meeting point on the Vydaelia side of the large river.

Yannuvia said, "There's nothing for it."

The Wandmaker flew effortlessly over the wall and out over the sea. About a hundred Yardley paces into the sea several pairs of Carcharians awaited orders to continue to aggravate the seaward wall personnel. The invisible Wandmaker approached the shoreline and looked at the bustling area around the millpond. Carcharians had erected crude structures. A single four-armed warrior walked among them and barked orders. Quunsch had accurately depicted the area. Yannuvia flew to a hundred paces from the shoreline and fifty feet above the sea and still far from the cavern's ceiling. He remembered his destruction of Fort Melphat and torturing the Droll Doblay. Aulgmoor paid the price of a thousand lives for killing his mother Carinne. He regretted nothing. The Tree Shepherd's assessment was spot on. Fire wizard…

Words entered the Wandmaker's mind.

"I give you my blood through which you will receive all you seek. You in turn give to me your all."

Ø ∞ Ø

The Wandmaker rolled the precious bit of sulfur in his hand, bided time, and allowed Merry Bodkin and her lot to get into position. There was little traffic coming from Doug-less. The Carcharian's Quartermaster had set up by the command tent. Stockpiles of weapons and shields, including a cache of wyvern-hide shields, lay orderly stacked. The four-arm walked toward his command hut and several others followed. Some sort of meeting was afoot. Several Carcharians came in from the sea and joined the meeting.

It was time. Yannuvia slipped the Master Wand into his robe.

Yannuvia uttered the arcane phrases, crushed the sulfur, and made complex motions with his hands. A ball of blue flame formed in the air above the working Carcharians. The flame illuminated the area. Doomed warriors looked up just as white hot flames streamed from the now visible Wandmaker's extended hands toward the command tent. In an instant a massive explosion enveloped the area in a radius of fifty feet. The water boiled at the shore. Smoke and steam rolled out over the water. Screams filled the air. Shouts rang out from Vydaelia. Sergeant Major Klunkus led a formation of seventy Rangers, Gruusch, and Bluuch toward the outcropping. At the same time shouts came from the edge of the river. Merry Bodkin's group charged into the small group of stunned Carcharians walking to and from Doug-less. With Yathle, Quunsch, and Loogie's help, the sixteen formerly invisible fighters easily dispatched seven Carcharians without suffering casualties and now blocked land escape to Doug-less. The guards at the edge of the outcropping pulled back. Klunkus's troops charged forward.

On the seaward allure Clouse shouted **"Grove veer cleave land"** and white light streamed from the tip of the Wand of Lightning into the pair of Carcharians approaching the wall. Both died instantly. The number "five" appeared in Clouse's mind.

When the fireball ended, eighty-one Carcharians were dead and many others suffered burns and smoke inhalation. The surviving Carcharians were in disarray. The guards posted at the outcropping turned and ran around the corner. Klunkus's troops ran toward the outcropping and then maintained their position about thirty paces from the point of the outcropping. His plan had been to lure the enemies into a charge and within bow range of the western wall allure.

The Carcharians drew into defensive positions and stood back to back. Yannuvia fired Magick Missiles repeatedly. The spells were lethal to already injured Carcharians. The battle seemed won.

Then Fishtrap stood up from beneath the pile of wyvern hide shields and held a wyvern hide shield in all four hands. He'd suffered burns to his legs and face. The massive four-arm angrily shouted, "Make a stand, you riff raff. All those to my right arms form two ranks facing the east. Act like Carcharians. Everyone left of me take up bows and spears! Kill the Sorcerer!"

The Wandmaker evaded several thrown spears and arrows. Taking evasive action prevented his spell casting. His legs began to feel heavy. He drifted downward a bit. The effect of the Fly Spell was ending. Merry Bodkin's group was closer so he drifted downward toward them. Fishtrap saw the descending Wandmaker, threw a smoldering shield aside, grabbed a spear from a fallen warrior, and hurled it toward Yannuvia. The projectile passed so close that Yannuvia smelled the weapon's charred shaft. The Wandmaker landed with a thud behind Loogie, Quunsch, and Yathle.

Fishtrap bellowed, "Ranks to the east! Advance! Ranks to the left, follow me! Kill them all!"

Klunkus had halted his advance a few paces short of the verge of the outcropping. After the guards retreated, Yannuvia descended, and shouts followed the fireball, the Sergeant Major, Jonna, Joulie, Tariana, Tanteras, Andra, Alistair, Gordon, Leftbridge, and Stewart and thirty other Drelves moved forward cautiously. Jonna and Stewart hazarded a peak around the corner. Carmen, Gheya, Petreccia, Myrna, Bret, and Maverick formed a rear guard and kept bows drawn with arrows nocked. Sergeant Major Klunkus ordered his troops forward, and his force turned the corner. Forty Carcharians were organizing into two ranks near the millpond. Rangers switched to bows and fired into the cluster of Carcharians. The Vydaelians outnumbered the surviving Carcharians.

Brace heard the explosion and saw the commotion on the shore. Yannuvia's fireball spell dwarfed the effect of exploding Duoth bombs. Brace sent Monty and Bradlee to check on Fishtrap's status. Clouse saw them, directed the Wand of Lightning, uttered **"Grove veer cleave land"** and sent another lethal blast into them and dropped Monty and Bradlee. The number "four" appeared in Clouse's mind.

Merry Bodkin's group blocked retreat along the seashore. The Wandmaker again fired mauve rays into the beleaguered Carcharians. Two more fell. Merry Bodkin, Yathle, Quunsch, Loogie, Breeley, Liammie, Jannette, Scottie, Morris, Goodman, Ridgway, Thalira, Gebek, Yebek, Ringway, and Songway now had the added burden of protecting the Wandmaker. Klunkus's troops arrived in numbers and faced the Carcharians who were advancing from the billabong. Veteran Rangers filled the front rank and three tiers of archers formed behind them. The front rank knelt and the archers fired from behind them into the advancing Carcharians.

Fishtrap threw two more shields aside, picked up three spears, kept one shield in front of him, and charged toward Yannuvia's location. Seventeen two-arms followed his lead. Yannuvia fired Magick Missiles in succession. The shield afforded the charging four-arm some protection. The spells had surprisingly little effect on the massive Carcharian.

Fishtrap stopped about ten paces from the Rangers and said, "Clear my path! The sorcerer is mine!"

Two-arms charged forward. Merry Bodkin, Breeley, Liammie, Jannette, Scottie, Morris, Goodman, Ridgway, Thalira, Gebek, Yebek, Ringway, and Songway readied with swords and shields. Yathle, Quunsch, and Loogie favored spears and tridents. Six Carcharians closed on Yathle, Quunsch, and Loogie. The three refugees from Dougless tried to stay between the attackers and Yannuvia. Ridgway, Thalira, and Morris formed a rank behind them. Yannuvia fired two Magick Missiles and injured two Carcharians attacking Merry Bodkin. Merry made an opportunistic stab with her short sword and felled one attacker and managed to avoid the second's blow. Now it was one on one as Merry Bodkin, Breeley, Liammie, Jannette, Scottie, Goodman, Gebek, Yebek, Ringway, and Songway each faced a Carcharian. The Rangers were quicker and veterans of many battles with larger Drolls. The Carcharians matched the Drolls' strength, but lacked their agility and swordsmanship. Their large spears and tridents served up deadly force, but served it slowly and crudely. Merry Bodkin's group repeatedly wounded their larger opponents. Gebek took a glancing blow to his shoulder which knocked him to the ground and relieved him of his shield. The Carcharian raised his spear to end the fight but Merry Bodkin quickly slapped his spear with her shield and gave Gebek a chance to regain his footing. Fishtrap menacingly shouted obscenities at

Yannuvia, who pondered the value of his learning Gruusch's language. Ridgway, Thalira, and Morris gamely stepped forward and engaged three Carcharians, leaving for the moment Quunsch, Yathle, and Loogie against one opponent. Quunsch's battle prowess was readily evident. The big half-Bugwully kicked his opponent with his powerful left leg and stabbed the off-balance victim. The two-arm fell to his knees and Quunsch finished him with a heavy blow to his head. Morris evaded several lunges from his foe and managed to get close enough to inflict a deep wound on his leg. Fishtrap walked forward and swatted Morris aside, knocking the Ranger into the cavern wall. Quunsch was quickly on Morris's opponent who stepped between Quunsch and Fishtrap. Quunsch threw the two-arm backwards into Fishtrap. The two-arm charged angrily but Quunsch evaded him and clobbered him with his spear. Quickly Quunsch jammed the spear into his chest and ended the fight. Yathle bested his foe and turned to help Thalira. Ridgway had little success and spent most of his time dodging blows. Loogie and his foe were well matched and both scored blows. Fishtrap ripped spears in his lower left and lower right hands through the air. He struck Yathle's right arm with a glancing blow. Thalira thrust her short sword into her opponent's forearm. The wound was not critical but it kept the Carcharian from doing further damage to Yathle. Yannuvia hit Fishtrap with a Magick Missile. The spell had little effect. Thalira dodged the Carcharian's spear, but her huge opponent smashed into her with his shield hand and knocked her asunder. Yathle fought with only one effective arm, but the new opponent had attacked Thalira and left himself vulnerable. Yathle shoved his spear through the opponent's armor and brought him down. Ridgway's opponent also disdained his weapon and grabbed Ridgway and threw the Ranger against the wall. Yathle turned to Ridgway's opponent. Both Loogie and his opponent scored hits. Loogie dropped to one knee. The Carcharian drew his spear back but Yannuvia hit him in the face with a Magick Missile and opened a grievous wound. Loogie pushed his spear into the Carcharian and brought him down. Loogie then collapsed. Dark green blood poured profusely from his side. Yathle stood against Ridgway's opponent and fought one-handed. The opponents exchanged blows three times. Yathle lost his spear on the third attack and dropped to the ground. Quunsch leaped into the air and slammed both feet into Yathle's opponent's chest, and knocked the Carcharian backward. The drop kick had been one of the half-Bugwully's favorite moves in the arena. The Carcharian fell backward. Quunsch finished him with a hard blow to his throat. The six two-arms with Fishtrap had been defeated, but Quunsch was out of position and left Fishtrap a clear path to the Wandmaker. Yannuvia backed up. Merry Bodkin had scored several successful attacks against her opponent and leapt into the air and hit him across the face with the hilt of her sword. The haymaker stunned the Carcharian, who dropped to his knees. Merry thrust her sword through his throat. This briefly freed her to intercede for the Wandmaker.

She was no match for the four-armed Carcharian.

Fishtrap grabbed her with a large hand and growled, "I'm going to rip off your head and **** down your neck! Say good-bye."

Yannuvia hit Fishtrap with another Magick Missile. The spell only annoyed the four-arm. Fishtrap paused for a moment and left Merry kicking and struggling in the air. Suddenly Quunsch flew through the air and landed both huge feet into Fishtrap's torso. The blow freed Merry Bodkin from his grasp and she rolled aside gasping and holding her throat. Fishtrap righted his body and cursed. Quunsch hurled his body toward the four-arm again, but this time Fishtrap was ready and grabbed Quunsch with three arms and raised the spear in his fourth hand. Quunsch broke free but was off balance. Fishtrap clobbered him with both left arms and sent him flying towards the water. Quunsch lay motionless. Fishtrap turned toward the injured Wandmaker and muttered, "You're a** is mine now!"

Yathle, Loogie, Merry Bodkin, Morris, Ridgway, Thalira, and Quunsch were incapacitated. Breeley, Liammie, Jannette, Scottie, Goodman, Gebek, Yebek, and Ringway, and Songway battled against eight Carcharians. The Rangers scored repeatedly but the larger opponents withstood the attacks.

Yannuvia sent three ineffective Magick Missiles into Fishtrap. The four-arm threw his spear down and declared, "I'm going to choke the life out of you. Make your peace sorcerer."

Yannuvia turned to run but the bigger Carcharian was quickly on him and knocked him to the ground. The sounds of battle seemed distant. His ears rang. Fishtrap reached down and grabbed his robe and pulled the Wandmaker up with his left lower hand. He then placed both his right and left upper hands around Yannuvia's head. Quunsch leapt through the air and slammed both huge Bugwullyish feet into the four-arm and knocked Fishtrap and Yannuvia down. The big Carcharian fell on Yannuvia's right leg. The sickening crunch told The Wandmaker at least one bone was broken. Both Fishtrap and Quunsch stood. Yannuvia managed to crawl to the cavern wall. Years of ridicule and frustration welled up in Quunsch. The bulky legs that brought him so much teasing proved effective weapons. Quunsch leapt and kicked Fishtrap repeatedly. The bigger four-arm retrieved a spear, but Quunsch repeatedly outmaneuvered him. Fishtrap lunged forward and missed. Quunsch went into one of his patented leaps and wrapped his powerful legs around Fishtrap's throat. Fishtrap flailed his four arms but Quunsch brought him to the ground and squeezed tighter. His finishing move ended many battles in the arena. After several minutes of struggling it ended Fishtrap's life. Exhausted Quunsch slumped over the dead four-arm. Yannuvia sat up. Gebek and Goodman lay on the ground. The Wandmaker was unable to walk and his head throbbed, but Magick Missiles required neither incantation nor material component. Yannuvia poured them into Breeley, Liammie, Jannette, Scottie, Yebek, Ringway, and Songway's opponents. Two badly wounded Carcharians fell. The odds were now 7 on 6, and the Rangers fought exhaustion. Excruciating pain overcame Yannuvia and he leaned back against the rock wall. To the east of the millpond, archers had inflicted many casualties before the hand to hand conflict began. Bluuch and Gruusch swayed many battles. Once the hand to hand battles favored the Vydaelians, Bluuch and Gruusch broke away and sped toward the Wandmaker. They arrived too late to help Quunsch. The massive four-arm Bluuch quickly ended three battles. Gruusch ended two others. The final Carcharian Taktaki fought on. Bluuch asked the young warrior to surrender. Taktaki uttered expletives and swung mightily at Jannette and knocked the Ranger down. Bluuch smote Taktaki with a single spearing.

Scottie and Yebek had broken arms. Breeley's nose was broken. Liammie suffered a shallow stab wound on his arm. Merry Bodkin sat beside Yannuvia with sword at ready and coughed repeatedly. Quunsch lay by the fallen four-arm and breathed heavily. Yathle, Loogie, Jannette, Morris, Goodman, Ridgway, Thalira, and Gebek were down. Loogie lay in an ominous pool of dark green blood. Yathle's arm was misshapen. Ringway and Songway were unhurt but breathing heavily from exhaustion.

Klunkus's charges won battle after battle and thinned the Carcharians numbers by the millpond. Sergeant Major Klunkus offered quarter, but the frenzied Carcharians refused to stop fighting. The death of their leader only spurred them on. Some disdained shields and took up fallen comrades' weapons and fought like berserkers with two weapons. The Carcharians battled till their last warrior fell.

Veteran two-arm Phoodle came out of the sea and charged toward Yannuvia. Gruusch intercepted him. Enraged Phoodle knocked Gruusch down and raised his trident to end the young Carcharian's days. Mighty Bluuch stepped in and drove two spears through Phoodle.

Ø ∞ Ø

Brace saw his friend Phoodle fall. The big two-arm griped his spear and pondered charging the shore. There was a chance he might spear the sorcerer before the newcomers killed him. No... four-armed Bluuch patrolled the rocky beach. He'd just share his friend's fate. Brace opted to return to Doug-less to inform Lunniedale of the debacle. Hopefully the blame would fall on Fishtrap, who was already dead.

Ø ∞ Ø

Sea elf Squaddie Faryn followed Brace.

CHAPTER 40

After Fishtrap

202 Carcharians had died.

After the battle, Vydaelians gathered nine extruded stones. Noble Loogie succumbed to his wounds. His nodule was 1.6 times heavier than the eight from Morris, Gebek, Eyesen, Myrna, Vasor, Rettick, Hummitch, and Ayden. Scores of Vydaelians poured from the western wall to gather and aid the injured. Bluuch and Gruusch headed up a squad of twenty reserves who watched the shore leading to Doug-less. Clouse arrived with the Wand of Lightning. Fisher received the nine graparbles, labeled each as to its source, and carefully stored them separately. Rangers carried the bodies of the fallen into the citadel. Quunsch struggled to his feet and insisted on carrying the injured Wandmaker to the inner ward of the quadrangle. Once all wounded were attended, the Vydaelians gathered the fallen Carcharians and searched through the wreckage. Most gear and weaponry were ruined. The Rangers gathered six wyvern hide shields and several undamaged spears and tridents and nets, which would prove valuable to their Carcharian allies. Gruusch gathered the four-arm's bling. Among his possessions was a chain bearing a pink semicircular stone. The Drelve-Vydaelians respectfully collected the remains of their enemies and ignited a pyre.

The pyre burned for more than two rotations of the Day Glass.

Sergeant Major Klunkus rushed about the quadrangle giving orders and placed reserves on the allures and at the verge of the outcropping to watch the sea and the west. The wounded and bodies of the fallen were inside the inner ward. Fisher collected the nine graparbles and kept them separated and then entered the inner ward to attend the injured.

Elders Dienas, Yiuryna, and matrons busily looked after the injured. Once the casualties were inside Vydaelia's walls, Klunkus organized a search of the ruined Carcharian outpost. Most gear and weaponry was destroyed in the Wandmaker's fireball. Klunkus first concentrated on keeping the perimeter watched. Clouse assisted by saying **"Jar old ford"** and touching young Rangers Fexa, Fenideen, and Wilfrise. This imparted "haste" on the trio. He then plucked eyebrows, used gum Arabic, conjured, incanted, and placed Invisibility Spells on Fexa and Fenideen. The young Rangers positioned at the outcropping to monitor the Carcharians' pyre and the land route from Doug-less. Wilfrise was hasted but visible in order to facilitate alerting the allure of approaching enemies. The invisible Rangers eased a bit further around the corner and stood quietly. Clouse then went to the inner ward. Jonna, Joulie, Tariana, Tanteras, and Andra positioned on the western allure and stayed on high alert. Alistair, Gordon, Leftbridge, Stewart, Carmen, Gheya, Petreccia. Bret, and Maverick stood and intervals and watched the sea. Gruusch and Starra stood with them. Peter, Blair, Dennis, Bernard, and Noone kept eyes toward the Duoth passages. During the entire battle Blair saw Duoths peeking out from the passageway on only two occasions. A well placed arrow chased the pudgy marshmallow man back up the passage.

Clouse took the Wand of Healing. There were plenty of candidates. Fisher had already been hard at work dressing wounds, and administering potions to ease pain and unguents to stop bleeding and battle infection. The Wandmaker Yannuvia's leg was immobilized. Morganne gave him enhancing root tubers and tea. Quunsch sat disgruntled against the wall. He'd insisted on going into the water to chase after possible survivors, but Klunkus ordered him into the inner ward, where he promptly collapsed from fatigue. Clouse approached Yannuvia with the Wand of Healing.

The Wandmaker said, "Clouse, I'd rather you attend the others."

Fisher interrupted, "No, Wandmaker, you are most critical to our survival. If he improves your status, then you'll be able to help us, and we do need help. Clouse, proceed with the healing spell."

Clouse said **"rut fir ford bee haze"** and touched Yannuvia with the Wand of Healing. An orange aura covered the Wandmaker. Several small cuts and scratches healed completely. A snapping sound emanated from his injured leg, and the wince left Yannuvia's face as his pain abated.

The spell did not fully repair the bone, but it aligned the fragments and began the healing process while eliminating the pain. The Wandmaker stood with his splint.

Clouse said, "I should give you the Wand of Healing. I can use the healing dweomer."

Yannuvia said, "I knew the healing dweomer when Fisher entered the chrysalis, so you knew it when you emerged with him. Unfortunately casting the spell requires conjuration, incantation, and mistletoe. My mind is weary and I have very little mistletoe in reserve. So it's best we use the Wand of Healing. The Wand of Healing was created on the first day of the Dark Period. Magick touches you. It should have as many uses in your hand as mine. Use it as long as you can. Yathle is badly injured. Touch him next."

Half sea-elf Yathle sat dejectedly on a bench with his injured arm wrapped in a sling. Clouse approached the two-armed Carcharian, said **"rut fir ford bee haze,"** and touched Yathle's injured arm with the wand. The arm snapped and straightened.

Yathle said, "Thank you. I miss Queen Piara's touch. Can you do anything for Loogie?"

Loogie's body lay with the slain Vydaelians.

Yannuvia said, "Death is Nature's servant. Restoring life is beyond Magick. We can only honor his memory. He, and you, fought well. You, Loogie, and Quunsch saved me and many others."

Yathle said, "My arm feels weak, but it no longer hurts."

Clouse cautioned, "The bone will require time to heal. You must keep it in the sling."

Yathle hung his head and nodded.

Merry Bodkin sat up against the wall, rubbed her throat, and coughed. Angry bruises and several lacerations covered her neck and shoulders. Matron Pamyrga cleaned the wounds and applied unguent. Clouse uttered **"rut fir ford bee haze"** and touched Merry. Wounds closed and she took a deep breath. She spoke in a hoarse voice, "It was my command. I lost three of our people. Loogie, Morris, and Gebek no longer draw breath. But for Quunsch and Yathle I'd have joined them in death. I'm not worthy."

Clouse flatly answered, "You slew Carcharians and helped keep the Wandmaker alive. Stand tall."

Scottie suffered a broken arm. Clouse said **"rut fir ford bee haze,"** used the wand, and alleviated the Ranger's pain. Matrons placed the gimpy arm in a sling. Yannuvia suggested Scottie retire to his quarters, but the Ranger replied, "My eyes are fine. I'll go to the wall and watch the sea."

Breeley's broken nose and sprained wrist were attended by Matron Suthyia. The Ranger declined aid from Clouse and urged the green guy to go to others. Liammie's arm laceration was bandaged and he also set off for the wall. Clouse approached Yebek, said **"rut fir ford bee haze"** and touched the Ranger's broken arm. Yebek's physical pain abated but he mourned his brother Gebek who lay by Loogie. Jannette, Goodman, and Thalira were knocked out by the Carcharians and suffered concussions. The three had multiple bruises and knots on their heads, but all three were coming around. Ridgway remained unconscious. He'd been thrown into the rock wall. He suffered a broken leg and suffered nasty lacerations on his head.

Yannuvia assessed Ridgway's wounds and pulled a precious piece of mistletoe from his scant supply. He crushed the mistletoe, conjured, and sang a lyrical incantation. The "heal serious wounds" spell closed the wounds on Ridgway's body. The Ranger moved about but did not awaken. Yannuvia said, "Only time will tell. I had to try." Clouse said **"rut fir ford bee haze"** and touched Ridgway with the wand. The Ranger's breathing became more regular.

Sixteen Rangers from Klunkus's force were wounded. Clouse used the Wand of Healing on seven and improved their wounds. After touching the last, the number "Thirteen" appeared in Clouse's mind. Clouse attempted to use the wand on the next Ranger, but after he said **"rut fir ford bee haze"** words appeared in his mind. Clouse understood 17711 dialects through his Menderish legacy. The language was that of the Omega Stones and the phrase instructed the Wand of Healing would be without power until it was again touched by grayness. Clouse informed the Wandmaker, "Until the next wandmaking ceremony and the activation of the central sphere, the Wand of Healing is dormant. It's given thirteen uses. I've used them."

Yannuvia produced mistletoe and shared it with Clouse. The duo casts heal spells on the remaining nine wounded rangers. Most recovered to the point of resuming duty. Two sustained head wounds and remained with Ridgway under close observation. The Wandmaker retained enough mistletoe to cast only three more spells. The Vydaelians now relied heavily on the skills of Fisher, Clouse, and the experience of the elders. Starra and Sharchrina worked alongside the Drelve-Vydaelians. Bluuch and Gruusch lingered around the area.

Matrons covered the bodies of Loogie, Morris, Gebek, Eyesen, Myrna, Vasor, Rettick, Hummitch, and Ayden with bedcovers. Yorcia sat by her life mate Hummitch's corpse. Lynnae's wrapped body rested nearby.

The Wandmaker limped alongside Sergeant Major Klunkus, Gruusch, and Bluuch. The foursome walked through the busy quadrangle. Dragging Bluuch away from Starra was difficult, but the four-arm realized security of Vydaelia was paramount to protecting the princess and fulfilling his obligation to the departed Piara.

CHAPTER 41

Return to Doug-less

Two-arm Brace swam furiously back to Doug-less and never looked back over his broad shoulders. From his position offshore the commander of the seaward assault on the newcomers saw the carnage.

Ǿ ∞ Ǿ

Squaddie Frayn of Graywood observed from a bit further back from shore.

Ǿ ∞ Ǿ

Brace lamented that the small newcomers fought tenaciously and wielded powerful Magick. Traitorous Carcharians contributed greatly to the forces of Doug-less's defeat. Cursed Queen Piara and her lot! Fishtrap, Phoodle, Monty, Bradlee, and over 200 of his kind were slain. The braggart Boggle had escaped death by getting shot in the a** by an arrow. He'd been led back to Doug-less only moments before the sorcerer brought destruction from above the water. Brace approached the hidden entry to Doug-less, dove deeper, and made his way past the guards and into the Circle of Willis.

Ǿ ∞ Ǿ

Frayn went to the secluded reed area and found young Bryni waiting. He dispatched the youth to Graywood to keep Commandant Inyra apprised of happenings across the seas. A Carcharian defeat was a sea elf victory!

Ø ∞ Ø

The most experienced two-armed warriors now guarded the Circle of Willis. Double shifts stood at all times. Tippie, Caanno, Tilertoo, Ambroo, Nuttin, Hunnie, Ruutchie, Draacks, and Fraaid watched the circle. The guards on duty dutifully checked Brace. Now he had the ignominy of facing King Lunniedale.

Top Guard Clootch met Brace just beyond the Circle of Willis and was first to hear his glum report. He briefly consoled his old friend and said, "Lord Crudle arrived just hours ago in anticipation of a victory by his son Fishtrap. King Lunniedale called for Seabee mead."

Brace said timidly, "Maybe I ought to wait to give them the bad news."

Clootch replied, "Best get it over with! Boggle already blurted out some news of casualties when he returned. He squawked like a wounded sea chicken when they carried him into the birthing area for treatment. I hope the arrow in his a** didn't injure his brain!"

Brace answered, "My sentiments exactly. Quunsch bested him repeatedly. Our teasing the half-Bugwully came home to haunt us. Bluuch proved a cornerstone of their defense."

Clootch said, "I'd have thought it'd be Urquhart. I miss his four arms most."

Brace said, "Never saw him. I suppose Urquhart was within the citadel. The walls of the newcomer's fortress exceed the strength of the structures we've encountered. They fight in organized, efficient manner. I followed orders, but I know I wasted the lives of many warriors."

Clootch and Brace made their way through the crowded common area of Doug-less. New arrivals bolstered the Carcharians numbers by the moment. Crudle had arrived with five hundred warriors and the promise of five hundred more. The call for war had gone to all corners of King Lunniedale's realm.

The guards stepped aside and allowed the duo entry to the king's council room. Brace tentatively stepped through the door. King Lunniedale did not like bad news and had been known to take it out on the messengers.

Lunniedale sat at the table. Four-arm Crudle who was almost as large sat with the King. Gruusch's father Viceroy Phederal, Commander Gurgla, Heraldo, Reefa, Mountain Giant Guppie, recently promoted Commander Tapasbar, important members of Crudle's entourage, and the King's inner circle sat around the table. Seabee mead flowed freely. Attrition had necessitated promotion of numerous two-arms to positions of import.

King Lunniedale glowered at Brace and said, "If you aren't going to ****, get off the pot, Brace. Report!"

Guffaws filled the chamber.

Brace gulped and told the gloomy tale of Fishtrap's defeat. He embellished the roles of Quunsch, Bluuch, Yathle, and Loogie. He relayed the Magick assaults from the flying sorcerer and greenish sorcerer on the allure. He described Loogie's death in detail. Finally he gave a glorious description of Fishtrap's battle and sang praises of Crudle's late four-armed son. Brace concluded, "Had Quunsch not back-stabbed him, noble Fishtrap would have slain the newcomer's flying sorcerer. Phoodle saw Fishtrap fall and charged into the enemies. Bluuch cowardly stabbed him from behind. Our warriors fought gloriously!"

Lord Crudle stood, slammed his four hands into the table and cursed, "****! ****** *******! Back-stabbers! Cowards! Traitors! My son! They must pay!"

Mountain Giant Guppie growled, "So my amulet is in the hands of the newcomers! It matters little compared to the deaths of so many with whom I shared mead."

Lunniedale's wrath was immeasurable. The King shouted, "Brace, you are sea chicken ****! Why are you not lying as carrion on the beach with Crudle's son Fishtrap and my warriors? At least you are standing within range of my throwing spear!"

Brace took a deep breath, puffed out his chest, ripped open his wet tunic to expose his bare blue-green hide, and resolutely said, "My king, if my death consoles you, so be it. I thought of charging the shore. Phoodle barely made it ashore before the cowards backstabbed him. My death meant nothing on the shore by the millpond. At least I have served the purpose of informing you of your warriors' brave stand and the collusion of the b**** Queen's allies. Had only I been given the chance to ram my spear into her lecherous chest! Take my life now if it pleases you!"

King Lunniedale clutched the long spear in his favorite hand, his lower left and breathed deeply. All around the table grimaced. Brace held his position.

The irate King lowered the spear and said, "**** fire! I may have found a warrior that's worth a ****! Join our table, new Commander Brace! Have some mead! Then gather a hundred warriors post haste and go attack those ******** across the sea. I want their heads! Phederal, you might take something from Brace's bravery! Send that ******* that got shot in the a** back into battle! I don't want to hear of anyone running away from the battle."

Lord Crudle echoed the King's sentiments, "I never thought I'd want to see a two-arm command! Avenge my son! I'll ready a thousand warriors to swarm over their walls and kill them all! ****** *******!"

Brace thought he'd draw his last breath. Instead he was the first two-arm in his generation to attain the rank of Commander. He closed his tunic, stood straight, and announced, "My King, I will forego the mead! I go now to raise an assault force. We'll depart immediately!"

Top Guard Clootch said, "My King, permission to speak!"

Lunniedale sat down heavily, gulped from his big mug, and said, "What is it Clootch?"

Clootch asked, "My King, permission to turn over my guard at the circle and join my friend Brace in battle."

King Lunniedale said, "I'll be ******! Two warriors with backbones! Permission granted! Promote Hunnie to Top Guard."

Clootch said, "Done!"

Clootch and Brace turned and left the chamber room. Crudle wailed inconsolably.

Brace addressed his friend, "That was pretty dumb, Clootch."

Clootch said, "Yes, it was. Are you not too tired to proceed?"

Brace said, "Giving the King bad news is risky business. I thought I was a goner! Being tired and in command is better than dead. Who'd you choose to attack?"

Clootch said, "Crudle's men are fresh and loved Fishtrap. They'll fight tenaciously. We'll pick Tapasbar's squad. They are veterans."

Word spread quickly through Doug-less of the debacle. Every warrior with Crudle volunteered for the assault force. Tapasbar's squad energetically joined. Boggle limped out of the infirmary in the birthing area with the arrow freshly removed from his butt and reluctantly picked up his gear.

The Carcharians formed ranks and exited Doug-less through the Circle of Willis. The Mountain Giant Guppie and his cave warg Fenrir waited on the shoreline and offered to join.

Clootch asked, "Are you going to employ the phalanx like Fishtrap?"

Brace said, "Didn't work very well, did it? I followed Fishtrap's orders and used my seawall attacks to create diversion and a nuisance. Still we managed to get a ladder to the wall. Boggle made it to the top before Quunsch clobbered him. A newcomer shot him in the a** as he ran away. I'm going to attack the sea wall in force. It's a long expanse but they can only put a few defenders at any one place, and only fire a few rounds of arrows as we charge from the sea."

Clootch said, "The problem I see is the ladders. Swimming with ladders will impede our advance."

Brace said, "Boats!"

Clootch said, "Carcharians don't use boats! We swim much faster than we can row."

Brace said, "Ladders don't mind riding on boats. Gather supplies and at least twenty ladders. Have the three pontoon boats brought up from Soggy Inlet. The old boats were captured from the troglodyte chieftain Oogum long ago. The King uses them to transport mead and other niceties to Doug-less. I understand Heraldo and Reefa used them to travel to Doubling to the north and east of Cane Bisque Bay."

Clootch argued, "Won't the sorcerer just singe the boats with Magick?"

Brace said, "His power is limited. He sat rather helpless on the shore after he sent the devastating fire storm against Fishtrap's force. He sank from the air. Had he the capability he'd have flown away from the fray. Instead he relied on his colleagues to bail him out and save his a**. Many gave their lives protecting him, including the fool Loogie. If he wastes Magick on the boats, all we've lost is some cypress wood and he's used spells that might have been used on us."

Clootch said, "Serving as oarsmen is beneath Carcharians. Conscripted troglodytes and Bugwullies usually fulfill those tasks."

Brace said, "They will do so again. I want my warriors rested and ready to fight. Swimming is second nature to us. We'll get across the sea before the boats and rest in or on the water and feed on the sea's bounty. When the boats arrive with the ladders we'll attack in force. They will outnumber us. But attacking a short segment of the wall will lessen the effect of their superior numbers."

Clootch said, "I'll send for some Trogs and Bugs. Boggle still complains about his sore a**! He can serve as oar master on one of the boats. I doubt he wants to meet up with Quunsch again."

Brace asked, "Are you sure he can serve as oar master?"

Clootch said, "How hard is it to say one, two, three, four, grab those oars and row some more, you scumbags? Besides, I'll assign Cutthroat from Tapasbar's squad to master one boat, and I'll command the third and watch over them. You must get your materials timely!"

Brace said, "I'm counting on you."

Clootch pondered, "I'll be there. I don't want to miss the traitor's comeuppance."

Brace agreed, "Agreed! Bluuch, Loogie, and Quunsch were in the thick of it. Loogie fell. I did not see Urquhart, Piara, Starra, and Sharchrina. Say what you will about him, Quunsch was undefeated in the arenas. He used his abilities in his battle with Fishtrap. Urquhart likely stands by the former Queen or her daughter. He watched over them constantly. Bluuch uses all four arms well. I'd not want to meet any of the three one on one."

In the King's council room Lord Crudle's grief turned to anger and festered. Crudle roared, "I'll gather two companies and lead them myself!"

Lunniedale warned, "Brace and Clootch have already departed. They employed the old ships."

Crudle said, "They are attacking from the sea. They'll soften up the enemies. We'll attack from the west!"

The massive four-arm stormed out of the council room.

The Mountain Giant Guppie was chagrinned over the loss of his amulet and opted to follow Crudle. Fenrir the cave warg tagged along.

Ø ∞ Ø

Frayn rode his pottyhippomus and followed Brace's ships.

CHAPTER 42

"Join Add Yams"
The Magick Missile Wand

The Wandmaker Yannuvia, Sergeant Major Klunkus, Fisher, Clouse, Jonna, Joulie, Dienas, Yiuryna, Tanteras, Willifron and two-armed Gruusch, four-armed Bluuch, Alistair, Gordon, Leftbridge, Stewart, Peter, Blair, Dennis, Bernard, and Noone regrouped in the outer ward of the quadrangle of Vydaelia. The entire community remained on high alert. Fexa and Fenideen remained "invisible" and carried sticks, which they tapped on the stony ground. Others saw a stick floating eerily in midair and noted the invisible Rangers' location.

Gear salvaged from the Carcharians included two dozen undamaged spears, water tight containers of crude oil, a few bows and quivers, large squid bladder suits, packs, knives, and mostly worthless bling. Gruusch produced the four-arm's bling. He carried ornamental garb typical of royal Carcharians and wore a necklace around his neck. The necklace was made of purple mooler hide and suspended a pink stone. Yannuvia's Defect Magick Spell produced strong auras.

The Wandmaker said, "The amulet projects strong Magick. We should proceed cautiously with an item worn by an enemy. Most Magick does not affect Fisher and Clouse. The amulet should be safe in the hands of a *reflector*. One of you should carry it."

Fisher commented, "I'm burdened. Give it to Clouse."

Clouse accepted the amulet and placed it around his neck. He suffered no ill effects. Rangers stored other items after the Carcharians picked from the spears.

The group turned to Bluuch.

Bluuch's four arms outweighed his sea elfish blood and gave him privileged status in Doug-less. He'd seen prominent visitors to King Lunniedale's realm and recognized the four-armed commander of the Carcharian raiders as Fishtrap, the son of Lord Crudle, leader of the Cane Bisque Bay Carcharians. Crudle was Lunniedale's strongest ally. The death of his son certainly would bring reprisals. Yannuvia and Klunkus anticipated renewed aggression. The Wandmaker devised a plan to extend the wall to the outcropping and build an allure to allow vision of the approach by the millpond.

The Wandmaker again used the Wand of Masonry with its **"Wood row will son"** command and softened stone in the rock wall and created building blocks. Over the course of a rotation of the Day Glass, the Wandmaker produced three score blocks, which was just enough to lay the base of the wall from the outcropping to the edge of the sea. Yathle used his one functional arm to carry boulders. Clouse announced the beginning of the Dark Period was imminent. Yannuvia paused in his block making and made his way to the geodesic dome that contained the Central Sphere and 88 stones. Fisher, Morganne, Clouse, Jonna, Joulie, Dienes, Yiuryna, and 26 other Vydaelians accompanied the Wandmaker.

Holding the Knock Wand in his right hand, the Wandmaker walked to door of the geodesic dome, touched the door, and said **"cow vine cool ledge."** The door opened, and the group entered. Protocol dictated all but a selected few Rangers attended the wand making ceremonies, but recent events forced most able bodied Rangers to guard duty. Many matrons attended the wounded. 34 Vydaelians including the Wandmaker entered the dome.

The Wandmaker emptied his right hand, kept the Master Wand in his left, walked to the center of the dome, touched his spell book *the Gifts of Andreas to the People of the Forest* with the red and blue tipped wand, and said, **"Hairy true man."**

The Central Sphere drifted downward. At the moment the six-foot diameter sphere began to move, the 88 smaller stones froze in their orbits. The six-foot diameter sphere approached Yannuvia and stopped with its center four feet from the floor and also four feet from the Spellweaver. Slowly the triumvirate of runes on the Central Sphere faded. The surface of the sphere changed to a brilliant reflecting surface. The Wandmaker's image appeared on the Central Sphere and eighty-eight smaller stones.

Slowly Yannuvia's visage disappeared and the trio of runes reappeared on all 89 stones. At the exact moment the runes reappeared, another wand appeared in Yannuvia's right hand. One of thirteen stones that shared an orbit of 48-foot diameter eerily floated from its orbit. The little stone moved toward the Wandmaker's right hand, where he held the new featureless wand. Yannuvia placed the wand in his pocket, extended his hand, and grasped the small spherical stone. The stone softened and meld to the shape of his hand. The Wandmaker held a Stone of Magick Missiles.

Yannuvia had created new wands with each dark period, as calculated by the Day Glass rotations and the internal clocks of Fisher, Clouse, and Piara. During the Approximation he created the exceptional USA Wand. Kirrie's visage visited his dreams and claimed to be a messenger and sister of Grayness. She reported the Wandmaker's nodule had reached its maximum size and could get no larger. When the Dark Periods arrived he would be able to create wands, but they would share the same power. He now knew that power was Magick Missile Spells. When Grayness returned the Central Sphere and four score and eight stones would direct him to create another exceptional wand, his nodule would then *tell* him what to do, and Grayness would recharge expended wands.

Yannuvia released the stone. The Stone of Magick Missiles regained its spherical shape and eerily hovered near his right hand. Next he removed the new wand from his pocket and held it in his right hand. Very small runes appeared on the new wand.

Ǿ ∞ Ǿ

On the surface of the Central Sphere, the runes faded, Yannuvia's image briefly reappeared and faded, and then a phrase written in Old Drelvish appeared.

"Join add yams."

The Stone of Magick Missiles wobbled back to its original position in an orbit of 48-foot diameter with twelve other stones.

Another aura of Magick followed. The Central Sphere returned to its position thirty-four feet above the floor and precisely over the center of the hemisphere. The eighty-eight small stones resumed their rotations around the Central Sphere. The observers felt an itch in their left hands and curiously glanced at the little nodules at the base of their left fifth digit. The nodules increased in size by one graparble. Yannuvia's nodule did not change. Yannuvia took the spell book, used the red and blue tipped wand, and painstakingly etched Wand of Magick Missiles, *1-eleven*, and the command "**Join add yams**."

The Wandmaker placed the Wand of Magick Missiles in his deep pocket and said, "In the hand of everyone but Clouse and me, this wand has thirteen uses. It should be used only in an emergency. In 29 rotations of the Day Glass we must again enter the geodesic dome. Let's get back to work."

The Wand of Healing emitted a gray aura. The Healing Wand regained 13 uses during the wand making ceremony. It was an unexpected boon. None of the other wands regained expended usages. Yannuvia led the group out of the geodesic dome.

CHAPTER 43

Debating Strategy

Yannuvia walked with the assistance of a cane and turned toward the western wall.

Fisher asked, "Where are you heading Wandmaker?"

Yannuvia replied, "I want to get back to preparing the new wall. We've only begun the construction."

Fisher platonically said, "There are more pressing issues."

Sergeant Major Klunkus, Elder Dienas, Elder Yiuryna, Bluuch, Yathle, Quunsch, and Gruusch joined the Wandmaker's party.

Klunkus said, "Wandmaker, we lack adequate personnel to defend the walls we have. Now we have lost ten of our first line defenders, nine Rangers and noble Loogie. I stood by Hummitch at the Battle of Lone Oak Meadow. Everyone is tired, but we know another attack might be coming soon. Might our energies be better spent reinforcing the existing walls?"

Elder Dienas added, "Noble Klunkus makes a valid point Wandmaker. Nine of our own and noble Loogie have fallen. We don't have the luxury of the forests of Alms Glen and Lost Sons to lay them to rest. The only soil is the onyum patch area. We must attend those we have lost and return them to the forest."

Fisher added, "We should concentrate on strengthening existing defenses."

Yannuvia slammed his cane against the wall and said, "Do you question my judgment?"

Fisher answered, "Yes."

Yannuvia responded, "Why am I not surprised by your answer?"

289

Fisher added, "Let's assess our situation. Bluuch, what do you think will be the King of Doug-less's next move?"

Yannuvia scoffed, "I just fried over a hundred of his warriors with a single spell! He lost over two hundred altogether including his commander! I'd say he'll be licking his wounds!"

Bluuch said, "Wandmaker, Carcharians live for war and fighting. By now word has reached Doug-less of the battle. Envoys will carry word to Lord Crudle of his son's death. Crudle sent over a thousand warriors against the rebellious overlord Skullbuster."

Klunkus said, "Skullbuster? Odd name…"

Bluuch replied, "Not really. He was good at it."

Dienas asked, "Good at it?"

Bluuch said, "Skull busting. Skullbuster ruled over lands beyond Cane Bisque Bay in Reed Creek Delta. He'd subjugated troglodytes and coerced them to do mundane tasks. He made a big mistake and defied King Lunniedale. Lunniedale and Crudle sent Fishtrap with two legions to quell the resistance. When it was over Skullbuster fed the sea beasts. Losing two hundred warriors will not faze the King, but losing a four-armed son will rile old Crudle. We only faced a probing force. Their purpose was to wear us down. They were doing a pretty good job of it until the Wandmaker's spell."

Yiuryna said, "I agree with Dienas that we must honor our dead. We must continue our Drelvish traditions. We must give our friends back to the forest, albeit, the onyum patch is not much of a forest."

Dienas said, "It's the only forest we have."

Yannuvia said, "Fisher, you have said little about Carcharians. What say you? What knowledge do Menders share of our enemies?"

Fisher said, "We've had Carcharians to study since Gruusch arrived and Piara's party followed. I've learned more from them than reflecting on my forebears' experience. There was no need to probe my mind for obscure memories. But if you insist…"

Yannuvia said, "I insist!"

Fisher said, "As I've said before, I have little insight into this area. A Mender walked these shores and encountered Duoths, Sea Elves, and Carcharians. My knowledge confirms Bluuch's information. They will be back and probably in greater numbers. Their actions from the sea were merely toying with us. They never attacked in force and still nigh breached the wall. Carcharians will be comfortable attacking from the sea. I'd imagine that's where they'll come from."

Bluuch said, "I agree."

Clouse said, "I'd confirm Fisher's impressions."

Sergeant Major Klunkus said, "Let's honor our fallen colleagues. I must remind you of our vulnerability. We must be ready. Bluuch, what about Loogie?"

Bluuch replied, "He has no living family. I'd like to honor him with a pyre and then let him rest with those with whom he fought and died."

Dienas said, "So be it."

Klunkus looked anxiously toward the sea and said, "I'll keep guards at all times along the wall and at the outcropping. Quunsch, Fexa, and Fenideen have volunteered to go beyond the millpond to give us advance warning. Quunsch is hiding in the reeds and Fexa and Fenideen remain invisible. Prepare our fallen. We must proceed with haste."

Fisher said, "What of the graparbles that I carry?"

Jonna said, "Wandmaker, why have you told Fisher to keep the little stones separate?"

Yannuvia said, "We've seen them unite. We don't know the effects of additional stones. The fourth did nothing apparent. We've yet to activate all five. Our benefactor suggested 'planting' the graparbles. I'd like to test them. Fisher, please place the stone extruded from Loogie in close proximity to one of the others."

Rocks coming from Rangers consistently reverted to the size of a single graparble regardless of the size they'd attained. Loogie's rock was outwardly identical but 1.6 times heavier than the others. Fisher said nothing and took the heavier graparble from Loogie and placed it near Lynnae's rock. The little rocks clanged together and lay side by side. Fisher removed Lynnae's stone and placed Hummitch's stone by Loogie's. Again nothing happened.

Yannuvia said, "Place each graparble with the person it came from."

Fisher asked, "Why?"

Yannuvia answered, "Why not?"

Fisher shrugged and did as the Wandmaker asked.

The bodies of Loogie, Morris, Gebek, Eyesen, Myrna, Vasor, Rettick, Hummitch, Ayden, and Lynnae were lovingly prepared and wrapped in linens. Matrons soaked the linens with oil. The bodies were placed in the onyum patch and given individual pyres. The ashes were buried with their graparbles.

After the ceremonies Yannuvia, Fisher, Clouse, Dienas, Yiuryna, Morganne, Jonna, Joulie, Sergeant Major Klunkus, Bluuch, Gruusch, and Yathle gathered in the outer ward.

Yannuvia said, "I feel strongly about extending the outer curtain and enlarging our fortified area. I'll create building blocks from the wall behind the inner ward. Excavating the stones from this wall increases the area within the inner curtain and our living area in the inner ward. This will allow growth. I'd like to get started."

Klunkus said, "Wandmaker, our energies…"

Fisher interrupted, "We've already trod on this ground. I have an idea."

Yannuvia said, "Typical Mender fashion!"

Fisher said, "Yes. I am Mender. What else can I be?"

The Wandmaker said, "Get on with it!"

Fisher said, "You brought about the destruction of the Carcharian force with a fire spell. By your admission your supply of sulfur runs thin. The wands have finite usage. Hand-to-hand fighting led to ten deaths and fifty other casualties. A direct assault on the seaward wall by a force equal to or larger than the one we just faced will most certainly breach our defenses. We lack forest to hide in. We have two choices."

The Wandmaker asked, "What do you mean?"

Fisher said, "We cannot stand alone. We can either give up and leave or make alliances."

Yiuryna commented, "We've nowhere to run."

Sergeant Major Klunkus queried, "Allies? We have our few friends from Doug-less, but there's no other."

Fisher said, "The Duoths."

CHAPTER 44

Duoths

First contact...

The first Duoths encountered by the Vydaelians were *Candler26* and *Montgomery32*. Like all Duoths, *Candler26* and *Montgomery32* communicated telepathically but were incapable of verbalizing. The pudgy beasts also read the thoughts of most other creatures. As a result other ilks considered Duoths mute and mindless. *Candler26* tentatively eased his rotund abdomen around the corner of the stone passage to peer toward the Tree Onyums. The strangers had appeared 12480 minutes earlier. Duoths flawlessly measured the passage of time, and the spheroid white beings were familiar with the invariable heart rate of the *minute* minutemen. Many people counted sixty heartbeats of the tiny minuteman as a minute. In the world above, 960 such minutes passed during a cycle of the yellow sun Meries, one light and one amber period. 480 such minutes also passed in one rotation of the Day Glass.

$$Ø \infty Ø$$

Ranger Merry Bodkin spotted *Candler26* peeking around the corner. *Montgomery32* was adjusting to his new title as Onyum Grower and his name. A week earlier he had been stand-by *Jenkins222*. The erstwhile stand-by's predecessor *Montgomery31* had fallen victim to Unduothers, a term the Duoths used to describe anyone other than a Duoth. *Montgomery31* had been careless and the veteran *Candler26* cautioned the novice onyum grower to be careful.

Montgomery32 and *Candler26* mutely communicated and monitored goings on in Vydaelia. At the time the onyum patch was outside the first wall constructed by the Drelves.

There was not a lot of variation in Onyum Growers' names, but the numbers after the names differed quite a bit. The *Candler* nameline had been more fortunate than Montgomery, but both fared better *Bacons*. There had been 98 *Bacons*. It seemed Unduothers had a particular fondness for *Bacon*. Duoths' leader *Mose14* worried *Montgomery31* may have been taken before he was able to clean up his metabolic waste. Duoths carefully guarded their excrement. Duoth excrement was not malodorous and had many unique characteristics. There was great healing power in Duoth Dropping Soup. A pale visitor joined Duoths for a time. Lou Nester created healing potions and unguents. Duoth leader at the time *Mose6* was unable to read his thoughts.

Montgomery32 found it hard to believe that the leader of Duothdom was unable to read an Unduother's thoughts. Even a novice like him could read the thoughts of most of the creatures he encountered. The veteran *Candler26* confirmed the strange but true story that the pale wanderer created a barrier to his mind. The traveler enjoyed speaking aloud and told many stories. Because Duoths saw inside Unduothers' minds, Duoths seldom have to use their innate ability to translate spoken word. *Mose6*'s encounter with the pale Lou Nester was one such instance. *Mose6* passed along the stories the visitor told. Lou Nester averred he was a Mender, professed neutrality, asked many questions about dried Duoth droppings, and told of an upper world. *Mose6* implied the Mender asked too many questions. According to the Mender, spell casters used Magick like Duoths used Duoth Dropping Soup to remove poison and cure wounds.

The thought chronicles of *Mose6* declared Lou Nester left after he learned he could not effectively communicate. *Mose6* recorded in his thought annals that the pale visitor wandered off to the east and encountered the Giant Amebus. In his unfortunate liaison with the hungry Amebus, the Mender was badly injured but escaped. *Mose6*'s last recollection placed the Mender in the company of sea elves. Thoroughly dried Duoth Droppings exploded on impact. Weaponized excrement! Duoths collected them for their value and to keep them from falling into the wrong hands. The Mender never learned that dried Duoth droppings became explosive sling bolts.

Montgomery32 was just beginning Onyum Grower training and was *Jenkins 222* a week earlier. As youths, Duoths were taught the value of hygiene and told to police up their excretion. Elders collected the droppings and made soup from them. That their droppings could be used as weapons was only taught to Onyum Growers.

Montgomery32 actually grew up in Brunswick and worked in the tater patch by Cane Bisque Bay. The industrious Duoth had more training than any other *Jenkins* and dug taters with the best of them, and it was Jenkins group's turn to step up and become one of the thirteen Onyum Growers.

Drelves constantly watched over the onyum patch. The newcomers had planted several plants in the ground of the onyum patch. *Candler26* and *Montgomery32* stayed on high alert and watched for Carcharians, whom they called "Frogmen" or "Unduothers." Carcharians attacked from both land and sea and considered Duoths delicacies. Duoths considered them the most dangerous Unduothers for Carcharians breathed in and out of the water, like frogs, and were called many names including Amphibimen, Frogmen, Carcharian, Sahagin, Sharkmen, and Sea Wolves. Duoths' forebears named them Unduothers because they are about as near our opposites as possible. Seems they were always hungry, and Duoths were always on their menu. Of the 25 departed *Candlers*, only 7 died of natural causes or old age. Unduothers killed the others. Amphibimen slew *Montgomery31*.

Duoths rarely received visitors. Duoths had a collective society, but the care and cultivation of the precious onyums was entrusted to a group of thirteen Duoths designated as Onyum Growers. These thirteen were given the names *Emanuel, Candler, Treutlen, Bulloch, Wheeler, Montgomery, Evans, Tattnall, Toombs, Telfair, Jeff Davis, Appling, and Bacon.* At any given time, in all Duothdom, there was only one Duoth bearing each of the thirteen names.

Seven pods of Duoths served as stand-bys for the role of Onyum Grower. These seven pods were *Jenkins, Screven, Dodge, Pierce, Wayne, Long, and Laurens.* The leader of Duoth's society, who was always named *Mose*, appointed Duoths as stand-byes. *Mose* assigned eight Duoths to each stand-by pod. All members of the seven stand-by pods were taught basics of the Onyum Growing trade, but some knowledge, such as drying and using Duoth Dropping Bombs, were restricted to

Onyum Growers. The recipe for concocting Duoth Dropping Soup was more general knowledge. When one of the thirteen Onyum Growers met with an untimely or natural death, one of the stand-byes replaced him and assumed his name *plus one*. The seven pods alternated the honor of promotion to Onyum Grower when the need arose. Not all stand-byes became Onyum Growers. Some lived out their lives as stand-byes. When a stand-by became an Onyum Grower, died of natural causes, or met an untimely death, another Duoth entered the pod and assumed the next numbered name and role of the stand-by. Stand-byes served other important roles, including working in a large communal large cabbage patch in another area of the underworld, digging taters in Ty-Ty and Brunswick, tending and harvesting from the jellyroll forest, and brewing Duoth Dropping Soup. Regarding the thirteen Onyum Growers and seven pods of stand-byes, Duoths and numbers changed but the names remained the same. *Montgomery32-Jenkins222* was the 32nd Onyum Grower named *Montgomery* and had been the 222nd stand-by named *Jenkins*. The current *Mose* was *Mose14*.

Outsiders knew little of their reproductive physiology, but Duoths produced little Duoths. All in all, the doughy critters were quite affectionate. To other ilks, Duoths looked alike. Duoths knew instantly whether another of their ilk was male or female. The little beasts mated for life and enjoyed a long life span. The occupational hazards of Onyum Growers and Stand-byes oft shortened the lives of Duoths so assigned. Duoths that lived in hamlets like Brunswick, nestled by Cane Bisque Bay toward the eastern ocean, faced extraordinarily difficult hazards. Many stand-bys came from Brunswick, particularly those named *Jenkins* and *Screven*. Just as they had the ability to form orifices in their doughy flesh, the little underworlders formed arms with stubby little digits when the need came up. Again, Duoths modified their doughy bodies when necessary. Limited shape changers…but always just modified Duoths. Duoths preferred their characteristic rotund doughy and grayish white appearance and usually maintained this look. Duoths cultivated onyums only in the onyum patch. Most underworld creatures did not fancy onyums, but predators such as the Carcharians did fancy Duoth. Usually the Duoths' telepathic sense gave them ample warning, and they avoided the attacks by the sea beasts. Unfortunately the erstwhile *Montgomery*, the 31st to bear the name, had let his guard down. *Candler26* and *Montgomery32* came to the shores of the great underworld sea to the Onyum Patch to attend the crop, harvest some onyums, and assure their fallen comrade had left nothing of himself behind. The highly intelligent Duoths readily saw through Clouse's illusory forest. But they also saw armed Drelves watching the path.

Candler26 and *Montgomery32* opted to return to Ty-Ty and consult with *Mose14*. Merry Bodkin saw *Candler26*. *Candler26* had to relieve himself. The older Duoth paused. Noiselessly a small rounded protuberance developed on his equator. Gradually a spheroid emerged from the Duoth's middle. The material was grayish with white spots. When it reached a diameter of two inches, the material separated from the Duoth, fell to the ground and rolled away! There was no smell and the only sound was a slight clank when the round excretion hit the cavern passageway's floor. The dropping rolled away before *Candler 26* could catch it. The duo sped away.

CHAPTER 45

Unduothers' Plans

Wandmaker Yannuvia, Mender Fisher, Clouse, Elder Dienas, Elder Yiuryna, Morganne, Jonna, Joulie, Sergeant Major Klunkus, Lodi, Merry Bodkin, Tariana, Tawyna, Bluuch, Gruusch, Quunsch, Starra, Sharchrina, and Yathle were gathered in the outer ward of Vydaelia and discussing Fisher's idea of approaching the Duoths.

Yathle startled said, "Duoths are food… and cantankerous."

All Carcharians in attendance nodded agreement.

Yannuvia scornfully added, "Logic and reason have abandoned you, Mender. Duoths have injured nigh as many of our folk as Carcharians. You've sat with me at the dinner table and munched on roasted Duoth!"

Fisher said, "Yes, and it was delicious."

Dienas said, "I prefer the fruits of the forest and sea and avoided the meal. How can you consider Duoths a resource for anything more than food for our friends from Doug-less?"

Klunkus said, "Furthermore, the marshmallow men don't communicate."

Morganne said, "The Duoths coordinate their actions. They are not mindless foragers."

Fisher said, "I've watched them. Duoths employ tactics and bring in allies like sea lions and the Giant Amebus. Their actions are purposeful. They don't speak, but they certainly communicate. We should treat with the Duoths."

Bluuch said, "I'd rather have Duoth for a treat. You suggest negotiating with a delicacy!"

Fisher said, "Your point is well taken, Bluuch. However, the Duoths share our fear of Doug-less and its monarch. The enemy of my enemy is my friend."

Yannuvia followed, "An overused adage, Mender. An enemy is still an enemy. Duoths murdered our colleagues in our first days in Vydaelia."

Fisher said, "I bore witness to these events, but our situation is not tenable. I'll approach the marshmallow men."

Morganne added, "Did not the Duoths bring harm to the Mender that preceded us. Why'd they treat you any different?"

Fisher answered, "I emerged from a chrysalis with some knowledge of Lou Nester's journeys. Accessing the collective knowledge of Menders is not like reading a book. Deciphering a recipe for a poultice differs from understanding a chapter in someone's life. Menders don't consider personal information important. Lou Nester underwent confinement in this realm. My visions of Lou Nester's encounters with the Duoths are inexplicably unclear. He had difficulty communicating with the Duoths. I don't really know what happened to him. Grayness clouds my vision. Perplexing..."

Dienas said, "Are you saying you see other Menders' paths more clearly than this Lou Nester fellow's?"

Fisher said flatly, "Yes. I'm Mender. Another Mender endured confinement and brought me into the world. That Mender is to me as I... and the Wandmaker are to Clouse."

Clouse said, "In a sense I have two fathers."

Fisher said, "You are Menderish and Spellweaverish. As to your Mender nature, all Menders are your progenitors but no one is your father. The Wandmaker and I are merely 'fatherish.'"

Yannuvia asked tartly, "Spoken in true Mender fashion."

Fisher replied, "Menders don't often speak of their line. I see no need to discuss my lineage. Lou Nester lived for a time among the Carcharians and acquired a taste for Duoth."

Yathle quipped, "I can see how that could happen."

Fisher said, "He accompanied Carcharians on a hunt and encountered Duoths in a tater patch. A Duoth bomb exploded. The next them he remembered... he was surrounded by Duoths. He lived among the Duoths before I came into being. Maybe that's why my visions of him lack clarity."

Starra said, "My instructors spoke of the Mender's time in Dougless. My mother utilized some of his creations. He was on an ill-fated hunt when Duoths attacked. The hunting party returned without him and didn't know his fate. Many stories are told of hunts."

Sharchrina added, "Most are embellished!"

Fisher matter-of-factly added, "True of most hunters and fishermen."

Bluuch said, "Duoths like taters almost as much as onyums. Taters and onyums grow wild. Duoths don't farm them, they just eat them. There's a big tater patch in Reed Creek Delta. We hunt there a lot. The largest known tater patch is at Brunswick near Cane Bisque Bay, but it's very hard to access. The Cane Bisque Bay Bomber protected the Duoth settlements along Cane Bisque Bay, but my grandfather told me of good Duoth hunting in the Hills of Lithonia to the north and Doubling to the east beyond Cane Bisque Bay. Urquhart knows more of Duoths than I do."

Yathle added, "We smote the Cane Bisque Bay Bomber, but there could be more than one."

Clouse commented, "The one we killed had to come from somewhere."

Yannuvia said, "Mender, You've withheld information."

Fisher said, "I've never told you lots of things. I lived among the Kiennites and served Drelvedom's greatest enemy General Saligia. Nevertheless I still serve you loyally. I'm Mender. Ultra-rare whitish Menders are among the oldest folk of the World of the Three Suns. Given the opportunity, a Mender will heal both a warrior and the warrior's enemy. Mender's nature precludes haughty eyes, a lying tongue, hands that shed innocent blood, feet swift to run into mischief, deceitful witness that utters lies, and sowing discord among brethren. Menders are neither loyal nor disloyal. Menders do not display lust, gluttony, greed, sloth, wrath, envy, and pride. Likewise Menders do not show signs of chastity, temperance, charity, diligence, patience, kindness, and humility. Menders do not seek adultery, fornication, uncleanness, lasciviousness, idolatry, witchcraft, hatred, variance, emulations, wrath, strife, seditions, heresies, envying, murders, drunkenness, reveling, 'and such things.'"

The Wandmaker said, "Enough about Menders. You don't know so much about your forebears' footsteps."

Joulie said, "So... we really don't know whether Duoths bore ill will toward your predecessor."

Fisher said, "Correct."

Yathle entered, "But we know they taste good!"

Fisher said, "Correct. But we need them as allies more than food."

Yannuvia said, "All of us recognize our peril. I still feel the marshmallow men are animalistic killers."

Morganne and Tariana chimed in, "Duoths are defending their homes and lives! You eat them!"

The Carcharians disagreed.

Yannuvia said, "We agree to disagree. How do you propose to communicate with them?"

Fisher said, "The Omega Stones. They allow us to peer into one another's thoughts. They affect those of us who ordinarily reflect Magick. I'll carry the stones to their domain."

Yannuvia said, "You are delirious! They'll only kill you and steal the stones!"

Fisher said, "Possibly! But I'm willing to take the chance. They'll probably negotiate for onyums. You have a spell to supplement the onyum supply. Also, we captured the odd container which they used to draw out the baneful large bubbles. Its effects were most damaging to Carcharians. I'd bet they'd like to have it back. We have no use for it. I've been unable to reproduce the soapy substance that forms into the bubbles."

Bluuch said, "I wouldn't give that infernal thing back to them. It's said in Doug-less the bubbles are made from Duoth p***!"

Yannuvia said, "Yes, Create Food and Water has increased our supply of onyums. It won't help if you're dead and they have the stones."

Fisher said, "What good have the Omega Stones been other than allowing us to speak chaotic evil and learn each other's secrets? We have five. Bluuch still holds the stone given him by Piara. The Wandmaker holds one. I have the other three. I'll take only three. Maybe I'll be able to communicate with Duoths and see into their thoughts. If they are mindless killers... I'll know."

Joulie said, "You'll be dead too."

Yannuvia said, "We need to talk more about your plan. I can't help but ponder that you know more than you are telling? Have you been visited in your dreams?"

Fisher said, "Not lately."

Klunkus said, "Mender, you have aided us many times. My concern is the safety of our folk. Wandmaker, we face strategic shortages. We don't have BJ Aires to construct arrows. If he were here, we lack raw materials. After the battles with the triskaidekapod, Duoths and their allies, and the Carcharians, our Rangers have retrieved as many arrows as possible to reuse them. We salvaged what we could from the Carcharians' armaments. Their spears serve mainly as a resource for our allies. I worked with BJ. He taught me many things, but I'm no BJ Aires when it comes to making arrows. The wood is poor. Nothing in the onyum patch provides a resource. Battling the Carcharians hand-to-hand bodes poorly for us. My tactical experience relied on the forest as an ally. I'm leaning toward supporting your idea Fisher, but I must know that you are telling us everything you know about this realm."

Morganne followed, "My quiver only holds eleven arrows. Sergeant Major Klunkus makes very good points."

Fisher said, "I have no reason to keep secrets from you. When I emerged from my chrysalis, I shared memories from his and all other Menders' timeline. We traveled in red and blue light and perceived the passage of only a moment's time. The Dreamraider says we traveled 13 changes of seasons in the World of the Three Suns. Before my experiences traveling in red and blue light was previously unbeknownst to Menders. We arrived on the rocky shores of an underground sea in a massive cavern illuminated by luminescent lichen overhead. Realms like this are commonplace. Lou Nester's time line tells of such a place. I did not know we trod the same ground until recent events. I saw Duoths for the first time with you. Like me, Lou Nester first met them as an entrée on a dinner table. Starra tells us he may have been knocked out by a Duoth bomb. Accessing Lou Nester's timeline only gives me sparse knowledge of Duoths and adds little to our state of affairs. Gruusch was my first contact with Carcharians. Lou Nester also made little note of Carcharians. Seems he almost made the table as a main course. Piara and Starra tell us his creations helped Doug-less."

Yannuvia asked, "How did Lou Nester get to this realm?"

Fisher said, "Lou Nester arrived in this realm in a different manner. A Mountain Giant assisted him. He sought a dark place for confinement, not an easy task in the night less world of Parallan. The Mountain Giants live in the caves and caverns beneath the Great Southern Range.

Lou lived among them and they became beholding to him. He came here with a rogue giant."

Yannuvia persisted, "How'd Lou and the Mountain Giant get here?"

Fisher flatly replied, "Don't know. Lou experienced *dreams*."

Yannuvia impatiently asked, "Dreams! Sounds familiar! What happened when Lou Nester encountered the Duoths?"

Fisher said, "Lou Nester's experiences with Duoths are ill defined. He left them and explored the east. There's a dark area in his time line. Then his time with the sea elves appears. He lived with them until his confinement. It's unclear again. A second Mender emerged with him from the chrysalis and soon left. Two Menders can't serve the same master."

Dienas said, "But both you and Clouse are with us!"

Clouse said, "I'm only Menderish and Fisher and I don't really serve Vydaelia."

Fisher said, "I do."

Jonna asked, "What happened to the Mender who came out of Lou Nester's chrysalis?"

Fisher said, "The Mender who emerged from the chrysalis with Lou Nester left in the same manner that Lou arrived. The sea elves led him past Doug-less and he waited for the Giant. Giants accept the comings and goings of Menders. The new Mender passed for Lou Nester and left with the Giant. Like Lou Nester he vowed to keep safe the location of the sea elves that helped him. I can't see through the veil that covers this knowledge. The new Mender left the giants and wandered the World of the Three Suns until he was captured by Kiennites. He served them many years."

Jonna observed, "Sounds like you, Fisher."

Fisher replied, "Yes, it does."

Yannuvia raised his eyebrows and commented, "Almost too much to be a coincidence, Fisher. Where did you come from?"

Fisher continued, "Menders don't reveal their origins. Confinement is a very private affair. Many Menders follow similar paths. Like Lou Nester I required a dark place for confinement. I was following his path when our pathways crossed and I wound up at Lost Sons. Our encounter with the Baxcat and Leicat and your efforts to save me forever changed us. I've scanned the common knowledge of Menders and read many tomes. Nowhere can I find anybody like me, the Wandmaker,

303

and Clouse. Queen Piara shares many of our traits. But she is gone, and my and our past is not pertinent now. We must make safe our present. The Carcharians will be back and in greater numbers. If we sit and wait for more attacks from Doug-less, we'll share the same fate. With your permission, Wandmaker, I'll make preparations to seek them out."

Jonna protested, "We need your healing skills!"

Fisher said, "Clouse can fulfill my role. I've stockpiled what I can from the onyum patch. The Wandmaker can expand and enlarge my plant material."

Clouse closed his eyes and said, "When I concentrate, I see hazy images. Your words, Fisher, make these images clearer. You are more experienced. Should I not be the one to approach the Duoths?"

Fisher said, "No, you are only Menderish... but also Drelvish and Spellweaverish. You are too green both literally and figuratively. The Duoths may find my paleness reassuring."

Yannuvia said, "I agree with Jonna. I don't feel we can spare anyone."

Jonna reiterated her concerns.

Elder Dienas asked, "Should we part with the Omega Stones?"

Fisher suggested, "The crescent shaped stones have similarities and differences. They allow us to peer into one another's minds. Bearing false witness has never been my nature. That's not necessarily true of most non-Menders. The stones either compel the truth or allow others to tell when it's not being told. They've done little more than act as divisive items. The Duoths attack in organized manner, and, in my opinion, cultivated the onyum patch. Using the stones might allow us to communicate with them."

Yannuvia quizzically responded, "Why'd we want to communicate with them? They've cost us lives and property! I might add, they taste pretty good, too!"

Fisher calmly replied, "I won't argue about their culinary value. The collective knowledge of Menders contains little knowledge of Duoths. They were here first and have brought powerful allies into the fray against us. The sea lions were tough, and it took the help of the Dreamraider to overcome the Giant Amebus. What else might they bring against us?"

Morganne added, "I agree. If you managed to reach and communicate with the marshmallow men, you might know things that could help us."

Sergeant Major Klunkus still favored his gimpy leg and said, "Bear in mind, the marshmallow men are dangerous, Mender. We can't stand against their explosive devices. Morganne's excursion ended badly. We lack numbers to pursue them."

Fisher said, "I'm Mender and a liability in a fight. I won't bear arms. I've studied all options. Going to the Duoths is our best chance of securing help."

Elder Yiuryna added, "But your healing skills are needed."

Fisher said, "Clouse performs well. My supply of panacea is exhausted. I need other sources of raw materials. The Wandmaker, Clouse, and the Healing Wand are more important."

Elder Dienas said, "We don't know all the properties of the stones. I don't like the idea of Duoths holding devices that allow them to see into our thoughts."

Bluuch said, "But Elder, the Wandmaker and I are holding stones. Princess Starra's scarf tells her when stones are near. She'll know if someone tries to spy on us. We're setting here a few steps apart and I cannot see into the Wandmaker's mind unless he activates the rock. By the way, when can we try it, Wandmaker?"

Yannuvia said, "Uh, no, Bluuch. I'm good. But your point is well taken." Yannuvia still pondered the four-armed Carcharian's response to learning of his relationship with Piara.

Fisher quietly added, "There is also a distance factor. The devices must be in close proximity, within 13 paces to be exact."

Yathle said, "Duoths lack mouths, ears, eyes, and noses. They just feel their way around. I see no means of their helping us. You will become sea fodder. They blow us up with Duoth bombs, burn us with Duoth bubbles, and ally with giant globs and sea lions to fight us and bring down our walls. But for the flying she-beast, Duoths and their allies would have likely destroyed us before the forces of Doug-less arrived."

Fisher said, "How do you suppose they communicate with the sea lions?"

Bluuch said, "I support Yathle. Sea lions are beasts. You can train sea horses and sometimes dawg fish. Duoths probably subjugate them by threatening to blow up or burn them."

Starra added, "Our forebears say sea lions and Duoths have always run together."

Bantering continued. Finally Yannuvia relented.

The Wandmaker said, "You are not bound to us. You have free will. Know that I am opposed to your plan. Bottom line… we will know if the Omega Stones are near and they have limited value." Yannuvia recalled three stones were necessary to activate the *Three Stones effect* that enabled bearers to see into one another's mind.

The Carcharians continued their objections. The Elders continued to question the wisdom of parting with the three Omega Stones.

Yannuvia scoffed, "Fisher, go your own way. Take the stones. We can spare no other to go with you. You are on your own. I want to get on with construction of the new wall. Remember the first passage to the Duoths' realm is blocked."

Fisher said, "I ask for no help. I'll make ready."

Yannuvia said, "So be it. I'm getting back to work."

Morganne said, "I'll review our route with you."

The meeting broke up. Fisher made ready. The Wandmaker produced building rocks, which were thirty-four inchworm lengths long, twenty-one inches wide, and thirteen inches high. Clouse called the interlocking bricks "automatic binding bricks." The bricks locked together by means of eight round studs on their tops and eight hollowed out areas on rectangular bottoms. Each stone interlocked over two neighbors beneath it. The blocks snapped together so tightly that separating them required extraordinary effort. Every able-bodied Drelve worked to place the heavy stones. Vydaelians continued construction of another wall at the verge of the outcropping and began construction of a sea wall running from the former outer curtain toward the outcropping. Rangers worked incessantly. Defending the longer sea wall was beyond their capability, but the extended wall allowed for future growth and provided another barrier to attack from the west. Clouse dispelled the Illusory Terrain Spell he'd cast on the western wall. The area was now inside the outer curtain.

CHAPTER 46

Ty Ty

The first passage leading from the Duoth's home Ty Ty to the onyum patch was hopelessly closed by the newcomer's Magick. The second passage was damaged when Morganne's party captured the ill-fated Duoth *Long206*. Standing guard in the cubicles on either side of the second passageway to the east of the Onyum Patch was the responsibility of Stand-byes, Duoths who were subordinate to onyum growers and stood ready to step up should an onyum grower fall. Numbered Stand-byes were next in line to become Onyum Growers. Unnumbered members of a numbered Stand-by's pod assisted the numbered member. After the arrival of the newcomers, Duoth leader *Mose14* dictated numbered Stand-byes stand guard. *Long207* and *Dodge191* drew the duty of watching the cavern. It was young *Dodge191*'s first important assignment. The cubicles were only five feet wide and a similar height. A narrow archway above the passageway connected the two observation posts. A passage connected the western observation post to the northern wall of the great central cavern of Ty-Ty east of the huge tater patch. The entrance to the passageway that led from Ty-Ty to the cubicles was revealed only to Onyum Growers and Stand-byes. Secret sliding stone doors enabled the occupant of the western cubicle to both exit to the sea and retreat toward Ty-Ty. The secret doors were imperceptible to all but the most discerning creature. In both small cubicles, small slits cut in the stone allowed the Duoths inside to peer out toward the sea. The narrow slits were smaller than murder holes that archers fired through in drum towers and bartizans. Duoths couldn't squeeze through the slit. When the Duoth guards were in position, their bodies filled the openings and made the apertures imperceptible to passersby in the outside cavern. The cubicles and passages had been damaged in a battle with Morganne's party. The skirmish had cost the Duoths *Long206*. Duoths had labored to reconstruct the guard posts and clear the passageways. Efforts to hide the secret doors were redoubled.

Long207 sat in the cubicle to the west of the passage and *Dodge 191* watched from the other.

Ø ∞ Ø

Fisher reached the observation point and looked around. He took a deep breath, shrugged, and thought aloud, "Here I am."

Ø ∞ Ø

Dodge191 and *Long207* observed the Mender.

Dodge191 silently commented, "He is alone and bears no weapons. He also carries onyums!"

Long207 answered, "I'm famished. Let's take his onyums!"

Dodge191 replied, "He must be watched! We should not give away our position!"

Ø ∞ Ø

Fisher listened intently. The barking of a dawg fish broke the silence. The Mender hoped to find Duoths and avoid sea lions. Fisher pulled out and nonchalantly munched on an onyum. Fragrant aromas wafted to the sensitive membranes of the nearby Duoths.

Ø ∞ Ø

Long207 thought, "I've checked thoroughly and find no other nearby thought patterns. I've got a bomb if we get in trouble! Let's get the onyums!"

Dodge191 and *Long207* bolted from their hiding places and pounced on Fisher. The Mender wrapped an arm around each Duoth. His arms pushed into their doughy flesh. The Duoths extended pseudopods and wrapped around the Mender. Both sent silent distress messages and in moments other Duoths arrived.

308

Fisher released his grip and stopped struggling and said aloud, "I only want to talk. I mean you no harm."

The Duoths remained silent.

Bullock37, who seemed to be in command, muttered, "You dummies, you gave away our positions!"

Long207 defensively said, "He is alone and carries onyums. His thoughts are very hard to hard."

Evans47 said, "It's one of those pale skinned blokes. *Mose6* told of one. Let's whack him and feed him to the sea lions."

The Mender heard nothing.

Fisher said aloud, "I have gifts for your leader."

The Duoths understood his spoken words.

Long207 said silently to the others, "How does he know we have a leader?"

Evans47 silently answered, "Everybody has a leader. Get him into the passage and close the doors. We'll deal with him there."

Dodge191 thought, "What if he is a sorcerer?"

Bullock37 answered, "He would have attacked us by now! Besides, I've seen the sorcerer. I narrowly avoided getting singed by one of his spells. This bloke is much too pale."

Fisher said aloud, "Take one of the stones I carry. Just be sure to leave me one. It'll confirm my intentions."

Evans47 said, "He is a sorcerer!"

Bullock37 said, "Let's subdue him and take him to Ty Ty and Mose14."

Evans47 said, "You are a fool to take him to Ty Ty."

Bullock37 said, "If he makes any trouble I'll burn him with Duoth bubble solution."

Dodge191 excitedly commented, "Onyum Grower *Bullock37*! Onyum Grower *Evans47*! He carries the bubble decanter! He does carry three odd rocks not much larger than a Duoth bomb."

Bullock37 said, "I still doubt he has good intentions. But at least we can reunite the bubble decanter and bubble sword, our most effective weapons against the Carcharians."

The Duoths secured Fisher by wrapping appendages around him and lifting him from the ground and made for Ty Ty. The Duoths scurried down narrow curving passages with remarkable speed. Fisher's impeccable sense of direction was stressed to maintain his orientation. After a short trip the party reached a brightly lit grotto. A massive tater patch dominated the area where they entered. It was a Carcharian hunter's dream. Duoths moved about the area tending the patch and performing countless tasks. The leaders *Bulloch37* and *Evans47* reported to other Duoths. The Mender was the center of attention. *Evans47* raised the Duoth bubble decanter into the air. The pudgy Duoths extended arms above their shapeless heads and noiselessly bounced up and down. The collective obviously worked in coordinated fashion. Passages exited from the huge grotto to the southwest, east, and southeast. When the Mender looked back toward his entry point, he saw only solid wall. The door was disguised much as the lookout sites bordering the sea. *Bulloch37* turned the decanter over to another Duoth and scurried to the southwest passage. In a little while he returned with colleagues. Duoths carried Fisher toward the southwest passage. The passage extended for a hundred paces and came to an intersection. The group carried Fisher to the south in the leftward passage. The passage angled back to the east and came to a rather ornate door. *Bulloch37* formed an appendage with digits and opened the door. The door opened to a circular room with a large table. *Bulloch37* closed the door and went to the table. Four Duoths restrained Fisher with rope-like extensions of their bodies. Fourteen other doors lined the walls of the circular room. One larger door sat directly opposite the entry door. The thirteen other doors looked identical. Three Omega Stones rested on the table. Twenty-one little chairs sat around the table. *Bulloch37* took his seat. Duoths sat silently in all the chairs. One larger chair sat in front of the ornate door opposite the entryway.

21 Duoths gathered in the room of the round table. Many changes had occurred since the last council of Ty Ty. In the battle with the newcomers in which the Giant Amebus was destroyed, ten of thirteen Onyum Growers fell, including *Tatnall28*, the renowned Ty Ty bomber. Only *Montgomery33*, *Bulloch37*, and *Treutlen41* survived. Mose14 promoted ten Stand-byes to Onyum Grower. Three Duoths went from top tater picker to Onyum Grower without tenure as Stand-bye. Two

Duoths from Laurens, Jenkins, and Wayne pods rose to Onyum Grower status. Neophytes now filled all Stand-bye positions. *Mose14* presided over the meeting that now included Onyum Growers *Candler28, Montgomery33, Emanuel31, Treutlen41, Bulloch37, Wheeler28, Evans47, Tattnell29, Toombs25, Telfair59, Jeff Davis33, Appling41,* and *Bacon100.* The Stand-byes were *Jenkins226, Screven152, Dodge191, Pierce180, Wayne 170, Long 207,* and *Laurens201.* Most Stand-byes never became Onyum Growers, but the odds of ascending to the job were increased of late.

The Duoths released Fisher and allowed him to stand.

The Mender said aloud, "I returned your weapon. The stones on the table are a means we might use to communicate."

Mose14 used his languages ability to understand Fisher's spoken word. He silently conversed with the Onyum Growers and Stand-byes. Fisher had arrived unarmed with the bubble decanter and onyums. *Mose14* extended his body, surrounded an onyum, and took it inside his body. The other Duoths shared the onyums Fisher brought. The marshmallow men silently bantered. Finally *Mose14* nudged the Duoth to his left, *Bacon100.*

Bacon100 shuddered and muttered, "Why me? Bacon always goes into harm's way!"

Mose14 replied silently, "Better you than me! Take the rock!"

Bacon100 extended part of his body and formed an appendage. He tentatively wrapped his pseudo-arm around the Omega Stone and pressed on the stone. Grayness filled the chamber and dimmed the light from the dense population of lichen.

A single rune appeared on the smooth crescent shaped stone.

$$\Omega$$

The rune persisted for thirteen minute minuteman heartbeats. Then the single letter faded, and three runes appeared on the surface of the rock, which briefly emitted gray light.

$$Ǿ \infty Ǿ$$

The runes faded after 21 heartbeats and the single rune reappeared. The pattern repeated three times.

The Duoth *Bacon100* stared at Fisher and then twisted toward *Mose14.*

Bacon100 communicated, "I feel charismatic. Perhaps it's time to seek a mate."

Next *Mose14* extended a blob of his body and motioned to Fisher's guards. One of the guards pushed Fisher. The Mender approached the table and picked one of the identical stones. Was it the fifth that had not revealed its nature, Jonna's strength stone, or Gruusch's charming stone? Fisher slowly extended his hand and grasped the stone on the left. The stone meld to his hand. Grayness again sprayed the room.

A single rune appeared on the smooth crescent shaped stone.

$$\Omega$$

The rune persisted for thirteen heartbeats. Then the single letter faded, and three runes appeared on the surface of the rock, which briefly emitted gray light.

$$\acute{\text{Ø}} \; \infty \; \acute{\text{Ø}}$$

The runes faded after 21 heartbeats and the single rune reappeared. The pattern repeated three times.

The *Two Stones effect* occurred, though the speech was silent.

Fisher looked toward *Bacon100* and said aloud in the chaotic evil language of the stones, "Hello, *Bacon100*, for I see that is your name."

The Mender saw into the pudgy marshmallow man's thoughts. It was odd to sense thoughts in the bizarre language, but Menders understood 17711 dialects.

Bacon100 extended the stone toward Fisher and said silently but the Mender understood the telepathic words, "Hello, Mender. You speak the truth about the stones. I have relayed this thought to my leader *Mose14.*"

Mose14 extended an appendage and gripped the third rock.

A single rune appeared on the smooth crescent shaped stone.

$$\Omega$$

The rune persisted for thirteen heartbeats. Then the single letter faded, and three runes appeared on the surface of the rock, which briefly emitted gray light.

$$Ø \infty Ø$$

The runes faded after 21 heartbeats and the single rune reappeared. The pattern repeated three times.

The *Three Stones effect* occurred.

Mose14 thought, "I see we'll all *think* the truth, Mender. Speak aloud. My colleagues can decipher spoken word even when they cannot see into another's mind."

Fisher thought, "I mean you no harm. My comrades share something in common with you."

Mose14 said, "Yes, they want to have us for dinner. Literally!"

Fisher said, "No, the need to fend off the forces of Doug-less."

Mose14 said, "You must think me a fool, Mender. My people have seen the Carcharians among you. I lost 10 Onyum Growers during the last battle. Your greatest task will be convincing us to not kill you."

Fisher said, "What good would that do?"

Mose14 said, "It might help my angst!"

Fisher said, "I returned the decanter in good faith. The onyums are a gift of my leader the Wandmaker."

Mose14 said, "If I had a mouth, I'd laugh! You are giving us that which we have labored to produce! Who do you think grew the onyums? It's our onyum patch! You are the trespassers and transgressors!"

Fisher said, "You never communicated!"

Mose14 countered, "Neither did you."

Fisher replied, "Point taken! All information available to us branded you as scavengers and nuisances. Prey animals!"

Mose14 said, "Who told you such?"

Fisher said, "Well, my ties to the common knowledge of Menders and Carcharians…"

Mose14 incredulously answered, "Did you consider the source? We did encounter a Mender! He came seeking our flesh!"

Fisher asked, "Did you harm him?"

Mose14 said, "Not intentionally. He was stunned by a Duoth bomb. His hunting companions left him in the lurch. I could not see into his thoughts, but we brought him here. There were barriers to communication. We interpreted his spoken word but the communication was one way. He shared potions and unguents with us. We shared taters, onyums, and jelly rolls with him. He was seeking a dark place with soil. The onyum patch satisfied his need for potting soil but it was too well lit to meet his needs. He had to move on. He went east. Our erstwhile ally the Giant Amebus ate first and asked questions later. The Mender that preceded you Lou Nester literally crossed paths with the Giant Amebus. The Amebus read minds too, and couldn't read his. It didn't know he was there and ran over him. He didn't know what hit him. The Amebus felt bad about it and carried him across the sea and deposited him on sea elves' doorsteps. That's the last we heard of him. The Mender benefitted us. We did not harm him. Can you say the same about yourself and Duoths?"

Fisher said, "I… don't think I harmed Duoths…"

Mose14 followed, "You speak the truth to the best of your knowledge. Have you shared our flesh with the Amphibimen?"

Fisher said, "Yes."

Mose14 replied telepathically, "The truth is refreshing. It's rare to hear it from Unduothers! Deny you are allied with Carcharians!"

Fisher said, "Truthfully, we number Carcharians among our ranks. There are outsiders like me. The sea elfish queen of Doug-less fled and sought sanctuary with her daughter, niece, and five loyal to her."

Mose14 thought, "Aha! I've caught you in a lie! You mind lists nine names altogether."

Fisher countered, "I was about to say another Carcharian arrived before the queen. He survived an attack from a triskaidekapod. His name is Gruusch. The Carcharians among us are refugees. They think you are mindless non-communicative beasts and consider eating you akin to eating a fish. I see now they… and we have been wrong. You have 13 Onyum Growers, seven Stand-byes, and seven pods, and one leader… telepathic communication… ability to read minds. That's how you communicate with the sea lions. How do they speak with you?"

Mose14 followed, "You see in my thoughts that they don't speak to use directly. We've developed hand signals over generations. The current monarch Linus threw everything he had into the last battle. Sea lions hate Carcharians as much as we do."

Fisher said, "We have our common ground."

Mose14 said, "We might wait until the Carcharians wipe you out and just regain the Onyum patch."

Fisher said, "They will resume preying on you. My leader the Wandmaker has the power to augment the natural production of the onyums. He can produce more than you'd ever grow. He's promised access to the onyum patch. And... if Vydaelia falls, the onyum patch will likely be destroyed."

Mose14 said, "Your stones let you down again, Mender. He has not given his blessing to your mission to us."

Fisher said, "He has not."

Mose14 said, "That gives you more credibility and your leader less. I'm not sure how much influence you have in your citadel, Mender. Why don't you just stay in Ty Ty and work with us? Does not Vydaelia enjoy the services of another Mender, the one called Clouse or Green Guy?"

Fisher said, "I'm considering it. But I have someone to serve. I owe the Wandmaker my life. Clouse is Menderish. He is neither Mender nor Drelve."

Mose14 said, "That also gives you credibility. You also owe the Wandmaker your slight tinge and bit of feelings. You disagree with your leader... your Fire Wizard. Magick is a difficult Master to serve. Perhaps this green guy will also be seduced by Magick."

Fisher said, "Magick is also finite. We lack numbers to repel the Carcharians many more times."

Mose14 thought, "I see your fears. The Carcharians are relentless. We have been safe in Ty Ty for the most part, but our allies thin. The Amebus is gone. I'm unsure that it left spores. They can take generations to mature anyway."

Fisher noted, "You have three Amebus bombs."

Mose14 thought, "But lack the strength to use them. The sea lions are decimated."

Fisher said, "Your colleague *Bacon100* informs me of your Duoth bombs, bubble sword, and settlements in Brunswick. We have mistreated you. My leader the Wandmaker has suffered losses and carries great responsibility. The guilt I feel now comes to me through my link to him."

Mose14 thought, "We are you going to tell me about your winged ally, who destroyed the Amebus?"

Fisher said, "I'll concentrate on the Good Witch. That's all I know of her."

Mose14 thought, "I know you think the truth. Standing before me is an individual who has eaten my kind and helped keep us from the onyum patch. Why am I not ordering your death? Deep inside... you know what I'm thinking. I trust you. I do not trust your leader. I certainly don't trust your Carcharian allies. I can treat with you, Mender Fisher. This language is disturbing. You may speak. I have the ability to decipher spoken word. But we'll need these marvelous rocks to give you access to my thoughts. My council and I have enjoyed the onyums, but my people have long been without our favorite food. I'll consider an alliance... but your Wandmaker must provide us an immediate supply of onyums and allow my people access to the onyum patch. He must reopen the first passageway to Ty Ty."

Fisher said, "I'll present your offer. I'll refrain from..."

Mose14 thought, "You need not say it. I sense your regret."

The leader extended two small legs and stood. Around the table the twenty Duoths stood, formed small hands, and applauded.

Fisher bowed respectfully.

Ø ∞ Ø

CHAPTER 47

Green Sea Elf in Gray Vale

Piara again faced her inquisitors.

Commandant Inyra, Nurse Nila, Nila's son Lieutenant Liani, Squaddie Agarn, and gray sea elfish guards Horton, Rory, Adric, and Turlough gathered in a cozy cabin on the outskirts of Graywood, the conurbation established by the progeny of the Gray Matron and resumed discussions with the erstwhile Queen of Doug-less. Piara's emerald greenness contrasted with the subtle gray-green tint of her captors' skin. The Gray Matron Alexandrina was an outcast from sea elf community Elder Ridge and Inyra's great-great-great grandmother. Piara was taken as a child from Elder Ridge by Carcharians. Inyra carried the ornate scepter UK, which was quite similar to the USA carried by the Wandmaker in Vydaelia. Initially Piara's arrival with four-armed Carcharian Urquhart had set the folk of Graywood against her. Urquhart slew eleven sea elves in a furious fight that left him dead and Piara unconscious. A twelfth sea elf Fytch eventually died from his wounds. The sea elf Giryn died after attacking Piara and Urquhart as they traveled across the sea. Inyra initially also held Piara accountable for the 13 deaths. The gray-green captors had dumped Urquhart's body in the sea and retrieved the little nodule that extruded from his left hand. Lieutenant Liani also found the amulet that the Dreamraider had given Piara. The folk of Graywood bore little nodules in their left hand. In contrast to the Vydaelians, the gray-green sea elves came into the world with the little nodules, which did not increase in size. Like the Vydaelians at death the nodules left the gray-green sea elves. The Graywood folk interred the nodules with the ashes of fallen comrades in an area called Gray Vale. Piara had envisioned the area though images she shared with the long dead great-great-great grandmother.

Earlier talks had formed some solid ground. But for the greenness of her skin Piara was the spitting image of likeness of the Gray Matron on the ornate door of the edifice in Gray Vale. Piara's amulet was an exact replica of that worn by the matron's image. Slowly Piara and Inyra established fragile trust. Piara received a visit from the Dreamraider Amica, who shed some light on bygone events and confessed to some of her actions. Piara relayed her visions of the inner tomb and the means of entering it. Inyra detailed stories of her, and his ancestor. Slowly trust grew. Bryni's reports of Squaddie Frayn's observations of the newcomers' battle with the Carcharians furthered Inyra's trust in Piara and positive feelings toward the newcomers.

Sabrina served sea biscuits, sea bee honey, booderries, and purple fruits with pits.

Piara addressed her grayish-green sea elfish captors, "My resistance to Magick stems from my great, great, great grandmother. I was taken from the sea elf village Elder Ridge and scarcely remember stories I was told of her. She gave me more than her looks. I see ... some of her thoughts. It's as though I've shared some of her experiences. My great-great-grandmother, great-grandmother, grandmother, and mother did not have this connection with my great, great, great grandmother. My folk lived in the shadow of Doug-less and foolishly thought we could evade the Carcharians. This place... I've seen the gray valley in my mind's eye many times. I've seen it through her eyes, but I don't know her."

Inyra reiterated, "Four generations have come and mostly gone since the time of my great, great, great grandmother. There are legends of the tomb in Gray Vale. Everyone who witnessed the creation of the Mender's Tomb developed a nodule on their left hand. Since that time the nodules have been passed along and are present at birth. They do not increase in size and leave us at death. Experience taught us that the nodules merge if brought together. Merged nodules are inert. They will not grow if planted. However, if we place extruded gray pebbles with the remains of those who bore the nodules in the forest surrounding the Mender's Tomb, trees sprout from them. These trees produce purple fruits. We just ate some of them. The pits within the fruits are not seeds. Trees only grow from gray pebbles planted with the individual that bore the nodule that burst open in death and expressed the rock. The pits will not produce trees if planted. We use the pits in many remedies. Ground up purple pits was a major ingredient in the mixture that saved Piara from the Fawagy and Irukandji poison. This knowledge passed down from the Gray Matron and those who witnessed the creation of the tomb. We recently planted 12 nodules. The Carcharian extruded a gray stone when he passed. But it's heavier than those that passed from our ilk.

Piara said, "Folk in Elder Ridge don't have the little nodules. I've seen Gray Vale many times in my mind through my ancestor's eyes."

Inyra said, "Your association with the Carcharian still vexes me, but otherwise I am comfortable with your story. We'll proceed to Gray Vale. I'd like to test your theories. Your visions are quite accurate. You're only missing some details."

Piara, Inyra, Nila, Liani, Horton, Rory, Adric, and Turlough exited the cabin and walked through the array of cozy cottages. Familiar light from luminescent lichen overhead provided light to Graywood. Moving from Graywood toward Gray Vale the seven gray-green and single emerald green sea elf traveled onto a rocky path that ended in stairs at the end of the common area and ascended the stairs. Inyra and Nila walked ahead of Piara with Liani and the four youths following behind. The wide stone path meandered through 200 paces of stone and finally exited onto an open area, which widened before them. Looking above one saw no ceiling, only grayness with occasional points of light. The ground changed from stone to soft gray soil. Green foliage changed to deep gray leaves. Taller trees and bushes rimmed the entire roughly circular area, but a valley filled with gray trees made up the greatest part of Gray Vale. A hill in the center of the valley obscured the far side of the circular vale. Gray plush grass covered a rim that extended several paces. At the edge of the gray moss, the terrain inclined gently at about fifteen degrees for thirty paces and reached the floor. The floor of Gray Vale extended several hundred paces, rose gently in several areas, and circled the central knoll. A grassy upslope began where the floor ended and extended fifty or so paces to the top of the central hill. Many small rivulets coursed through the landscape. A gentle breeze crisscrossed the surprisingly warm valley. Overhead deep blueness intermingled with ever-present gray light. Potting soil filled Gray Vale. Lichen did not provide illumination in Gray Vale, and the overall illumination exceeded the great cavern with the sea. The Gray Vale Stone Circle rested upon the gray grasses in a flattened area halfway up the hill. The circle had five small stones and one large alignment stone. The huge monolith was a rectangular slab and had been arranged radially to the circle and is aligned with the NE-SW circle axis. It totally dominated the site and sat very close to the tiny circle of five stones, and the whole site was perched on a little terrace halfway up the hillside. The five slab-like stones of the ring were tangentially placed. A winding path meandered toward the octagonal structure on the hill. Halfway up the duo passed the stone circle.

The eight-sided edifice that sat on the hillock was made of coal black stone. 13 gray trees circled the eight-sided building. Gray grass and stands of gray trees covered the area. 13 soft mounds filled the area at the fringe of the forest. The trees bore purple and gray leaves and purple fruits, which the group had eaten earlier. Overhead fathomless grayness took the place of sky and ceiling. Piara had described the path to Gray Vale and the area in accurate detail.

Inyra said, "It's time to test the accuracy of your visions. From time to time the grayness is accentuated and wondrous things occur. The structure on the hill is the final resting place of the Gray Matron and one very dear to her."

The group crossed the floor of the Vale and started up the winding path. When they reached the Gray Vale Stone Circle Inyra touched each of the five small stones once and the large stone five times. Nila and Piara followed his lead. Then they continued on to the crest of the hill. The black stone of the tomb stood out against the grayness of Gray Vale. The trio looked upon sealed doors that made up one of the edifice's eight sides. The door faced the circle of one large and five smaller stones. A strikingly detailed image of a beautiful matronly gray-green sea elf occupied much of the door.

Piara said, "Am I gazing into a looking glass? But for my greenness, she could be my twin."

The sea elfish Commandant Inyra said, "Only a bit older. The resemblance is remarkable. She's the Gray Matron."

Piara said, "I've… seen her face many times in my mind. My great-great-great grandmother…"

Inyra said, "My great-great-great grandmother…"

Piara said, "May I hold the amulet I carried?"

Inyra hesitated. Then the Commandant produced the Twin Stone and its purple thread. The Twin Stone changed from gray to deep purple and emitted purple auras. The amulet around the engraved figure's neck also changed to purple and emitted similar purple hues. Auras surrounded Inyra. Again he felt chilled and the urge to place the amulet around his neck. Instead he extended the amulet to Piara who accepted it in her left hand. Auras now surrounded the former queen. Piara placed the amulet around her neck. It faded from sight, but she still felt its slight weight. The amulet around the figure on the door faded from sight.

Liani, Horton, Rory, Turlough, and Adric watched from a few paces away. Liani blurted, "Sorcery!"

Piara said, "No. It always fades."

Nila scolded, "My son, the Gray Matron was labeled a sorcerer."

Inyra asked, "Is the amulet the key to entering the tomb?"

Piara said, No, but its twin rests within the structure. The circle holds the key. The amulet may afford some protection. Perhaps I should go first."

Inyra said, "Let's test your entry suggestion."

Piara walked to the Stone Circle. The circle had five very similar small stones and one large alignment stone. The huge monolith was a rectangular slab. It has been arranged radially to the circle and is aligned with the NE-SW circle axis. Piara shared Mender's uncanny sense of direction. The large stone totally dominated the site and sat very close to the tiny circle of five stones. Piara stood in the center of the circle. She moved forward and touched the monolith, then returned and touched one of the little stones. Then she went back and touched the monolith twice. She then touched another stone thrice. Next she returned to the monolith and touched the big stone five times. She followed by touching a third little stone eight times. Next she went back to the monolith and touched it thirteen times. Then she went to the fourth stone and tapped it twenty-one times. She returned to the monolith and touched it thirty-four times. Lastly she went to the final stone and methodically touched it fifty-five times. A gray slightly raised stone circle of 13 foot diameter formed within the circle of stones. Humming sounds emanated from the circle and gray and purple lights flashed about its surface.

All but Piara jumped back. She remembered the Dreamraider's visit.

Inyra tossed a small stone onto the newly formed gray circle. The stone disappeared.

The Commandant said, "I'm opposed to stepping onto the stone circle."

Piara said, "I will go, but I should go alone. I'm drawn to the tomb. No one else should be in harm's way."

Inyra said, "I'll go with you."

Nila quickly protested, "No! You are our leader! We cannot spare you."

Piara agreed, "Yes, it's my task."

Inyra said, "We don't know that. We've only just met you. I must attend our interests."

Squaddie Agarn said, "I'll go with her. My closest friend Fytch fell by the Carcharian's hand. I'll assure she stays on course."

The humming sound intensified and the purplish lights dancing on the surface of the circle brightened.

Piara said, "The circle is changing! There's nothing for it. I must go."

Piara and Agarn stepped onto the circle and moved to the center of the circle. Piara said to Agarn, "Tap your left foot eighty-nine times." She carefully counted and tapped her left foot eighty-nine times. Purple and gray auras flashed about the circle of stones. Piara and Agarn disappeared.

The former queen felt tingling sensations throughout her body. Her long green hair stood on end. She heard a muffled scream.

Piara stood on an identical circle inside the well-lighted tomb. Agarn's lifeless body lay beside her. A graparble lay beside his corpse. She picked up the graparble and quickly looked upon the inner works of the tomb. She stepped off the gray circle and it disappeared. The dead gray-green sea elf now lay on the black stone floor.

Trapped!

Alone!

Uncanny… she sensed so much familiarity. The tomb was bigger on the inside. Both time and space were distorted. Walls between the doors bore images of her great-great-great grandmother and another who looked remarkably like Fisher… only the bloke in the tomb's image was paler. On three walls there were identical doors which were not visible from the outside. Two sarcophagi sat near the wall opposite the three doors. They were made of black stone, like the walls and doors. A simple black rod and little piece of black stone sat on the sarcophagus on the left. Another Twin Stone rested on a thick tome which sat beside the black rod. A small purple bag lay beside the tome. A huge stone called heel stone dominated the area of the tomb opposite the sarcophagi. The heel stone was a single block of sarsen stone. It was sub-rectangular, with a minimum thickness of 2.4 meters. (A meter is 39.37 inchworm lengths.) It rose to a tapered top 4.7 meters high. A further 1.3 meters was buried in the ground. Gray soil made up the floor of the tomb where the gray stone circle had formed and then disappeared. The rest of the floor was the same black stone that formed the walls and sarcophagi. The heel stone sat 77.4 meters from the sarcophagi and was nearly 27 degrees from the vertical. Its overall girth was 7.6 meters. It weighed 35 tons. A ton was… very heavy! Piara shared Fisher's uncanny sense of weights and measures.

CHAPTER 48

Tomb Dreamraider

In the cabin at the foothills of the Doombringer Peaks Kirrie stared out the window and watched a rambling bramble bush snare a careless yellow hare. Meries sat high in the sky and gave its bright light to the Light Period. Her companion snored and fought to stay asleep. The Dreamraider's protuberant tummy interfered with her comfort. Occasionally she formed an illusion of her svelte form, but it did little good. Amica moaned and sat up.

The grumpy Good Witch said, "Oh, ****! Someone has entered the tomb unprotected. Are you up for a trip?"

Kirrie said, "Sure. It's rather boring sitting here and listening to your snoring. I am getting used to my daily beverage. I drink from the esyuphee sack every day. The smoky waters of Fire Lake warm me. The esyuphee sack refills each time. I feel strong."

Amica said, "Good! You are stronger and I don't feel up to the task."

Kirrie asked, "How much longer will you carry your...uh, burden?"

Amica answered, "A while, and it's not a burden. Let's just say I'm enjoying an altered state of health."

Kirrie asked, "By the way, what are you carrying?"

Amica curtly replied, "It's not a what! I carry my child, and he or she comes from good stock and will be exceptional!"

Kirrie answered lackadaisically, "I'm sure, just as I'm sure you don't feel up for a trip. Whom shall I visit? The Wandmaker again? The Sharkman? How about the ***** Morganne? I'd love to give her a nightmare."

Amica answered, "You have no connection to her. You are a novice. This time you will have a focal point inside a nice tomb."

Kirrie said, "Why did anyone fall asleep in a tomb? I'm OK with sneaking into their dreams, but... why?"

Amica said, "You are stronger. Your daily drinks have drawn you closer to me... to Grayness. There's a powerful focal point. This time... *you* are going...not just your mind."

Kirrie replied, "Am I capable? I've been closer to death more times than I'd like of late, but I don't fancy going into a tomb. Why'd we want to enter a tomb before our time?"

The Good Witch said, "Some unfortunate has entered the tomb unprotected and activated the Glyph of Warding. I hope it wasn't that ***** Piara. I'd given her credit for more sense. I'd told her the amulet gave protection. Surely she didn't go without it."

Kirrie said, "Piara? The Carcharian's Queen? The one whose daughter the four-armed Bluuch was told to guard? I saw images of her in Bluuch's mind. Quite pretty! Maybe prettier than you, Good Witch! Why'd she enter a tomb? Whose tomb? You're not making much sense. Tell me what to do."

Amica said, "If you're finished with twenty questions and comparing me to that green ****, I'll get on with it. A Glyph of Warding guards the tomb. You'll need protection. Prepare a beverage as you would when the sphere returns."

Kirrie said, "Why? The chalice and sphere are not here."

Amica said, "Still... prepare as you would if they were."

Kirrie one after the other poured uncolored, yellow, red, and green potions into a large mug and then decanted smoky fluid from the purple esyuphee hide sack into the cup. Auras filled the cavern with each addition. Kirrie eased the vessel to her pale orange lips and gently sipped the smoky warm effervescing liquid. Goose bumps covered her carroty skin and she felt chilled to the bone. She tipped the cup and quaffed the remainder of the liquid.

Amica said, "I'm going to place a Protection Spell on you."

The Good Witch uttered guttural phrases and placed her hand on Kirrie's shoulder. Kirrie felt little shocks throughout her body. Amica grasped the locating stone, blew hot blue breath onto the stone, and whispered unsettling phrases in the language of the Omega Stones. Gray and mauve auras flashed from the little rock. Then the Dreamraider uttered another arcane phrase. The locating stone developed a deep purple hue and vibrated softly. She gave Kirrie the locating stone and said, "Don't lose it. I just told it where to go."

Kirrie said, "Nice little purple rock. What's next?"

Amica said, "Now take the Omega Stone."

Kirrie said, "I get it. The Omega Stone will guide me."

Amica said, "No. dummy! The Locating Stone will guide you. The red and blue tiles are your pathway. The Omega Stone will tell you what to say. Squeeze the **** thing!"

Kirrie gripped the stone. It bent to the shape of her hand.

A single rune appeared on the little stone.

$$\Omega$$

After 13 heartbeats the rune faded and the triumvirate appeared.

$$Ø \infty Ø$$

The trio of runes persisted for 21 heartbeats. Thrice the pattern repeated...13 heartbeats, 21 heartbeats...then the stone's surface was again smooth.

Kirrie marveled, "It's a memory bank. It stores memories."

Amica said, "Well, it stores information! It'll tell you want to say."

Words entered Kirrie's mind.

"I give you my blood through which you will receive all you seek. You in turn give to me your all."

$$Ø \infty Ø$$

The Good Witch gave Kirrie a flattened blue stone tile and placed a red tile on the floor.

Amica said, "Step onto this red stone tile and you'll leave this cabin and arrive in an eight-sided structure outside the World of the Three Suns. Share the Omega Stone's information with those within the... uh, edifice. After you attend your business, place the blue tile on the floor and return here."

Kirrie said, "Sure, and I'll return a lot older! Also, when we left the grotto behind the falls you had no idea how much time would pass.

The púca dropped red sand on the tile and it led us to the tree in Alms Glen, but thirteen years had passed."

Amica then said, "That was different! I'm in control now and know where you are going. In a prior visit I left a focal point inside the octagonal edifice. The potion you drank and my protection spell should stop you from aging. I've given the locating stone direction. Keep it safe! Don't lose it! Tell the visitors to the tomb their means to escape. When you have finished, do not follow their course. Place the blue tile on the floor, think about me and this place, and step on it. Now step on the tile and take another step into Grayness."

Kirrie said, "There's nothing for it."

The she-Drelvish, Fire Wizardish, erstwhile Teacher of the Drelves stepped on the red tile. Redness surrounded her. Phrases entered her mind.

"I give you my blood through which you will receive all you seek. You in turn give to me your all."

Ǿ ∞ Ǿ

Deep red ripples coursed through Kirrie's mind. Then she heard a soft thud. Her soft shoes rested on a stone floor in an eight-sided chamber. The floor and stone were made of black stone. She was not alone.

Ǿ ∞ Ǿ

Piara looked frantically around the brightly illuminated chamber. Three of the eight walls had doors. Then red light filled the chamber. An orange-skinned female stood in the chamber. She stepped off a red tile and picked the tile off the floor. She looked remarkably similar to female Drelve-Vydaelians.

Piara said, "Redness! Don't try to fool me! I'm not sleeping! Is this another of your guises, Dreamraider?"

Kirrie said, "I am here at the behest of your benefactor the Samaritan Good Witch. Pay heed to what I say."

Piara said, "She left my dream hurriedly. I've had visions of this place. Why should I trust you over my intuition?"

Kirrie said, "Do you know how to get out?"

327

Piara said, "I have an idea. My instinct yells me to touch the Heelstone."

Kirrie said, "How many times? How can you be sure you don't suffer your companion's fate?"

Piara answered, "I...I can't."

Kirrie surreptitiously gripped the Omega Stone. Words formed in Kirrie's mind. She said, "Then listen! Touching the heel stone thirteen times produces the gray circle that allows exit from the tomb to the stone circle on the hillock and also induces the formation of images on the three doors. Be wary of the doors. They open gates to other realms. Opening such gates requires precision. Making a mistake brings consequences. Traveling through gates oft comes at a price."

Piara asked, "What images form on the doors? Other realms? All visions I've seen through my great-great-great grandmother's eyes are of my world. Before I met the newcomers at Vydaelia I had no concept of 'other realms.' Where do the doors lead?"

Kirrie gripped the stone and said, "What lies beyond these doors does not concern you, Piara of Elder Ridge. Stick to your business at hand. You wanted to learn of your ancestry. The opportunity to do so has landed in your lap. If one makes a mistake while attempting to open the doors and chooses the wrong sequence...the door leads to a grotto behind a waterfall. Without a means to exit the traveler wastes away in the grotto. With a means to exit and a focal point one might end up... somewhere and sometime else."

Piara said, "Who are you?"

Kirrie said, "I'm another piece of your Wandmaker's past. Remember well what I've told you."

Kirrie placed the blue tile on the floor and stepped onto it. Blueness flashed through the tomb. But for Agarn's corpse Piara was alone. She picked up the second Twin Stone, black rod, black stone, and tome. She held the tiny bag of little weight. To her surprise, the bag accommodated the rod, stone, amulet, and tome.

There was nothing for it.

Piara went to the heel stone and touched the heel stone 13 times. Images formed on the three doors. An image of a red-bearded giant formed on one door. Another door bore an image of a tall man with a cherry red birthmark on his chin. An image of a female fire demon formed on the third. The gray stone circle reappeared in the center of the tomb! Piara stood in the center of the gray circle and tapped her left foot 13 times. Purplish auras surrounded her. In an instant she stood in the center of the Gray Vale Stone Circle outside the tomb in Gray Vale. Only young sea-elf guard Horton stood near the circle. Piara stepped off the gray circular stone and it disappeared.

Horton marveled, "You are finally back! We had given you up for lost. Commandant Inyra ordered one of us to stand guard."

Piara asked, "How long was I in the tomb?"

Horton replied, "A season of growth."

Piara asked, "How long is a season of growth?"

The young gray-green sea elf guard replied, "Sorry. It's the time required for a seedling to spring from one of our planted stones."

Piara said, "Time! How much time?"

Horton thought hard and replied, "My teachers say it's 832040 minute minuteman heartbeats."

Piara replied, "That's a constant measure of time. I'm familiar with it. That would equal 30 rotations of the Day Glass in Vydaelia, the length of one of the newcomer's Dark Periods. I have a very accurate sense of time. I was in the tomb precisely 987 minute minuteman heartbeats."

Horton respectfully followed, "My lady, we rotate guards every 17711 heartbeats. The guard has changed 47 times since you and Squaddie Agarn stepped onto the gray circle. Where is Agarn?"

Piara said, "I must speak to Inyra immediately."

Horton said, "I'm not to leave my post."

Piara said, "I'm here now. The circle has disappeared. Bring Inyra. I must talk to him about the tomb."

Horton persisted, "Where's Agarn?"

Piara answered, "He's not coming back. Fetch Inyra."

CHAPTER 49

The Adjuster Arrives

Blueness surrounded Kirrie. She felt a bit chilled but otherwise no worse for the wear. She stood in the cabin in the foothills of the Doombringer Range. The Good Witch lay on the bed and moaned, "I thought you'd never get back!"

Kirrie said, "You said I'd not age! How long was I gone?"

Amica answered, "About 5 minutes! I was speaking of my need, *Fire Wizard!*"

Words entered Kirrie's mind.

"I give you my blood through which you will receive all you seek. You in turn give to me your all."

Ø ∞ Ø

Memories awakened in Amica's mind…

The Dream Raider inched closer and gently stroked the Wandmaker's shoulders. She deftly pushed her chest against him and cooed, "Work is done. There's only the two of us. I'll say anything you want to hear. I'll see everything through. I'll do anything you want me to…just to win the love of a guy like you."

Yannuvia momentarily enjoyed the warmth and softness of her touch. The deep gray light made her all the more beautiful and enhanced her already overwhelming pheromones. Amica gently exhaled her enticing breath onto his left cheek and delivered a soft kiss.

Blue flames flickered in Yannuvia's eyes and matched the Dream Raider's.

Why resist?

The Dreamraider's tryst with the Wandmaker was coming to fruition. Her stomach tightened in ever increasing intensity and decreasing interval. She managed, "I never thought I'd want to see the Mender, but I could use him now. You'll have to help me."

Kirrie said timidly, "I've no experience in bringing young into the world. Can't you just use Magick?"

The Dreamraider grimaced as another contraction began and said, "This falls into Nature's realm. In some ways I'm just as feminine as you. This is one of them. We can use the waters of Fire Lake. The warmth will comfort me."

Kirrie decanted smoky waters from the esyuphee sack. The sack predictably refilled. The she-Drelve used moistened raiment to sponge the bright red sweat from the Dreamraider's brow. Amica maintained her Good Witch guise.

Kirrie asked, "Why don't you change into something more comfortable. I won't be alarmed.'

Amica panted and answered, "One form is as good as another. I think it's time."

Kirrie readied for the worst. What was about to make its appearance? The Dreamraider acted much as a laboring she-Drelve matron. She maintained her composure remarkably well.

Amica took a deep breath, then panted several times, and said, "It's time. Help me!"

Kirrie said, "I know nothing about birthing nymphs! Oh, well! What the ****! Stay on your back. Do you want a pillow?"

The Dreamraider said, "Yes! A pillow! That'd be nice!"

Kirrie opened the door and plucked a large chunk of orange door moss which grew around the cabin and snatched up unwary insects that tried to make their way inside. Kirrie stuffed the ultra-soft moss behind Amica. The Dreamraider leaned backward and sank into the moss. Kirrie retrieved the esyuphee sack containing the smoking waters of Fire Lake and sat the container by Amica. More red sweat dripped from the Good Witch. Beads dropped to the floor and smote a meandering creepy crawly that had evaded the door moss. The Good Witch struggled to maintain her composure.

Amica muttered, "Give me the container!"

Kirrie said, "I thought it was for cleaning!"

Amica said, "I need a drink!"

Kirrie added, "I'm not sure that's a good idea. Drelvish matrons always kept laboring she-Drelves' tummies empty."

Amica said, "That's one place our similarities cease. I'm not Drelvish."

The Good Witch quaffed quite a good bit of the smoky liquid and nestled into the soft moss. Her pain came closer and closer together. Each time she concentrated on her breathing and used the Omega Stone as a focal point. After a time... the Dreamraider said, "It must be time! I can't hold back! I must push!

Amica pushed. Kirrie made ready. In a few moments a soft cry rewarded the Dreamraider's efforts. Kirrie performed the midwifery role admirably.

Kirrie said, "Well, congratulations, Mom, you are like us in many ways!"

Amica sighed and said, "Yes, the Wandmaker certainly knows so."

The cries intensified.

Amica closed her eyes tightly and asked tentatively, "What... is it?"

Kirrie said, "It's a beautiful nymph... uh, child... demonling... uh, whatever it is you have."

Amica impatiently asked, "Come on, Kirrie, and is my child male or female?"

Kirrie said, "It's... male."

Amica took a deep breath and asked, "Is he OK?"

Kirrie said, "Rather robust little bloke! Seems hungry!"

Amica gave a sigh of relief and said, "Describe him. Does he look like... who does he favor?"

Kirrie answered, "Hard to say! He is beautiful. Hold him while I finish up."

Kirrie expertly divided the umbilical cord and passed the babe to his mother. Amica opened her eyes, placed both hands around the infant, and held him on her flattening tummy. Lesser contractions followed. Kirrie attended the new mother's needs and used the remainder of the smoky waters to cleanse. She briefly left Amica's side to retrieve another bundle of door moss. She released it and the door moss scurried along the floor and cleansed the area thoroughly. The Dreamraider cuddled the small bundle. The crying stopped. Amica studied the babe. He had mostly Drelvish features, including orange-ish skin, fine silver-gray hair covering his smooth little head, and red-orange eyes. Two miniscule horns rose from his little head and a tiny tail with an innocent barb on its tip playfully swayed back and forth. Amica checked his tiny hands and feet and thankfully noted six fingers and toes. Normal! Thank Grayness! A tiny nodule sat at the base of the infant's sixth left finger.

The Dreamraider murmured, "Like his daddy!"

Kirrie frowned.

The infant sneezed. His visage changed. The new look included pale skin, blue eyes, blond hair, and five fingers and toes. The little nodule sat at the base of the fifth left finger, but the little horns and tail were absent. A little burp produced another visage with fiery red skin, a longer tail, forearms ending in little talons, and smoke trickling from its little nose and backside. Amica placed him on her shoulder and comforted him. Her touch brought the little bloke back to his original form. Amica put the child to her breast and he received his first nourishment.

Kirrie said, "I'll be ******! Never thought you had it in you, the beautiful matronly thing. The little blighter adjusts his form on a whim."

Amica said, "Good observation! I've pondered names. 'Adjuster' works well."

Kirrie said, "Suppose your Master will be happy about having another minion."

Amica said, "The Master's eye is blind to events in the World of the Three Suns. I'm going to keep him in the dark for a bit."

Kirrie asked, "What about his Daddy?"

Amica added, "Him as well."

Kirrie asked, "Is your son a Spellweaver?"

Amica said, "No. He was not born in the Gray Light. He is Drelvish and may be Spellweaverish. From what I've seen he's certainly "Fire Demonish. Only time will tell his strength and alignment. For now… he has no worries. He has two Fire Wizards to protect him."

Kirrie replied, "That he does."

CHAPTER 50

Preparations in Vydaelia Land and Sea

A fortnight plus one day earlier in Vydaelia…(30 rotations of the Day Glass)…

832040 minute minuteman heartbeats earlier…

Wandmaker Yannuvia, Morganne, Knightsbridge, Mender Fisher, Clouse, Elder Dienas, Elder Yiuryna, Morganne, Jonna, Joulie, Sergeant Major Klunkus, Lodi, Merry Bodkin, Tariana, Tawyna, Peter, Blair, Dennis, Bernard, Noone, Alistair, Gordon, Leftbridge, Stewart, Bluuch, Gruusch, Quunsch, Starra, Sharchrina, and Yathle concluded their meeting in the outer ward of Vydaelia. Fisher had recanted a tail of two Menders from his insight into the common knowledge of Menders. Clouse shed little additional light. Fisher pressed to seek out the Duoths and try to communicate. Yannuvia disagreed but relented and allowed Fisher to set out alone and in possession of three Omega Stones. Truth be known the Wandmaker bade the stones good riddance. They had been of little value. Communication with the Carcharians was not an issue after their experiences in the geodesic dome. The Omega Stones had added nothing to defensive and offensive capabilities and posed a threat to revealing secrets within the Wandmaker's mind to other community members. Bluuch rigidly held the stone Piara had left with him and tarried near Starra and Sharchrina at all times. The Wandmaker retained an Omega Stone. Fisher held the other three. Clouse wore around his neck an exceptional amulet, which had been taken from the fallen four-armed leader of the Carcharians' failed assault.

The Wandmaker set about creating more building blocks to extend the wall. Klunkus and other veterans preferred to strengthen existing defenses, but Yannuvia mind was set. Morganne had led a party to explore the region to the east and gave Fisher what information she could. The Mender set out alone.

Yannuvia worked two rotations of the Day Glass and without stopping. The expanded wall took shape. Elders Dienas and Yiuryna insisted Yannuvia rest. The Wandmaker yielded and went to the Day Glass enclosure and joined Morganne for a time. Sleep was fitful. Knightsbridge refused relief and dutifully stood by the door whilst the Wandmaker rested. Yannuvia awakened and went back about his business.

Near the end of the next period guards on the wall shouted, "Vessels approach!"

Sergeant Major Klunkus shouted, "Sound the general alarm! All Rangers report to stations! Youths and elders to the inner ward!"

Yannuvia joined Klunkus on the allure facing the sea. Three boats neared Vydaelia. Quunsch and Gruusch stood by the Wandmaker.

Quunsch said, "The King's ships!"

Three penteconters approached. The ships had a single row of 25 oars on each side. Troglodytes and Bugwullies manned the oars. Troglodytes were about the height of tallest Vydaelians (60 inchworm lengths) and had spindly but muscular arms and squat legs. Trogs had some lizard-like traits, with reptilian heads and forearms, a spinal chest and a long slender tail. Ladders and weapons were stacked on the decks and a single Carcharian barked commands.

Yannuvia asked, "What are they up to?"

Klunkus said, "Fexa and Fenideen have reported no activity to the west. I'm going to call everyone into the outer curtain."

Quunsch squinted and declared, "I make out old Boggle. I guess he didn't get enough last battle."

Gruusch said, "Clootch sits atop the middle ship. Is that old Cutthroat on the third ship?"

Ø ∞ Ø

Brace welcomed the sight of Clootch's ships. Keeping his charges hidden and patient had been quite a challenge. The ships' approach had increased activity on the wall.

Brace declared, "Gruusch! He has survived, only to serve the newcomers! Traitorous lot!"

Clootch, Boggle, and Cutthroat barked commands.

Ó ∞ Ó

Squaddie Frayn from Graywood watched from a distance.

Ó ∞ Ó

On the allure young Tawyna said, "They are in bow range? Shall we fire?"

Gruusch added, "Wandmaker, why don't you hit them with a spell?"

Yannuvia was already firing Magick Missiles at Cutthroat and Boggle. The unerring spells walloped the oar masters. Both dropped to the deck and took cover.

Archers took assigned positions along the allure. Then scores of Carcharians came from deeper water and swarmed over the boats and pulled ladders into the water. Troglodyte and Bugwully oarsmen left their positions and moved in front of the ladder bearers. Groups of three Carcharians carried each ladder and formed up behind the oarsmen.

Jonna said, "They are using the oarsmen as shields."

Quunsch said, "Go ahead and shoot. You wouldn't want to run into a troglodyte in a dark corner. They serve out of fear, but if they breach the wall, the Trogs will attack you viciously. They hate sea elves and you guys look a lot like orange sea elves."

Klunkus ordered the archers to fire at the approaching enemies. From this range most arrows hit their marks. A hundred and forty Troglodytes and ten Bugwullies led the ladder bearers toward the wall. Bowstrings twanged. Soon fifty or more Troglodytes had fallen. The enemies fanned out to approach the seaward wall. The Carcharians wore thick hide armor, which provided some defense against the arrows and diminished the seriousness of their wounds.

Merry Bodkin said, "They are attacking all along the wall. At least we can outnumber them at each site."

At the last moment the ladder bearers converged on a section of wall about forty paces wide. The Carcharians charged relentlessly. Well-placed arrows felled a half dozen warriors but soon twenty ladders slammed into the wall and Troglodytes started to climb up. Larger

Carcharians followed. Sixty Carcharians carried the ladders and two ranks of twenty followed them. The rear ranks hurled spears toward the wall and forced the Rangers to duck behind the merlons. Rangers managed to throw back a few ladders but sheer numbers of the heavy ladders proved effective. Troglodytes scurried up the ladders. The unarmed Troglodytes didn't fare very well, but they made a clever ploy to allow their taskmasters to enter the conflict. Ladders concentrated in the short section of wall enabled the enemies to reach the wall walk and engage the defending Rangers hand-to-hand. Klunkus ordered Rangers to concede the section of allure under attack and descend to the outer ward or move along the allure. Archers formed ranks in the outer quadrangle and fired into the Carcharians as they reached the allure. Arrow supplies became precariously low. Yannuvia still limped badly and followed Sergeant Major Klunkus to the outer ward.

Then Fexa yelled from the western wall at the outcropping, "Carcharians! Hundreds of them!"

Lord Crudle's companies had reached the millpond and approached the partially constructed wall. Fexa, Fenideen, and the other Rangers hurriedly retreated to the former outer curtain and entered the quadrangle. Crudle's fresh warriors easily transgressed the partially constructed wall and made for the former outer curtain. All the while Carcharians and a few surviving Troglodytes spilled over the merlons onto the wall walk on the seaward wall. Klunkus ordered everyone to positions near the inner curtain and recalled everyone from the eastern wall. Yannuvia and Clouse attacked the enemies with Magick Missiles. The Wandmaker gripped the red and blue tipped master wand and readied the sequence to summon the Dreamraider. She'd said she'd come three times. So far he'd used the power twice, while the triskaidekapod attacked and to fend off the Giant Amebus.

Quunsch said, "We'll put up a fight. Their survivors will have something to tell their spawn about." The half-Bugwully hurled a spear and dropped a larger Carcharian just before he stabbed Ranger Tariana, who had slipped and fallen on the allure. Tariana rolled aside and scurried down the wall stairs and just evaded a thrown spear from the allure. Quunsch hurled another spear and felled a second two-arm. Gruusch and Bluuch arrived from the inner ward and hurled spears. Bluuch hurled two at a time and smote four invaders in rapid succession.

Gruusch threw half as many but also enjoyed deadly accuracy. Starra and Sharchrina arrived with bows and fired effectively.

Bluuch threw again and said, "Starra refused to stay in the inner ward. We'll fight till the end."

Knightsbridge stood beside the Wandmaker.

Yannuvia sternly said, "I ordered you to stay by the Gay Glass enclosure and guard Morganne."

Before Knightsbridge could answer a bowstring hummed and an arrow felled another Carcharian. Morganne said, "I'll stand with my brothers and sisters."

Yannuvia shouted, "No! Your time of delivery is near!"

Morganne wore her favorite orange walking dress. The fabric stretched over her protuberant tummy. Her long red-orange hair fell down her back. She wore in her hair the ribbon given her by elder Yiuryna at her ceremony of life-time commitment with Yannuvia.

Morganne said, "That won't matter if they breach the inner curtain and invade the inner ward."

She fired another arrow and dropped another enemy from the allure. Soon the Troglodytes had fallen. Carcharians on the allure threw spears. Bluuch dropped his weapon and held four shields and shielded the Wandmaker's party. Six spears clanked off the shields. Quunsch deftly gathered the spears and hurled them back toward the allure and scored four lethal hits. Morganne fired nine more arrows and dropped eight enemies. With an empty quiver she drew a short sword and stood by Yannuvia. Many archers were running low on arrows. Clouse and Yannuvia repeatedly sent Magick Missiles into the Carcharians on the wall walk. Usually two spells brought the big warriors down. Clouse readied the Wand of Lightning. The green guy uttered **"Grove veer cleave land"** and directed the wand toward the allure. A beam of light streamed from the tip of the wand and exploded on the allure, where it sent eleven Carcharians to their doom. The number "three" appeared in Clouse's mind. The force of the spell knocked several ladders backward and sent Carcharians climbing up them down onto the rocky beach. The enemies sustained various injuries. Some were knocked out of commission. Only a dozen or so Carcharians remained on the wall walk. Clootch ascended one of the remaining ladders and stood on the allure. He barked orders and the surviving warriors made for the wall stairs and charged toward the Wandmaker and the Carcharians loyal to him. Clouse readied the wand of lightning again but Yannuvia bade him wait.

Bluuch said, "We can handle this rabble!"

Bluuch, Gruusch, Quunsch, Starra, and Sharchrina drew swords and charged toward the enemies. Sergeant Major Klunkus, Jonna, Joulie, Merry Bodkin, and Tariana joined the assault. Bluuch overwhelmed his two-armed opponents. Quunsch's legendary battle prowess again showed evident as the big half-Bugwully quickly beat two Carcharians into submission. Young Gruusch fought well. Starra and Sharchrina had received weapons training and stood toe-to-toe with their two-armed opponents. So far all the assault had accomplished was the depletion of theVydaelians' arrow stores and a scant amount of Magick. The quicker Drelves kept their larger opponents at bay until Bluuch, Quunsch, Starra, Sharchrina, and Gruusch ended their battles and came to the Rangers' aid. Clootch stood on the wall and saw his minions falling one by one. The Carcharian allies were turning the tide into the defenders' favor.

Clootch reached for his throwing spear. He saw the spell casters in the midst of the cluster of warriors. One used a device to foment Magick. The other had to be the sorcerer that was Fishtrap's bane. Clootch took aim and hurled the spear. Morganne's state prevented her charging the advancing Carcharians. Instead she stood by Yannuvia with sword drawn. She saw Clootch's movements on the wall. Bluuch and the others had moved away from Yannuvia and left Clootch a field of fire. The throw was accurate! At the last second Morganne stepped in front of the spear. A sickening thud told the spear found a mark. The ugly weapon sank deeply into Morganne's side. She moaned and fell by Yannuvia. The Wandmaker extended his left hand and uttered arcane phrases and sent a mauve ray toward the wall walk. The ray struck Clootch and obliterated him. Yannuvia collapsed.

At that moment the last invader fell to Bluuch's mighty hand.

Clouse rushed to Morganne and Yannuvia.

Morganne gasped, "Is he … dead?"

Clouse answered, "No. He's entered a fugue state. I recognized the incantation. He sent a Disintegrate Spell into the Carcharian. It's an eighth level spell and should have been beyond him. He is unconscious, much as I was after the fight with the Giant Amebus."

Morganne gasped, "Clouse, save my baby!"

Klunkus sent warriors to form a defensive line facing the western wall, where the shouts and hammering of Crudle's warriors were heard. Others ascended the stairs to defend the breach. The seaward attack had been thwarted. Only a few wounded or injured Carcharians hobbled their way back toward the three boats. Brace stood on the middle ship and stared at the wall. Clouse, Starra, and Jonna and Joulie carried Morganne to the inner ward. Fexa and Knightsbridge carried the prostrate Wandmaker.

Sergeant Major Klunkus asked Clouse as he retreated toward the inner ward, "Can you call the Dreamraider?"

Clouse answered as he ran; "Only the Wandmaker knows the means to summon her using the red and blue tipped wand. I'll try to save them. Do what you can to keep the enemies at bay. Starra stay with the others. Take the Wand of Lightning. Its command is **"Grove veer cleave land."** Use it wisely. We have three uses left."

Matron Pamyrga met them in the inner ward which bustled with activity. Already wounded Rangers filled the area and overwhelmed the matrons, elders, and youths. Fisher was sorely missed. Clouse kept his hand over Morganne's wound. The spear entered her body in the right lower chest. He hesitated to remove it. Sometimes a penetrating weapon tamponades bleeding and gave healers a little precious time to attend the wounded. The Wandmaker's breathing and pulses were normal. His color was ashen and he was in stupor and did not respond to stimulation. Morganne's breathing was labored and her pulse was weak. Clouse took the Healing wand and uttered **"Rut fir ford bee haze"** and touched Morganne with the wand. Small scratches on her arms healed. Her skin moved around the impaling spear and slowed the bleeding. Clouse handed the wand to Pamyrga and instructed her to use it on the Wandmaker. The Healing Wand had regained usages during the last Wandmaking ceremony. The green guy conjured and uttered an incantation and touched Morganne. His Healing Spell produced little effect. Her breathing remained shallow. Pamyrga uttered **"Rut fir ford bee haze"** and touched the Wandmaker. Yannuvia did not respond.

Clouse muttered, "Were only Fisher or, I hesitate to say, the Dreamraider here! It took her touch to revive me!"

Ø ∞ Ø

Scores of slain Carcharians and Troglodytes were strewn along the allure and the stone ground of the outer ward. No Bugwullies made it into Vydaelia. Brace had no command remaining. His assault had served its purpose. The two-armed Carcharian again debated his course. From his vantage point on the boat Brace heard the shouts and tools of Crudle's forces smashing the wall. Arrows no longer coursed through the air. A devastating spell hit his friend Clootch and nothing remained of his body. Hopefully Clootch's last attack proved effective, but he obviously had not eliminated the perpetrator of the Magick that destroyed him. Injured Carcharians climbed onto the boat. Brace realized he had lost over a hundred warriors including Clootch, Cutthroat, Tippy, Cannoo, and Tilertoo. Boggle still waited on the next boat.

Ø ∞ Ø

Sergeant Major Klunkus struggled to organize defenses. Rangers hurriedly gathered expended arrows from the fallen enemies and the few errant shots. There were scarcely enough for a single volley. He took a page from Fishtrap's tactics and formed his defenders into a phalanx with shields facing outward. Quunsch, Gruusch, Bluuch, and Sharchrina gathered a few spears to throw. Starra clutched the Wand of Lightning. The slim instrument looked rather natural in her slim reptilian hand. Pieces of stone began to fall from the western wall. Yannuvia's construction had withstood the Carcharians' axes admirably, but the persistent attackers were making progress. Klunkus's defenders were positioned about eighty paces from the wall. Archers positioned in the rear. The Sergeant Major opted to dispense the arrows among twenty archers to give more shots when the enemies broke through. There would not be time for many rounds. Hand-to-hand combat was inevitable. A large piece of stone fell from the wall. A Carcharian peeked through the opening creating by the break. Quunsch moved forward, heaved a spear mightily and struck down the interloper. His comrades removed his body and continued to chip away at the wall. Another large piece of rock separated and crashed to the ground. Every able bodied Vydaelian gathered in the outer quadrant to fight. Only elderly, matrons, very young, and Clouse remained in the inner ward with the infirm. Unfortunately the infirm included the Wandmaker and Morganne.

The wall gave way.

Two Carcharians came through. Archers struck them down. The chipping resumed. Another segment of wall broke and created a breach wide enough for four Carcharians to enter abreast.

Sergeant Major Klunkus said, "Aim carefully. Make every shot count. I can see we are outnumbered. Be ready Starra."

Four Carcharians passed though the breach. Archers again struck them down. Then Crudle ordered a defensive formation. A cluster of warriors passed through with interlocked shields. The mini-phalanx stepped deftly across the rubble and moved into the outer ward of the quadrangle.

Sergeant Major Klunkus shouted, "Now, Starra!"

Starra uttered in Carcharian tongue **"Grove veer cleave land"** and directed the Wand of Lightning toward the advancing Carcharians. A flash of light escaped the tip of the wand and slammed into the enemies. Several went flying back through the opening and all 36 were killed. The large bodies crashing into the fractured stone and the force of the Lightning Bolt further weakened the wall. The number "two" appeared in Starra's mind.

From the allure Fenideen shouted "Get down!"

Klunkus said, "Shields up!"

Scores of thrown spears flew over the damaged western wall and crashed among the defenders. Most fell short but two found marks. Vydaelia lost two more defenders, Trando and Lapril. Graparbles fell from their hands.

The Carcharians returned to chipping away at the wall. Soon their efforts were rewarded. Another large section fell. Now the opening accommodated over a dozen wide-shouldered Carcharians. Crudle ordered the formation of a standard phalanx. His loyal warriors obeyed without question. Carcharians hustled to remove debris. The full phalanx of a hundred warriors advanced through the opening. Starra uttered **"Grove veer cleave land"** and sent another lightning bolt into the advancing warriors. The devastating spell disrupted the formation and sent Carcharians flying. Over forty were killed, but the others hustled to regain formation. The number "one" appeared in Starra's mind. A large four-armed Carcharian named Fleugzog jumped onto the wall walk and shouted. The warriors moved toward the defenders. Starra again said, **"Grove veer cleave land"** and sent another beam of electricity into the Carcharians and scattered them. This time few survived and they simply tried to crawl away. The phrase "grayness is necessary" appeared in Starra's mind. The Carcharian princess threw the wand aside and grasped a trident. The four-arm Fleugzog on the allure wailed and hurled a spear toward Bluuch. Bluuch raised his shield and deflected the spear. Quunsch fired a spear toward the four-arm on the allure, but he evaded it. Carcharians outside the wall formed ranks. Lord Crudle ordered them to move forward. The warriors entered the breach in the wall twelve abreast and moved toward the defenders. A Mountain Giant moved into the opening after the tenth rank.

Guppie's loud voice thundered. "Which of you scumbags holds my amulet? I'm going to eat your heart!" The cave warg Fenrir walking beside Guppie and growled menacingly. More Carcharians filed in behind the giant and cave warg.

Sergeant Major Klunkus said "There's nothing for it. It's hand to hand now. Stand tall, my friends. Let's let them know they were in a fight."

Gruusch gripped Starra's hand for a moment and said, "Fight well, my love."

Bluuch sighed and said, "I fight for my Queen, though she is not here." The big four-arm gripped the Omega Stone briefly and prepared four weapons.

Jonna and Joulie grasped hands.

Jonna said, "We're together."

Joulie added, "To the end, my sister. We'll honor our father Banderas with our effort."

A whistling sound came from behind the defenders. An explosion rocked the ground forty paces in front of the defenders and dropped four Carcharians in the front rank.

Tariana asked, "Has the Wandmaker aroused?"

Bluuch answered, "No! That was a Duoth bomb!"

Yathle added, "Typical for the cowards! Attacking us while we're vulnerable and just to get onyums for their bellies."

Sergeant Major Klunkus said dejectedly, "So much for Fisher's mission! We can do nothing about it! We have more enemies before us than we can handle. The Duoths will have their way. At least their attack took several enemies with us."

Then three more Duoth bombs sailed overhead. These exploded in the advancing ranks of the Carcharians and sent many flying. Then large filmy bubbles drifted over the defenders and floated toward the Carcharians. A Duoth, *Laurens201,* stood on the inner ward allure with the bubble sword and bubble decanter and repeated created the large bubbles and waved them toward the attackers. More Duoth bombs fell into the attacking Carcharians and splintered their ranks. Guppie took the brunt on an explosion and fell. When the giant fell, the cave warg ran away. *Long207, Jenkins226, Wayne170, and Pierce180* ran to the side of the defenders. *Long207* passed a Duoth bomb to Quunsch and extended a pseudopod toward the four-arm on the wall. Quunsch shrugged and hurled the bomb toward the allure. The round bomb landed by the four-armed Carcharian Fleugzog and blew him to smithereens. The surviving Carcharians broke formation. Bluuch gave a yell and the defenders charged into them. *Laurens201* moved to the western edge of the seawall and floated bubbles into the partially enclosed area beyond the western wall. The bubbles burst over the Carcharians that remained in the area. Onyum Grower *Telfair59* scooted beside *Laurens201* and hurled a Duoth bomb into the area. The bomb exploded near Lord Crudle and his second in command and nephew Tosser. The force of the blast hurled Tosser into his Uncle and sent the pair sprawling on the ground. When Lord Crudle fell, the paltry force that remained fell into total disarray. Individual Carcharians refused to surrender and fought relentlessly, but there was no organization to their efforts.

Fisher approached the rear ranks with Onyum Growers *Candler28, Bacon100, and Evans47.* Jonna saw the Mender and ushered him into the inner ward. The Onyum Growers hurled Duoth bombs over the wall into the beleaguered Carcharians who remained around Lord Crudle and Tosser. One of the bombs exploded near the commander and killed Lord Crudle. Bluuch, Quunsch, Yathle, and Gruusch fought tenaciously and felled multiple opponents. A lucky throw from a downed Carcharian struck Yathle in the back. The noble two-arm fell. The graparble fell out of his left hand. Like Loogie's it was 1.6 times heavier than those that fell from Drelves.

Ǿ ∞ Ǿ

Wounded and injured Carcharians made their way to the sea and tried to reach the waiting ships. Brace and Boggle watched the carnage unfolding. Both saw Fleugzog get blown off the wall and Lord Crudle and Tosser fall to the barrage of Duoth bombs.

Boggle marveled, "The newcomers have allied with Duoths! Food! As an ally! Hardly any of Lord Crudle's force remains alive, but they are still fighting. We can offer little. Let's get the **** out of here."

Brace sighed, "Who's going to row the boat, *******? All the oarsmen died in the battle. Are you going to tell King Lunniedale about the defeat? I faced him once with bad news. I'm not relishing the thought of doing it again."

Boggle said, "We can't just stay here. More of our fellows fall by the minute. Now the newcomers are coming through the wall to pursue us. Look out! There's a Duoth bomb headed this way!"

Ø ∞ Ø

Bluuch and Gruusch were infuriated by Yathle's death and charged through the defect in the wall after the Carcharians. Sergeant Major Klunkus sent Rangers with them. Quunsch joined his newfound Duoth buddies on the wall walk, accepted another Duoth bomb, and hurled it toward the ships. His throw was spot on and blew up the easternmost penteconter.

Ø ∞ Ø

Brace and Boggle dove into the water and abandoned the ships A few injured Carcharians filtered into the water and swam away. On the shore Crudle's forces battled to the last man. The Carcharians refused the offer of quarter.

Ø ∞ Ø

Squaddie Frayn followed the rag-tag survivors back to Doug-less and watched them enter. Shortly thereafter Carcharians exited Doug-less in large numbers. Frayn recognized several of Lord Crudle's entourage who took the route toward Reed Creek Delta.

Young Bryni mused, "Like rats deserting a sinking ship, Squaddie Frayn. Why are they leaving in such numbers? Normally Carcharian dignitaries travel by ship, but their boats did not return."

Frayn answered, "Their forces were just thrashed by the newcomers and their allies. One of the boats was destroyed. The others fell into the hands of the defenders. Doug-less does not pose a threat to us for the moment. I'm a bit overdue for a visit to Graywood and long to see the trees of Gray Vale and share a mug of mead with my friend Commandant Inyra. I need to let him know about the battle. You and Auvi will remain hidden and watch the Carcharians. Send word if anything changes."

Frayn made for Graywood.

CHAPTER 51

Another Aftermath

748 Carcharians died in the assault. All the Troglodyte and Bugwully rowers fell. Only Brace, Boggle, and nine wounded swimmers struggled to make their way back to Doug-less.

Yathle and 13 Drelves died. Trando, Lapril, Adama, Byron, Shelley, Bysshe, Fallie, Bollen, Bickum, Bendet, Chex, Glyten, and Perian joined Miclove, Owings, Buck, Borger, Houston, Bart, Killian, Geber, Eyesen, Myrna, Vasor, Rettick, Hummitch, Ayden, Lynnae, and Loogie in giving their lives to defend Vydaelia.

Fisher entered the inner ward and found a flurry of activity. Clouse worked feverishly with gravely injured Morganne. Matron Pamyrga and Elder Dienas sponged the unresponsive Wandmaker.

Clouse said, "I'm glad to see you."

Fisher replied, "Actually the Duoths did lots more than I did. Their bombs turned the tide of the battle. I would have thought the Wandmaker would have summoned the Dreamraider before things got this far."

Clouse answered, "He likely would have had he not made the same mistake I did and cast a higher level spell. He's in a bad way, but his vitals are steady. Morganne on the other hand hovers near death. I've stopped the bleeding but I fear removing the spear."

Fisher said, "Wise move, but it's likely a mortal wound."

Clouse said, "The last thing she said was 'save my child.' Is it possible?"

Fisher said, "The common knowledge of Menders tells of taking offspring through the mother's abdomen. But the results are not good. I tapped that knowledge in my time at Aulgmoor. When is her confinement time?"

Clouse said, "The matrons say any day now. She refused to remain in hiding and fought beside us. In fact she took down ten Carcharians before she stepped in front of a spear meant for the Wandmaker. The spawn is active. I feel much movement within her stomach."

Fisher said, "We will probably lose Morganne if we attempt to take the child."

Clouse said, "We'll lose both of them if we don't"

Fisher said, "Have you used the healing available to you?"

Clouse said, "Yes. There's been little effect."

Fisher said, "We can try. Bring me a vorpal blade and sewing material. I've attained some knowledge of the innards of Drelves, but this is new to me. I've brought Kiennish young into the world through their mother's abdomen, usually when the child is pointed the wrong way when the time to come into the world arrives. Mender's panacea and stout ale helps the mother-to-be through it."

Clouse said, "There's nothing for it. She's growing weaker."

Fisher said, "Let's carry her to the Quartermaster Enclosure. My supplies are there. I'll... we'll do what we can."

Pamyrga and Dienas chimed, "We'll assist."

Knightsbridge, Leftbridge, Alistair, and Stewart gently carried Morganne into the Quartermaster Dome. Fisher, Clouse, Pamyrga, and Dienas followed.

Fisher and Clouse were laboring to save Morganne's life. Fisher rubbed unguents around her chest wound's edge and placed Mender's panacea in her parched mouth. Clouse used the Wand of Healing, pronounced **"rut fir ford bee haze,"** and touched Morganne. The wound's edge tightened and bleeding slowed.

Morganne aroused a bit and managed, "Save my baby!"

Fisher said steadily, "We'll lose you if we take the child."

Morganne repeated, "Save my child."

The Wandmaker's life mate faded and lost consciousness.

Clouse repeated, "You said you've taken a child from its mother."

Fisher answered, "Well, yes, in Aulgmoor, but circumstances were different, and the results were still poor."

Clouse said, "We must remove the spear, but it's near her heart."

Fisher uncharacteristically cringed and said, "It still must be done. She's unconscious. I'll remove the child. Remove the spear and immediately thereafter use the Healing Wand again. Hopefully it will slow bleeding and give me time to prepare the wound."

Fisher readied the vorpal blade.

Pamyrga gasped, "No, it'll kill her!"

Fisher said, "Morganne's my friend, too, but she's likely already lost to us."

Fisher moved with speed and precision. In moments a little girl was taken from Morganne's stomach. Clouse just as expertly pulled the spear and immediately used the Wand of Healing, said **"rut fir ford bee haze"** and touched the ugly chest wound. The chest and abdominal wounds' edges pulled together a bit and bleeding slowed.

Morganne again aroused and said, "My baby! Is my baby well?"

Clouse stammered, "Uh, no, Morganne. She is not breathing. Dienas and Pamyrga are working with her."

Morganne struggled, "She... my Carinne. Please save her."

Fisher quickly sutured the abdominal wound and asked, "Clouse, do you still possess the white rock I gave you in Lost Sons?"

Clouse answered, "Yes, I have the Mender's Stone. I've saved it least we lost the Wandmaker. You used it to restore the tree he destroyed in Alms Glen. But I'm not fully Mender."

Fisher answered, "That's alright. It doesn't always work anyway."

Morganne moaned, "Please. Allow me to touch her."

Pamyrga leaned forward and placed the still unbreathing infant within her stricken mother's reach. Morganne touched her tiny hand and said, "She's cold and purple!"

Pamyrga cried, "I'm trying!"

Clouse took the white rock from his pack and gripped it. It softened and bathed the area with white light. Runes appeared on its surface.

Ó ∞ Ó

Clouse moved the Mender's Stone towards Morganne's chest wound. Morganne grabbed Clouse's hand and said, "No, not me!"

Clouse said, "But..."

Morganne grimaced and said, "Do it, Clouse! Try to save Carinne!"

Clouse sighed deeply and said, "I'm not really sure how this works, but here goes."

The green guy touched little Carinne with the white rock. Deep gray auras surrounded them. The infant gasped and gave a robust cry. The runes faded from the white rock.

Ø ∞ Ø

Morganne smiled weakly, touched tiny Carinne again, and said, "Tell Yannuvia that I love him and forgive his transgressions. He has responsibilities as a father now. Tell him to make Vydaelia strong and safe for my daughter Carinne."

Morganne then closed her eyes, took one agonal breath, and breathed no more.

Clouse and Dienas wept. The Wandmaker's blood touched Fisher and cursed him with feelings. The Mender cursed his newfound emotions and said, "I know I have a heart now, for I feel it breaking." Snow white tears flowed from Fisher's pale eyes.

Pamyrga emerged from the Quartermaster Dome with a small bundle wrapped in a soft purple glowworm silk blanket. She rushed into the nursery in the inner ward, Matrons labored to help injured Rangers. The bodies of the fallen had been gathered and placed along the inner curtain. In a little while Elder Dienas, Fisher, and Clouse emerged from the Quartermaster Dome. Dienas immediately went to helping matrons. Clouse placed Healing Spells on three wounded Rangers. The wounded were stabilized. Clouse and Fisher exited the inner ward and approached Klunkus. Quickly Jonna, Joulie, and the Carcharians joined them.

Jonna asked, "What of Morganne?"

Another milky tear betrayed Fisher's attempt at stoicism. Clouse cried openly.

Fisher said, "Morganne is dead."

Jonna and Joulie broke into tears. Sergeant Major Klunkus cleared his throat and sighed.

Jonna asked, "She carried the Wandmaker's child. What...?"

Fisher answered, "She is strong. Matron Pamyrga carried her to the nursery. Yorcia is giving her... nourishment."

Clouse said, "She is beautiful. She has Morganne's eyes and the Wandmaker's nose and pointed ears. She has six fingers and toes and a little nodule at the base of her sixth left finger. Fine silver hair covers her head. Morganne aroused for a moment after the little nymph took

350

her first breath. She touched the baby and smiled. With her last breath she muttered, 'Tell Yannuvia I've always loved him.' I didn't tell her of the Wandmaker's state. She died with her left hand touching the baby."

Jonna said, "A feminine child… Morganne had chosen names. She wanted to honor the Wandmaker's mother if she bore a female child. The babe's name then is Carinne."

Sergeant Major Klunkus gathered his thoughts and managed, "What of the Wandmaker?"

Clouse said, "Physically, he is fine. He remains unconscious. I've tried Healing Spells and stimulation. We can only watch and wait."

Starra asked, "Can't you summon the Dreamraider?"

Clouse answered, "Only the Wandmaker knew the means to summon her."

Sergeant Major Klunkus said, "Fisher, what of the Duoths?"

Fisher said, "I promised them two things."

Sergeant Major Klunkus asked, "Which were?"

Fisher replied, "First, a generous supply of onyums, and secondly, they will not be eaten."

Sergeant Major Klunkus said, "I doubted the wisdom of your mission to the Duoths. You and they arrived in the nick of time. I'll speak for the Wandmaker and say those terms are certainly agreeable. Can you relay to them our gratitude?"

Fisher said, "They know. The fact that Carcharians are within spear range and haven't attacked them confirms it. The Duoth leader *Mose14* received me and I treated with him. He maintains an Omega Stone. The Onyum Grower *Evans47* carries an Omega Stone. I can communicate with him through the devices. As I suspected, Duoths are likely intelligent. They cultivated the onyums."

Sergeant Major Klunkus said, "Tell them to attend their dead and avail them the onyum patch. We must remove the bodies of the dead enemies and prepare to honor our dead, but security remains our first priority."

The quadrangle of Vydaelia took on macabre character. Nineteen Duoths clustered along the seaward wall. Onyum Growers *Wheeler28, Montgomery33, Toombs25, Tatnall29, Candler28, Evans47, Bacon100, Emanuel31, Telfair59, Jeff Davis33, Appling41, Treutlen41,* and *Bulloch37* and *Stand-byes Laurens201, Jenkins226, Wayne170, Dodge191,*

Pierce180, and *Long207* stood silently. *Telfair59* and *Emanuel31* held Duoth bombs in pseudopods. An errant Carcharian spear had impaled young Stand-by *Screven152* and he lay on the western allure. Bluuch, Quunsch, Gruusch, Starra, and Sharchrina gathered around Yathle's body and stood about thirty paces from the Duoths. Starra sobbed softly and gently rubbed Yathle's body. Bluuch held Yathle's extruded graparble in his left lower hand and methodically tossed it into the air. Quunsch stared hungrily at *Screven152* and the cluster of silent marshmallow men. Rangers gathered their fallen comrades and the little graparbles. Jonna and Joulie carefully kept the little stones separated and designated by person. Other Rangers carried fallen Carcharians and Troglodytes into the area between the breached western wall and the partially finished wall at the outcropping to the west. Sergeant Major Klunkus supervised the activities and stationed Peter, Blair, Dennis, Bernard, and Noone on the western wall and Tariana, Tawyna, Merry Bodkin, Willifron, Petreccia, and Tanteras along the seaward wall. Two vessels sat about a hundred paces out to sea. Quunsch's thrown Duoth bomb had decimated the third penteconter. Watchers on the allure saw no activity in the sea and the observers on the western wall saw only lifeless bodies in the cleared area to the west. Klunkus's charges gathered precious expended arrows and weaponry from the Carcharians. Ranger Gordon carried messages back and forth from the inner ward.

Quunsch's stomach growled. The big half-Bugwully muttered, "There's Duoth within my reach! I'm so hungry!"

Starra scolded, "They saved us! We were goners! You must restrain your wants!"

Quunsch moaned, "What a waste! He's just lying there."

Starra sternly said, "Quunsch!"

Quunsch, "I'll behave!"

The entire community remained on high alert and went about their tasks. The Duoths silently positioned on the walls and in the opening in the western wall.

The Wandmaker remained unconscious.

CHAPTER 52

Piara's Delivery

Piara insisted, "Horton, I must speak to Inyra. Agarn is not coming back. He's lying dead in the tomb. Magick protects the edifice! I'm back! There's nothing to guard!"

Horton said, "I suppose you are right. Inyra is back at Graywood."

Piara and Horton made their way back to the common area of Graywood. Nurse Nila, Lieutenant Liani, and guards Rory, Turlough, and Adric joined them. Inyra questioned Agarn's fate.

Piara said, "I did nothing to harm him. If you recall, I wanted to enter the tomb alone."

Inyra said, "True. Describe what you found."

Piara described the inner working of the eight-sided edifice in great detail. She left out Kirrie's visit, but did reveal the items she brought out of the tomb, including the second Twin Stone amulet, the black rod, clump of black stone, and the tome. Inyra listened intently.

The gray-green sea elf Commandant said, "We've heard stories of the Rod of Ooranth and Stone of Ooranth. They are said to be the artifacts used by the Gray Matron's parents to construct the tomb. The runes on the outside of the old tome are not sea elfish. I cannot decipher them."

Piara said, "I can. The runes say 'Alexandrina's memoirs.' They are written in the language of the Omega Stones."

Liani said, "Say again?"

Piara said, "I am fluent in 17,711 languages. I can translate the writing in the tome."

Inyra asked, "Why weren't you injured?"

Piara said, "The amulet I wear provides protection. Marvelous little device! It helped guide me to my ancestor's realm, your Gray Vale, and its identical sister. I found its twin in the tomb."

Inyra asked, "Why were you within the tomb for 832040 heartbeats?"

Piara said, "From my perspective, I was only in the tomb for a very brief time."

Nurse Nila said, "I believe her story about the time. Her pregnancy is no further advanced than when we last saw her."

Inyra asked, "What is the power of the twin amulets?"

Piara said, "I don't know. Yet. I hope studying the tome will shed light on the power of the twin sister amulets. I held both amulets in the tomb, but only wore one."

Inyra said, "We now possess the second amulet. Perhaps you should place both around your neck."

Nila warned, "The visage of the Gray Matron on the tomb's door only wears a single amulet. Is it safe for her to wear both? Remember, she carries a child."

Piara said, "I'll do it."

Before Nila could object Piara placed the second Twin Stone Amulet around her neck. Pleasant mauves auras enveloped the stones and a low pitch drone flowed from the artifacts.

Inyra asked, "What do you feel?"

Piara recalled the Dreamraider's words from her dream in Vydaelia:

"Marvelous little device! It has an identical sister. It'll lead you to its twin. Keep it safe and hold it close. It'll both guide and protect you. Pay heed to the twin speak when the sisters are together. The sisters are the keys to unlocking many doors, dissuading Magick, and saving time."

Perplexed Piara answered, "Nothing... I thought they'd communicate."

Inyra said, "Maybe I should hold one."

Piara removed the second Twin Stone from her neck and gave it to Inyra.

Liani shouted, "Commandant, we can't afford to lose you! Allow me!"

The Commandant ignored the warning, took the amulet, and placed it around his neck. Now intense gray auras surrounded Piara and Inyra.

The *Two Stones Effect* occurred!

The Twin Stones mimicked the larger Omega Stones and exerted the *Two Stones Effect* on the Commandant and Piara. Piara's *Menderish* nature did not prevent the effect. Inyra and Piara began to speak the unnerving language of the Omega Stones and spoke truthfully.

The *Three Stones Effect* occurred!

Piara and Inyra saw into one another's minds.

Piara said, "I don't understand. There are only two identical stones. This effect required three activated Omega Stones."

Inyra muttered in gibberish speech, "I see your Mind's image of the Omega Stones. These are not Omega Stones. They are speaking to us! But more than that... I see... everything you have said is true. Your baby's father is... the leader of Vydaelia! Your other child is the spawn of the liege of Doug-less! Piara of Elder Ridge, you do get around!"

Nila quizzically asked, "What are you saying?"

Piara replied, "I understand you. Two Omega Stones empower communication in an old dialect and compel the truth. Three Omega Stones enable the bearers to look into their colleagues' minds. We never discovered the effect of four and five stones, and I never knew of more than five of them together. Now the Twin Stone 'speaks' to me. The Twin Stones mimic ALL effects created by multiple Omega Stones. Nothing special happens with four. Five stones produce a *Protection from Magick* effect. Six and seven do nothing special. Eight Stones effect enables *Continual Light*. I don't know what that means. No added effect from nine, ten, eleven or twelve Omega Stones, but thirteen stones produces *Time Saving Effect*. Time will remain constant when passing between realms. 14, 15, 16, 17, 18, 19, and 20 do nothing more. 21 Omega Stones will irreversibly form into a Xennic Stone. Xennic Stones helped the Gray Matron create UK and revolve in the geodesic dome in Vydaelia."

Inyra said aloud, "It'd be hard to get twenty-one people carrying twenty-one rocks to do anything together. So it's mostly moot."

Piara thought, "You understand me. When we hold the Twin Stones, we need not speak aloud. The Twins Stones produce these effects as a pair, but apparently only if worn by two individuals. I wonder... I am not touching you."

Piara grasped Inyra's arm. The Commandant tensed briefly and then relaxed, and silently responded, "I know what you are doing. I feel no different."

Inyra said aloud, "Release me. I want to check distance between us. The Commandant walked toward the door, exited the cabin, and took a few steps outside into the Graywood common area. When he reached a distance of thirteen paces all discernible effects dissipated save a sense of the second twin stone's location.

He reentered the cabin and said, "You entered the tomb without being harmed, so the Protection from Magick is inherent in each Twin Stone. Time passed differently for you in the tomb, so the Time Saving effect requires both stones. We'll learn other effects by trial and error."

Piara said, "The tomb was brightly lit without an apparent source. Perhaps a single amulet can give light in a dark place."

Inyra asked, "What if you desire darkness?"

Piara said, "I suppose you *think* it off."

Nila muttered, "I haven't understood a word either of you have said."

Inyra insisted, "I want to see the inside of the tomb."

Nila said, "Her delivery time is nigh. Piara should rest and take nourishment."

Piara said, "I feel well. I'm not opposed to entering the tomb again, but it'll be more productive after I have read the tome. Allow me some time. It's several hundred pages of writing."

Inyra said, "I still can't read the writing on the tome."

Piara commented, "It's written in Mender and cursive chaotic script. My Menderish traits help me read languages. Apparently wearing a Twin Stone doesn't avail one the ability to read the language."

Piara pondered, "These aren't twin stones. They are two of triplets."

$$Ø \infty Ø$$

In Vydaelia Clouse noted a drone from the Amulet he wore. The pink stone vibrated. Mauve auras enveloped the stone. The stone shrank and transformed to purplish gray color. The green guy said aloud, "Two of three sisters are reunited."

$$Ø \infty Ø$$

Inyra relented and the group left Piara in the little guest house. Horton remained outside her door. The sea elf studied the tome intently. The beautiful flowing cursive writing belied the guttural spoken words. The Gray Matron's words detailed her time in Gray Vale. The intensified gray light in Gray Vale that heralded the Mender's entry and exit from his confinement chrysalis mimicked that of an Approximation of a Gray Sun Andreas in a World of Three Suns.

Piara studied.

The highly intelligent sea elf read quickly and absorbed the tome's information.

The inner tomb's heel stone was identical to another in a distant place called Stonehenge. Touching the heel stone reproduced the gray circle that allowed exit from the tomb to the stone circle on the hillock and also induced the formation of images on the three doors. These images provided mechanisms to open gates to other realms. An image of a red bearded giant forms of one door, which leads to giants' realm. Another door bears an image of a tall man with a cherry red birthmark on his chin. The door leads to a stone circle at a place called Uragh Wood in a simple world. An image of a female fire demon forms on the third. It leads to a circle on a green island in a world of three suns. If one chooses the wrong key…the door leads to a grotto behind a waterfall. Without a means to exit the traveler wastes away in the grotto. With a means to exit and a focal point one might end up… somewhere and sometime else. Sometimes traveling through gates comes at a price.

The Rod of Ooranth and Stone of Ooranth appeared to the Mender Lou Nester and Alexandrina's parents in Gray Vale. The origin of the artifacts and their name remained unknown. The command **"Jams Gar Field"** activated the power of the Rod of Ooranth. The tome detailed the construction of the scepter UK that Inyra carried. The powers of the artifact were detailed.

Whilst the gray light concentrated on Gray Vale, four stones gathered around the Menders, Edward, Victoria, and three year old Alexandrina. The four stones hovered and then revolved around the quintet at about Victoria's eye level. The stones revolved 13 times and then migrated to the area of the stone circle, where they began to revolve around the five stones. Intense gray light illuminated the area around the five stones. A purple light flowed from the larger stone and concentrated on the area in the midst of the five stones. A circle of grayness formed on the soil between the stones. Then a gray sphere appeared and hovered directly over the center of the circle on the ground. The sphere emitted auras and droning sounds. The four stones continued to revolve around the stone circle. The quintet made their way down the hillock to the circle on the ground. One by one they stood on the stone. The six-foot diameter sphere hummed more loudly. Purple rays flowed from the sphere onto little Alexandrina and moved back and forth from the child to the center of the circle. Little Alexandrina left her mother's side and walked to the center of the circle and stood beneath the hovering sphere. One of the stones left its orbit and moved to the child's side. Runes appeared on the stone.

Ø ∞ Ø

The surface of the sphere changed. First the sphere reflected Alexandrina's face and then letters appeared on its surface. The first phrase read "Xennic Stones." The phrase read **"Win Stone Church Chill."**

Alexandrina uttered the phrase. The Black Rod of Ooranth hovered briefly and then slipped into the child's tiny left hand. She reached out and touched the hovering stone. The rock decreased in size and she gripped it and uttered "Curse Stone." The Curse Stone meld to the shape of her little hand. She touched the stone with the black rod. Then the black stone of Ooranth hovered and moved near the child. Alexandrina gripped the curse stone in her right hand, held the rod of Ooranth in her left hand, and touched the hovering black stone and said **"Win Stone Church Chill."** A section of black stone shaped like the rod of Ooranth hovered in front of her. The stone of Ooranth dropped to the ground. Alexandria released the curse stone from her hand. It resumed its original spherical shape and returned to its orbit. A second stone left its orbit and drew near her hand. The surface of the sphere again reflected her face and then the phrase **"Wood row will son"** appeared. Runes appeared on the stone.

Ø ∞ Ø

Alexandrina touched the second stone, which again shrank to fit the size and shape of her tiny hand. She said Stone of masonry, touched the hovering replicated rock with the rod of Ooranth and said, **"Wood** row will son." The young sea elf released the Stone of masonry. A third stone drew near her. The sphere reflected her charming face and they displayed the phrase **"Lend dawn john son."** Runes appeared on the stone.

Ǿ ∞ Ǿ

Alexandrina said "Light Stone." She touched the Light Stone with the rod of Ooranth, then touched the hovering length of black stone, and said, **"Lend dawn john son."** She released the Light Stone and the fourth stone drew near her. The sphere showed her face and then the phrase **"Eyes Inn Hour."** Runes appeared on the stone.

Ǿ ∞ Ǿ

She uttered the phrase, touched the fourth stone with the rod of Ooranth, and accepted the new stone in her hand, and declared it the Battle Stone. She touched the hovering length of black stone and said **"Eyes Inn Hour."** The hovering rod transformed to a scepter with an ornate handle and vorpal blade. The child released the Battle Stone and Black Rod of Ooranth. She uttered **"Win Stone Church Chill"** and reached out and grasped the scepter. Her face again appeared on the rotating sphere above her head. Then runes appeared.

UK

Ǿ ∞ Ǿ

The Xennic Stones left Gray Vale.

Midway into the book the handwriting and language changed. Piara quickly recognized the written language of Menders. The author identified himself as Lou Nester. He detailed his journey. Lou Nester came into the world Parallan in a cave in the Doombringer Mountains. Early on in his life he served a Droll clan named Korcran. Lou helped them learn to use an artifact called them Summoning Stone of Fire, which enabled them to subjugate Firehorses. Lou then wandered to the Kiennites' realm and briefly served the liege of Aulgmoor. Lou's nodule enlarged and he meandered to the south. Menders could not seek confinement in the place they arrived. Piara had not seen this in her brief contacts with the common knowledge of Menders. Lou traveled to the land of Mountain Giants. He clandestinely followed a Mountain Giant into the underworld realm, where he was captured by Carcharians and narrowly missed being the main course. Quick thinking and his skills enabled him to save a Carcharian princess and gain favor with the liege of Doug-less. Lou discovered a taste for Duoth in Doug-less and accompanied Carcharians on hunts. On one such hunt, a Duoth bomb exploded near him and rendered him unconscious. His fellows abandoned him, but the Duoths found him and nursed him back to health. Lou tried as he might but was unable to communicate with the Duoths and parted with them on mutually good terms. He was injured in an encounter with the Giant Amebus and awakened under the care of sea elves in Elder Ridge. The sea elves said a Samaritan placed Lou on their doorstep. Lou lived among them at Elder Ridge for a time, but eventually confinement beckoned and the sea elves led him to Gray Vale. From there the accounts rendered by Inyra had been accurate. Lou's account of the creation of the scepter UK echoed Alexandrina's. The tome then detailed Lou Nester's potions and experiments. Much of the detail was beyond Piara's reckoning. She was, after all, only Menderish. Lou Nester emerged from his chrysalis with a second Mender, who chose the moniker Darner. Darner left after a season and Lou only knew of him through the common knowledge of Menders. Piara's new Mender knowledge entered the common knowledge of the ilk. Other Menders *saw* her path. Lou Nester made entries about young Alexandrina and her Menderish traits, which confused him, much as Clouse confused Fisher. Lou's health deteriorated and he supervised the construction of the eight-sided structure.

The language changed again to the Chaotic Evil writing of the Omega Stones. Alexandrina's penmanship was evident. The tome detailed the keys to passing through the three doors and entering the alien realms. The giant's realm… the Dark Sorcerer… the Fire demon… Piara committed the mechanisms to memory.

The sea elf studied the tome for the equivalent of three rotations of the Day Glass. Sabrina brought her nourishment, Nila checked on her every period, Inyra sent queries, and the young guards rotated shifts watching her. Finally Piara finished and sent word to Inyra.

Inyra arrived. Nila protested but Piara agreed to reenter the tomb. The small group returned to the stone circle outside the eight-sided tomb. Piara and Inyra placed the Twin Stones around their necks and walked to the Gray Vale Stone Circle. The circle had five very similar small stones and one large alignment stone. The huge monolith was a rectangular slab arranged radially to the circle and aligned with the NE-SW circle axis. The large stone totally dominated the site and sat very close to the tiny circle of five stones. The whole site was perched on a little terrace halfway up the hillside. Piara and Inyra stood in the center of the circle. The duo moved forward and touched the monolith, then returned and touched one of the little stones. Then they went back and touched the monolith twice. They then touched another stone thrice. Next the pair returned to the monolith and touched the big stone five times. The brace of sea elves followed by touching a third little stone eight times. Next The Commandant and erstwhile Queen of Doug-less went back to the monolith and touched it thirteen times. Then they went to the fourth stone and tapped it twenty-one times. They returned to the monolith and touched it thirty-four times. Lastly they went to the final stone and touched it fifty-five times. A gray slightly raised circle of 13 foot diameter formed within the circle of stones. Humming sounds emanated from the circle and gray and purple lights flashed about its surface.

Piara said, "Let's test our theories. We'll enter, retrieve Agarn's body, and exit. I want to see how much time passes."

Inyra acquiesced to her suggestion.

The pair stepped onto the circle, tapped their left feet four score and nine times, and was instantly transported into the center of the tomb. They stepped off the circle and it disappeared. Agarn's lifeless body rested on the floor. The tomb was unchanged. Piara and Inyra went to the heel stone and touched it thirteen times. The circle reformed along with the three doors. They went back to the circle gathered Agarn's body, and tapped their feet thirteen times. In an instant they were back in the Gray Vale Stone Circle outside the tomb. Those gathered before still waited.

Piara asked, "How long?"

Horton said, "89 heartbeats."

Inyra said, "Sounds about right."

Agarn looked like he had simply fallen asleep. His body appeared to have ceased living no more than an hour ago.

Nila said, "We'll proceed with his ceremony of interment."

Inyra yearned to explore further but agreed with the nurse.

The ceremony required preparation. Agarn's graparble rested in the infirmary. Nila supervised transport of the corpse to Graywood and made formal preparations. The nurse insisted Piara take rest. The tired sea elf agreed. In the equivalent of a rotation of the Day Glass, the community gathered and Agarn's procession made its way to Gray Vale. Piara acquiesced to Nila's request and did not attend the ceremony.

Inyra employed UK and repeated his actions from Fytch's ceremony. The Commandant and Nurse had a go about delaying further exploration, but Nila persevered. Piara took a needed sleep. After a few hours Sabrina carried food to Piara, who made ready for Inyra's arrival.

Nila knocked on the guest cabin's door. Piara bade her enter, and the nurse entered with Commandant Inyra and an older gray-green sea elf that bore many scars. Piara and Inyra wore the Twin Stone amulets. *The Two Stones and Three Stones* effects occurred.

Inyra said, "I have news. My lead Squaddie and loyal friend Frayn has returned to Graywood. He has watched your friends from Doug-less."

Piara interrupted, "I've repeatedly told you that I have no friends in Doug-less. I am a wanted criminal. You have seen into my thoughts and know I speak the truth."

Inyra said, "You speak the truth. You won't be sorry to learn that the forces of Doug-less have taken two devastating defeats at the hands of the newcomers. The second cost them dearly. Frayn informed me that Lord Crudle, leader of the Reed Creek Delta and Cane Bisque Bay cluster of Carcharians and his notorious son Fishtrap have been killed along with over 700 frontline Carcharian warriors. Crudle was second only to King Lunniedale in power and meanness. His minions fomented many of the raids against our folk and tormented sea elf communities in the Reed Creek Delta."

Frayn said, "The newcomers allied with Duoths and repelled everything that the forces of Doug-less threw against them. The fighting was tenacious."

Piara asked, "Frayn, what about the newcomers' casualties?"

Inyra said, "I sensed a bit of angst in your question."

Piara tartly answered, "My daughter lives with the newcomers! During my time in Doug-less I met Lord Crudle and his son. The world is better off without them."

Frayn said, "A few Carcharians fought with the newcomers, but I observed from a distance and was too far away to determine gender."

Piara said, "Did the Wandmaker's Magick stem the tide?"

Frayn said, "During the first battle one of the newcomers flew over the water and sent devastating Magick into the Carcharians. He eventually went to the shore and had a close call. Only a concerted effort by his colleagues saved him from the four-armed menace Fishtrap. A Carcharian with Bugwullyish legs eventually brought down Lord Crudle's son."

Piara said, "My friend Quunsch saved the Wandmaker! Did Quunsch survive?"

Frayn said, "Yes, at least the first battle. The Carcharians fought to the last bloke. The Sorcerer was hobbled and limped toward the walled citadel. The newcomers suffered casualties."

Piara asked, "What of the second battle?"

Frayn answered, "A larger force attacked from land and sea. Three ships carried warriors. Lord Crudle led the ground assault. The Carcharians fought viciously and breached both the seaward and western walls."

Piara said, "I'd imagine they felt the brunt of the Wandmaker's Magick."

Frayn replied, "I saw nothing to match the explosion that killed so many Carcharians in the first fight. There were several small blasts that followed flashes of light. I thought the Carcharians had prevailed. Then the Duoths arrived."

Piara gasped, "Oh, no! The Vydaelians were attacked on two fronts. Were Duoths in league with Carcharians?"

Frayn said, "No, Duoths fought on the side of the Vydaelians. Many Duoth bombs tore into the forces of Doug-less. The Carcharians suffered a devastating defeat. Only a handful swam back to Doug-less. They left their boats behind. I followed their retreat. Shortly after the survivors entered Doug-less many Carcharians departed including many of Crudle's folk. I left responsible observers to monitor comings and goings of Doug-less."

Piara sighed and commented, "Strange days! Duoths fighting beside Carcharians and newcomers! The lack of Magick bodes poorly for the newcomers. Did you see anyone... flying?"

Frayn said, "Not in the second battle! Their walls sustained great damage and they suffered more casualties."

Inyra added, "They are vulnerable."

Frayn said, "Not as weakened as Doug-less. King Lunniedale's allies are deserting him. His most brutal ally and veteran commander are dead. Do you not tire of the specter of Doug-less hanging over us? We abandoned the sea urchin fields after our mothers were taken. That tragedy has bound us like brothers Inyra. My line hails from Kibler Valley. My entire village was destroyed by minions of Doug-less in my grandfather's time. The Gray Matron took my people in and made them welcome in Graywood. Time grayed our bodies. Those of us born here have nodules of grayness. A fire burns within me. The flame won't be extinguished until Doug-less pays for its transgressions. I relished the death of every Carcharian. King Lunniedale is vulnerable. We have an opportunity Inyra."

Inyra replied, "We lack the strength to take on even a weakened Doug-less."

Piara added, "The entry to Doug-less is guarded in many places."

Inyra said, "You managed to get out."

Piara said, "It took some doing. The Circle of Willis is nigh impenetrable."

Frayn said, "I watched Crudle's force exited the cavern wall. I know the location of the secret entry."

Inyra said, "But you don't know how to open the door, and the twists and turns we'd encounter once inside."

Piara said, "I am a resource for knowledge of Doug-less proper. You probably speak of what Lunniedale calls 'the giant's entry.' I was not privy to such information. There is a secret door that enters into the King's sitting room. I always figured it was a quick getaway for the King."

Frayn said, "Your knowledge of Doug-less is quite a boon."

Inyra said, "My friend, you have always been a zealot regarding Doug-less and its King. As Commandant I can't afford that luxury. So much has happened in the past few time periods. What started as the tragic loss of thirteen of our folk against the Carcharian has culminated in our learning of the Gray Matron's progeny Piara. Through her we have gained access to the tomb and the Gray Matron's journal. Already Piara has learned so much."

Frayn said, "Some of those thirteen were my dear friends. Had I been here I'd have been in the thick of it. I'd have never accepted this beautiful lady's explanation for her predicament. I fear I'd have smote you, Piara."

Piara said, "Zealot, indeed."

Frayn said, "Lady Piara, I am primarily a soldier. My friend Inyra is more a statesman and politician. Inyra tells me you are like us among the King's most wanted."

Inyra said, "It's true."

Frayn said, "Inyra also tells me about the Twin Stones. Might I wear one?"

Inyra removed the amulet and placed it around Frayn's neck. The veteran squaddie stared at Piara. The *Two Stones* and *Three Stones* effects occurred. Frayn sighed, "My grayness! The depth of your minds exceeds even your beauty, Piara of Elder Ridge. Many of your thoughts are beyond my reckoning. But you clearly are of the Gray Matron's line. Your thoughts of the newcomers reassure me and strengthen my conviction of the course we should take. The newcomers share our enmity for the Carcharians. The Duoths most certainly do. We must seek an alliance with the newcomers. They have somehow managed to communicate with the Duoths. Duoth bombs are a means to weaken the stone walls that surround Doug-less."

Piara said, "Those are ambitious thoughts, Frayn. I feel your hurt. You have long served your people in harms' way, much as Urquhart and the rest of my purple gang served me."

Frayn added, "I see the images of your purple gang in your mind. The large four-arm Bluuch and half-Bugwully Quunsch are the warriors who played a big part in saving the sorcerer you call the Wandmaker... oh, the father of your child. It's reassuring that you do not carry another Carcharian. Your daughter's image is pleasing to you. I find it hard to look upon a Carcharian with anything but hatred."

Piara said, "My daughter's physical features are Carcharian, but she is half sea-elfish and shares my demeanor. The four-arm Urquhart came from a sea elfish mother. My daughter Starra, niece Sharchrina, Yathle, Loogie, Bluuch, Quunsch, Urquhart, and I left Doug-less under duress and to seek my daughter's love Gruusch, who survived an ill-fated scouting mission. The newcomers conditionally accepted us. We gradually gained their trust."

Frayn said, "These folk are loyal to you and oppose King Lunniedale. It'll be tough, but I will work with them."

Inyra said, "Frayn, we have not made any decisions. We have just discovered a means to enter the tomb. I want to explore now."

Frayn said, "My friend, as Commandant the final decision is yours. I'll obey your orders. But we cannot read the tome. We face unknown dangers in the tomb. We face a lingering constant threat from Dougless. I make a practical point. The lady is laden with child. I have no midwifery skills, but I'd surmise Piara is near delivery. Shouldn't we delay exploring the tomb until she delivers?"

Piara insisted she felt well enough to explore the tomb in Gray Vale.

Frayn removed the Twin Stone amulet from his neck and returned it to Inyra, He said, "Lady Piara, I accept your word from this point. I'll use the amulet only when necessary to explore."

Inyra insisted, "I had in mind exploring with Piara. We only have two amulets."

Piara said, "The three of us will have to always enter as twosomes. Someone can exit alone with both stones to facilitate bringing in a third person. Every time you enter or exit the tomb you must be wearing the Twin Stone or else suffer Agarn's fate."

Frayn persisted, "I have the fastest pottyhippomuses in the east. Inyra, we could treat with the newcomers whilst Piara is waiting delivery. She shouldn't place her child at risk."

Nila agreed, "Her delivery can come at any time. It's a small child but I think she is at term."

Piara, Inyra, Frayn, Liani, and Nila bantered a bit. Piara was adamant about going into the tomb. Frayn and Nila yielded to the Commandant's authority and agreed to make preparations. Inyra and Frayn exited the cabin to gather gear.

CHAPTER 53

Mose14

In Vydaelia rangers worked constantly to repair the hole in the western wall. Clouse used the Wand of Masonry with its **"Wood row will son"** command to create some new building blocks. Yannuvia had created the wand on the first day of a Dark Period and it had unlimited uses in his hand. Clouse used the device 13 times and the device became inert. However, the new blocks helped fill in the wide hole in the wall. Rangers placed the bodies of the Carcharians and their minions near the millpond and ignited a pyre. Morganne's body was carefully wrapped and placed with the other fallen Drelves and Yathle. Morganne's nodule was indistinguishable from others. The Duoths remained in Vydaelia. Young Stand-byes-in-waiting ferried messages back and forth to Ty Ty and carried onyums to the Duoths' home. The best tater digger in the Screven pod was promoted to *Screven153*.

After a rotation of the Day Glass a contingent arrived from Ty Ty. *Screven153* escorted the leader *Mose14* who sought out the Mender. Fisher and *Mose14* met in council and the Mender took *Mose14* to the stricken Wandmaker.

Mose14 presented Fisher with a treasured glob of Mender Panacea, which had been a gift to the Duoths from Lou Nester. He also gave Clouse a sizeable amount of sulfur, the critical ingredient or material component for Clouse and Yannuvia's fire spells. Clouse emerged from the chrysalis with knowledge of the Drelvish Spellweaver Fire Spell, but it had done him no good, because he lacked the sulfur. The Duoth's generosity gained him Vydaelia's confidence and acceptance. Rangers allowed *Mose14* to approach the Wandmaker. Fisher relayed to the others his communications with *Mose14*, who kept an Omega Stone gripped in a folded section of his doughy body. *Mose14* also presented a terrine filled with Duoth dropping soup. *Mose14* applied the thick unguent to Yannuvia's eyelids and lips. The Duoths' leader then carefully decanted small sips of the remarkably fragrant soup into the Wandmaker's mouth. Then he formed a tube-like structure with his tissue and extended the reed-like pseudopod into the Wandmaker's mouth. Slowly he poured the soup down his extended and narrowed tissue. Yannuvia awakened. The startled Wandmaker pulled the Duoth's thin pseudopod from his throat and coughed. Fisher and Clouse quickly reassured him. The Mender and Menderish green guy carefully assessed the Wandmaker who seemed no worse for the wear and soon adjusted to the sight of Duoths meandering around Vydaelia. Sergeant Major Klunkus took the Wandmaker aside and told him of the Duoths' arrival to turn the tide of the battle, Morganne's death, and the birth of little Carinne. Clouse shared the bounty of sulfur with the Wandmaker and returned the Wand of Masonry. Clouse still wore the amulet taken from Fishtrap.

Yannuvia walked away to the solitude of the bathing stream. He then went to the nursery, looked upon his beautiful daughter Carinne, and thanked Yorcia for her surrogate care of the nymph. He then returned to the outer ward. Klunkus, Dienas, Yiuryna, and Pamyrga had already begun the preparations for the ceremonies to honor the fallen. Yannuvia gazed upon Morganne's body. He then went to *Mose14* and extended his left hand while gripping the Omega Stone with his right. He sent thoughts to the Duoth leader and received them in return. *Mose14* extended a pseudopod and gripped Yannuvia's hand.

Yannuvia thought, "Death to Doug-less and its King!"

Mose14 returned silently, "Death to Doug-less and its King!"

Bluuch said aloud, "Death to Doug-less and its King!"

The big four-arm gripped the Omega Stone in his left lower hand, laid his massive left upper hand on the Wandmaker's shoulder, and said in the language of the Omega Stones, "You'll make things right with my Queen, Wandmaker!"

Yannuvia gulped and said, "I intend to do so."

A party of Duoths arrived from Ty Ty with three Amebus bombs. A fourth bomb rested in the inner ward from the Amebus's attack. Clouse intercepted and prevented its explosion.

Yannuvia shook the Duoth's hand again and sent the thought, "That will be a good start!"

Fexa and Fenideen arrived with choicest onyums and presented them to *Mose14*, who greedily absorbed them into his pudgy body. Duoth's buried *Screven152*'s body in the Onyum patch.

Quunsch muttered quietly, "**** of a turn of events!"

Gruusch held tightly to Starra.

Clouse held tightly to Jonna.

Sergeant Major Klunkus held tightly to Joulie.

Yannuvia held tightly to his anger and hatred.

Rangers and Quunsch anchored the brace of ships that Brace had left behind.

$$Ø \infty Ø$$

Brace, Boggle, and a haggard lot of wounded survivors made their way to Doug-less.

CHAPTER 54

Three Doors

Inyra carried the scepter UK. Frayn was equally comfortable with bow and short sword. The veteran shouldered his bow and carried his short sword in a sea mooler sheath. The leaders of Graywood expectantly approached Piara's cabin. The expectant mother had a surprise for them.

The first pains gripped the erstwhile queen of Doug-less's abdomen. Nila was correct. Piara's time to deliver had come. Inyra fumed, but the Commandant relented and returned to the observation area with lead squaddie Frayn.

Nila led the sea elf to the infirmary and tended her expertly. Purplish fruits and unguents eased Piara's pain. Nila assisted the birth of Piara's progeny. A beautiful pale green, pointed-eared little girl! She had smooth green skin like her mother. Her little pointed ears mimicked the Wandmaker. A little nodule sat at the base of her tiny sixth left finger, a trait shared with her father. She also had the Wandmaker's nose. Yannuvia's contact with the Mender Fisher led to the arrival of Clouse. The Wandmaker's tryst with Menderish Piara resulted in the birth of beautiful Clouse-ish tiny... the only name that came to Piara's mind... the only appropriate name... Alexandrina!

Then the new mother rested.

Piara awakened and sat on the soft bed in the guest cottage in Graywood and gently rubbed Alexandrina's soft little head as the babe slept. Piara was a veteran of motherhood, having raised Starra in the austere conditions of Doug-less and assisted many new mothers in the birthing rooms. Her midwifery skills were second only to her mothering skills. The infant's most telling features were the fine silver hair on her little round head and the little points on her ears. She had the

Wandmaker's little nodule and nose. Her beautiful smooth skin was pigmented identically to her mother and Clouse. What secrets did the little girl have in store?

Inyra was insisting on exploring the tomb. Piara felt the need to stay with little Alexandrina. Her last foray into the tomb lasted 30 rotations of the Day Glass in Gray Vale while she only sensed the passage of a few hundred heartbeats. The Twin Stone Amulet protected Piara. The second Twin Stone gave them another means to enter safely. Traveling in and out of the tomb with a single amulet distorted time. She and Inyra had learned from the Twin Stones that moving in and out of the tomb with both Twin Stone amulets "saved" time. The Gray Matron and Mender's journal had also shed great light. Caring for the baby the past few Day Glass rotations had taken Piara's mind away from grieving Urquhart and worrying over Starra. She wanted word of Vydaelia. Piara had spent time between care of the babe Alexandrina reading the journal and studying the chapters about the three "doors' or "gates." She'd learned about the tomb's defenses. A Warding Glyph protected the tomb from entry. Poor Agarn did not have a chance. Piara learned much of Greywood's folk from peering into Inyra's mind during the *Three Stones effect*. Frayn was very knowledgeable about the sea and its denizens. The veteran squaddie wanted to strike back against Dougless while the Carcharians were weakened by their battles with the Vydaelians. Inyra had scouts like the bloke Giryn she and Urquhart had encountered scattered about the great sea. The Graywood sea elves had contacts in the Endless Fen.

A knock at the door interrupted her thoughts.

Nila entered and said, "She grows more beautiful by the moment. Commandant Inyra is waiting outside."

Piara said, "Send him in."

Inyra entered with Liani, Adric, and Frayn. Nila took Alexandrina to the nursery.

Inyra said, "Your child is doing well. The points on her ears are interesting. She has a nodule of Grayness. But for the pointed ears... she shares your resemblance to the Gray Matron."

Frayn said, "She looks like us. Admittedly she's a little greener and has pointed ears."

Piara said, "Alexandrina is thriving, but she is too young for me to leave."

Frayn said, "You gave her the Gray Matron's name."

Piara said, "To honor her."

Frayn said respectfully, "She is as beautiful as her mother. She is a citizen of Graywood. I'll protect her to my fullest."

Piara said, "Thank you, Frayn."

Inyra said, "The stone circle in Gray Vale is under constant guard. Scouts have returned. An exodus continues from Doug-less."

Piara said, "I also want to learn about the three doors and study the tomb further. I'm studying the journal I found in the tomb. The tome is written in two very difficult languages and by two different hands. Knowing languages is second nature to me. Translating them to sea elf requires great effort. There is a section about the three doors. I cannot read it. Reading it requires the *Read Magick* function of the amulets. I tried wearing both of them. It didn't work, but I have learned that the Twin Stones are not just twins. They are two of triplets. The third amulet is in this realm. In fact, I sense it's in the direction of Vydaelia."

Inyra took and amulet and commented, "Yes. Twin Speak now reveals the existence of the other sister stone."

Piara added, "The Mountain Giant Guppie who visited my former mate Lunniedale wore an amulet around his neck. When the giant had too much sea bee mead, he'd gloat of the amulet's protective powers. But it was a large pink stone. I doubt the giant would ever willingly part with it. It was precious to him."

Frayn commented, "I have seen this giant entering Doug-less. He uses the secret passage as you surmised. The big bloke usually put the amulet around the cave warg's neck. I saw him heading toward Vydaelia with the second attack wave which was led by Crudle. Neither the giant nor the cave warg was wearing the collar. However, Crudle's son Fishtrap did have a collar around his neck. I thought nothing of it. Carcharians always enjoy bling. When I think about it, it was probably the giant's amulet."

Piara said, "Then the third sibling locating stone likely lies in the hands of the Vydaelians. Evidently the *Read Magick effect* requires all three amulets."

Inyra said, "I know nothing of Magick. These artifacts perplex me, but shouldn't it look the same? You described a large pink stone around the big bloke's neck."

Piara said, "I'm not a sorcerer. But Twin Speak implies the third sister sheds light on the matter."

Inyra said, "Shouldn't we call it *Triplet Speak*?"

Piara managed a chuckle and answered, "Not until we have all three of them."

Inyra muttered, "Another reason to treat with the newcomers. I shan't resist any longer. You win, Frayn. I should have listened to you in the first place. Long have our people suffered at the hands of the Carcharians. Most of the raids against our villages came from Reed Creek Delta and Crudle's folk. But the King of Doug-less always calls the shots and partakes of the spoils. I say, 'Death to Doug-less and its King!'"

Frayn said, "Death to Doug-less and its King!"

Piara asked, "How will you travel?"

Inyra said, "My trained pottyhippomuses, I call sea stallions can traverse the narrowest part of the sea quickly. The sea stallions can outrun most every predator."

Piara said, "Urquhart and I used a pottyhippomus in our travel. He was a very gentle beast."

Frayn observed, "The numbers of Carcharians in the sea is dramatically diminished. That's not all good. Boxjellies and other predators will be more brazen. But there aren't too many of them."

Piara insisted, "My older child… I've got to know."

CHAPTER 55

New Allies

Sergeant Major Klunkus supervised the repairs of the western wall of Vydaelia. Rangers used blocks originally formed to extend the wall to fill in the defect. The Wandmaker relished the ample supply of sulfur gifted by Duoth leader *Mose14*. In return Yannuvia went to the onyum patch and repeatedly cast Create Food and water Spells to amplify the onyum supplies. Duoths carried their cherished bounty to Ty Ty. Yannuvia also opened one of the secret doors in the eastern wall to allow the pudgy marshmallow men easy access. Fisher and Clouse supervised distribution of the fruits. Duoths treated the onyum plants with utmost respect and carefully avoided injuring any plants in the area.

Clouse wore the transformed amulet. Odd phrases formed in his mind and informed him that "two sisters are near" and "one is nearer." The odd language suggested "planting" the graparbles of their fallen comrades with their ashes. Early on the nefarious Dreamraider had suggested simply planting the graparbles before they merged.

Yannuvia, Bluuch, and *Mose14* carried Omega Stones. Clouse's little amulet made him privy to the *Three Stones effect*. Yannuvia ordered the community to gather for a ceremony to honor Morganne and the other fallen members of the community including Yathle and 13 other Drelves. Morganne, Yathle, Trando, Lapril, Adama, Byron, Shelley, Bysshe, Fallie, Bollen, Bickum, Bendet, Chex, Glyten, and Perian joined Miclove, Owings, Buck, Borger, Houston, Bart, Killian, Geber, Eyesen, Myrna, Vasor, Rettick, Hummitch, Ayden, Lynnae, and Loogie in giving their lives to defend Vydaelia. 12 year old Eyterlie and Matron Liorra were killed by an Amebus bomb. Four year old Drelvling Cabot,

Matron Chryssie, Nauryl, and Dara died in the Amebus conflict. All told 37 Vydaelians had died.

Yathle's larger and 13 smaller graparbles were arranged carefully on a purple blanket. The Wandmaker held Morganne's graparble in his right hand. Yannuvia recalled his greeting to Morganne when he returned from his first walkabout,

"Morganne of Meadowsweet, Teacher of the Drelves, I must say you are pleasant to look upon. I spoke to Sergeant Major Rumsie during the celebration. You underestimated the value of your contribution to the defense of the realm. You are a worthy replacement for Edkim."

Twenty Duoths spread out along the seaward and western wall allures. Onyum Growers *Wheeler28, Montgomery33, Toombs25, Tatnall29, Candler28, Evans47, Bacon100, Emanuel31, Telfair59, Jeff Davis33, Appling41, Treutlen41,* and *Bulloch37* and *Stand-byes Laurens201, Jenkins226, Wayne170, Dodge191, Pierce180, Screven153,* and *Long207* stood silently and watched the approach to Vydaelia. Most held Duoth bombs. *Evans47* held the bubble sword and decanter.

Yannuvia, Fisher, Clouse, Dienas, Yiuryna, Sergeant Major Klunkus, veteran Beaux, Joulie, Jonna, Bluuch, Quunsch, Gruusch, Starra, Sharchrina, *Mose14,* Tariana, Tanteras, Andra, Alistair, Gordon, Leftbridge, Stewart, Peter, Blair, Dennis, Bernard, Noone, Pamyrga, Willifron, Carmen, Gheya, Knightsbridge, Yorcia holding little Carinne, Merry Bodkin, Bret, Maverick, Rayhall, Andra, Petreccia, Lodi, Katryca, Fexa, Fenideen, Tawyna, Breeley, Liammie, Janette, Scottie, Phurro, Barcay, Baley, Banques, Gryer, Morris, Goodman, Ridgway, Thalira, Yebek, Thyatira, Ringway, Songway, Kala, Maggiemay, Rudyard, Navita, Gillian, Riandie, Chelsea, Merena, Woltza, Marthaygra, nymph Buckaroo, nymph Kellianne, nymph Leyden, nymph Megynne, nymph Kimberleigh, nymph Clayenne, Shorticia, Wayback, Sherman, Suthyia, Debbehall, Dapoole, Arthal, Peabody, Hallenoates, Wilfrise, Serratia, Fletcher, Bowman, Glynnice, Amyrla, Xavi, Eustace, Byron, and the rest of the community of 211 individuals gathered in the inner quadrant near the rock wall behind the four geodesic domes.

The Wandmaker stared at the little stone that extruded from Morganne's nodule. He stood and tried to speak, "Morganne bravely served Drelvedom at the Battle of Lone Oak Meadow and tended enhancing plants in Green Vale. She served Vydaelia. She carried my child, saved my life, and gave her life…"

He was unable to continue.

Sergeant Major Klunkus stood, placed his hand on Yannuvia's shoulder, and finished the eulogy. Yannuvia silently crushed a bit of sulfur in his hand, uttered lyrical phrases, and extended his left hand. White hot flames left his digits and hit the rock wall and softened the stone. He used the Wand of Masonry and uttered the command **"wood row will son"** and further softened the stone. He skillfully directed the wand and created a remarkable likeness of Morganne's face in the wall. He placed the graparble that came from her body in the softened stone in the likeness's neck and pronounced, "This serves as a memorial to the heroine Morganne of Meadowsweet and Vydaelia, life-mate of Yannuvia the First Wandmaker."

The Duoth leader *Mose14* produced two red diamonds and gave them to Yannuvia. Yannuvia inserted the rare stones in the eyes of the image. Starra placed a priceless blue oyster pearl necklace around the likeness's neck and said, "This is as unique as was Morganne. It was a gift from my mother. It had belonged to her great-great-great grandmother."

Yiuryna stood and led the community in a solemn lament. Yannuvia muttered **"wood row will son"** and hardened the stone which set the stones in place. The community proceeded to the onyum patch, where Dienas and Yiuryna lovingly placed the ashes of each fallen community member with their graparble in the soil. Yathle was placed beside Loogie. Quunsch angrily ripped the graparble from his left hand. Quunsch's graparble was indistinguishable from Yathle's. Fisher and Clouse attended the wound, which rapidly closed. Fisher placed the half-Bugwully's stone in the soil. The Mender typically gave no reason for his action.

The Wandmaker led the community from the onyum patch to the Quadrangle.

Mose14 tapped the Wandmaker's leg with a pseudopod.

The Wandmaker activated his Omega Stone.

Mose14 communicated, "Sea creatures approach. *Wheeler28 and Montgomery33* report a group of pottyhippomuses approach. The seahorses have no malicious thoughts. They bear riders, sea elves from Graywood."

Rangers ran up the wall stairs and joined the Onyum Growers and Stand-byes. Several blue-green pottyhippomuses rushed toward the seawall. The seahorses carried gray-green creatures with features remarkably similar to Piara.

From the allure Tariana said, "They are coming fast. Should we attack?"

Mose14 relayed, "They come in peace."

Yannuvia said aloud, "Good thing you can read their minds, *Mose14*. Otherwise they'd be toast."

Yannuvia, Sergeant Major Klunkus, Bluuch, *Mose14*, Clouse, and Joulie ascended the wall stairs.

Inyra and Frayn stopped their steeds about twenty paces from the shoreline. Inyra shouted in the language of the Omega Stones, "I will treat with the Wandmaker."

Clouse muttered, "I see in his mind. He has news of Piara and seeks an alliance."

Yannuvia said, "I carry a stone, Clouse and can see into his mind. The question is why you see into his mind. Bluuch, the Duoth leader, and I carry stones. You do not, but the amulet around your neck radiates mauve auras."

Sergeant Major Klunkus warned, "I count eight of these blokes, Wandmaker. I neither trust them nor those confounded stones you carry. Now the Carcharian commander's amulet comes into play. Be careful!"

Yannuvia brazenly stepped from behind the merlon, stood in plain sight, and shouted, "Know that I am the Wandmaker of Vydaelia and Fire Wizard of Drelvedom. State your business!"

Frayn replied, "Know that I am Frayn of Graywood and you address Inyra, Commandant of Graywood, who is descended of the Gray Matron. You shall show him respect."

Mose14 communicated, "You have both common enemies and acquaintances. They've knowledge of Piara and her spawn."

Yannuvia muttered, "Spawn."

Bluuch muttered, "Spawn?"

Yannuvia released his Omega Stone and shouted, "You may approach, Inyra. Come alone!"

Frayn replied, "That's not going to happen. I'll be with my Commandant."

Sergeant Major Klunkus said, "Approach without weapons, Frayn of Graywood."

Frayn answered, "We'll comply. You outnumber us. May my squaddies gain respite within your walls. We encountered a Boxjelly some ways back. We'll bring yellow and blue jellyfish as barter."

Quunsch said, "I could use something sweet, seeing how Duoth is out of the question!"

Tawyna smacked the big half-Bugwully's hand and said, "Quunsch!"

Eight gray-green sea elves led their plesiohawgs toward the shoreline. Rangers on the allure of the seaward wall kept bows at ready. Tawyna descended the wall stairs and opened the door. Frayn entered first and looked Tawyna in the eyes. Inyra followed. The Commandant wore a Twin Amulet around his neck. As a precaution the other remained in Graywood with Piara. Liani, Bryni, Horton, Adric, Turlough, and Rory followed. Tariana, Peter, Blair, Dennis, Bernard, and Noone and the younger squaddies led the pottyhippomuses to the inner ward and bathing stream where the visitors might rest. Bryni and Turlough presented sea biscuits and yellow jellyfish nectar. The Vydaelians shared luscious onyums.

On the allure Quunsch moaned, "The only thing I like better than Duoth is fresh plesiohawg! Oh the pain! Give me a **** sea biscuit!"

Tawyna patted his broad back and consoled him.

Frayn and Inyra stood shoulder to shoulder and faced the Wandmaker, Sergeant Major Klunkus, Clouse, *Mose14*, and Banderas's daughters Joulie and Jonna. Carcharians Bluuch and Gruusch towered behind the leaders of Vydaelia. Starra and Sharchrina stood nearby. Quunsch and Tawyna remained near the door.

The amulets around Clouse and Inyra's necks emitted mauve auras. Starra's scarf produced its runes, but the scarf was within range of the Omega Stones carried by Bluuch, Yannuvia, and the Duoth *Mose14*. Yannuvia and Bluuch gripped their devices and Clouse watched intently. The *Two Stones effect* and *Three Stones effect* occurred.

Inyra spoke in the language of the Omega Stones, "There is no reason for me to speak. You know why we are here. We know of your relationship with the Gray Matron's great-great-great granddaughter Piara. You know her daughter Alexandrina has been born. This language works to your advantage Wandmaker. The confused looks on the faces of your constituency tell me they don't understand us. Only the handsome green guy, you, the big four-armed Carcharian, and the Duoths understand what I am saying. Duoths and Carcharians! Strange lot in this walled citadel, Wandmaker! Your alliances bolster your prowess in war. We of Graywood are counting on your help."

Yannuvia answered in the language of the stones, "Everyone in Vydaelia is loyal to me."

Inyra continued, "Oh, but most don't share your secrets, Wandmaker. You grieve your lost mate, but how much of your feeling is guilt about your infidelity. The big Carcharian has an axe to grind with you. His thoughts are tormented. He saved you! Would lay down his life for you! Such loyalty in a Carcharian! To you and his queen!"

Bluuch said in the language of the stones, "I will protect Starra with my life. The Wandmaker's people welcomed us. I will fight for him."

Yannuvia said, "I've battled many foes. The Carcharians are second to none in strength and ferocity. The Carcharians neither ask nor give quarter."

Inyra added, "And they will be back as soon as they regroup. The King of Doug-less will not rest until you are destroyed."

The Wandmaker grimly muttered in Drelvish, "I do not intend to let that happen."

Frayn raised his fist and shouted in sea elfish, "Death to Doug-less and its King!"

Quunsch shouted, "Death to Doug-less and its King!"

Bluuch shouted, "Death to Doug-less and its King!"

Yannuvia yelled, "Death to Doug-less and its King!"

Mose14 thought, "Death to Doug-less and its King!"

Inyra smiled and said in sea elfish, "Death to Doug-less and its King!"

The chat grew throughout Vydaelia. In the bathing stream area, young gray-green sea elves clasped forearms with young Rangers.

Fisher pondered, "I'll have lots of work to do."

Leftbridge shouted from the eastern wall, "War machine! Sea lions! Sea lions approach with a trebuchet!"

Mose14 thought, "King Linus sends assistance at my behest. The machine can propel the Amebus bombs."

Sergeant Major Klunkus ordered, "Stand down! Allow them entry! Stay alert!"

Inyra looked at the pudgy Duoth leader and said, "I like this more all the time."

Gordon and Stewart opened the eastern door and allowed eight sea lions to enter with the war machine.

Klunkus said, "I've been on the wrong end of these many times. Our old enemy general Saligia of Aulgmoor loved these devices and used them to pound away at our forest defenses. Walking on their rear legs and using their forelimbs to maneuver the device makes the sea lions look quite similar to our old wolf-faced enemies the Drolls. Trebuchets are likely better at battering down walls. Why didn't the Duoths use them against us?"

Mose14 replied, "We had a Giant Amebus."

Clouse relayed *Mose14*'s response to the Sergeant Major.

Klunkus said, "Makes sense. How'd the sea lions get it?"

Mose14 thought, "Unduothers manufactured it. Sea lions captured it and brought the trebuchet to the Endless Fen."

Klunkus pondered, "Unduothers?"

Clouse replied, "Everyone who isn't Duoth."

The Wandmaker, Inyra, Frayn, *Mose14*, the Carcharians, Sergeant Major Klunkus, Clouse, Fisher, and veteran Rangers went to the inner ward for further discussions. Matrons prepared fruits of the sea. The Wandmaker shared enhancing root tubers with Inyra.

Inyra said, "Little Alexandrina has your pointed ears, nose, and shares our nodules. Grayness touches her. She has her mother's beauty. The child enhances all of Graywood."

Yannuvia said, "My daughter Carinne also has her mother's beauty."

Inyra said, "I offer support of my squaddies in an assault on Dougless. More than 200 armed motivated fighters! Most like me have lost loved ones to Carcharian raids. In return I ask for the amulet that your green friend wears. It's important to my people."

Clouse said, "The amulet has spoken to me since your arrival. Twin Speak tells me the amulets have great power. Should someone possess all three?"

Inyra answered, "We have learned the Twin Stones or Triplet Stones, if you will, amplify their powers when they are together. You share what Piara and I have learned. Two stones reveal the existence of a third and require the third to fully produce their effects; Piara cannot travel and leave Alexandrina. I must take the amulet to her."

Clouse asked, "What do you hope to learn from this tomb? You already know it's the resting place of your matriarch. Is translating the matriarch's journal so important?"

Inyra answered, "Yes."

Clouse said, "Then… when matters are settled here, I'll return to Graywood with you. We'll learn together."

Inyra concentrated and said, "Your mind is complex, green guy. I can't see around all the corners. Magick touches you. But I find nothing evil within you, and Piara speaks highly of you."

Frayn and Klunkus entered into detailed tactical discussion. Squaddies Horton and Adric took to the sea on plesiohawgs and left for Graywood. Fisher and matrons prepared unguents. *Mosel4's* generous gifts of raw materials had supplied the mender with ingredients needed for many of his unguents, including Panacea and sleep poultice. Rangers finished repairing the western wall. After two rotations of the Day Glass, Horton and Adric returned with Inyra's force of two hundred gray-green sea elves. Some rode pottyhippomuses, others came in on small vessels pulled by sea moolers, and others used various and sundry modes of water transportation. Horton and Adric brought in two sea moolers and yoked them to haul three Amebus bombs. King Linus's octet of sea lions remained deployed to maneuver the trebuchet. Bluuch, Gruusch, and Quunsch prepared weapons.

Gruusch and Starra approached the Wandmaker and Elder Yiuryna and asked to be joined by a ceremony of life-long commitment. Yannuvia gave his blessing and Yiuryna performed a simple ceremony. Their closest friends, Clouse, Jonna, Joulie, and Sergeant Major stood in attendance. The union was sealed by a kiss. Gruusch then returned to preparations. Starra and Sharchrina reluctantly agreed to remain in the quadrangle.

Frayn and Sergeant Major Klunkus expertly organized people and resources. The Wandmaker impatiently paced while other made ready. Bryni and Turlough shuffled back and forth to monitor activities in the sea and around Doug-less. Carcharians trickled from the stronghold. No one entered.

CHAPTER 56

Doug-less

The united force of Drelve-Vydaelians, Duoths, Carcharians, sea elves, and sea lions advanced by land and sea. Squaddies rode upon pottyhippomuses and sea moolers. Vydaelian archers utilized the two boats left by Brace's assault. Sea moolers pulled the crafts through the waters. The squaddies fanned out in a semicircle around the seaward entrance to Doug-less and formed a blockade. The ships anchored the blockade. The land force marched along the water's edge. Frayn identified the location of the secret entrance. Yannuvia checked for Magick traps and found none. He then used the Wand of Masonry and said **"wood row will son"** and softened the stone wall. Bluuch and Gruusch easily removed the softened stone. Tariana, Willifron, Merry Bodkin, Peter, Blair, Dennis, Bernard, and Noone checked the passage. It meandered for a ways and was unoccupied. Sergeant Major Klunkus stationed guards to block the exit.

Sea lions moved the trebuchet into position. Bluuch and Quunsch placed the first Amebus bomb on the device.

On Klunkus's command Bluuch fired the trebuchet. The Amebus bomb sailed through the air, slammed into the wall of the cavern just to the west of the known approach to the Circle of Willis, and created a massive explosion. Huge boulders fell out of the wall.

Bluuch reloaded and fired a second time. The second bomb blasted into the same area and exposed the inner sanctum of Doug-less. The third bomb fully exposed the large southwest living area of the Carcharian stronghold. Some areas of the ceiling caved in. Finally Bluuch loaded the Amebus bomb caught by Clouse. The fourth bomb obliterated the remnants of the cavern wall and laid open the innards of Doug-less.

The Wandmaker sighed and recalled his lost friends and loved ones.
The Teacher Edkim…
His mother Carinne…
Banderas…
Clarke Maceda…
Diana Maceda…
The water sprites Illarie, Condee, and Ellspeth…
Meryt…
Bryce…
Zack…
Debery…
The Lone Oak…
The Red Meadow…
The Tree Herder Old Yellow…
Vioss and Bystar…
Scores of his people…
Betrayals…by his brother Gaelyss, Kirrie, the nefarious Saligia…

Yannuvia was born in the light of the Gray Wanderer Andreas. The erstwhile Spellweaver had drunk from the Cup of Dark Knowledge and tasted the Seventh Nectar. Mender's blood had touched him.
Drelvish…
Menderish…
Spellweaverish…
Pointed-eared, ever so slightly greenish…
First Wandmaker…
Fire Wizard!

Yannuvia took the Wand of Flying, used the command **"Run nailed ray gun,"** and flew into the air. Unlike the battle with Fishtrap the Wandmaker now had an ample supply of sulfur. Carcharians rushed to the breach in their community's wall with weapons. Yannuvia flew safely out of spear range and shouted, "Here I am, ********!" The taunted Carcharians hurled spears and curses at the Wandmaker. More gathered in the large exposed cavern.
The Wandmaker shouted, "For Morganne!"
He then conjured, crushed sulfur, uttered disturbing phrases in the language of the Omega Stones, and sent devastating blasts of blue flames

into the gathered Carcharians. Massive explosions ripped through the room. No Carcharians survived.

The Wandmaker drifted downward and flew just above the rubble. Klunkus shouted, "Wandmaker, wait!"

Yannuvia flew into the smoking cavern. He flew past many charred remains and went up a passage to the northeast. Klunkus and Frayn led ground forces into the area but were far behind Yannuvia. Yannuvia passed into the huge common area of Doug-less. Carcharians of all ages were running in all directions. The veteran Draacks threw a spear at the Wandmaker and tried to organize defenders. Several Carcharians rallied to his side. Yannuvia dodged Draacks's spear, then directed his hands forward and sent blazing rays of fire across the common area. The flames immolated Draacks and his motley crew. Explosions alerted the entire community. Guards ran from the circle of Willis and cut off the Wandmaker's retreat. However Klunkus, Frayn, and Quunsch arrived and engaged the guards. Numbers favored the invaders. Klunkus and Frayn broke off and went into the common area. They found a berserk Wandmaker. Yannuvia floated thirty feet above the ground and just below the ceiling of the well-lit area, spun in circles all the while sending spell after spell into the hapless Carcharians. The temperature of the huge cavern increased. Survivors ran to the north toward the council room, which was locked from the inside. Carcharians banged on the locked door to no avail. Yannuvia sent a rain of fire toward the door and destroyed those trying to enter it. Bluuch and Gruusch joined Quunsch and the large group of Rangers that first entered the cavern opened by the Amebus bombs. The invaders beat the enemies back to the Circle of Willis. Guards broke off, dived into the water and attempted to get away. When they exited to the sea they ran into a rainstorm of arrows fired by sea elves on pottyhippomuses and Vydaelians on the boats. A few Carcharians made it to the reeds but Bryni had organized Graywood sea elves that easily overwhelmed the beleaguered Carcharians. Inside Doug-less females and young fled to the birthing area and barred the doors. Gruusch led Rangers to the guard chambers and soon overcame the few guards remaining. The Rangers suffered minimal casualties.

Yannuvia sent another Fireball into the door to the council room and blew it off its hinges. Phederal, Heraldo, Brace, and Tapasbar made a last stand to defend the monarch. Boggle ran out the back of the chamber into King Lunniedale's personal quarters. He sneaked into the secret passage that led out of the room and snaked his way along the passage. He reached the last corner only to find guards posted by Sergeant Major Klunkus. Boggle turned back to run toward the King's chamber. Sometimes a blind squirrel finds a nut. As he ran along the passageway Boggle's left hand brushed against the hidden door that Mountain Giant Guppie used to enter the realm. Boggle opened the door and passed though. Unfortunately he lacked protection and was instantly destroyed.

Yannuvia sent another Fire Spell into the northeast corner of the common area. The Fireball exploded and blew open the secret passageway that ran from the King's chamber to the birthing area and guard's quarters. Rangers rushed into the secret passage and searched right and left.

Klunkus shouted, "Wandmaker! Come down! They are defeated! Please!"

Words entered Yannuvia's mind.

"I give you my blood through which you will receive all you seek. You in turn give to me your all."

Ǿ ∞ Ǿ

The ancient Tree Shepherd's comment then resonated through the Wandmaker's thoughts.

"Fire Wizard!"

The Wandmaker eased to the ground and settled by Sergeant Major Klunkus. Rivulets of blue smoke flowed from Yannuvia's fingertips. He asked, "Have you found that son of a dawgfish Lunniedale?"

Klunkus said, "Doug-less is riddled with secret passages. This immediate area is secured. 500 Carcharians died in the common area and another 300 in the area destroyed by the Amebus bombs. Gruusch, Quunsch, and Bluuch are clearing the area around the Circle of Willis. Our Carcharian allies' knowledge of Doug-less has been very helpful. Elderly, female, and young Carcharians fled into the birthing chamber. The secret passage that you opened led to the King's private chamber. He is not there. In the other direction the passage leads toward the birthing room. Rangers found the secret door in the rear of the room that leads to the outer passage where the Giant enters. There is an unusual door midway along the passage. A Carcharian tried to pass through it but he was smote. Our people closed the door. That passage exits along the sea in the secret door Frayn pointed out and you opened. We've searched all areas thoroughly. The King must have used another passage to escape. Four Carcharians are holed up in the council room. We have them blocked in from both sides."

Yannuvia said icily, "Why haven't you taken them out?"

Klunkus pleaded, "Yannuvia! My friend! We've rained death on them. Doug-less is destroyed. I'd like to offer them quarter."

Yannuvia replied, "Do you think they'd offer you quarter?"

Klunkus replied, "I'm sure they would not. Still… we are Drelvish!"

Yannuvia said, "I am a Fire Wizard. You are Vydaelian!"

Klunkus said, "You are also the leader of our people and we need you. I ask that you return to Vydaelia."

Yannuvia said, "Do you know the King is not in the birthing chamber with the females and children?"

Klunkus hung his head and said, "I don't."

Yannuvia icily said, "I'm going to eradicate this den of snakes."

The Wandmaker ignored the Sergeant Major's pleas and walked toward the Circle of Willis. Yannuvia said, "Clear all our people out."

Klunkus ran ahead and ordered everyone back from the circle. Bluuch, Quunsch, and Gruusch had already cleared all the areas except the birthing room. The Wandmaker stood at the opening to the north and sent a Bolt of Flame toward the top of the Circle and collapsed the ceiling. This closed off the entry to the birthing chamber and blocked the undersea access to the ruins of Doug-less. Now the only access to the birthing chamber was the secret passage that led from the King's chamber. Klunkus sent Bluuch, Gruusch, and Quunsch with Rangers into the birthing chamber. The invaders cleared the area. Captives were lead to the smoldering common area.

Frayn joined the leaders and reported, "The group in the council chamber refused to surrender. They are all dead, but it cost me three squaddies Tuffy, Micks, and Micks' son Myron, and your Ranger Phurro."

Bluuch wiped a tear from his eye with his right upper hand, struggled to regain his composure, and reported, "Typically the adults fought till the end. Females stood by their mates. That's the way of…

my people! Every leader of Doug-less except the King is accounted for and dead, including Gruusch's four-armed father Phederal."

Klunkus said, "We have about a hundred females and young. The male guards are all dead. They refused quarter. Also… there were six dead sea elves and two slain Bugwullies in the birthing area. They were dead before we entered."

Yannuvia said, "They killed their captives, just as they killed our women and children and ravaged sea elf villages."

Bluuch said, "I cannot allow the killing of women and children."

Frayn commented, "Odd sentiment for a Carcharian!"

Bluuch suggested, "Queen Piara would say it's my sea elfish lineage."

Frayn said, "I'm not interested in killing children. The Carcharian settlements on Reed Creek Delta are accessible by boat. We can send them by the two boats to join their kind, but we'll fight them again someday."

Yannuvia said, "Get everyone out of this retched place. I'm going to make it so no one perpetrates mischief from these wretched walls again."

Klunkus and Frayn evacuated the area. The Carcharian survivors were placed on the boats and given oars. Older children and females took the oars. Frayn's squaddies failed to note the height and muscular definition of the largest captive. Carcharian females did not grow to seven feet in height.

The Wandmaker tarried in the vacated common area. He sent delayed blast fireballs into the four corners of the common area. Yannuvia exited the breach in the cavern wall just as the first of four massive blasts rocked the underworld cavern. The ceiling collapsed throughout Doug-less. Dust and rubble belched from the aperture. Only the secret corridor that led from the King's chamber to the sea remained open. It was now a passage leading to a dead end filled with rubble, but the unusual door was still accessible.

The organized assault cost the lives of seven squaddies from Graywood named Tuffy, Micks, Micks's son Myron, Divaq, Krunk, Munnie, and Rockie. Frayn's squaddies carefully gathered their bodies and graparbles. Rangers Phurro, Barcay, Baley, Banques, and Gryer lost their lives. Other Rangers carefully gathered their graparbles and bodies.

Most of Inyra's squaddies returned to Graywood from the ruins of Doug-less. Inyra, Frayn, Bryni, Horton, Liani, Adric, Rory, and Turlough returned to Vydaelia.

The two shiploads of Carcharians never reached Reed Creek Delta. Charred wreckage washed up near the sea urchin farms. Neither bodies nor survivors were found.

CHAPTER 57

Triplet Stones

The victors returned to Vydaelia. Ceremonies were held for the fallen. Inyra's fallen squaddies were placed with their graparbles in the soil of the onyum patch. Duoths took a bounty of onyums and returned to Ty Ty. The sea lions returned to their homes in the endless Fen, but left the trebuchet in Vydaelia. The leaders gathered for a somber meeting. The Wandmaker remained silent throughout the gathering. Klunkus and Dienas carried the conversation.

When the common business concluded, Inyra said, "We have fulfilled our part of the bargain. Now I must insist the third amulet go with me to Graywood."

Clouse answered, "With the Wandmaker's permission, I'll return with you."

Yannuvia said, "The amulet Clouse wears was taken from an enemy. It has changed since it came into his possession. I am not opposed to its leaving Vydaelia. Clouse has free will."

Clouse, Inyra, Frayn, and Liani made ready and picked four stout pottyhippomuses for the return journey to Graywood. Horton, Adric, Rory, and Turlough remained in Vydaelia as liaisons.

Jonna joined the foursome, selected Adric's steed, and said, "You aren't going without me."

Three gray-green sea elves, orange-hued Jonna, and greenish Clouse made for Graywood. Other than a brief conflict with a Boxjelly, the trip was uneventful. The quintet went straightaway to Piara's cabin. Little Alexandrina greeted them with a smile and rather loud burp. Piara, Clouse, and Inyra donned the Triplet Stones. The three amulets gave off mauve auras. *The Two Stones, Three Stones*, and *Read Magick effects* occurred. Jonna was not privy to the thoughts Piara revealed to Clouse.

Piara asked, "What of Starra?"

Jonna replied, "She has taken an oath of life-time commitment with Gruusch. They have become pillars of the community. Vydaelia has faced hard times since you left. Starra has stood tall."

Piara said, "How is the Wandmaker's health?"

Jonna coolly answered, "He has borne great burdens. His leg was injured in the first battle with the Carcharians. In the second battle he suffered a psychic injury similar to that Clouse suffered in the battle with the Amebus. The Duoth leader *Mose14* came to his aid. Duoth dropping soup is rather remarkable. The Wandmaker grieves the loss of his life-mate Morganne. Their daughter Carinne was born as her mother died."

Piara said, "I'm so sorry."

Jonna quipped sardonically, "I'm sure you are."

Piara blushed and persisted, "What of my fellow refugees?"

Clouse answered, "Loogie fell in the first battle and we lost Yathle in the second attack from Doug-less. Both fought well. Bluuch has been stalwart. Quunsch grows stronger by the day. Gruusch has done well. Your niece Sharchrina has also proven a valuable asset. I see your thoughts. I'm sorry about Urquhart."

Jonna and Frayn exited the cabin. The lead squaddie gave the she-Drelve-Vydaelian a tour of Graywood and Gray Vale. Piara and Clouse studied the writing. Inyra had difficulty deciphering the script. The protected symbols indeed detailed the three doors in the eight sided tomb.

Piara and Clouse learned from The Gray Matron's journal.

The inner tomb's heel stone was identical to the one in a place called Stonehenge, which the Gray Matron had visited after traveling through one of the doors in the tomb. Touching the heel stone thirteen times not only produced the gray circle that allows exit from the tomb to the stone circle on the hillock but also induced the formation of images on the three doors.

On the first door an image of a red-bearded giant formed.

To open the gate, one places two amulets in the giant's eye sockets. You insert the stone in the left eye socket first. Then the right eye socket. When the amulets are in place a huge ax appears in the giant's left hand. One touches the blade of the axe twice. The axe disappears and a dagger takes its place. One touches the dagger thrice. The dagger disappears and a gisarme appears. One touches the gisarme five times. The gisarme is replaced by a broad sword. One touches the broad sword eight times. A table made of blue wood appears in the tomb. A small cabinet filled with phials filled with varying colored liquids appears. The liquids are green, purple, uncolored, yellow, red, and green. The green potion is a potion of diminution. Drinking it reduces one's height to ten per cent its original. However, one's mass is not changed and he retains all attributes, including strength. The potions are additive. Drinking a second reduces to one per cent. The purple potions reverse the green. Drinking a purple potion does not increase your base size. It only tastes like grape juice. Uncolored potions are the trinity, the base of other potions. The clear potion has a slightly bitter taste. Yellow potions taste like pinanas, rich elongated yellow fruits. The yellow potion is highly nutritious. The red potion tastes like cherry juice. It enables one to control red giants and comes in handy in this realm. When the potions appear, one drinks in order uncolored, yellow, red, and green. This reduces your height. One then drinks the purple potion and regains his height. You then remove the amulets from the giant figure's eye sockets. The door opens. The potions protect one while passing through the gate. The amulet is superfluous.

That door led to giants' realm in a world of a single sun. The Gray Matron also visited this realm. The door in the tomb opens via a trap door beneath the bed in a room. The room is filled with man or elf-sized furniture and materials. The room has four walls of fifty feet. Bizarre tapestries and drawings cover the walls. Some depict a great sea in an underworld cavern illuminated by fluorescing ceilings. Our realm! Other drawings depict a sky filled by three suns, a dark sun, bright yellow sun, and a faint gray sun that almost filled the sky. Drawings of buildings in Graywood dominate the tapestries. The eight-sided tomb on the hill in Gray Vale dominates one tapestry. Figures of gray-green sea elves, the residents of Graywood, intermingle with the structures. It's a panorama of Gray Vale and its folk. Runes written in the language of the Omega and Twin Stones describe the structures. The Gray Matron placed tomes on book shelves, including the history of Gray Vale and the creation of the scepter UK. Another volume told of her exploration in the World of Three Suns and mentioned places like Ooranth, Alms Glen, Ornash, Mirror Lake, Alluring Falls, and Aulgmoor. Still another spoke of black-robed monks from a place called Calamitous Forest and spoke of them as allies. The language of the Triplet Stones is similar to a writing called 'old Elfish." Powerful Magick protects the door on both sides. Passing through to get back into the tomb in Gray Vale requires either the Triplet Stones amulet or the sequence of drinking potions in the order, uncolored, yellow, red, green, and lavender.

The door leaving the entry room to the giant's realm is merely locked. Passing beyond the locked is deemed quite hazardous. Drinking a red giant control potion is highly recommended. The Gary Matron's journal says little of the realm beyond the locked door.

Regarding the second door in the eight sided tomb, touching the heel stone 13 times creates the figure of a tall man with a cherry red birthmark on his chin. The wayfarer's cowl hides much of his face. Differing runes from an old language on their hand-holds differentiated three otherwise identical staves that hover near the robed figure. The staffs aligned to the north, south, and east. Each of the three staves bore four sets of runes about their circumferences at their midpoints.

$$Ø \infty Ø$$

The old language is from a world called Sagain. The runes of N, S, and E on ends of the artifacts represent direction. The triumvirates of runes at the staffs' midpoints were alien. The staves represent three of a set called *"The Staves of the Four Winds."*

Opening the door requires three Triplet Stone amulets. They must touch the hand-holds of the three hovering staffs. When this is done, another blue wood table appears. It has a shamrock, sprig of mistletoe and a bit of wet red sand on it. One must take up the shamrock and mistletoe and throw the red sand onto the door. The red sand allows safe passage through the gate.

This door led to a stone circle at a place called Uragh Wood in a simple world of a single sun and moon. The circle at Uragh Wood is identical to the Gray Vale Stone Circle outside the tomb in Gray Vale. When you got to Uragh Circle, you placed a shamrock and a sprig of mistletoe in the center of the circle. You touched the monolith, then one of the little stones. You waited a while and then touched the monolith twice. Then you touched another stone thrice. One touched the monolith five times, followed by touching a third little stone eight times. Next it was back to the monolith to touch it thirteen times. Then it was to the fourth stone twenty-one times. You went the monolith again and touched it thirty-four times. Lastly you went to the final stone and touched it fifty-five times. After eighty-nine heartbeats you received a signal from the Sandman. The Sandman appeared to the Gray Matron, but sometimes the three staves appeared alone.

The three staffs appeared identical save one thing. At the tip of each staff a single rune appeared. The Sandman aligned the staffs to the north, south, and east. The differing runes signified these directions. He placed the artifacts in the exact center of Uragh Stone Circle and allowed them to touch at their bases. If the Sandman wasn't there, the staves appeared and did it anyway. Each of the three staves bore four sets of runes about their circumferences at their midpoints.

Ø ∞ Ø

When the three staves touched they emitted an eerie purple aura that persisted for a time. The Sandman counted to 144, and a gray featureless stone appeared at the point where the three staves came together. If he didn't appear, one just waited for the stone to appear. The three staves rose from the ground and moved into the sandman's flowing dark robe or just disappeared if he wasn't there. Red liquid oozed from the gray stone and soaked the soil around the little rock. Sometimes the sandman spoke in riddles, and sometimes he simply counted to 144 and then stared aimlessly toward the west. When he finished counting the stone disappears. He then allowed you to gather the soaked sand. When the Gray matron received the gift of the sand, he said to her, "Remember to thank the Staves of the Four Winds, the Windward Staves, children of the Bloodstone, the Source of Magick."

The Staff of the West Wind, also called the Staff of Stone, was missing. The tall Sandman wore a robe and cowl that hid his face. His most telling features were his fathomless eyes. The Gray Matron learned nothing of the missing staff.

The red sand allowed safe passage back to the circle in Gray Vale. One sprinkled red sand in the center of the circle and reversed the pattern of touching the stones. The Triplet Stone amulets also provided protection.

An image of a female fire demon formed on the third door. It led to a circle on a green island in a World of Three Suns, from which the Vydaelians hail. Touch one of the Triplet Stone amulets to her left hand, then another to her right. Press the third to her lips. The visage changed to a kindly matronly female with smooth skin and flowing hair. Touch an amulet to her right hand, then her left hand and the third to her forehead. The door opened. The table with the phials of liquid appears. One drank potions in the order uncolored, yellow, red, green, and purple. Drinking the potions provided protection. Wearing the amulet also availed some protection.

You stand on a circle of flat, smooth gray stone near a replica of the heel stone at Stonehenge. A little yellow sun danced around an amber sky. Light ran from a large shadowy spiraling hole overhead and a deep gray speck appeared low in the sky. Miniscule gray rays from the tiny speck enhanced the grayness of the stone. When you step off the circle of gray stone, the stone circle disappears. Lush green foliage including bracken, bilberry, bell heather, and ling heather surrounded the area. A wood white, the prettiest moth in all the Emerald Island, fluttered about. To get back home, you returned to this place. The heel stone's twin served as focal point. You touched the false heel stone thirteen times; went to a point thirteen paces from the stone, and sprinkled a bit of red sand. The gray circle then reappeared under your feet. Next thing you stood in the middle of the Uragh Stone Circle. You get back to Gray Vale by following the same process as the second door.

If one chose poorly and made a mistake in opening the doors, the doors led to a grotto behind a waterfall. Without a means to exit the traveler wasted away in the grotto. With a means to exit and a focal point one might end up… somewhere and sometime else. Traveling through gates came at a price.

Piara and Clouse relayed the information to Inyra. Frayn warned of reprisals from other Carcharian realms. Squaddies kept up vigilance and searched in vain for King Lunniedale.

CHAPTER 58

Happy Family

Yannuvia sat in the soft grass by the bathing stream. Little Carinne played on her back and looked up at the luminescent lichen. The babbling stream calmed her. Yorcia's care had been exemplary. Carinne was thriving and taking her first steps. Rangers had completed the extension of the outer curtain and enclosed the area all the way to the billabong. The walls had been reinforced and heightened. Yannuvia had created 12 Magick Missile Wands. All used the command "**Join add yams.**" Yannuvia listed them in his Spellbook as I-*11* and added a notation for each additional device. Since the destruction of Doug-less, the community had not been attacked. The Duoths tended the onyum patch and the new growth. Purple-leafed saplings grew from planted Drelves-Vydaelians' graparbles. Gray-leafed trees had sprouted from the graparbles of Inyra's fallen squaddies and bore nutritious fruits akin to enhancing root tubers. Loogie and Yathle's graparbles had sprouted into robust saplings. To this point the deep green-leafed saplings had borne no fruit. Quunsch's ripped out graparble had sprouted into a gnarly bush with small berries. Fisher was still trying to figure it out. Quunsch had not developed another nodule. The citizenry's nodules had stopped enlarging when the Wandmaker's did so. Squaddie Frayn led scouting parties into Carcharian territories in Reed Creek Delta and confirmed the Amphibimen lacked leadership.

Starra was with child. Word had been sent to Graywood. Clouse and Jonna remained in the gray-green sea elves' settlement.

A voice interrupted the Wandmaker's thoughts, "It was time she met her father."

Piara arrived with Alexandrina. Alexandrina toddled over to Carinne and uttered a long spiel of gibberish. Carinne answered and extended her little hand to touch Alexandrina's little pointed ears. Alexandrina did the same in turn. The children wrapped little arms around one another and hugged. Yannuvia stared at Piara. The winsome sea elf remained as beautiful as ever. She walked over to Yannuvia and kissed his cheek.

Yannuvia said, "You left without saying good-by."

Piara said, "It was complicated."

Yannuvia asked, "Are you here to stay?"

Piara answered, "That depends on you. Word came to me of Starra's conception. I can help her with my mothering and midwifery skills. And as I said, Alexandrina needs to meet her people."

Yannuvia asked, "Is she... exceptional?"

Piara said, "She is exceptionally beautiful. Clouse and I have watched her. She has a way with plants and animals. We think she is Menderish. She was not born in gray light and cannot be a Spellweaver."

Yannuvia said, "She is beautiful. Her greenness mimics her mother. Are Clouse and Jonna well?"

Piara replied, "Yes. Clouse works with Nurse Nila and studies the Gray Matron and Lou Nester's texts. So far no one has explored beyond the gates in the tomb. Inyra recognizes the Carcharians remain a threat. King Lunniedale was never found. The survivors from Doug-less never reached Reed Creek Delta. Frayn found some wreckage. Troglodytes filtered into the wetlands near Graywood after the fall of Doug-less. Commandant Inyra won't allow them in Gray Vale and Graywood proper. Many were homeless and given simple tasks to do in the outlying farms. Given direction they are hard workers. Graywood sea elves again harvest from the sea urchin beds on the route to Doug-less. Jonna works with Frayn to shore up defenses. Clouse and Jonna will return if needed."

Yannuvia said, "I do not grieve the lost Carcharians. We would have fought the young when they grew up. As to the King... it was rumored he escaped with the females and children. If he did, then the tragedy that befell the other survivors claimed him as well. Fisher remains with us and Joulie has visited her sister on occasion. Jonna and Clouse may serve Graywood as long as they want. Squaddies Liani, Bryni, Horton, Adric, Turlough, and Rory and Rangers Tariana, Peter, Blair, Dennis,

Bernard, and Noone are serving as messengers. The pottyhippomuses provide good transportation."

Piara covertly inched closer and asked, "How goes the Wandmaking?"

Yannuvia answered, "Until Grayness returns I'll be limited to creating only one type of wand. It turns out its Magick Missiles. We now have 13. These wands are as powerful as arrows and shore up our defenses. These identical wands cannot recharge, even in the grayness of Approximation. Other wands have different properties. For instance... we had exhausted the uses of the Wand of Healing. However, it fortuitously recharged during the ceremony that created the first Magick Missile. It recharges in the presence of grayness. *Mose14* also gave us a generous supply of Duoth bombs. Fisher and *Mose14* have modified Duoth dropping soup. It's entirely sterile and sweet smelling. It's helping us with many common maladies."

Piara slipped her arm onto the Wandmaker's shoulder and softly asked, "How is your health? Is your nodule painful? Your leg wound?"

Yannuvia enjoyed her pheromones and answered, "The nodule will grow no larger. My leg no longer hurts. I've crammed a lot of living into my seasons."

Piara turned to face him and kissed him gently.

Another voice echoed from the wall, "Well, isn't this sweet, Kirrie?"

The Good Witch, a visage of Kirrie, and another toddler appeared. The little boy toddled over to Carinne and Alexandrina. He babbled and they babbled back. He touched Carinne and briefly mimicked her form. He changed back, touched Alexandrina and mimicked her visage. He then returned to his male façade and babbled more. The little girls laughed at his antics.

The Good Witch commented, "He has his Daddy's way with the ladies. It was time for him to meet you. Looks like we got here at just the right time, Kirrie!"

Yannuvia asked the Good Witch, "He is obviously exceptional. What is his name?"

Amica replied, "Adjuster! More formally, Jar Dee Ans! But he answers to lots of names."

Kirrie quipped, "Like his mother."

Amica smiled wryly and added, "He likes Dee."

Kirrie wore an amulet identical to the Triplet Stone amulets.

Yannuvia said, "Hello, Kirrie."

Kirrie nodded and said, "Hello, Fire Wizard! The conquering hero! Not much left of Doug-less!"

Yannuvia answered, "We did what we had to do."

Kirrie silently asked, "What was the fate of the Carcharian's leader?"

Yannuvia answered aloud, "No word! I think he stowed away on one of the ships. The penteconters from Doug-less never made it to Reed Creek Delta."

Kirrie smiled wryly and replied, "Probably victims of a sudden maelstrom."

Yannuvia surreptitiously gripped the Omega Stone in his pocket. The amulet around Kirrie's neck hummed and emitted mauve auras. Runes appeared on Yannuvia's stone. He saw into Kirrie's thoughts and confirmed he was looking at his old childhood friend. Kirrie's smile widened.

Yannuvia *silently* gasped, "You! Lunniedale's bane!"

Kirrie *thought* back, "I didn't want to miss out on the fun! He was getting away. Didn't want to see a repeat of old Saligia! I see you searched for them and would have done the same thing had you found them first."

Yannuvia answered, "There were over a hundred Carcharian women and children on those boats!"

Kirrie replied, "Yeah, yeah, and yeah! And their nefarious leader! By the way, they call their young minnows. They were enemies you'd fight another day."

Kirrie's thoughts confirmed her amulet was one of *Quintuplets!*

Yannuvia said aloud, "Five!"

Kirrie answered, "Yes, there are five siblings. Any two become Twin Stones and activate their effects. Piara carries one. Another rested in the Mender's Tomb and now hangs around Commandant Inyra's neck. Clouse wears a third courtesy of the fumbling Mountain Giant and by way of the Carcharian commander. I wear a fourth. Fisher brought the fifth to Lost Sons. It revolves around the Central Sphere and provides a focal point."

Yannuvia said, "The Xennic Stone differs. It's larger and can't be differentiated from its four-score and seven fellows."

Kirrie answered, "The Twin Stones have the ability to change their shapes and appearance. They become invisible if they chose. The giant's amulet was large and pink for a time."

Yannuvia muttered aloud, "Piara!"

The Wandmaker turned and faced the sea elf. The amulet around her neck also emitted mauve auras.

Piara's silence did not obscure her thoughts. In her mind Yannuvia read, "Elderly females and children! Wanton killing! Fire Wizards!"

Kirrie laughed, "Fire Wizard!"

Yannuvia said, "Fire Wizard back at you."

Words appeared in Kirrie's mind.

"I give you my blood through which you will receive all you seek. You in turn give to me your all."

Ø ∞ Ø

Words appeared in Yannuvia's mind.

"I give you my blood through which you will receive all you seek. You in turn give to me your all."

Ø ∞ Ø

Yannuvia released his grip on the Omega Stone. Piara stared fearfully at the Wandmaker and Kirrie. Kirrie munched on an enhancing root tuber and shared another with Dee, Carinne, and Alexandrina. The three children laughed and hugged Kirrie. Then they moved to the Wandmaker and threw their little arms around his legs.

The Dreamraider Good Witch sauntered over, placed an arm around both Kirrie and Piara, and said, "Well here we are. We're all just one happy family."

Yannuvia's left hand throbbed. Gray light filtered through the top of the geodesic dome that housed the Central Sphere.

Mender Fisher walked into the bathing stream area and announced, "Wandmaker, I've sent for Clouse. The time for your confinement approaches."

Ø ∞ Ø

In the distant future...

Ravenna Nocerre nervously entered the room. The red-haired elf approached the hidden door under the bed. High Priestess Knarra and

Mage Roscoe warned of protective Magick. Most of her party had fallen victim to traps. Giants killed the others. The Captain of Donothor's elite Ranger force was alone. She'd managed to reach the odd chamber. Ravenna recalled Knarra's words... *"I'll take two clear potions, two green potions, two lavender potions, two red potions, and two yellow potions. Put every other potion that we have found in this dungeon with the others in the cabinet."*

"I know you took four potions for the monk's release and two lavender potions for Pheye. Why did you take the other four?" Ravenna asked.

"We may want to enter the trap door in the green elves' room someday," the priestess answered flatly.

That day had come.

Ravenna drank in order uncolored, yellow, red, green, and purple potions. She placed the Amulet of Protection around her neck. The artifact emitted mauve auras and runes formed on its surface.

Ø ∞ Ø

The little stone and chain then faded from sight. Ravenna stepped through the door. Consciousness left her.

When she awakened, Ravenna Nocerre, Donothor's greatest Ranger, was alone within an eight-sided room. A tomb! Sarcophagi sat against the wall behind her. Three doors without opening mechanisms sat in three walls opposite the obsidian caskets. Most of the floor was the same black stone that made up the walls. A circle of gray soil and 13 foot diameter filled the center of the brightly illuminated chamber. A large stone sat opposite the sarcophagi.

The heel stone dominated the area of the tomb opposite the sarcophagi. The heel stone was a single block of sarsen stone. It was sub-rectangular, with a minimum thickness of 2.4 meters. A meter is 39.37 inchworm lengths. It rose to a tapered top 4.7 meters high. A further 1.3 meters was buried in the ground. Gray soil makes up the floor of the tomb. The heel stone sat 77.4 meters from the sarcophagi and was nearly 27 degrees from the vertical. Its overall girth was 7.6 meters. It weighed 35 tons. Ravenna Nocerre had a knack with measurements.

Ø ∞ Ø

Printed in the United States
By Bookmasters